VALOR OF STEELE

CARRIE THOMAS

Cover Design: Kate Farlow @ Y'all That Graphic

ISBN: 978-1-957700-42-7

Also by Carrie Thomas:

Sucker for Payne

Piper

Stephanie

Nicole

Travesty

A Forever Kind of Thing

Learn more at CarrieThomasBooks.com.

CHAPTER 1
TREVOR

RICHARD FULLER, the CEO of the American Fighting League, stuck his hand out for me to shake just in time for the ravenous paparazzi to capture the money shot. "You're going to regret this, Steele," he said, as a wide grin crossed his face, revealing perfect white teeth. It was as if he found the thought of me fucking up my life humorous.

But I knew that grin. I'd been dealing with that grin for years. It was nothing more and nothing less than condescension.

I could do condescension.

Matching his grin, and procuring my spot as alpha, I gripped his hand twice as hard as he did mine. "I don't think so."

I'd dissected the pros and cons of retiring from the pro circuit a million times before making my final decision. Over the last twelve months, I'd been methodical and precise. In the end, I mostly used common sense, though.

I wasn't old by any means, but going hundreds of rounds in a cage was hard on the body. Three minutes felt like ten in your twenties, and twenty minutes in your thirties. And I had nothing left to prove. I'd secured my place as champion. There wasn't anywhere to go but down. If I stayed in the league, my demise would be inevitable. No one remained number one forever, and I wanted to go out on top.

I could admit, leaving everything I'd ever known behind made me a little nervous. Sure, being a professional cage fighter had awarded me financial security for the rest of my life, but there was something terrifying about an unplanned future. I'd never been good at twiddling my thumbs.

As I walked around the grand ballroom of the Plaza Hotel, taking in professional athletes, celebrities, and white-collar dudes alike, melancholy filled my chest. Yet deep down in my gut, I knew it was time. There was a whole other generation of fighters coming up in the league. Leaving it to them was the right thing to do.

I found my friends in the corner of the ballroom, in a booth large enough for ten people. My best friend, Conner Payne, and his wife, Willow, were snuggled close like the newlyweds they were. She sat on his lap, grinning ear to ear, with his large hands spanned across her mid-section, holding her back close to his front. Payne was protective of her, and I couldn't blame him. His wife was the best thing to ever happen to him. I would have kept my ride or die close to my vest too.

Gage entertained the crowd by trying to fit as many pieces of shrimp as he could into his mouth. I often wondered what kind of panty whisperer he had to be. The number of women he pulled in with his antics was astonishing. I chuckled when he choked on the seventh shrimp.

Glancing to my right, I spotted Navie Fuller at the end of the booth, perched with perfect posture, like an aristocrat. My gaze roamed her body, lingering on her long, tan legs that appeared smoother than silk, crossed perfectly at her ankles. Damn, she was a looker. She'd recently become fast friends with Willow, and I was man enough to admit I was selfishly a fan of their friendship. It meant Navie was around a lot more.

Nodding in her direction, I smiled then scanned the crowd, realizing it would be the last time I had to endure a black-tie event. I'd never liked them, but it was the way Richard ran things in the business, so I always complied. As a retiree, I would no longer be committed.

After a few moments, I made my way to the stage I'd been ignoring most of the night. Blocking the spotlight with one hand, I took a deep breath, hoping to gather my thoughts before stepping up to the mic stand. I didn't like grand gestures, preferring to keep my private life private, but I couldn't leave my own retirement party without a few words of appreciation.

When I cleared my throat, the chatter in the room quieted, and I peered out to the crowd. Bright flashes blinded me, clicks from at least ten photographers snapped one right after the other in rapid succession. Hopefully, they would leave me alone after my public farewell.

"I'd just like to take a second to thank you all for honoring me tonight. I'm honestly humbled. I may not be fighting anymore, not professionally anyhow." I paused as bouts of laughter broke through the crowd. "But you'll be seeing me around. I plan to give back, to be a part of this world for as long as I'm able. Fighting saved my life. And all of you were a part of that in some way. Thank you, all of you, for the ride."

Cheers erupted, and glasses were held high in appreciation. I waved, giving the attendees one final nod. Random handshakes and pats on the back overtook me with each table I passed, bringing my target destination insight. A lopsided grin spread across my cheeks as I reached my friends, my family. Sliding my left hand into the pocket of my black slacks, I brought my right hand over my mouth, contemplating the right words, knowing my gratitude for them would be more intimate than the thoughts I'd just shared with a room full of people I barely knew. I wanted Payne and the rest of my crew to know how much I valued them and the friendship we all shared. For someone like me—someone who was completely alone in the world—they meant everything to me. I had no family to support. No mother to call after a fight and no wife waiting for me at home, who'd tell me, even on my worst days, how much she loved me.

"It means a lot to me," I started, then cleared my throat, hoping the bout of emotions bubbling up from inside would disappear. The last fucking thing I needed was for my voice to crack, giving Gage a solid opportunity to bust my balls. Not one to express vulnerability, I deepened my voice. "The support you guys have given me. Thank you for coming tonight. Thank you for showing up. I look forward to whatever the future holds, because I know you guys are going to be around for it all." Sincerity and sadness tinged the words. I was exhausted. The finality of my decision had been weighing on me for over a year and I was more than ready to bid my farewell to the party honoring the stressful decision.

Willow leaped off Payne's lap and into my arms. "We're so proud of you!"

I hugged her tight, pleased that my best friend had found a woman like her. She couldn't have been a better match for him. She was soft, where he was hard. She was vocal when he was quiet. Willow was exactly—one hundred percent—everything Payne needed. "Thanks, doll. I appreciate the love."

"Man, I hate to see you leave the league. But, silver lining, now there's a spot open for me." Gage grinned, giving me our secret handshake. I grinned too, knowing he'd probably make it. If he could keep his dick in his pants long enough to sign the contract.

I peered at Navie over Gage's shoulder. Her hair was swept halfway up, with wild, loose curls flowing down her back, while the black cocktail dress she wore sculpted her trim body as if it had been tailored to fit her. With her father's bank account, I was sure that had been the case. Richard Fuller was the richest man I knew. He was also one of the smartest. He'd built his business from the ground up with a prayer and twenty-thousand dollars. He'd also somehow managed to keep the meatheads in said business away from his beautiful daughter. Not that it mattered, but I wouldn't have gone there anyway. I learned a long time ago not to mix business and pleasure, and Navie was my boss's daughter, which meant she was obviously off limits.

Except that wasn't the case anymore.

Navie stood and took two steps in my direction, causing me to focus more on her and less on my contemplations. "Congratulations, Trevor."

"Thanks, Navie." Wrapping an arm around her, I brought her into my side for a semi-hug.

Her fragrance hit me like jab to my gut. Sweet, but not too strong. A hint of vanilla and peaches flowed through my nostrils, refreshing, as if she were a solitary living flower in the dead of winter. I breathed in deep, hell bent on never forgetting it.

Shit.

I just sniffed a woman. I was officially losing it.

My fingertips slipped from her back to her hip of their own accord. My hand seemed to have a mind of its own, following the path of least resistance, gliding down her hourglass shape. She glanced up at me, her baby-blue eyes clouded with an underlying allusion of lust. Her body stiffened then relaxed under my fingertips. With my face just inches away from hers, I could feel her warm breath tickle my face.

Exhaling, I attempted to sort myself out. As if I didn't have enough on my plate, the weight of the evening seemed to crash headfirst into my libido.

Navie stepped back, creating distance between us. My hand fell to my side, suddenly chilled from the loss of her warmth.

I made eye contact with Payne. "I'm going to head home. I'm beat."

"Congrats again, man. I'll see you tomorrow." Payne addressed me, but his chin was planted firmly in his wife's shoulder, his nose nuzzled closely behind her ear.

Nodding to my friends, I waved, then made my way toward the lobby. As I walked out of the hotel, I loosened my tie, not worried in the slightest that photographs were being taken of me. The second my fingers pulled on the fabric, I breathed deep, feeling immediate relief from the chokehold that had threatened to strangle me the entire night.

"Steele, how do you feel?" One photographer asked as he followed behind me, seeming to work double time to keep up with my gait.

"Excellent," I answered, even though what I really wanted to do was flip the bastard off.

My thoughts scattered but paused on the hug I'd shared with Navie. She felt so right in my arms. The way her hips flared, protruding from her trim waist, had created an amazing spot for my hand to rest upon. God, I needed to release some pent up energy. The fact that I was growing harder by the second from the feel of her *fully dressed* body was more than pathetic. Especially while I was being chased by vultures.

"Steele, will you keep your contract with Fight-Might?"

Reaching out, I grabbed his arm before he fell flat on his back. "Whoa, watch out there, buddy." I should have let the dude trip over the curb. "Of course. I drink Fight-Might every morning for breakfast. I love the stuff."

"There's talk about a Steele-Martinez fight in the works for pay-per-view."

Stopping my steps, I turned toward the photog who'd insisted on digging for an exclusive. The others stopped too. "If I answer this question, will you all go away?"

"Yes," they all agreed in unison.

I chuckled and shook my head. "I'm retired as of tonight. The only connection I'll have to pay-per-view in the future is by being a paying customer."

"Thanks, Steele."

"You bet."

It wasn't every day the paps left me alone after a few questions, but thankfully, most of them scurried around the corner, happy to have the latest scoop on the insane rumor that had taken mere hours to take root. Apparently, Martinez had taken it personally that I'd retired before agreeing to fight him. He challenged me three hours after I made my announcement. My responding publicly to his challenge was petty, but it gave me satisfaction that he'd never have the pleasure.

"Hey, handsome." A female voice carried from behind me.

Glancing over my shoulder, I watched as Amelia Farris slid into my path, her bright red gown shimmering from the light posts in the parking lot. Like a lion with its prey, Amelia seemed to always be lurking in the corner, waiting for the perfect opportunity to pounce on her latest victim. She was a groupie. A well-known cage bunny, who'd made it perfectly clear to those of us in the league—and everyone outside of it—that she was willing to do just about anything to become famous. I'd been with women like her more than once, and it always turned out the same. Two perfectly agreeable people with totally different agendas. They wanted me for publicity, and I wanted them for the obvious.

"Amelia."

"You're leaving early."

I crossed my arms, my body tensing of its own volition in some weird defense mechanism. I glanced back to the entrance of the hotel, making sure the photographers had gone back inside. "Yeah, it's been a long day."

Amelia stepped closer, chewing on the side of her lip. She didn't fool me. I knew exactly what she was doing. My gaze dropped to her glossy lips, but I quickly refocused, not wanting to linger there. Navie's face entered my mind. The same face that had me hard a few minutes ago, intent on living rent free inside my mind. Unlike Amelia, she'd not approached me, desperately vying for my attention. Navie's subtlety was one of her best attributes as far as I was concerned. It made her seem elusive and mysterious, which was one hundred percent a plus in my book.

"Stuffy events tend to make the day feel long." Amelia's fingers slid the length of my loosened tie.

At the sound of a vehicle revving its engine, I peered at the hotel again. We weren't the only two people in the parking lot anymore. Valets began to pull cars around to their owners, while taxis filled the aisles. It wasn't just the fact that I didn't want to be Page Six's cover story. Amelia had totally ruined my Navie-vibe. The one I planned on reminiscing about in the shower as soon as I got home.

"Sorry, I won't be good company tonight."

"Your loss, Trevor Steele." She winked and walked away, not slighted in the least.

Shaking my head, I unclenched my arms and hopped up into my lifted Jeep. At least I didn't have to end the night feeling like a dick-head. Or a reality TV star, because even though I didn't have one of those sleazy photographers in sight, I knew they were lurking, waiting for the money shot. They always were.

As I took the on-ramp to the interstate, I glanced over at the Manhattan skyline. I loved the city and usually enjoyed the benefits of the luxurious hotels there when I had to visit New York, but I wanted to sleep in my own bed, surrounded by my own things. There were few moments in life where I'd actually felt the need to protect myself but leaving my career as a cage fighter—the one and only thing I'd ever been able to count on, made me feel an overwhelmingly sense of loss. Like I'd have to grieve it somehow. I supposed there was no place to start that process like a three-and-a-half-hour drive home to Boston.

Creep played on the radio, stirring up ancient, forgotten memories. My mother had been the biggest Radiohead fan in the world. She owned one CD; Pablo Honey, and every time we rode in the car, she played it. She'd purchased it for fifty cents at Goodwill. I'd never forget the first time she sang along, nodding her head and matching Thom Yorke's lyrics word for word. She sang loud and proud, creating our own silly bubble inside the car. I should have known something was up. My mother had a habit of creating the best moments right before the other shoe dropped. After her impromptu concert, she dropped me off at the YMCA, and forced me to meet with Pastor Dave, who she swore was going to be *good for me*. I grinned at the thought of him. Pastor Dave initially thought I was the devil's spawn. He told me as much.

I admitted to him before he died that I had been an asshole to him on purpose. He didn't take offense, seeing that I was just twelve when we'd first met, and it wasn't like he couldn't read the writing on the wall. My mom felt guilty because my dad wasn't around. I'd caught on to that fact early on, but the day she dropped me off with Dave and practically begged him to teach me boxing, karate—anything resulting in male-bonding time—I knew for sure she feared I'd never become the man I was supposed to without a father around.

Three days a week, I'd trained with Dave one-on-one, learning everything from Brazilian jujitsu to judo. The day of my fifteenth birthday, he told me, "Young man, it'd do you some good to channel all that anger."

Looking back, it was obvious I had issues, and the chip on my shoulder grew larger at his words. I had gone a long time by that point without a man in my life. Hell, I was the *man* in my life. I raged against the machine for sure, but somewhere along the way, Pastor Dave's advice took root. Not only had I learned to defend myself through training with him, but I figured out over the years where to place my emotions and how to let them go through the physical release.

Dave died shortly after my mom, but he made the biggest mark on me as a man. I struggled over the years, contemplating ways to honor him; to do something positive with my good fortune, but volunteering the way he had, didn't appeal to me. Not in the local YMCA way.

Finally, after a couple of years in the league, inspiration struck. I realized I didn't have to give back to the community the same way Dave had, I could find my own path of making a difference. The gym started small, but for me, even helping train one guy who had fight in his veins and determination in his eyes was enough.

Pulling into my gated community, I took a deep breath, then sighed, proud of my personal accomplishment. I'd really created something cool. Within five years, I had over thirty guys who trained in my gym seven days a week. Their single goal was making it to the pro circuit. I helped where I could personally, but the real draw to my gym was that I hired professional trainers who pushed the athletes to reach their maximum potential. Giving the guys that one-on-one time was what ultimately made the difference. More than a handful of fighters who'd trained with me and my team ultimately made it to the big show, and I was pleased by that.

Unlocking my front door, I pushed forward, noting the quietness. Instead of turning the lights on, I tossed my suit jacket onto the counter, and unbuttoned my crisp, white button-down. Peering between the blinds over the kitchen sink, I watched the water in my pool smoothly dance from the late-night breeze. I loved my house and everything in it, but sometimes, the silence made me wonder what it would be like to actually share my personal space with someone. Would I still enjoy the quiet nights or revel in the noise from a couple of kids? I didn't know the answer to that, and I knew from past experience it wasn't smart to question my existence.

No regrets.

Pouring myself two fingers of whiskey, I sat at my kitchen table, alone in the dark, with nothing but my own thoughts surrounding me.

Toasting myself, I savored the liquid burn all the way through my chest.

To the end of one chapter, and the beginning of another.

The light streaming in through the wall of windows awakened me, forcing me to squint as I opened my eyes. I blinked, trying to recall why I hadn't made it to my bed. I'd fallen asleep on my couch, still half-dressed from the night before. So much for my Navie-induced shower time. I crinkled my nose, noting my own filth. I smelled of shrimp and stale liquor. At the thought of liquor, I considered a shot of whiskey. Pushing up on my elbows, I grimaced. Screw the hair of the dog. I needed to do something productive. Stretching, my back popped, giving my spine a much needed release after spending the last six hours lying flat on my back. Before I could mobilize, someone knocked on my front door.

Pulling the large oak door open, I rolled my eyes when I saw Payne, who stood silently wearing a shit-eating grin.

"Morning, sunshine," he teased and held up a white paper sack from my favorite bakery, along with a white foam cup of coffee.

"You're going to make someone a real nice wife someday." I winked and shut the door behind him.

"Get bent. Willow made me bring this shit to you because she was concerned about how you'd *feel* this morning. You know, with everything going on and all," he grumbled.

"So, this blueberry muffin is a pity muffin?" I pulled it from the bag, my mouth already watering, and took a huge bite. I couldn't contain my smirk, knowing Payne was most definitely annoyed that his wife insisted on taking care of me.

"Just text her later and tell her you loved it. That's all I need you to do."

I chuckled. "I will. I'll be at the gym in a bit. Are you going now?"

"Yeah, I was on my way when she called, begging me to check in on you."

"Your wife loves me."

A scowl formed between his eyebrows. "She fucking loves *me*, asshole. She *likes* you," he called over his shoulder as he headed toward the front door, obviously not in the mood to visit.

"I saw her first!" I yelled at his back.

"She's not into pretty boys." He turned around quickly and held up a finger. "Oh, I almost forgot. I need a favor."

"Shoot," I said, as I swallowed the hot coffee, while meeting him in the hallway.

"Navie."

He had my full attention at the mere mention of her name. I swallowed the coffee, more than curious. "What about her?"

"She wants to train at the gym."

Shocked, I pinched my brows together. Why would Navie want to train at my gym? Navie Fuller—as in Richard's daughter. A woman who had personal access to every gym available on the west coast, not to mention every fighter in the AFL. Something didn't add up. My gym was clear across the country. Thousands of miles from California—located in the heart of Boston. It wasn't like the weather in Beantown could have enticed her, which threw up a huge red flag for me.

Although, the thought of her in any proximity to me caused me to grin, the view alone worth more than I cared to admit. Navie Fuller. In *my* gym. With me. That could be hot. Then I remembered all the other assholes who'd be around her too. Gage came to mind, along with Tommy. I grimaced, not liking the direction my thoughts were taking me. Gage was a fucking horn dog, and Tommy schmoozed his way into the heart of every woman within a fifty-mile radius. He was private, so it wasn't like he flaunted it like Gage did, but that asshole got plenty of ass. I'd seen him with a different girl the last three weekends alone. Kendra, Taylor—and I couldn't remember the other one. All of them beautiful, and none of them the kind of woman he'd take home to his mother.

"I'll talk to her," I agreed.

"Cool. I appreciate it. After everything that happened with Willow, I feel like I owe Navie, you know?"

I did know, but I still wasn't past giving him a hard time. "But if I allow her to train at my gym, I would be the one repaying her, not you."

"Well, you're the one with the fucking gym, and I don't have anything else to offer her."

I smirked and took another bite of the gooey goodness he'd brought me. I didn't eat sweets very often, but when I did, I fucking went all out. Willow knew that, which was why she sent her husband over to my house the morning after a somewhat depressing night, knowing without a doubt I'd give in.

"I've got to jet. Willow's going to beat my ass if I don't get the oil changed in her car today. The light's been on for two days, and she's freaking the fuck out."

I whistled. "Two days, you say?" Shaking my head in disappointment, I frowned. "Such a horrible husband."

"Shut the fuck up. I'll see you at the gym."

I stood in the doorway, as he was seeing his way out. "I have the power to deny Navie access. You'd think someone asking for a favor would talk nicer to his friend."

"You're not going to deny her. She's Willow's friend, and I know for a fact you can't say no to my wife."

"Touché, asswipe."

Payne ignored my name calling and continued down my driveway until he reached his truck. Kicking the front door closed, I walked back to my kitchen, absentmindedly finishing off the muffin.

I was shallow enough to admit the idea of having Navie around worked for me personally. But professionally? Something was amiss. Why would Navie want to train? As far as I knew, she was head of public relations for the AFL. It wasn't like there was a women's league she could compete in. And if she was only planning to train for fun, why would she choose my gym? She had unlimited options. Plus, as far as I knew, she spent most of her time on the West Coast. I had to decide if having Navie around was worth the chaos at the gym. Not that Navie would bring drama on purpose, but when a woman entered the tight-knit circle of guys training for their shot in a sport professionally, especially in a small gym, all bets were off. Particularly when said woman looked like Navie Fuller.

CHAPTER 2
NAVIE

TAKING IN MY EMPTY APARTMENT, I groaned, wondering out loud what I was doing with my life. Who the hell ran away from home at twenty-five years old? I did. I ran away because having it all, according to my family, obviously wasn't enough for me. Running my fingers through my hair, I exhaled and leaned across the island in my tiny kitchen. I had never felt so out of sorts. It was the weirdest feeling. Logically—even emotionally—I felt so light, I could have been floating through the air. Mentally, I was exhausted. There hadn't been a time in the last thirteen years when I'd stood up to my father or disobeyed him in any way. I'd always done precisely what he asked because I wanted to make him happy even if it meant that I wasn't.

Gymnastics.

Karate.

Stanford.

Master's Degree in Business.

All of it had been his vision and ultimate decision, not mine. And instead of resisting his demands; trying to figure out who I was as a person, like most people my age, I relented because he was my dad; the only parent I had left. There was an exceptional amount of guilt that came from that.

My father expected a lot from me, and he didn't mince words when he reminded me of it. My brother, on the other hand, got a free pass because he was born with a penis, which meant all he had to do was come of age and my father would gladly hand over the reins to the multi-million-dollar company he'd built from the ground up. The daughter—me—could help with the public relations.

Gross.

It would literally blow his mind to know my intentions now that I had taken the plunge and moved to Boston. I tried to tell him, but my words had fallen on deaf ears. From an early age, I'd dreamed of entering the cage, just like David Lennon or Michael DeLange. Watching those fighters week after week had shaped my idea of true heroism. Of course, I'd had to watch from afar, but I never missed the chance to study the athletes my dad hired. Even the bad ones. At the age of seventeen, it occurred to me that my interest with the business was not in the realm my father had hoped for. No, I wanted to fight. I wanted to be *one* of them, not the one who cleaned up their messes after a night of ill-advised, string of bad decisions.

My enthusiasm had grown over the years and was unparalleled. The way the athletes' bodies moved so gracefully—the intense challenge of preparing to be a winner—I craved that experience. The look on their faces when they won the very match they'd trained hours a day for—it just seemed like the epitome of accomplishment. I yearned to feel that. Accomplished.

Rinsing the paper coffee cup out, I filled it again, not entirely satisfied because I'd settled for a thirty-dollar pot instead of my high-end, latte maker, which was on its way from California. That had been one thing I hadn't waited on the movers for. I couldn't function without my morning coffee, even if it was basically ground beans with zero extras. The caffeine would have to be enough—at least for a little while.

I pulled my hoodie over my head and reached for my keys. I told myself over and over that everything would be okay, even though I didn't fully believe it. I couldn't recall a time I'd ever been more nervous. Trevor Steele wasn't someone I knew that well. He was extremely private, one of the fighters I'd never learned much about. Of course, he was one of the most popular fighters in the AFL, but he'd remained an anomaly for me up until a few months ago when I became close to Willow. Of course, she had a ton of stories about him, and I'd even been around him a couple of times, but Trevor still felt three times removed for me. In a six degrees of Kevin Bacon kind-of-way.

Working in the AFL had afforded me certain privileges, but unless it had been business-related, I had no reason to keep tabs on Trevor. He ran in different crowds than a lot of my dad's athletes. He didn't give in too much where his private life was concerned, and coming from a family that thrived in the spotlight, I completely understood that.

I hadn't told Willow the extent of my plans, for fear of it appearing like I was taking advantage of my relationship with her. She had the complete and total hook-up with Trevor, and I needed his help, not his pity. I would admit too, I didn't want to jinx myself. I knew I was capable of excelling in the sport if for nothing else, because I cared about it so much, yet deep down, I wondered if Trevor would be open to my training at his gym.

Unfortunately, being in the business had also taught me about sexism, which seemed ridiculous in today's world, but I knew first-hand it still existed. I had to try though. There had been two reasons I chose to leave my cushy life in California and move clear across the country in attempt at making my pipe dream a reality. One, I trusted Trevor over every other fighter I'd ever come in contact with. Even without knowing him personally, I knew he was a solid guy. There hadn't been so much as a negative statement about his character in over ten years. His reputation preceded him. And two, he was the reigning champion. If anyone could train me to be a winner, it was him.

Parking my Range Rover in the gym parking lot, I took a moment to compose myself. With as much video as I'd watched plus the hours I had spent at past fights, one would think I would be able to waltz inside and get to work straight away. Regrettably, my nerves were taking a dump on my confidence exactly five minutes prior to one of the most important first impressions I would probably ever experience.

Dammit. Just go inside.

Grabbing my bag, I slipped out of my SUV and prayed I didn't look like a fool on my first day. Entering the building, I felt dozens of eyes on me from every direction, pinpointing me like lasers. I wasn't sure if it was because they recognized me, or if it was because I seemed to be the only female there. Ultimately, I was the outsider, and if I hadn't already known that, the attention I'd garnered walking inside solidified it. Taking a deep breath, I stilled and tried to ignore the attention as I searched for Payne.

I found him, unaware that I'd arrived, pumping out reps like a machine on the bench press, his earbuds secure in his ears. I disregarded the stares from the other athletes and headed straight for him, knowing once I reached him I would relax.

"Hey," I said, bumping his leg with mine.

He rose from under the press and pulled his earbuds out. "You made it."

I nodded and glanced behind me. Luckily, most of the nosy onlookers had gone back to their workout. "I really appreciate you putting in a good word with Trevor for me."

He shrugged and wiped his face. "I owed you one."

"Still."

I hated to collect, especially since Willow was quickly becoming one of my best friends. And if I was being honest, assisting her when she'd been attacked in the bathroom by an ex-con at one of Payne's fights had been a natural response. I hadn't come to her aid with any ulterior motive. But the fact remained, I needed a place to train, and Trevor was the one person my father wouldn't consider a joke. His reaction when I asked to train with his athletes back home hadn't been misconstrued. My giving it a go amused him if nothing else. Not to mention, I didn't have any aces up my sleeve. My father owned everyone. And every contact I had either worked for him or owed him something. But Trevor wasn't indebted to him in any way since my dad no longer signed his paychecks. It seemed to me, he was my only chance.

With my dad still the CEO of the American Fighting League, no one on the West Coast would so much as scrap with me. My father had made sure everyone on his payroll knew it would be career suicide to indulge me. It was totally different with Preston, my brother.

He'd ridden on the shoulders of almost every fighter in the league over the last decade. Sparred with them, taken private lessons, and even refereed a charity event once. Not me, though. I sat in the VIP booth and listened to my dad pitch his latest idea to an interested investor, while taking notes and smiling at all the appropriate moments.

I loved my father, but the differences in the way he treated my brother and me was beyond chauvinist. Even as kids, he'd allowed Preston to compete in karate tournaments and attend fighting events, proudly displaying our last name at the after parties. Me, not so much. He allowed me to take karate lessons, but I later found out the reason for that had been so Preston and I were at the same place after school. With him being a single dad, it was simply convenient. And the after parties were never discussed prior to the fight nights. Instead, his black Denali waited at the back door with Jeff, one of my dad's drivers, ready to carry out my father's strict orders to get me home safe, into the care of my nanny, Ms. Lisa. My dad never failed to kiss me on top of the head, with specific instructions to study hard and get some rest. It was insulting to say the least.

It seemed my father had his own idea of who I was supposed to be, and that was what he expected of me. Forget that I had a mind and heart of my own.

It wasn't like I had my mother around to remind him. I'd never forget the police officer who came to the door the night she died. Tall and sort of hefty, he'd worn a brown, felt hat. I noticed the dark stains on it from the rain. She'd been just seven miles from our house when she ran off the road and her vehicle overturned into a ditch. She'd gone to the store for a few ingredients so Preston and I could bake cookies. That was it. Cookies for my mother's life. I still couldn't handle the idea of baking them on my own, even as an adult.

When I thought about how distant we'd become as a family since my mother's death, it made me miss her even more. If she were still alive, she would have made sure our family stuck together. She wouldn't have stood for my father limiting me or my brother becoming a brat.

I shook off the misguided thoughts. Reminiscing about my mom wouldn't bring her back, nor would it force my father to encourage me in my endeavors.

"I see you made it." Trevor Steele's deep voice echoed from behind me.

Swiping the fly-a-ways that had fallen from my ponytail out of my eyes, I turned to face him. "Yeah. Um—thank you for letting me train here." It would be a total lie if I said seeing him again after the hug we'd shared at his retirement party wasn't a bit uncomfortable. Mostly because I had liked it. I could still feel the warmth from his embrace if I tried hard enough.

He crossed his arms but remained relaxed. "What exactly are you expecting, Navie?"

There was absolutely no way I could indulge my secret dream. It was one thing when twenty-something-year-old dudes vied for his wisdom involving the league, but he would have thought I was a complete and total lunatic if I mentioned my plan to not only reach the highest level of cage fighting, but my full intention of creating a league all my own. "I just want a place to train."

He eyed me in silence, making me feel feeble. In an instant, I felt deflated, as if my hopes for him as an understanding and supportive person had been burst with a single question. He wasn't rude or anything, but asking me what I was expecting within the first two minutes of my being there made me feel like he was sizing me up. To top it off, he looked unperturbed, but his words were frank. As if he didn't have the time to humor me. I lifted my chin, even though I had the urge to look down.

Finally, he said, "Okay."

"Okay?"

He nodded and unfolded his arms. "Okay."

"Good. Awesome."

His gaze never wavered. "Awesome."

"I'm going to get started then." But I didn't budge.

"Cool." He hadn't moved an inch either, and I was annoyed. I didn't want him analyzing me. Not on my first day. I was anxious enough as it was.

"Okay, see you around." I fake smiled, hoping to shoo him off.

He ignored my dismissal and tilted his head to the side. "Does your dad know you're here?"

Payne grunted from somewhere behind me and moved to start his jumps. Glancing in his direction, I saw that he wasn't paying any attention to my conversation with Trevor. Good. Having an audience witness my being awkward would have made things worse.

I narrowed my eyes, not appreciating being treated like a juvenile runaway. "No."

"You know this puts me in a weird position, right?" Trevor's right eyebrow rose just a hair, making him appear boyishly cute.

Right… he was in the middle of chastising me.

Irritated, I decided to show him that I was a full-grown woman, capable of making my own decisions. I pulled my T-shirt over my head, more than over his inquisition. I'd made my mind up. I was living my own life. Besides, maybe if he saw me standing in nothing than my sports bra, he would leave me alone. I couldn't imagine he would appreciate his audience gossiping about him and the new girl.

It was a low blow, but all I had.

"How so?"

His gaze dropped to my chest.

Money.

With my hands on my hips, I waited him out, watching as his green eyes changed colors, the brightness almost the shade of freshly cut grass. The intensity from the storm raging behind his irises had me fighting the urge to grab my T-shirt off the floor to cover myself. It wasn't like I'd stripped naked, but his honest reaction gave me the same sense of scrutiny. But sports bras were how women competed. I'd seen it hundreds of times, and so had he. Even though my stripping down to training gear had served as an off-the-cuff defense mechanism, it seemed I'd not factored in my response to his. When he didn't hightail it away from me, I realized my move had one hundred percent backfired.

Fighting the urge to squeeze my eyes shut, I held my groan inside and somehow found the courage to remain silent. I only wanted an opportunity to see if I could make it in the male dominated world I'd grown up in. One that I knew front and back, inside and out. All I needed was someone who could help me with the physical part of it. Someone who would take a chance on me and my ability to learn. After leaving my resignation letter on my father's desk in a cowardly manner, I couldn't afford another blow to my confidence, even if it was from someone who didn't know me. The last thing I needed was another reason to believe I was an idiot for even trying.

"Never mind." He smirked, seemingly impressed with my poker face. "You're welcome here. If anyone gives you any trouble, let me know." Cool as a cucumber, the color in his eyes returned to normal, a natural olive green.

"Will do. Thanks."

Exhaling, I watched him walk away, my gaze lingering longer than necessary. Soon, grotesque smacking noises came from behind me. Glancing over my shoulder, I couldn't miss Gage thrusting his pelvis up and down, his lips drawn together as if he were a fish out of water. He didn't miss anything. Not one opportunity to embarrass someone, and he seemed to get off on the vulnerability of others. Payne was on the other side of Gage, annoyingly amused at the situation.

I blew out a frustrated breath, and quickly turned my back to them, embarrassed I'd been so side-tracked by Trevor's looks.

Pushing my earbuds into my ears, I resolved to make the most of the opportunity in front of me, intent on disregarding their antics, determined to get back to business. I did three sets of one hundred jump ropes, then quickly moved on to some strength training, and then finished up with a three-mile run. I knew the workout was nowhere near what I needed to be doing, but I had to start somewhere. Honestly, I wanted to learn from the guys but following them around intensely studying their regiment would probably be coming on too strong. I needed to discover exactly what they did in order to achieve their fighting success. But since it was my first day, and no one had offered to train me personally, I figured I'd just feel it out for a while. I couldn't very well beg someone to train me after just receiving the opportunity to use Trevor's gym.

What would I even say? *What? Like it's hard?* Insert quick hair flip. *Listen, guys, I know I've spent the last few years on the top floor of a fancy office building, creating kick-ass marketing for the AFL, but I feel like I'm ready.*

No.

To anyone on the outside, I was positive most of them regarded me as the spoiled daughter of one of the richest men in America. An office lackey in a pinstriped Chanel suit with sky-high Louboutin's to match. Little did they know I'd spent most of my life behind the scenes, wishing I was one of them. Watching them work their asses off for a specific goal, where the outcome was instantaneous, inspired me. My heart skipped beats at the prospect—my inner voice shouting from the tops of her lungs that she needed the physical connection to triumph, which made me feel so strong. I'd denied myself for so long. I saw no other choice but to give in to my secret aspirations, praying I would finally feel whole. That was the thing so many people misunderstood about me wanting to enter the cage. On most days, pride was all I had. The determination to win; to feel productive and feed my soul. I needed to prove the naysayers wrong. Especially my dad and my brother.

I supposed living in my father's shadow, not to mention Preston's, could have contributed to my need for wanting them to eat their hateful words, but trying to smother my belief that I could be more than a pretty face who could make out a schedule and write a decent memo, just made me feel worse. Like I was some fraud, living a life with no point to it. In my ideal world, the sky was the limit. I'd never told anyone; never said the words out loud before, but I hoped to take fighting in the cage as far as I could. Maybe I could even start a women's league back up. One that would stand the test of time because I knew exactly what it took to make it in the business, thanks to the unlimited time my father gave me inside the offices at headquarters. Not to mention my master's degree in business. There was that at least.

A tap on my shoulder broke me out of my reverie. "Hey!" Willow hugged me, even though I was a sweaty mess.

"How are you?" I asked, not surprised in the least to see her at the gym before Payne's workout was finished.

"Great. When will the movers be here?" She reminded me of the work I had to do once I got home to my new apartment.

"Friday afternoon, thank goodness. I underestimated the two suitcases I packed."

And boy had I ever. Unfortunately, I'd had Penny, my dad's housekeeper, help me pack when my father was at work. Penny tossed a couple pair of underwear, joggers, shorts, two sports bras, five T-shirts, and two pantsuits in my bags. She promised the rest of my belongings would be sent with the movers. I trusted her, but doing laundry every other day hadn't been my favorite part about moving across the country. I'd been in my apartment for almost two weeks, sleeping on an air mattress and living off ramen noodles and turkey sandwiches. It hadn't been as extravagant as my life in California, but it sure as hell had been more peaceful.

"How's your quest going?" I winked, knowing my friend was happy to finally be searching for the house of her dreams.

She scrunched her nose, appearing disappointed. "It's a pain. I'm still searching for our white picket fence."

I tipped my water bottle upward, taking a full swig as my gaze landing on Trevor over her shoulder. He was at the front desk talking to two guys I didn't recognize. He glanced at me as he spoke to them.

I looked away, giving Willow my full attention again. It seemed training in Trevor Steele's gym was going to take more concentration than I'd originally planned for. Already, I'd caught myself looking his way too many times to count, including the mortifying moment Gage had caught me and made the event public knowledge.

"Okay, so we'll see you around six, then?" Willow asked, referring to the time she and Lena, her best friend, would be over to help me shop for a couple of necessities for the kitchen.

I wiped my face with a fresh towel, absently wondering if Trevor washed his clothes at home with the same detergent. It smelled fresh, clean. Like him. "That sounds good, and seriously, I really appreciate you guys helping me."

"No problem. After all you've done for us? Girl, we've got you." She nudged my shoulder, then strolled off to the corner where Payne was working out.

I watched them for a few minutes, marveling at their easy interaction. Just seeing his face made her beam, and he was so aware of her and where she was in proximity to him. When she leaned back, he leaned in. When they took the first step to wherever they were going, their hands joined automatically. Their body language matched perfectly, always in sync.

"So...how was your first day?" Trevor's voice interrupted my thoughts.

"Oh. Fine. Good—it was good." I stumbled over my words, startled at being interrupted as I observed Payne and Willow.

"I noticed you stayed mostly stationary today."

He'd noticed. Probably because it looked like I didn't know what I was doing.

"Yeah. I thought I'd ease myself in. Would it be a big deal if I hung around some? To observe?"

"Not at all. We're all here for each other."

"Great. I have stuff to do this afternoon, but maybe starting next week I'll stay after my workout, if that's cool?"

"Like I said, we're supportive. You can hang around anywhere you'd like."

I licked my lips, not knowing what else to say. I wasn't sure why I was nervous around him. He certainly wasn't a stranger. But there was something different about Trevor now. Maybe it was the fact that he was no longer an employee of my family's business. Or it could have been that stupid hug we'd shared at his retirement party. The one that had my sense of smell searching for his scent wherever I was. Either way, his easy-going demeanor made it seem like he knew something I didn't, and I wasn't sure what that was, nor was I positive I liked it.

"I appreciate that. I'll see you around." I grabbed my bag and forced myself to walk away, tamping the dancing butterflies in my belly down through sheer determination.

My obvious attraction to Trevor was unlike anything I'd ever experienced before. I felt drawn to him, and walking in the opposite direction from him seemed wrong. As if my brain and body were working against each other, the sensation of utter disarray made me awkward. Plus, I sensed his gaze on me even when I reached the door.

Shaking off the distraction of my thoughts, I pushed the large, metal door open and walked out of his gym, breathing in the fresh afternoon air. Thinking of Trevor Steele in any other way than valiant would not be good for my end goal. I had to put training first and prove to myself I could live up to my potential. I had all but cut ties with my family and uprooted my whole life, chasing a dream. Not only was I aiming to be a female cage fighter, I was attempting to become one in a man's world—a world that my father owned and Trevor Steele still somehow ruled with his retirement being so new. Keeping those facts in the forefront of my mind made walking away from him easier. In fact, it made leaving Trevor Steele behind my only choice.

CHAPTER 3
TREVOR

"YOU HAVE TO HELP HER." Willow's sweet voice rang through my ears, sounding like an unrelenting little sister who needed her big brother's assistance instead of my best friend's wife asking me for a favor. I should have known I'd regret inviting them over for dinner just shy of a week after Navie had entered my gym for the first time. Willow never left anything alone until she knew every god-forsaken detail and was satisfied with the outcome.

I didn't *have* to do anything, not that I was willing to tell her that. I exhaled, blowing out a frustrated breath because, even though I knew I didn't have to help the beautiful woman I was attracted to, I knew I was going to. Which was so not a good idea. I had self-control, I wasn't a Neanderthal. But… I was still a man. A man who swore to himself after his first and only failed marriage, that he would never, and I mean—ever—go down that rabbit hole again. Getting so attached to someone made a man weak and considerably stupid. With that came vulnerability, and ultimately at their partner's mercy. Fun? I could do. Passionate rendezvous? I was so down. But a woman like Navie? No, the pleasure wouldn't be worth the pain. She was a woman with class, and I knew enough from talking with her, and observing her over the years to understand that she was not the kind of girl who would entertain my private, but extremely shallow, mantra of no strings attached. Which left me somewhere between an idiot and a glutton.

"Seriously, dude. She could obviously use a mentor. Plus, she stepped up big time when we"—Payne nodded at Willow—"needed her help."

I pulled a face as I stood up and made my way over to the grill. He wasn't wrong, but Payne didn't know my internal battle. I wasn't sure training anyone, let alone someone I was attracted to, was something I should be dealing with, especially when said attracter was Richard Fuller's daughter. Blowback from him could cause mass destruction for the guys who trained in my gym.

Glancing at Willow, I mentally gave in, even though I continued to search for reasons why entertaining Navie would be a bad idea. After a couple of silent moments passed, I couldn't exactly think of anything substantial. At least nothing that didn't make me look like a lustful asshole.

Still, I spoke the cons I could think of on the spot out loud. "I don't know what I can do for her. It's not like there are women knocking down the doors of gyms, hoping to get into their own league. I'm not even sure that's what she wants. She hasn't mentioned a personal trainer."

I resisted voicing the rest of my concerns. I was still confused as to why she'd shown up out of the blue. I'd never heard even a whisper that Navie was interested in training or fighting. To be honest, she didn't look the part either. She was sophisticated, beautiful, and more often than not, shy. Or at least reserved. She was definitely in shape, that much was obvious, but anyone with a set of eyes could see that strength wasn't one of her strong suits.

Plus, there hadn't been a professional league for women in years. There was a joke of one in Minnesota, some has-been ran for a couple of years, but he didn't promote it right and God only knew what he had those female athletes do for a fight night. I wasn't sure that was what she was looking for. But leaving six figures to *exercise* in my gym didn't add up.

Payne lifted a shoulder. "So what? Maybe she just wants to learn the craft. Maybe trying to go pro isn't her end game."

His words made sense. It wasn't like she didn't have the most difficult part in the bag with her father's standing. "She'd need a league first. Plus, if anyone could help her go pro in any capacity," I said, flipping the burgers on the grill, "it's her old man."

"I don't know the extent of it, but she's talked about fighting inside the cage before. She knows women who do it, but according to her, her father burned those bridges to the ground, after announcing publicly he didn't support a female league. He is such a prick." Willow patted Payne's shoulder. "Sorry, babe."

"Don't apologize to me. The man signs my paychecks, but that's about all."

Richard and I had a decent relationship during my time in the league. He was arrogant and a little boisterous for my taste, but all in all, he hadn't been hard to deal with. Plus, he'd always given me what I asked for, which put him in the decent boss category as far I as my career was concerned. But it was no secret he showed favoritism or at the very least, a difference between Navie and her brother. In fact, thinking about it now, Preston was always in the forefront, standing to the right of his father, where Navie only came along for the black-tie events. The whole situation rubbed me the wrong way.

I scowled, realizing I had never analyzed it before. It crossed my mind when I saw them at functions and Preston seemed to be his right-hand man. Navie, on the other hand, was nowhere to be seen. The few times she was around, it seemed like her father expected her there for superficial reasons. Richard never outright encouraged conversation from her the way he did his son, who was a total dumbass. I never focused on the issue, mainly because it wasn't any of my business.

Add in the fact I'd seen the YouTube video that had gone viral—the one everyone in the fighting circle had watched on loop for a solid week. They'd been in one of the VIP boxes at the Staples Center in Los Angeles, when Navie asked for her dad's permission to train with Evan Massingil. Standing tall in her lavender dress with a split up to her hip, she'd told her father she wanted more out of life, practically begging him to see her point of view. I couldn't imagine she'd wanted anything other than to be humored at that time. Her brother, Preston, had taken the liberty to record the whole conversation live, which he obviously found entertaining. Although when push came to shove in the PR nightmare, he swore publicly that someone hacked his phone and released the video, but anyone with common sense knew better. During their private conversation, Richard questioned his daughter's sanity and Preston told her Evan didn't have time to indulge a foolish girl's silly dream.

Furrowing my brow, I realized I'd never asked Evan about the situation.

"I don't know. She's a little closed off. Maybe I'll try to talk to her this week to see what's up."

"I mean she's a private person, but I know someone else who can relate to that." Willow paused, raising her left eyebrow. "She's a good person, Trevor. Trust me, I have an eye for these kinds of things." She grinned and planted a kiss on Payne's lips, the perfect exclamation point to her statement.

"I'll think about it." I sighed.

Willow puckered her bottom lip, not liking my response.

"Willow—babe..." I smiled my best reassuring grin, knowing she had trouble resisting my dimples.

"Don't you show me those stupid dimples. I'm immune now. Just give her a chance." Her face was crinkled with worry, probably already taking on the responsibility of Navie's best interests, because that's what Willow did. She mothered everyone around her, but none of us took offense. We loved her for it.

Just as we were about to eat, Willow's phone rang. Payne and I continued our argument over who was going to win the next main event on pay-per-view while she took the call.

"What do you mean, they didn't deliver your stuff?"

Payne and I eyed at each other, but before I could say anything, he was already behind Willow holding her hip for comfort.

"Well, that's just—I'll be over there in a minute. You stay right where you are." She shoved her phone in her back pocket and looked up at us. "We have to go."

"What's going on?" Payne asked.

"Not sure of the details. That was Navie. Instead of the movers showing up, her brother did. He bought the apartment building without her knowledge and kicked her out! We literally just got her settled."

"Why would he do that?" I asked.

It seemed my earlier concern wasn't so far-fetched. I'd never considered myself insensitive, but the idea of unwanted drama didn't appeal to me in any way. I was too old for asshole brothers and pissed off fathers—especially one who had the future of the guys who trained in my gym in the palm of his hand. I didn't want any unwarranted commotion and my clients didn't need it.

"Because her dad and brother treat her like an idiot. They literally think her only job is to interview well and show her cleavage when the league needs a boost. To be available twenty-four hours a day, handle their social media nightmares and to never have a life of her own. Her brother had her phone tracked. That little pissant." Willow crossed her arms, fuming.

Payne kissed the top of Willow's head. "Baby—calm down. We'll figure it out."

"You don't need to get involved," I chimed in. "Not with your contract at stake. I'll go help Navie," I volunteered before I realized what I was doing.

"I don't give a fuck about the contract," Payne argued.

Willow turned, looking deep into her man's eyes. "I know you don't, sweetheart, but I think Steele is right. You stay clear of it. I don't want any of this blowing back on you. Your career is just taking off and I don't want anything to jeopardize that. We'll help her out." Willow pulled Payne toward her by the back of his neck.

"I go where you go," he told her through clenched teeth, his brow set in a stubborn line.

Payne wasn't looking at me by any means, but I knew from the tone in his voice his declaration was for me as much as it was Willow. He wasn't leaving her. There would be no exceptions. Instead of arguing with him, Willow and I followed him out the front door, and jumped into his truck. There was no small talk as he maneuvered the side streets while Willow gave directions to Navie's apartment.

Payne parked in the first vacant space available. We followed

Willow up to the third floor in silence, where Navie opened the front door before we even knocked, looking beautiful… and defeated.

Even with her despondent demeanor, dressed in her loungewear, I'd never been more enamored by anyone. Her long hair was pulled into a messy bun atop her head, the shorter pieces curled as if they'd air-dried. Her black leggings molded to her body perfectly, and the light purple sweater she wore hung loosely off one shoulder, showing skin so smooth, impure thoughts muddled my mind, thinking of three different ways to touch it, fondle it, and taste it in less than thirty seconds.

She wore glasses. Thick, black frames shaped her face, making her appear younger, and honestly a little hipster, which wasn't typically something that grasped my attention. Except, the second I realized what I was doing, my breathing hitched, and smoldering heat sprang from my chest. Immediately, I reminded myself why we were standing inside her apartment. I wasn't there to take in her unique beauty. Or to ogle her ass in the fitted leggings she wore. And I certainly wasn't there to gaze at her piercing blue eyes outlined by the longest eyelashes I'd ever seen. She was a friend, of sorts, and we were there to help her with an issue she had in whatever way we could. I peered out the third story window, just before Willow grabbed the sleeve of my T-shirt. Apparently, she'd taken notice of my moment of reprieve.

"I'm sorry I don't have anywhere for you guys to sit down." Instead of being embarrassed, Navie held her head high, raised her chin even.

"What exactly happened?" Willow asked.

"My brother happened." Navie sighed. "He showed up, informed me the moving trucks weren't coming and that he was the new owner of my building. He handed me a bogus contract advising me that in five months, my rent would be five-grand a month, plus a ridiculous amount of service charges for things I don't even use. I threatened to call the police, and he left."

"Five fucking grand?" Payne scowled. "Why didn't you call us earlier?"

Navie shook her head. "Because I didn't want you guys involved in my family bullshit. He's trying to manhandle me into going back home. I've dealt with stuff like this my whole life, but this is a new low for him."

"A new low for Preston or your dad?" I asked, wondering if Richard was really behind the asinine attempt of tough love or if her brother was just being the dick I knew him to be.

"Both. My dad is—not as difficult all the time. He just thinks he knows what's best." She pushed both hands through her hair, then tightened her hair tie. "My brother is a different story. He knows I quit my job. That's why he bought the building. He thinks he can drain my bank account, and I'll be forced to go back home."

"You can stay with us." Willow looked to Payne, whose eyes were practically bugging out of his head. "Right, honey?"

He did not want company, that much was clear. Sharing his new bride clearly hadn't been on his to-do list, no matter how sweet Navie was. But I knew he'd relent because he loved Willow and he would do anything to make her happy.

He waited a beat before agreeing. "Sure."

I would have laughed out loud had the circumstances not been so bad. I'd definitely fuck with him about it later, though. There was really no reason for me not to offer up my place. They were newlyweds. I was alone and had the extra room.

"Look, I've got four bedrooms, and three of them I don't even use. You're more than welcome to stay at my place until you figure things out."

Navie's eyes grew a fraction, surprised. "Oh, no. I couldn't. I appreciate you—"

"Stop." Willow grabbed Navie's hands. "You have done so much for us—for me. We're all family here, and we take care of our own."

"Willow, I couldn't. I'm so thankful—I am—but I'll figure it out. I have some money put back to get by. I'll get a job and figure it all out."

"Where? Where will you get a job?" Willow wasn't a mother yet, but she had the mom voice down pat. "You want to eventually get inside the cage, do you not? How are you going to find a job that will pay rent when you have to train eight hours a day?" She pressed, surprising me by announcing Navie wanted to be a cage fighter. Even Navie's eyes widened in shock, and it was more than obvious Willow had spilled the beans. I shot Payne a look but remained silent.

Navie swiped her right hand across the top of her head, smoothing the frayed curls back in frustration. She glanced up at me, making eye contact, then glanced at the floor as if Willow's revelation had mortified her. "I don't know. I'll come up with something."

Willow turned to her husband in desperation. "Conner, do something." Her plea made my gut churn.

My face flushed, and the heat spread throughout my body. A foreign feeling caught me off guard. How in the hell was I jealous of my best friend and his wife for attempting to help someone in need? Clarity formed when I pictured Navie in my home, surrounded by my things. I imagined her in her pajamas leaning across my bar with a cup of coffee, or cozy on my couch in front of the fireplace watching *Friends* reruns. The thought made me…happy. Like, maybe it would be less lonely and actually nice to have someone to laugh with.

"You'll bunk with me," I blurted. It sounded harsher than I'd wanted it to, and I braced for her reaction.

Navie glanced up at me, her eyes squinted in anger. "I don't like being told what to do. That's what landed me in this situation in the first place."

"Fine." I cleared my throat. "I'd like it if you would stay with me, at least until you're back on your feet without your brother's interference."

Her annoyance disappeared and her face softened. "Trevor, I appreciate your offer. Really." She crossed her arms. "But I can't put you out like that."

"It's no imposition. I'm hardly ever there anyway," I lied.

"It's none of my business, but I think staying with Steele is best. He has the most room. And like he said, he's hardly ever there," Payne said, waggling his brows at me when the girls weren't looking.

I flipped him off, taking advantage of the girls' concentration on each other.

"I agree. Think of it this way—it's a new start, and it will give you time to adjust. Not to mention, if you stay in an apartment your brother owns, he has access to you. If you stay with Steele, there will literally be no pressure, and you won't have to worry about bills and such." Willow smiled, clearly pleased with the new arrangement.

"I'm not worried about the bills," Navie sighed.

"Just let us help. Get out of this environment so you can at least think straight. It will give you time to find a new place without worrying about what ways your brother or father will attempt to derail you."

Navie nodded once. She looked at me and her eyes softened, the slightest hint of blush blooming on her cheeks. "Okay," she agreed. "Only if you let me pay rent once I get a job."

"Done," I lied again.

Damn, I hadn't had ten conversations with her and had already lied twice. And I'd done it so flippantly to keep her feelings intact. I wasn't sure what that said about me, but I was fairly certain it wasn't good.

"It's settled then." Willow clapped her hands together. "We'll help move—" She looked around and frowned.

"So, other than a few belongings, that won't be necessary. I didn't even take the time to pack most of my clothes because I relied on the moving trucks, who are obviously not going to show up." Navie glanced around the apartment.

"It's cool. We can swing by a store and get anything you need." I tried to settle her nerves. She peered over at me but remained silent. I couldn't tell if she was offended or grateful.

Willow cut in. "We'll figure everything out. Don't worry."

Famous last words. Ironic, too, because when we all walked out of Navie's apartment complex and got into different vehicles, Navie and myself in hers, and Willow and Payne in his, I couldn't help but panic a little on the inside, because I was the dumbass who'd all but begged a beautiful woman to live with me. Me—a man who'd sworn off relationships and made it a point to keep females at arm's length. Especially females I was attracted to.

Needless to say, I was fucking worried.

I was worried for me, and I was worried for Navie, because as good of a guy as I liked to think I was, I'd failed someone before, and I didn't want to do that again. Not that things with Navie would even get that far, but I could feel the shift in the air when we were near each other. She felt it too; I could see it in her eyes, and even though we both seemed intent on ignoring it, I had a brain. And common sense.

Glancing out the driver's side window, I gritted my teeth. I had vowed a long time ago that keeping my own space was a must for my self-preservation when it came to women. And up until thirty minutes ago, I hadn't ever second-guessed that decision. But the thought of Navie suffering made me want to kill the person responsible and throw my guts up at the same time. Groaning, I realized I'd have to take my own trip to the store whether Navie needed to or not. Extra strength antacids were going to be a must.

CHAPTER 4
NAVIE

I WAS HUMILIATED. Not only had my brother basically forced me to make my personal matters public, he'd warned me my father would cut financial ties with me, leaving me with no trust, if I chose not to board his private jet back to California with him. Preston had lied about many things in the past, but the ultimatum he'd issued per my father hadn't been one of them. Before Willow, Payne, and Trevor had shown up at my apartment, I contacted my lawyer, who was also our family lawyer, and he advised me my father had changed his will twenty minutes after Preston stormed out of my apartment.

I'd saved for six months prior to moving to Boston, but the thought of not being financially stable had never crossed my mind. I never feared day-to-day expenses, knowing I could balance it all because I had something to fall back on if needed. Except that wasn't the case anymore since my family was pushing back.

It wasn't like I expected Payne, Trevor, or anyone else not to figure it out, but I hadn't told them or Willow that part of the story when they'd shown up after Preston left me high and dry. I wasn't sure why. Maybe I was ashamed, fearful they'd see me vulnerable, and much to my dismay—petrified. More than anything, I didn't want them to see me as a failure. None of them had grown up like I had. They were used to doing things on their own, making things happen for themselves. I wasn't.

With the disappointing turn of events, I knew my savings would dwindle with living expenses because there was absolutely no way in hell Trevor Steele or anyone else for that matter was paying my way. But I wasn't an idiot. Money would run out quickly, and I'd be stretched too thin, attempting to work to earn money, while simultaneously training to fight, which would leave me defeated before I even got started. I knew that much from growing up around the league. My father paid his fighters to train to be the best, and their job was to practice. If I was working, that meant I wasn't practicing. I hadn't even made a full attempt, yet the obstacles already made me feel like it was going to be a lifetime of one step forward and three steps back.

I closed my eyes, pushing back the frustrated, gut-wrenching wails on the inside, but the water in my tear ducts was too much for my poor lids to take. The realization of the whole situation crushed me like an ant under my shoe. My relationships with my family had never been perfect, but I couldn't believe how eager they'd become trying to force me to do what they wanted. One tear spilled over, then two. I hadn't said a word to Trevor since we'd both slid into my car, knowing we were embarking on uncharted territory. At least for me it was.

He was helping. I was helpless.

It wasn't ideal.

Not for someone like me. Not for a woman who'd just made the ultimate sacrifice to prove to herself that she could do anything she set her mind to. Not for the woman I thought I was becoming.

"Hey." The kindheartedness of his tone enveloped me, soothing my nerves.

I wiped away the tears and continued to stare straight ahead.

"You're going to be okay. It's all going to work out. I promise."

I swallowed and sniffed. "Thanks. I appreciate what you're doing."

"Don't thank me." He pulled into his circle drive and put my SUV in park. I hadn't resisted when he'd walked straight for the driver's side of my car outside my apartment.

He reached his large hand out, pulling mine from my lap, and squeezed it. "It's going to be all right. And hey, you might even enjoy a roommate like me. I mean, I can grill a kickass steak. And I don't leave my dirty socks in the couch cushions or anything."

I chuckled, thankful for the reprieve. I'd had a rough couple of weeks, and there was something so overwhelming about only having a suitcase full of mere basic necessities. I shook my head, reeling from the enormous decision I'd made to leave an apartment I'd just signed a lease on. I still had to deal with the legalities of the situation, and now that I was sitting in front of a massive house, owned by a man I barely knew, knowing we were going to be roommates, I wondered if I shouldn't have stuck it out for a few months.

"I know this is—strange," I began.

"Not strange. Timing is everything. What's supposed to happen will happen." Trevor leaned into the side panel of the driver's side door but hesitated then glanced over at me, capturing my full attention. "Don't ever be ashamed of who you are or where you're going. Everything happens for a reason. Follow your heart." He lifted his right hand, then spread it across the left side of his chest. "Don't ever doubt that massive thing doesn't know what's best for you." He winked.

I smiled at his words as he got out of my car. Maybe he was right. It was conceivable everything happening to me was part of a bigger plan. I could have made the right decision, following my instincts to leave California, then leaving my apartment which was tied to my brother. It was quite possible, having to fight for success was just part of the road to getting there. I stepped out, feeling somewhat lighter. Not only because I literally had two suitcases and the clothes on my back, but Trevor's assurance sparked something deep inside, something I hadn't felt in a long time: confidence.

As I reached the front door of his home, he nodded for me to go in in front of him. I smiled and nodded back at him, thanking him silently. When I walked into his house, I wasn't bogged down by the emotions I'd felt mere moments before. As uncomfortable as I was intruding on his personal space, I was still hopeful I could make a life for myself on my own.

"Help yourself to anything. I'll get groceries soon. Pick any room in the hallway. The last one on the left is mine."

"Thanks." I left him in the kitchen to check out the spare rooms. I figured a little space couldn't hurt.

The first room was obviously his home office. The second was a guest bedroom, but it was full of AFL gear and swag from endorsements. The last thing I wanted to do was impose further, so when I saw the third bedroom was adorned with nothing more than a bed and a chest, I decided on it. I walked inside, taking in the large windows that gave a breathtaking view to his backyard.

He had a pool.

A large grin spread across my face at the realization. Vivid images of Trevor taking a few laps, water running over his sculpted back burned inside my mind. Tiny droplets sliding down his tanned, toned muscles until they reached his—God, I was a total pervert. I wished I could have helped myself, but the thought of Trevor's naked body roused something deep inside me. Something feminine. And sensual. Gripping the sheer curtains, I pressed my forehead against the windowpane to cool off. Inwardly, I moaned. I shouldn't even allow myself to go there with my new roommate, and hopefully future trainer. I knew better, especially given my past.

My previous relationships with men had been few and far between. Mostly because I never knew who to trust. Growing up in the business, I realized early on that to some people—okay, most people—I was a means to an end. One hundred percent disposable to anyone climbing the ladder. To say I had trust issues, would be a huge understatement. Jeremy Tillman had solidified my skepticism. He'd all but swept me off my feet, claiming to have never seen anyone more beautiful. He was sly and charming. I fell for his act hook, line, and sinker. No one had ever been so unbothered by my family's name before. It was endearing—at first. After a few months, he began to insist on meeting my family, claiming he wanted to get to know them. Then, it became a weekly drop-in for Sunday dinners. Next, was weekend trips with my brother, for bonding purposes because Jeremy and I were getting serious. I saw through him by the sixth month, but continued to stay with him because the moments he and I shared in private somehow felt worth the few days a week I felt used.

Which was pathetic. Yet, my heart struggled for proof of more cons.

It wasn't until my father offered him a job the second he graduated college, when he'd proven to me that I was at the bottom of his priority list. He volunteered to travel every week for the sake of the league, even going the extra mile where my father was concerned, handling the Canadian office two months at a time. I quickly figured what kind of a future we'd have together. A non-existent one. Jeremy eventually moved there wagering deals on my father's behalf, and I was perfectly fine with that.

Luckily, during my years in grad school at Stanford, I found an easier rhythm. Instead of focusing neurotically on my private life, I put all of my energy into soaking up everything I could from the AFL. I went to every fight. Every function. Every interview. I trolled the headquarters office, pretending to work, while learning every department within my father's company.

Letting the curtain fall from my fingertips, I turned and leaned against the windowsill, determined to not think about the past.

The room was beautiful, even with minimal decorations. The bed was huge and appeared more inviting than my own back home. As I slipped my flip flops off, I took a chance to see if my observation was correct. Lowering myself slowly onto the mattress, as if it might crumble beneath me from my weight, I closed my eyes, bringing my arm to rest over my face as my body relaxed on what felt like a fluffy cloud.

"This room doesn't have a bathroom attached. I can move—"

Lifting my head, I pushed up onto my elbows, to find Trevor standing in the doorway, his hands griping the door frame on both sides, pressing his large torso through the door. His biceps bulged from the pressure he was putting on them by leaning forward.

I swallowed, my mind completely focused on his stature. "This one is good."

"Okay. Great."

I stayed silent, not knowing if I had the energy to sustain a conversation. I had nothing else to say except to thank him again, and he'd already told me he didn't want to hear it.

"I'll, uh, leave you to it then. For real, make yourself at home. I'll go get some food in a while, unless you're hungry now?"

I shook my head. "No, I'm good. I think I'm going to rest for a little while, if that's okay?"

Why was I asking his permission? I was the worst independent woman ever.

"Sure. I'll be around." He nodded and pulled the door closed.

I slid back on the bed until my head hit the pillow. Closing my eyes, I wrapped the throw from the end of the bed around me, feeling surprisingly comfortable. Physically at least. Mentally, there weren't enough hours in the day for my therapist, whom I'd forgotten to call in my hurry to leave California. I made a mental note to email her. I thought about calling my dad and apologizing, like I would have normally done. I didn't like turmoil, hence me leaving the comfort of his safety-net five years too late. He would likely return my title to me, and I'd have my belongings back in the blink of an eye, not to mention my nest egg. But those things were contingent on a life *he* wanted for me, not the one I wanted for myself.

I curled up on my side, hoping I hadn't made a mistake, even though I couldn't get Trevor's words from the car out of my head. I'd only ever been privy to seeing Trevor's playful side; his confident side. Which was why his being so serious caught me off guard. I couldn't stop my curious mind from wondering. Where had he learned so much about the heart, and what moments had shaped his perception on it? Because as simple as his advice was, it was profound, and it seemed to me the only way someone would know that kind of thing, was if they'd personally experienced it.

As I pondered my truth, the more powerful I grew. My heart knew what was best for me. And as much as my dad and brother wanted to control the outcome, they couldn't because I was my own person. It was time I started acting like it.

CHAPTER 5
TREVOR

I COULD ADMIT when I was wrong. Humbling myself had never been a problem for me because I understood people made mistakes. My expectations of others weren't so high that no one could live up to them. Including myself. But I'd made a colossal mistake letting Navie move in with me. There was no way I wouldn't fall for her. And dammit, I didn't want to admit that to anyone, let alone her. What kind of man would I look like? The kind who let a woman stay with him so he could eventually sleep with her? I couldn't swallow that, so I kept my thoughts and feelings to myself, practically choking on the lump of truth every time I was near her.

"What do you mean he's basic?" Navie asked one night after dinner, as she painted her toenails in my living room floor. "There is nothing basic about Leonardo DiCaprio. Nothing," she reiterated then blew on the lavender paint.

"I said what I said," I teased, knowing she'd have a comeback.

She'd forced me into watching *Titanic, The Departed, Gangs of New York,* and *What's Eating Gilbert Grape* all within a week. I was nowhere near as impressed with the dude's acting chops as she was. If it was even his acting that appealed to her in the first place. And if it wasn't, then I was even less impressed.

"You're just jealous."

I tossed a throw pillow at her face. "Of DiCaprio? Hell, nah."

Navie giggled and kicked her leg out. My grin fell, and I licked my lips, as my gaze caught a split-second reveal of her satin purple panties through the inside of the loose shorts she wore. Readjusting myself, I closed my eyes trying to focus on anything other than the mental image I'd already stored safely for frequent visits. I was only human, which was exactly what I had to tell myself so I didn't feel like a douche-canoe, copping glances at my roommate.

Navie didn't notice my indiscretion and jumped to her feet. "I need a Twinkie."

You need something, but it ain't a fucking Twinkie.

Instead of continuing my wayward thoughts, I felt it best to remove myself from the situation. The last thing either of us needed was me fantasizing about her. It wouldn't do any good, for one. Second, hooking up would further complicate an already complicated situation. I was a man, but it took me exactly one time to learn my lesson. Relationships were not for me, and I didn't know Navie that well, but I knew enough to know she wasn't the kind of woman who constantly doled out lush benefits to a friend.

When she returned to the living room, I pretended to be tired. "I'm going to turn in," I said, stretching.

"Party pooper! I thought we were going to watch *Shutter Island*."

"Rain check?"

Peeling the wrapper back on the Twinkie, she nodded. "Fine."

After locking the outside doors, I bid her goodnight. Leaning against my bedroom door after I closed it, I reveled in the silence, taking comfort in a moment of reprieve since I was alone. Squeezing my eyes shut, I told myself I just had to get my mind right. Navie wasn't an option. Not only was she staying with me, she was training in my gym. I wasn't the kind of guy who mixed training and indulgence. I'd watched enough of my buddy's crash and burn from the intoxicating mixture. I wasn't the sharpest tool in the shed, but the odds weren't in my favor for investing in something, even purely physical, that was doomed to fail.

Fourteen days passed, pushing my willpower to the brink. It felt like fourteen weeks. Fortunately, I had prepared myself from the beginning that things would need an adjustment period, so at least somewhere in the back of my mind, I'd found reason. At the gym, I gave Navie pointers, but mostly stayed in my office. At home, I cooked and kept our conversations light. All the while, escaping to my room before ten o'clock each night for a cold shower. It wasn't ideal, but it did the trick. Most of the time.

I lifted my gaze as Navie entered the kitchen for coffee and announced she was bored. "I haven't done anything fun since I've been here."

"What do you want to do?"

"I don't know. Something other than train."

Boston was filled with things to do, so coming up with something on the fly wouldn't be difficult. But I wasn't sure what she'd be interested in.

Before I could suggest something, she peered over the rim of her coffee cup. "You know, I've always wanted to go to Lexington."

I took a sip from my own cup and smiled in surprise. She liked history. It was my favorite subject in school, and I should have been embarrassed by the amount of money I'd spent on novels covering everything from the Revolutionary War to Benghazi, but I wasn't.

"We can go, if you'd like."

"Really?"

"Yeah, give me ten and we'll roll out."

"Trevor," she said and motioned toward her Dwight Schrute pajama pants. "I'll need more than ten minutes."

She looked so fucking cute. I realized I knew more about her than I'd thought. She loved *The Office* and Twinkies. Her clothing style leaned more toward sophisticated, yet she loved a good pair of jeans and sneakers. Her favorite color had to be blue. She wore the same tiny, turquoise earrings every day, unless she went out to dinner with Willow and Lena.

"Take as long as you need, but keep in mind the only people who are going to see you are tourists and those dressed in garb from 1775."

Crinkling her nose, she considered my words. "True."

Both heading toward the hallway, we met and nearly ran into one another at the entrance. Navie bashfully glanced up at me, while I grabbed her waist so as not to knock her down. "Where's the fire?" I asked.

"Sorry, I'm excited."

I shook my head, but grinned. "Ladies first."

Accepting my invitation, Navie scooted past me and hurried toward her room. I followed behind to grab my wallet and keys.

Twenty minutes later, she entered the living room and announced she was ready. My gaze shot straight to her hips, taking in the way her faded Levi's molded to her body. Her T-shirt was fitted, showing off barely an inch of her skin. Hopping off the couch, I turned out the lights and led the way to my Jeep.

As I backed out of my garage, Navie kicked her sneakers off and tucked her feet underneath her. "I can't wait to see everything."

"It's pretty cool."

"Will we be able to ask questions?"

Glancing at her as I made my way to the Interstate, I teased, "So you're that girl."

She bit her bottom lip, pulling it between her teeth. "I'm a geek." She shrugged.

So am I.

"Geeks are cool."

"No, they're not," she argued, while nudging my arm up off the console. "I'm going to leave this in here, okay?" She grabbed a tube of lip balm from her purse then applied it to her lips. Instead of waiting on my response, she opened the console, tossed the lip balm inside, then shut the lid.

"We should totally test this theory."

"If geeks are cool?"

"Nah, I know geeks are cool. I need to know what I'm working with here. I want to know the level of your geekiness."

She shrugged with zero fear. "Shoot."

"Who hangs out in the Fortress of Solitude?"

"Seriously?" she scoffed, almost offended. "Superman."

"That was an easy one," I told her as I turned onto Interstate 95. "Who forged the One Ring?" I narrowed my eyes in her direction, knowing if she knew the answer, she was my people. I caught myself grinning from her jaded facial expression. She was most definitely my people.

"Dark Lord Sauron, and before you insult me further, it was forged in the fires of Mount Doom."

Impressed with her feistiness, I decided to go in for the kill. "If you understand loopback, we're done here."

"Are you referring to a localhost?" she beamed, obviously impressed with herself.

Hell, I was too. I didn't know my ass from a hole in the ground when it came to technology.

"Wow. You really are a geek."

"Don't forget it. I have more useless knowledge up here"—she touched her temple—"than you can ever imagine."

For some strange reason, knowing that about her turned me on even more. She wasn't just beautiful, nor was she just a geek. She was a fucking boss—perfect in almost every way.

As I parked next to the visitor's center, Navie's eyes twinkled with anticipation. I couldn't remember a time I'd ever seen someone so thrilled to simply visit a town. Sure, I'd had my fair share of women who'd been happy with a paid vacation—or even a lavish gift, but the enthusiasm Navie showed for my driving her twenty-five minutes from my house made me feel peaceful. Honestly, a little enthusiastic myself because even though I'd been to Lexington before, I'd never been with Navie, and I had a feeling I was going to experience the historical place on a whole new level.

I found myself watching Navie more than anything. The way she took in our surroundings in an almost childlike manner made me feel like I was giving her something her heart desired. Observing her enjoy herself to the point of wonderment and awe cracked something deep inside my chest. Something I tried to ignore, when I knew for a fact it would come back and haunt me.

"Can you believe this was what alerted the militia to the common?" she asked, pointing to The Old Belfry.

"I know. It's hard to imagine a world like that. That's why I love history so much. Things were so simple back then."

"Simple to us." She lifted her phone in the air to capture a picture of the statues. "Their lives were probably just as complicated as ours but in a different way."

Nodding, I agreed. "Yeah, I suppose you're right. But they had less distractions."

"I would have loved living in the 1700s."

"You know men could whip their wives back then," I teased.

"Yeah, and women could poison their husbands because Lord knows they weren't cooking the meals."

I chuckled as we walked farther, until we came upon the Buckman Tavern. The tavern was one of my favorite places in Lexington. It held so much history, it was palpable.

"Your life would have certainly been different." I hadn't meant to re-open a wound, but Navie had obviously grown up with a cushy lifestyle. It wasn't that I didn't think she was capable of hard work. I just knew from experience starting from the bottom humbled a person. I assumed she'd never had to start anything before with such a disadvantage.

"Yeah."

Noticing her tone, I glanced at her. The sight wasn't pleasing to the eye. It was almost as if she would have preferred it that way; to be different from what she was. I didn't like the direction her thoughts seemed to be going, so I changed the subject.

Walking up to the front door of the tavern, I pointed out the bullet hole I thought was cool. "Check this out," I told her, as I ran my fingertips over the damaged wood.

"This is so neat," she whispered almost to herself as her eyes never leaving the building. "It's all so amazing."

We continued our tour, casually stopping when Navie wanted to capture a photograph or when she asked me questions in reference to the war or minutemen. We stopped at The Old Burying Ground, then at the Hancock-Clarke House where Paul Revere had ridden from Boston to warn Adams and Hancock the British troops were on their way. Navie took more images than should have been allowed.

"Let's get some lunch," I suggested.

"I'm starving." Lifting her hand, she pointed to our left. "Can we see what's over there after?"

I nodded. "Not to bring up business when we're sightseeing, but I thought I should check in with you. See what kind of schedule you want at the gym?"

"I want to train as much as possible."

"Train for what, exactly?" I hadn't meant to push her, but it would be easier to train her if I knew what she was training for. Willow mentioned her possible plans of ending up in the cage, but Navie had never confirmed that. At least not to me.

"I want to compete." Navie's eyes burned, causing the blue in them to darken. I wasn't sure if she was nervous or absolute. "Ultimately, I want to form a women's league. One that is prosperous and taken seriously. I know this business, Trevor. Inside and out. All I need is the experience inside the cage."

We had a few minutes to burn as we made our way to an outdoor restaurant, and I decided to dig a little deeper. "So, eventually you want to be CEO—like your dad?"

"No." She shook her head. "I don't want to be anything like him. Not in the way you're thinking," she told me, as we crossed the street. "My goal is to run a league after experiencing every part of it. Eventually, when I'm helping women who want to fight secure their dream, I want to have walked in their shoes."

I considered her words as I pulled a chair out for her under the umbrella of an outdoor eating space. I hadn't asked her if she was okay with a sandwich shop, but the relaxing vibe felt right. "I can respect that."

"Good. I know this is all—a little weird, but—"

"You're weird," I goaded.

"So are you, 'Mr. Paul Revere rode here from Boston to warn the British were coming.'"

I chuckled. It wasn't a lie. "You seem to be having a hard time admitting my knowledge of American history is vaster than yours."

Our waiter interrupted our conversation to take our orders. After ordering a BLT, Navie went back to our conversation. "I'm not even jealous about that."

"Good. Otherwise, the ride home might be a little awkward."

"Speaking of that. It's super weird."

"What do you mean?"

"Nothing with you is awkward, Trevor. You're like a human whisperer. You always know exactly what to say or what to do. It's kind of annoying, if you want to know the truth."

Smirking, I leaned forward on my elbows. "Navie Fuller. Did you just give me a back-handed compliment?"

"Don't get all beside yourself. Remember, I know a crazy amount of crap no one cares about. I can make you feel this small"—she held up her finger and thumb—"in no time."

"I don't need any help humbling myself. Retiring in my thirties has about done me in."

"I'm sorry."

Glancing up, I tilted my head at her sudden change in demeanor. "It's no big deal." I shrugged.

"Was that your plan all along? To be retired in your thirties?"

"Not really. I don't think I ever had a plan, to be honest."

"Why retire when you were killing it, then?"

Sipping my water, I thought about her question. I'd answered it so many times before, but I'd said the same thing every time, and it felt like it was no longer true. "I just—didn't want to fight anymore. I enjoyed it, but I lost the reason I was doing it. I know that sounds—cocky, but fighting for me, has always been a release. I began evaluating myself, kind of checking in, I guess you could say, and when I asked myself why I was doing it, there wasn't a clear answer."

"A release for what?"

"We're getting a little deep here," I joked.

"You're cool with me knowing what a geek you are but not the reason you retired? Your deflection tells me more than if you'd just answered the question."

I narrowed my eyes, but chuckled when she cocked her head to the side and grinned impishly.

"I forget how perceptive you are. It didn't seem like that would be a problem when you first moved in, considering you went straight to your bedroom and fell asleep by nine o'clock for the first week."

Her eyes grew wide in embarrassment. "How do you know I was asleep?"

"Because I opened the door and heard you snoring."

"You did what?" She threw a French fry at my chest. "I was tired. I've never worked out so much in my life."

"I get it." I held my palms up. "Still, we could pick up some Breathe Rites, if you want."

She laughed at my teasing, then handed me her phone. "Look at this one."

I inspected the Minute Men rock she'd captured when the sun hit it perfectly. "That's cool. But I think the bullet hole in the front door is my favorite," I told her as I scrolled through her photos.

"Will you take one with me?"

"Sure."

She leaned over her plate, bringing her face into view of the selfie I was taking. She smiled big, causing me to as well.

"There, the best one yet," I told her, believing it to be true.

She examined the photo. "I agree."

After our venture to Lexington, we fell into the easy rhythm of hanging out, away from the gym or my house. It started out as her offering to take me to Samuel Adams Brewery. Of course, that was a no brainer. Then that led to me wanting to match her kindness, where we enjoyed an afternoon game at Fenway. As the weeks passed, Navie became more relaxed in my home. She cooked. She read on the back patio. And even though I paid a maid four times a month to help out, my favorite thing ever was witnessing her clean the house, dancing freely while nineties rap blasted through her earbuds. She danced for hours, creating moves for each chore. I loved watching the ease with which she danced, especially when she didn't know I was watching. It was borderline masochistic.

Once, while I observed her from behind as she squatted to the ground then quickly popped back up to place a coffee mug in the cabinet, I realized I never wanted her to leave. Watching Navie without reservations made me want to be around her even more. A comforting sense of peace took root in my gut, making me feel less inclined to have such a hard boundary where someone being in my space was out of the question. Since she'd moved in with me, time passed in an odd manner. It felt like two days and two years all balled up in a glorious mixture of lust, like, and fun. She lit up my house. Every fucking room came alive when she entered it.

As I spent my afternoon holed up in my office, contemplating a workout schedule for her, I groaned aloud, not satisfied with my assessment. I'd only ever considered workouts for men, which were a hell of a lot more intense. I had to come up with the best way to ease her into fighting. A career in the league was not easy. Personally, it was the hardest thing I'd ever sustained, but Navie's drive and outright willpower matched any fighter I knew. That alone was enough for me to want to help her, whichever way the chips fell. Although, now that I knew her, I would admit I probably cared more about her schedule than any I'd created before.

I preferred Tommy training with her over Gage, for multiple reasons—the main one being that Gage had *offered* to let her shadow him. I knew that douchebag well enough to know he wasn't offering out of the kindness of his heart. He had an ulterior motive, and if I had anything to say about it, his motives were going to stay inside his pants where they belonged. I'd scowled at him the last time he winked at her, and I was pretty sure he caught my drift, because he didn't offer his services again. Or wink at her. Or look in her general direction. The asshole did look in my direction, though, and caught me looking in hers. Then he winked at *me*. I flipped him off, knowing there was no need in denying my annoyance. He'd just keep fucking with me until I said something about it just to prove a point.

After checking in with two trainers, I found Navie outside the cage, recording Tommy as he sparred. "Hey, what's up?"

"I've been practicing rolls all day. I realized the craziest thing. You know I've been stalking the guys in the gym for weeks, but I feel like my style may be closest to Tommy's. Everything he does, my instincts go there too. I'm just getting a little video to study for later."

"Yeah, he's more about the groundwork," I agreed, pleased with her eagerness.

"I love how smooth he is." Her eyes sparkled in appreciation. "Everything he does is so fluid. I want to be like that."

She was barefoot. I hadn't meant to look. I didn't want to look. I'd seen her bare feet many times, and every single time I saw them, it was like a punch straight to my gut. They were petite; dainty almost—and I wasn't even a feet guy. But hers were sexy. Her toenails were perfectly manicured, and her tanned skin always appeared so smooth, like the finest silk.

I shook off the thoughts, remembering I was in the gym. I watched as she moved around the outside of the cage, enjoying her enthusiasm too much to tell her that her video would be shit because nothing she was capturing would be in focus. So I just smiled, even though she didn't see me because her eyes were glued to Tommy and his opponent.

"Did you get that arm bar?" Tommy asked her, stepping out of the cage.

"Yes. We have to work on that next."

I grimaced. She seemed a little more excited about rolling around with Tommy than she did learning a new move.

"I got you, girl."

"I brought an extra sandwich. Want to break for lunch?"

Opening my mouth, I meant to question her thoughtfulness where he was concerned, but nothing came out. Tommy grinned at her and put her in a soft headlock.

"Eww, you're gross," she told him, but giggled as if her face being buried in his nasty-ass armpit wasn't appalling.

"You love me."

Wait just a damn minute.

When had they become so close? Had I covered my tracks so well that he had no idea he was pissing me the fuck off? Or did he just not care?

Biting my tongue, I swallowed, swearing I tasted blood. Well, there was that. Not only was I restless about the schedule, now I had a mental picture of their level of comfort with each other to ponder.

Instead of pushing him out of the way, like I envisioned, I went back to my office, knowing I needed to concentrate more on her schedule and less about my feelings on her friendships. I sighed and leaned back in my chair, turning an old rubber band ball from hand to hand. I wasn't sure Navie truly understood the amount of work she'd have to put in just to gain a match. Since female fighting wasn't in the forefront of the sport, I knew she'd have a long road ahead of her.

An hour later, I was satisfied with the first draft. I took a break, checking in with a couple of fighters and their trainers on the floor. I looked on—impressed with Payne's routine. He was a fucking beast. Richard had two trainers come in from Las Vegas to work with him. I missed being his primary sometimes. Especially when I needed to burn off some energy. Like now.

Thinking about Richard brought me back to Navie. She'd come to the gym early to make up for the time she'd lose due to her job interview in the afternoon. She hadn't mentioned where she was interviewing, which annoyed me, but not enough to be nosy about it. I could've made things easy for her and just offered her a job at the gym. She was there most of the time anyway. But after the way she'd acted about staying with me in the first place, I figured I needed to let her work the job thing out on her own. If nothing else, I'd learned she didn't like a hand-out or me doing something for her that she could do for herself. Like the time I filled her tank full of gas once when she stopped at the corner convenience store. Or the time she struggled to lift a fan from the shelf at Target. I looked on for a solid, annoying five minutes as she stubbornly attempted to knock it off the shelf with a shower rod before I reached over her and did it myself. She ignored me the rest of the night.

Casually checking in with a couple of lightweights, I noticed that, when she and Tommy finished their session, she took a seat on the bench closest to the wall.

Approaching them, I asked, "What time is your interview?"

She pulled a sweatshirt over her head and slipped into her slides. "Four."

Screw it.

"You never mentioned where you were interviewing."

She looked up at me, and the little squint in the corner of her eyes told me she was surprised I'd asked. "Melton's."

I opened my mouth then closed it. *Melton's?* Melton's was a pub. Melton's was the Mecca for live music, which meant every horny band member from Boston to New York would frequent it seven nights a week. Melton's was a fucking brothel for guys between the ages of twenty-one and thirty. I felt my blood pressure rising at the thought of her being circled by vultures on a nightly basis.

She pulled the bottom right side of her lip inside her mouth. I didn't hear what she said next. As if I had gone deaf where I stood, my other senses took over. My sight was compromised by her lips. I watched, entranced as her pink tongue peeked out from beneath her white teeth, the view, leading my dumbass brain into a tunnel, like I was on a roller coaster ride at Walt Disney World.

Warmth spread from my chest to my stomach in a matter of seconds, right before the heat hit my dick. I straightened, a little disappointed in myself. I'd gone from righteous indignation to what–the–fuck, all from a little lip action. I swallowed, trying to tamp down the raw energy buzzing inside my body so I could focus on what she was saying.

She was still speaking, as normal as ever, even though I'd just completely blacked out for what could have been a full minute.

"It was all I could find on such short notice. The manager said I would be perfect, so it sounded like the interview is just a formality. I need money, Trevor." Her last words sounded wounded, like she knew what Melton's was, but beggars couldn't be choosers.

It killed me that I had plenty of money, yet she wouldn't accept it. I had what she needed, and I wanted to give it to her. Which was terrifying. My natural instincts regarding Navie floored me sometimes. I really didn't want to go there—to a place where feelings were involved, not after what had happened last time.

I'd gone three years without attaching myself to anyone seriously. Three years without the innate need or want to have someone by my side. Easy. That was what I'd been doing, and it worked. Or it had in the past. But none of those easy relationships had been with Navie. The hold she had on me already was baffling.

"I get it." I didn't, though. I'd prefer if she didn't feel like she had to work at a place that was going to hire her because of her looks. It seemed to me she was selling herself short, but I kept my mouth closed, feeling like I would be overstepping.

"Okay, I'm going to head to your house to get ready. Do you need anything?"

You.

"Nah, I'm good. Good luck."

I went to my office, not wanting to see or talk to anyone about anything. I was in the middle of a mind-fuck. I couldn't wrap my brain around the fact that I was in a funk and Navie had everything to do with it. Pushing her away seemed warranted. Yet feeling her perfect curves in my hands as I roamed her beautiful body, getting to intimately know every inch of her overtook me. The back of my neck throbbed, as short bursts of pain started at the base on my spine and wrapped around the sides of my head, pulsating the closer it got to my eyes. The *thought* of her gave me a headache.

The girl was straight up a pain in my brain.

I pushed some paperwork around on my desk, knowing I could find something productive to do at the office whether I wanted to or not, but I sat back in my chair, resigned. There was absolutely no fucking way I was going to get anything beneficial done. My mind was elsewhere and I didn't have the energy to regain any sense of focus. Pushing to my feet, I tossed a couple of scratch pieces of paper in the trash. If I was going to allow her to invade my mind, I was going to think about her in the comfort of my own home. As I made my way through the gym, I waved the guys off, telling the trainers to lock up on their way out.

Once I reached my house, where I could wallow in privacy, I barricaded myself in my bedroom for two hours, counseling myself about why kissing her would be a mistake. Then, I added the pressure of the guys to the mix to beef up the ridiculous risk.

"Trevor!" Navie called from the living room. I hustled out of my room eager to hear what she had to say.

My smile matched hers as she jogged down the hall. "I'm assuming it went well by the smile on your face?"

"Yes!" She leaped into my arms.

My reaction was delayed because she surprised me. Once it hit me that I was holding her, I wrapped both my arms around her and squeezed, relaxing in the perfect moment. If I could have had one superhero power in that instant, it would have been to stop time. I could have held on to her for days, feeling her warm, soft body pressed into mine. She pulled away and jumped up and down twice, grinning the entire time.

I licked my lips, realizing in the time we'd been around each other, I had never seen her like that. Navie was composed, always airing on the side of reserved. Even with Willow. She'd laugh and converse with everyone, but never fully seem to let loose. She never jumped up and down in delight. But she just had with me.

"I'm really happy for you, babe." I'd been so caught up in everything I was noticing about her that I hadn't realized what I'd said until I noted the look on her face.

Her eyes widened in surprise, then softened. Her gaze shifted downward, as if the term of endearment had embarrassed her. I grinned, amused by her sudden shyness.

"Thank you. I know it's not much, but now I'll be able to help out around here." I started to interrupt her, but she cut me off. "I know you don't need it. But I won't live here unless you let me contribute. My whole life, my father has had his thumb on me, taking care of everything. I've never been…independent. I want that so bad. I didn't know it until I moved here, but I do."

I nodded, remembering the feeling. The need to prove oneself left little room for accepting help, however willingly offered.

"I know it's not much, but it's a start."

"Okay, if that's what you want," I conceded.

"It is. And…" She pulled her bottom lip between her teeth, like she was about to spill a juicy secret. "Ethan, the manager, told me as long as I worked weekends, he'd try to work around my training schedule during the week."

I bet he did.

Having someone like Navie working weekends at the bar would be good for business. "Good." I kept the generic smile plastered to my face.

I'm going to keep my eye on that motherfucker.

"Let's go to dinner to celebrate. My treat." I placed my palm on my chest so I didn't grab her hand.

"Okay," she agreed.

"Cool. What do you feel like?"

"Oh, I'm good with whatever. I'm still buzzing, so it's probably better if you choose. I may have us eating junk food."

I grinned as she flew past me to her room to change clothes. I grabbed my wallet and shades off the entryway table, already making plans. I was treating her to ice cream after dinner. She deserved it, and I, oddly enough, was craving a sweet treat.

CHAPTER 6
NAVIE

"MARSHMALLOW CREAM CHEESECAKE concrete with extra marshmallow, please." I beamed, my mouth already watering. And I hadn't even had to talk Trevor into the savory treat. It was his idea. Go figure.

Trevor made a face, while glancing at the overhead menu. "That's…a lot of sweet."

"Just try it. I bet you'll love it."

Eyebrow raising just a hair, he glanced down at me. "A bet, you say?"

"I'm one hundred percent certain you'll love it. So, yeah. Name your price."

He placed a matching order with the teenager working the register and sidestepped to the left. I followed so the people behind us could order, still waiting on his response.

"When I win, you have to grapple for two weeks straight."

I shrugged. "No problem. I'm eager to learn anyway, I told you that."

"With me," he finished.

Oh damn.

I gulped, tripping over my thoughts. Ground work with Trevor Steele fit into the dreams-coming-true category for anyone in the fighting realm. The idea of grappling with him shot me straight to the moon but for different reasons. My heartrate picked up. I was so thrilled that he'd even consider it. And he'd offered that up as a punishment? Or was that a reward for him winning? God, I was so perplexed but elated too. Turned on, confused, worried, and psyched out, all at the same time.

"All right," I agreed. "But if I win, and you love the ice cream, like I know you will, then you have to get in the cage with Payne. I want to see you spar with him again, and I want to record it. That way I can watch it whenever I want." I'd probably given him too much. I'd shown my appreciation in many ways, but I'd never truly told him what a huge fan of his I'd been for so many years. I loved watching him fight and admired how he carried himself in and outside of the cage.

He was the best in the business, and he'd always held up his end of every bargain. If he gave his word to meeting a super fan, or visiting a children's hospital, he showed up. The press had their fun with his private life, linking him to every actress in Hollywood, including the ones who'd not quite made a name for themselves. If the lies they printed had been true, he would have had to have slept with no less than ten women a day, which I supposed was doable, but not likely with his schedule. Even with those rumors, I'd never heard a cruel word about him. Not from other people or the press, which made me trust him even more.

While he appeared to debate himself, I waited a beat before he stuck his hand out for me to shake. "You're on."

"So are you, Mr. Steele." I placed my hand in his warm one and smirked.

A teenage boy stepped up to the counter and called our numbers with less enthusiasm than I had on my yearly visit to my gynecologist. He didn't smile. He didn't recognize Trevor, or if he had, he obviously wasn't a fan, which led me to believe he didn't recognize him. The boy handed Trevor the overfilled cups like a robot. I would have burst into laughter at Trevor's face, but the anticipation of our bet was killing me.

As we took our seats on opposite sides of the booth, I folded my hands together and calmly leaned forward. Trevor nodded toward my ice cream, but I shook my head.

"I'm waiting on you," I said.

"We go at the same time…" He leaned back, spreading his arms across the back of the booth, signaling he was completely comfortable and willing to wait me out.

"Fine," I agreed and began our count down. "Three. Two. One."

We both dug in, my portion bigger than his. Our spoons reached our lips at the same time. I swallowed the thick, creamy goodness with my eyes closed. I was in food heaven. I reveled in the combination of dense, tangy cheesecake and sweet, fluffy marshmallow. The sweet escape didn't last long though.

Realizing I'd missed Trevor's reaction, I opened my eyes and found his irises burning like a wildfire in the dark of night, his right hand gripping the cup so hard, it protruded on one side. Instead of sitting in silence with my nerves bouncing around like a batch of microwave popcorn, I spoke up.

"Well?"

"Well, what?" His voice was hushed, as if he was straining to answer me.

I chuckled. "Do you like it, silly?"

"No."

I pinched my brows together. There was no way he didn't like it. "No? Did you even try it?"

"I did."

"I don't believe you. Everyone likes this mixture. And why are you acting weird?" I wiped my lips with the napkin he'd given me. He'd gone mute, and that concerned me. The fact that Trevor was so laid back was one of the things I liked about him the most. I never had to try around him. Yet the look on his face had me second-guessing our exchange. Typically, Trevor was playful; mischievous even. He didn't appear to be in a joking mood, though. His jaw was taut. His eyes steady. I swallowed when his tongue peeked out and licked his bottom lip.

"I'm acting weird because I feel like I just watched you have a foodgasm, and that got me thinking about the face you make when you orgasm. From there, it went downhill pretty fast."

Oh.

He coolly maneuvered in his seat, and I had a sneaking suspicion he was adjusting himself, but I couldn't see his hand under the table.

Covering my flaming cheeks with my hands, I swallowed the residual cream on my tongue. "That's—embarrassing."

"And I didn't like the ice cream, because I hate cheesecake."

"What? Everyone likes cheesecake." He shook his head, his eyes twinkling like sparklers on the fourth of July. I tried my best to ignore them and continued. "Why didn't you tell me that?"

"I didn't tell you…" he leaned forward, placing both his elbows directly in front of him on the table, "…because I wanted to win."

I narrowed my eyes, shocked by his level of deceit.

He nodded, his eyes fading to a dark shad of denim. He looked like a teenager, not a grown man. As I was thinking about what his admission meant, my head mimicked his. Which was stupid, but it happened. And I knew it was happening because after playing the whole scenario out over again and again in my mind, I was still doing it long after he'd stopped. My stomach muscles clenched.

Knowing I had to redirect my thoughts, I stated the obvious. "Okay then. You win."

"I win." He scooted the cup of ice cream to the side, making a show that he was done with the sweet treat and didn't intend on touching it again.

I finished my ice cream, not willing to waste the tasty goodness. Bursts of nervous energy, like electric shocks, pulsed throughout my body, seemingly stopping and shocking every few inches. The charged feeling stayed present the entire time I ate—his eyes fixed on mine, his gaze dropping to my mouth with each bite I took.

I had no words.

He seemed perfectly content watching me as I enjoyed my treat. He didn't talk about the weather. He didn't ask about the gym. Since informing me of the sexualized thoughts he'd had while examining my expression as I enjoyed my dessert, I hadn't been able to stop considering it. Which led me to scarfing the ice cream so fast, I was surprised I didn't give myself a brain freeze.

"Ready?"

Trevor grinned, his dimples sinking deeper into his cheeks. "Yup."

God, his dimples had to be the cutest things ever created. From the way his whole face changed when he showed them, my guess would be that he'd spent his whole life with girls and women alike telling him how awesome they were because if there was one thing I knew, it was that he was fully aware of the power he yielded when he showed them.

Trevor opened the door for me, placing his hand on my lower back as we exited the shop. I'd noticed he did that—touched me slightly—when we entered or exited a building. At first, I thought it was sweet, but I soon noticed his manners extended to Willow when she walked in front of him too. And Lena, Willow's friend. We'd met everyone for dinner not a week ago, and I'd been talking to Tommy about the next day's session. Trevor was ahead of me, walking out, and Lena was in front of him. I saw that he placed his hand at the small of her back, the same way he did with me. It was something a gentleman did when a woman walked in front of him. Not that I'd been privy to that growing up. When walking with my dad or brother, I was always in the back, trailing behind them. They were the important ones, the people everyone wanted to see, so they led and I followed.

"Hey. Where'd you go?" Trevor asked as he helped me into his Jeep, ducking his face down even with mine once I was settled.

I noticed he'd started doing that as well—opening my car door for me. He didn't do *that* for Willow or Lena, and he hadn't done it for me at first. But the last few times we'd taken the same vehicle, he had. And I liked it. I liked it a lot.

"Nowhere," I answered.

"Were you thinking about me kicking your ass for the next two weeks?" He placed his hands on the roof of his Jeep, completely relaxed, as he waited for my response.

I smiled at him. If he only knew.

"No, actually, I was thinking about you thinking about my orgasm face," I drawled sweetly. I knew he'd be shocked I said it. In fact, I banked on it. I had no clue what was going on with me. Why I suddenly felt moved to flirt with him openly; to force a reaction from him, but it was fun.

The smile he'd been brandishing slipped—trickling off his face until it was completely gone. He wasn't laughing now. But I chuckled hard on the inside, while keeping my facial expression neutral. He swore under his breath and closed the passenger side door. He walked —no, stalked—around the front of the Jeep and climbed in, shutting his door with a bit more force than required.

"No response?" I taunted.

He started the engine but glanced over at me before he put it in gear. "Oh, I've got a response, but I'm going to wait to give it to you."

My eyebrow furrowed. "Why?"

"Because you're not ready for it."

All at once, the poise I'd found somewhere behind my overactive nerves exited my body, floating out slowly, as if I were a balloon and his words were the pin. After the initial disappointment, annoyance spread inside me like tentacles. Who was he to tell me I wasn't ready? Like I was a toddler and couldn't handle the truth. It was just a reminder that sometimes I felt like he handled me with kid gloves, and I didn't like it. It made me feel inferior. It reminded me of situations with my family, and I hadn't left them behind only to experience the wretched feeling with someone else.

I picked at my nails indignantly. "Sounds to me like *you're* not ready for it, and you're blaming me so that you can somehow feel better about yourself." I fought the urge to squeeze my eyes shut. My comeback was more emotional than I wanted it to be. But he knew what I meant. I knew he did, because the moment I said it, his face fell again, but instead of surprised, he seemed annoyed.

The silence in the cab of his Jeep on the way home was smothering. The feistiness I'd felt a few minutes ago evaporated, leaving me numb. I'd overreacted. Or reacted in a way he didn't like. Either way, I was troubled. I'd read him wrong, clearly, and I'd made him uncomfortable, in turn, making myself feel foolish.

I quietly gathered my things when he pulled into the garage and met him at the door. Instead of opening it, he stood silently. A large indentation creased between his furrowed brow, and his lips pursed as if words were fighting to escape his grim-set mouth. The silence stretched on, agonizing while he contemplated his words.

Unfortunately, I didn't do well with arbitrary silence. "I—I'm sorry I said that. I was out of line."

He looked down at me. "No. You were absolutely right."

"I was?" I gripped the strap of my purse.

He opened the door, and we both walked inside, stopping at the bar in the kitchen when he flipped on the lights. "I know I send you mixed signals, and I'm sorry about that. It's fucked up. I'll stop."

Disappointment flooded my belly.

It's fucked up, he'd said.

He'd stop.

I nodded but didn't respond. Whatever had started between us was obviously ending. I completely understood he didn't want to go there with me, he'd made that abundantly clear, but I didn't get *why* he thought he couldn't.

I attempted a pathetic smile. "It's okay. I'm sorry too. I'm going to turn in. Thank you for dinner and the ice cream."

When he didn't respond to my apology, I turned on my heel and left him standing in the kitchen surrounded by his own silence, sure that was how he wanted it, and how I *needed* it. I'd endured enough. I was tired, disappointed, and self-conscious. Not exactly how I expected to end my night, but smart enough to know it had happened for a reason.

CHAPTER 7
TREVOR

"WHAT'S UP YOUR ASS TODAY?" Payne asked from the doorway of my office.

I blinked up at him, aggravated as fuck. Obviously, I wasn't hiding my frustration.

After our uncomfortable conversation, Navie and I had settled into a decent routine the past few weeks. Decent because it wasn't weird anymore. She, like me, had ignored the awkwardness until it wasn't awkward anymore. Now that she was working at Melton's, it wasn't like we had a lot of spare time on our hands at home anyway. She hadn't said it out loud, but I'd caught on to the fact she'd been picking up extra shifts.

"Nothing. What's up?" I answered, deciding not to dump my problems on my best friend. He had enough to deal with.

Payne closed my office door. "Seriously, what's going on?"

I grimaced. My past was catching up with me. The situation with Navie had me reminiscing on my relationship with Britney, my ex-wife. There were so many mistakes in that whole ordeal. Marrying her being the first, but so many after that too. And just thinking about the shit I went through divorcing her, I knew I never wanted to go through it again. It wouldn't be fair to Navie to make a go at a relationship if I never intended on marrying again. I knew that logically, but it still didn't make the decision any easier. I liked her after all. But I also figured most women liked to think that one day, calling herself a wife was appealing.

I blinked, debating on whether I should let Payne in on my secret or not. I'd never talked about Britney with him. Honestly, I didn't want to think about it, much less discuss my past blunders.

Back when I turned pro, the publicity that surrounded a professional fighter had hit me like a ton of bricks. I hadn't been prepared for it and learned quite a few lessons the hard way. I'd never in my life had anything to hide, nor did I care to, so when I was completely honest with the media, reporters took advantage of my transparency and twisted my words so they could make shit up for show. Not just that, but once I'd made it clear I was in a committed relationship, hordes of photographers followed me day and night trying to catch me in any compromising position they could. If they witnessed me standing next to a woman, I was automatically a cheater. Being interviewed by a female sports analyst? A flirt. Made-up stories like that eventually led to the falsity of my being a womanizer.

Every relationship I had my first couple of years in the league got burned to the ground and the media lit the match. They hadn't been as unkind to me as some of the other guys, which didn't say much, and it took a while for me to put everything into perspective. They shouldn't have had anything to do with my life, and the main reason I persisted on being low key.

With some experience under my belt, I made no secret that Britney and I were going to remain somewhat clandestine from the moment we began dating. I explained the media to her in depth so there would be no surprises.

She hated it. I hated it too, honestly. But it was their world, and we lived in it. I'd had a feeling, soul-deep, that we wouldn't last forever, because being in the public eye while trying to maintain an ounce of privacy was a difficult lifestyle to sustain, but I was willing to try with her.

And just like I predicted, they swallowed us whole. She'd ended it ten months after we took our vows. Licking my wounds in private, I remained silent on the entire situation, and after hitting rock bottom, I pulled myself up by my bootstraps and climbed my ass to the top of the fighting league, giving the public nothing personally and everything professionally.

During my divorce, I'd never felt so alone. The one person I thought I had—the person I wanted—left me without a backward glance. I was devastated. That relationship had been the cause of me losing others. The fear I had of giving my all to someone, and them shitting on it, had kept me from making any real attempts at having a family.

I would never make that mistake again, giving myself fully to someone. And Navie didn't deserve anything less than someone giving their all to her.

"I was just thinking about my ex," I admitted.

"Okay…" Payne drew the word out, clearly not understanding my predicament.

I shook my head. "Not okay."

"What's going on?"

"Just going through some shit."

I couldn't explain how Britney had done a number on me, and I was in the beginning stages of fucking up having any kind of relationship with Navie. I already had feelings for her, and they weren't going away. I wasn't sure what to do with them, I just knew she'd backed off considerably when I had, and I didn't like it.

His eyebrow rose, questioning, I was sure, the size of my balls. "Is thinking about an ex-girlfriend enough to put you in a funk?"

I folded my arms across my chest and shook my head again. "Ex-wife," I clarified.

Payne's face straightened in surprise. "The fuck you say?"

"It lasted less than a year. It was a mistake."

"How come I've never heard about this?"

"Never came up," I clipped.

I knew I could have told Payne more about the situation and he would have listened to every detail, but I wasn't in the mood, and he didn't press for more information.

Had I been able to separate my wants from my fears, I could have acted accordingly, but it all just resembled a jumbo mess inside my brain. Which was probably most of the problem; I was overthinking it. Any other time, I would have laughed at myself for acting so strange, but it wasn't funny to me. Being so caught up in Navie petrified me.

The thought of failing at anything with her was enough to keep her at arm's length. If we never let our feelings get too deep, then all our problems would be surface level, and I could tackle surface level.

But when I thought about how my heart sped up when she entered the room after taking her shower—small pellets of water on her chest because she hadn't dried off well enough—it made me want to give her more. When I pictured what her soft pink lips would taste like after she applied her "car" lip balm she left in the center console of my Jeep, I wanted to get more too.

But my marriage had shown me that no matter what you give or get in a relationship, if one of the two parties involved wanted to leave, they could, and they didn't have to give you a heads-up before they showed you their back. Not only had I been hurt when things didn't end well with Britney, I'd been ashamed I hadn't been able to make it work. Marriage was the one thing I'd ever completely failed at.

"You going to Melton's tonight?" he asked, changing the subject.

I frowned. I hadn't committed to going, but it was clear to everyone Willow was stressing about her friend's birthday. She wanted everything to be perfect for Lena, and I would have felt like an asshole if I didn't get the chance to hug the birthday girl myself. "I'll stop by."

"Good. My wife is going to give herself a fucking ulcer over this shindig. She's been on the phone all morning with Navie, going over every little detail."

"Yeah, Navie told me she switched shifts with someone so she could help out. I know how much it means to the girls. Plus, I haven't seen Lena in a while."

"Okay, man. I'll see you there." Payne rapped his knuckles twice on the desk and headed for the door, ironically with ease.

I sat back in my chair relieved. I had never discussed my divorce with anyone before, and Payne hadn't freaked out. Maybe holding my past inside caused my distress about it to intensify instead of healing. Leaning my head back, I sighed. Just when I thought I had actually figured something out, life was always there to prove me wrong.

Melton's was packed, but luckily Navie had been able to secure the back room for Lena's party. We had to bypass all the craziness up front, but it was a private party, so no one was forced to deal with the drunkards at the bar. Lena looked beautiful, strutting around in a pinstripe suit, gladly taking in all the consideration on her special day. She was over-dressed, and the center of attention. Just the way she liked it.

"Happy birthday, doll. You don't look a day over forty-two." I grinned, pulling her in for a hug.

"Shut up, asshole. I look like I'm twenty-five."

"Twenty-five plus five," added Gage.

She leaned over to take a swipe at him while still in my arms. I laughed, squeezing her harder so she couldn't reach him.

I still hadn't congratulated Tommy on his last win. Between his intense workouts with his trainer, helping Navie, and me dwelling on my own bullshit, I kept missing him. I glanced around the room, searching for him, but my gaze found Navie instead. And then I followed her illuminating gaze to Tommy. They were sitting together in the corner. A dark corner.

Heat surged through my body, and pricks of anger stirred low in my gut. It took me a minute to grasp how pissed I was at the sight. And miffed, I supposed. I'd pushed the odd sense of jealousy I had at the gym away, realizing I had no place to be angry. It was none of my business how close they'd become. Plus, I was the one who'd pushed her off on him for training purposes because I hadn't wanted to muddy the waters she and I were wading in.

"Hello?" Gage waved his hand in front of my face. "Earth to Steele." I could have kicked his ass for calling attention to my unwarranted possessiveness.

Our group, including Navie and Tommy, glanced up at his words. There I was, on display in front of the entire party, looking—no, *staring*—at Navie and Tommy, with what was surely a murderous glare.

I tamped down my irritation for being outed and stepped back. "What?" I snapped.

"Dude. You looked like you were having a seizure."

Payne unwrapped himself from Willow and stepped between us. "Gage, go see where the food is."

Gage held his palms up in surrender, then scurried toward the kitchen.

"Is the food really coming?"

"Yes. But Willow's got it. I just knew he'd get lost in some girl's panties on the way." I chuckled and eased my stance. "You good?" he asked.

I scanned the darkened corner where Navie had been, but she had since vacated.

He slapped my chest bringing my attention back to him. "Never mind, man. You're fucked."

"What are you talking about?"

He leaned close so I was the only one to hear him. "I'm talking about the fact that not two seconds ago, you looked like you were coming out of retirement to slit Tommy's throat. I'm talking about you clearing out this whole fucking room to find Navie. I'm talking about earlier in your office."

I sighed and stuffed my hands deep into my pockets. "I don't know what the fuck I'm doing."

"Can I give you a piece of advice?"

I gave a curt nod. Clearly, I needed it.

"Just go get her, man."

I shook my head, knowing his advice couldn't be taken. "Can't."

"You're torturing yourself."

Nodding to a party guest over his shoulder, I collected myself. "I'm cool."

I thought he'd continue on with how stupid I was being, but he didn't. He left me, in search of his wife, no doubt. That was one of the things I liked most about Payne—he didn't push. He always tested the waters first, and once he read the situation, he acted accordingly. It was one of his best attributes as a fighter.

"Hey." Navie's voice came to me like a whisper in the dark.

We were surrounded by people and conversations everywhere, but for a split second, it was like she and I were alone in the room.

"Hey." I made fists with my hands filling my pockets, so I wouldn't touch her.

She brought a glass to her lips, taking a quick drink of whatever she was having, then asked, "Having a good time?"

"Sure. Parties are my thing."

"So I've noticed." She surveyed the room and smiled. "I'm glad everyone could make it."

"Yeah, Lena's cool. She deserves it." Echoes of cheers and birthday wishes rang throughout the pub from where Lena blew out her candles.

"She does," she agreed. "Look, I, uh—"

"Don't. You don't have to say anything. I'm the one who should apologize. I know I've been a little off these last couple of weeks. I'm sorry I haven't been so involved in your training."

After our ice cream bet, I had punked out, knowing being so close to her would make me want her more. I should have said something to her. I should have come up with some kind of corny excuse about being too busy in the office to make good on our deal, but I hadn't. I'd ignored it, for selfish reasons, without any explanation. And just as I expected, she hadn't questioned me about bailing on her, she just continued on with her usual routine as if it had never happened.

"Oh, that's no big deal. I'm learning a lot. Between the trainers and Tommy, I'm making good progress."

"Good." I nodded. "That's good."

I'd never thought so hard about what to say to someone before. Talking, in general, had never been difficult for me, but with Navie, it was like I was a fourteen-year-old boy telling a girl I liked her for the first time. The fear circling my gut was unsettling.

If I wasn't going to make a go with her, it shouldn't still be bizarre. When I was around her, I shouldn't be pissed that she was getting close with someone else. But I was. And that let me know that even though I'd told myself a million and one times to just get over it, I couldn't.

"I may not be home later. I think I'm going to go pub crawling with Tommy and Gage. I need some fun in my life. As you know, I'm an old lady most of the time." She frowned. "Plus, my dad called me last night, and I need a distraction."

The mention of her father concerned me. "When?"

"Before dinner."

"Why didn't you say anything?"

She shrugged. "I don't know. I'm still trying to piece everything together."

Nodding in understanding, I exhaled under my breath. "Is everything okay?"

"Not really. He didn't seem to have an opinion on the fact that Preston bought the apartment building where I was renting and seemed even less interested in discussing why he changed his will."

"I'm sorry, Navie."

And I was. I wished there was something I could have done for her.

"Me too. It's just been so crazy. I know it will work out eventually, it's just getting to that point, you know? Plus, training and trying to stay focused…I just need to let loose for a bit."

I hadn't a clue how long my head had bobbed up and down. I just kept nodding at her words like she was speaking a foreign language, while trying to process my runaway feelings.

"Do you think it's a bad idea? I just thought—"

I straightened. "No. You deserve it. Go. Have fun. Crawl all night long."

Her eyes softened. We stared at each other for a moment before she wrapped her arms around me. I pulled her in close, inwardly moaning from her touch. I wanted nothing more than to leave the bar with her in tow. The primal need to take her home and make her my own came at me fast and furious. I swallowed hard and released her. Stepping back, I nodded once, and decided to make my exit. I couldn't be the kind of man who expressed my displeasure when she found solace with someone else yet did nothing to give it to her myself. That was a dick move, and one hundred percent not who I was or wanted to be. Forcing a smile her way, I tightened my lips and turned away from her, wishing I wasn't so troubled by my attraction for her. I found Lena, wished her a great birthday, and walked out the doors of the bar without so much as a goodbye to anyone else.

The drive home did nothing for my internal turmoil, nor did I feel any less anxious by the time I parked in the garage. Bypassing the television, I peeled my clothes off and crawled into bed, feeling more alone than I'd felt since Navie had moved in. I squeezed my eyes closed and rolled over, pissed at how I felt inside. Empty. Gutted.

Miserable.

Because even though she and I weren't an item, the fact that she slept mere feet from me every night gave me comfort. I knew she was there, and that had been enough for me. Until tonight. When she wasn't there.

Would I seriously be the douchebag who was content on letting the single real thing I'd felt in years get away from me just because I didn't want to take a risk? I'd always considered myself a solid guy—always one to help someone in need. The one who knew the right thing to say when someone struggled. Hell, my best friend was a recovering addict. I'd spent many nights with Payne searching for the meaning of life while simultaneously being his soundboard. But somewhere along the line, I lost that connection with myself, because I hadn't been in a situation personally where I needed to use my instincts. There hadn't really been a moment, other than deciding to retire, where I'd even attempted to psychoanalyze myself.

Lying in my bed, stripped of any and all contemplations of anyone else, forced to consider myself, and my own feelings, I rolled over and punched my pillow.

I tried to convince myself to leave the situation alone. But that just made me feel weak. I wanted to be with Navie and instead of admitting that, I was alone in bed before midnight on a Friday night. Not having her in my life the way I wanted her was more torture than never having her at all, even if she and I didn't work out. I couldn't just be in bed every night knowing she was right down the hall from me, or out with someone else, regretting not ever taking the chance.

The longer I laid there, the angrier I got. Different scenarios floated through my mind about where she was and what she was doing, not to mention who she was doing them with.

Dammit.

Tommy and Gage weren't supposed to make her happy. I was. And

I'd been a punk—a fucking weak-ass punk—by letting them give her what she needed instead of providing for her myself.

I growled, irritated that every ounce of my frustration was caused by my own actions.

Pulling my jeans on from earlier, I buttoned them, then quickly shoved my feet into my boots. Tearing through my house, I grabbed my keys off the side table without ever turning a light on. I hoped Navie was ready, because even though I knew enough about her to know I'd have to take things slow, I'd never been a half-asser. I went all in when something mattered to me, and now that the situation was squared away with me, convincing her that we should be together would be no different.

CHAPTER 8
NAVIE

"I'M FREAKING SWEATING! I think you're slacking, Tommy. This is more of a workout than what we've been doing in the gym." I laughed...again. I was laughing at everything because I was drunk. Somehow, I'd managed over the years to maintain a casual buzz while drinking. Except for a few times in college, I'd been able to control myself. But trying to hang with Tommy and Gage put me in a whole new ballgame, and if I planned to play, I had to pay.

My eyes watered. I could barely see a couple of feet in front of me. And I didn't care about that, not one bit. I felt lighter than air, freer than a bird, and happier than a squirrel who'd found a nut.

Tommy narrowed his eyes in a teasing way. "You shouldn't have told me that, doll. Be prepared for death come Monday."

"You're on!" I clicked my glass to his and downed the rest of my drink. "Where's Gage?" I asked, realizing our partner in crime had disappeared.

Tommy's eyebrow rose and wiggled twice. "I'll give you one guess."

Eww.

"He's disgusting."

"He is," he agreed.

"In a club? They barely clean these places. I should know, I work at one."

"He's probably catching something in the bathroom stall right now. Something even Ajax won't take off."

"Remind me not to drink after him."

Tommy bent at the waist and let out a howl. "You'd be hard-pressed to catch what he's currently acquiring by drinking after him."

"Still. I don't want to take that chance."

"Fuller, you crack my ass up."

We high-fived, even though I wasn't sure what we were celebrating. The music pumped through the club, the reverberation a steady hum. My body was so relaxed, I moved in perfect time with the beat even from our booth. Sitting down hadn't hindered my capabilities. We'd danced most of the night, in between drinks that was, and I loved every moment of it. Taking a break had been Tommy's suggestion, not mine. I was ready to go all night.

I had zilch in my brain: nothing to worry about, nothing to analyze. No situations with my family or feeling uncertain about my career choice. Not once did I think about my living arrangements or how I'd managed to cut my salary by three-fourths at a job I never imagined I'd have to do. After those first few drinks, I hadn't even concerned myself with Trevor or how unwanted I felt around him. I knew him well enough to know he wasn't trying to make me feel that way, but when he acted uninterested—at least personally, I couldn't help but finally see it for what it was. He didn't see me as girlfriend material. He'd friend-zoned me. It stung.

As much as I tried not to let the rejection affect my self-confidence, I couldn't seem to find a way around it. We'd never come right out and talked about it, but he'd stopped sharing the couch with me, choosing the recliner on movie nights. He had taken control of the cooking on most nights, keeping it simple with protein and vegetables. And there had most certainly not been any after dinner ice-cream runs. I remained quiet on the topic and let him set the pace, controlling every aspect of our non-relationship.

Gage quickly slid next to me in the purple, velvet booth. "Look, if a girl named Lindsey comes over here, you haven't seen me, okay?"

"Why would someone named Lindsey come looking for you?" I asked, even though I was positive the answer would disgust me.

"I may have scheduled a meet up with her in the bathroom but ran into a knockout on my way there."

"You did not cheat on a hookup before you actually hooked up."

Tommy burst into laughter, causing me to laugh too. Gage stared at both of us as if we'd grown two heads. "What the fuck? You guys got hammered without me?" he asked, sounding almost wounded.

"You've been gone for over an hour," Tommy told him, then finished off his drink.

Gage smirked at me and waggled his eyebrows.

I shook my head, convinced he was lying. "There is no way in hell you had sex for a solid hour. No. Way."

"Only one way to find out," Gage taunted.

"I guess I'll never know then," I teased.

"Damn, alcohol makes you mean, like Willow and Lena. You get ginger ale from now on." He moved to take the glass from my hand.

I held it high and away from him, and closed my eyes, "Negative, Batman."

After finishing the fruity drink I could barely taste, I placed the glass on the table and basked in the drunken buzz that had enveloped my whole body. I swayed back and forth like I was the only person in the room. Tendrils of my hair slipped through my fingers as I pulled my hair up into a high ponytail, even though I didn't have anything to tie it with. Twisting my hair into a loose bun, I sighed in contentment at the coolness on my neck.

Tommy interrupted my solace by calling my name. When I didn't respond, he tapped my arm until I looked at him.

"Steele's looking for you." He pointed to the front of the club where Trevor was peering through the crowd, eyes like lasers.

"Why's he looking for me?" Something must have happened. He'd never show up at a club at—I glanced at my watch—twelve thirty-seven, unless something had happened to Willow or Payne.

Oh, God.

Dread spread from my gut as flashbacks from the night Willow was attacked last year swirled through my inebriated mind. Standing from the booth, I quickly pushed my way through the crowd.

Stopping in front of Trevor, I caught my breath. "What's wrong?"

"I'm taking you home."

"Why?"

"We need to talk."

I shook my head, confused. My buzz was wearing off due to the adrenaline burst, but I still felt foggy. "Talk?"

He pulled me closer, his lips barely touching my ear, and whispered, "Yeah."

"Is everything okay?"

"Everything's fine." He touched my elbow and glanced around the club. "I just want us to speak in private."

Relief washed over me, realizing my friends were fine. But then—Trevor wanted us to be alone?

I felt like a bad friend, willing to leave Tommy and Gage so quickly, but the anticipation of what was to come outweighed trying to guess which girls in the club Gage had never hooked up with.

"Okay, um—let me go find Tommy." I turned away but Trevor grabbed my hand pulling me back to him.

"I've already texted him. He knows you're coming home with me."

"Oh. Well, all right then."

I was puzzled and plastered, but quickly coming down from my high, which was frankly, a little disappointing. But not overwhelmingly disappointing. Because more than anything, I desired to know what Trevor had to say that was so important it couldn't wait until tomorrow.

He helped me up into the seat of his Jeep and buckled my seatbelt. We sat in silence as he made his way onto the highway. I didn't know what to say because I was confused by his serious expression. I wasn't sure why he remained quiet, but the silence wasn't uncomfortable. In fact, it was relaxing. Dozing, I rested my head against the window, knowing we had a few minutes before reaching his house.

Rousing when he lifted me from the Jeep, I opened my eyes but remained mute. I lifted my arms to circle his neck and he brought me closer to him. I waited, still half asleep, while he unlocked the door.

"Sorry," I mumbled as he sat me on the sofa.

"Don't apologize." He turned the lamp closest to him on with a flick of his wrist and took a seat next to me.

I rose from my slumped position and kicked my heels off. Folding my feet underneath me, I pushed back into the cushions, feeling much more like myself after my power nap, and waited for him to speak.

He clasped his hands together, appearing wounded, like whatever he was thinking about was physically hurting him. His brows tightened and his frown deepened as he spoke. "I know I've been an asshole."

Seeing him so tormented made my belly sink. Him apologizing to me wasn't even close to the top five of things I imagined he was going to say. I felt like I needed to let him off the hook. "Trevor, you don't have to do this."

"I do, though." He considered me, and his unguarded gaze stopped the breath in my lungs.

Rendered silent, I stared at him.

"I've fought my feelings for you. I've pushed aside every natural instinct I have where you're concerned, because I thought I wanted something else. I conditioned myself to the idea of being alone."

He dropped his head, searching the floor, as if the hardwoods had his next words hidden beneath the boards. "I've known for a while how I feel about you. But when you left with Tommy and Gage, when you basically told me they were going to be the reason you felt better tonight, it made me feel like shit. *I* want to be the reason you feel better."

Oh. My. God.

"Trevor." My voice cracked. He'd never, *ever*, displayed so much honesty. And I wasn't firing on all cylinders at the moment. Panic grew within me.

What if I don't remember this moment?

Trevor chuckled. "I won't let you forget, I promise. I'll tell you every day if I have to."

Heat rose from my neck to my cheeks. "Did I just say that out loud?"

He laughed harder. "Yeah. Come on. You sleep on it, and I'll cook you a greasy breakfast in the morning to cure your hangover."

I pushed myself up off the sofa and began walking toward my room, but at the last second, I reached for his hand behind me. His palm slipped into mine; warm and inviting. I closed my eyes, lost in the sensation of him. Standing in the hallway, I pushed my bottom lip through my teeth, hoping I wasn't crossing a line. I wanted to be next to him, even if that meant just being in the same room for the rest of the night. I wasn't ready to let him go so soon after he'd confessed his feelings for me.

Turning toward his bedroom, I paused as we reached the threshold. "Can I sleep with you?"

Trevor's brows raised, as if he was surprised by my boldness. Then I realized how forward my question must have sounded. Damn alcohol. I held my laughter inside and cleared my throat. "Just sleep. I—I just don't want our time together to end after—what you said."

His eyes softened, almost appearing guilt ridden. Like I'd made him feel remorseful for waiting so long to share his feelings, which was not my intent.

"Of course."

I tilted my head up and gave him a nod as tension I hadn't realized I'd been holding in my shoulders drained from my body. I relaxed, oddly enough as we entered his room, me still in my club clothes, and him in a pair of faded jeans. The way they hung from his hips made me want to pull him closer to me by the belt loops. Trevor took his watch off and emptied his pockets. I watched, not convinced he wasn't putting on a show. He had to have known what seeing him in his own space, confidently going about his nightly routine was going to do to me.

He is so hot.

I'm hot.

Why is it so damn hot in this room?

Fanning my face, I blew out a deep breath, my body's reaction to what appeared to be a ginormous inconvenient hot flash.

Trevor chuckled and pulled a T-shirt from his dresser. He wadded it up and tossed it to me before slipping into his master bathroom. I stood silently, gathering my thoughts as he closed the door—I assumed to give me privacy. I wasn't sure, still stunned by the night's turn of events as I sat on his bed, trying to make sense of it all.

Holy hell.

I was wrecked. He'd just spilled his guts to me, something I was mentally bitching about not three hours ago, and I hadn't said anything in return. My hair was a rat's nest. My teeth hadn't been brushed. I hadn't had a shower, and considering all the sweating I'd done, I was pretty sure I had the odor of a teenaged boy's gym locker. I glanced around, looking for anything to spray that would knock the rank off me.

Second guessing myself, I chewed on the inside of my jaw. No, I couldn't do that. He'd smell it immediately, and probably think I was trying to cover something up. Like a fart.

The mere thought of farting in front of him had me wanting to faint from anxiety. I had to calm down. I turned my face into his pillow, concentrating on slowing my breaths and remaining sane.

In and out.

In and out.

I smiled after a few moments, the scent of his pillow creating an overwhelming whimsical swirl in my belly, entirely overtaking my previous anxiety. Lying on my stomach, I brought my arms under his pillow, lost in the aroma of him. My emotions were all over the place. I felt like a basket case, going from almost hyperventilating to laughing so quickly. I covered my mouth to keep from snickering out loud. I was giddy, and there was nothing I could do about it. Clarity formed in my mind, a tranquility I'd never felt before, as if my mind was doing yoga while my body sat on the sidelines. I bit my lip, already reminiscing about the sweet words he'd said to me earlier. *He* wanted to be the reason I felt better. I couldn't recall a time when anyone had said something so sweet to me.

I sat up straight, rubbing my palm across his midnight blue sheets. Quickly, I tugged my dress over my head. As I reached to unclasp my bra, I thought better of it and pulled his T-shirt over my head. It engulfed me, hitting me just above my knees. I smiled, knowing it would take minimal effort to get used to it all. His T-shirt. His bed. Him.

I crawled up to the head of his massive bed, pulling the covers out from under the pillows, reveling in the comfort from them, just as the bathroom door opened.

I leaned back on my elbows, and grinned. Trevor's bare chest gleamed under the overhead lights. I had him pegged for a nude sleeper, which could have totally been the case, except I was in his bed. He was probably just being a gentleman, but the fact that he had a pair of gray and black plaid pajama bottoms was, for some reason, sexy to me. The deep V disappearing under the waist band made me bite my bottom lip—hard. As if the sting from the pain would override my arousal.

He made his way to the bed, turning the overhead lights off by flicking a switch on his nightstand. Settling in, he placed his arm behind his head, relaxed.

"Is it bizarre that I'm in here?" I asked after a few moments of silence.

He glanced in my direction. "No."

"How long did you think about telling me how you felt?"

"A while."

"I'm not fishing or anything, I just feel like this came out of nowhere. You've been so…distant."

Trevor rolled his body toward mine. I swallowed, keeping my palms under my cheek.

"I'm really sorry about that."

"No." I shifted my weight, bringing my knees up to my stomach. "I didn't ask so you'd apologize again. I'm just curious."

"I get it, but I don't think I can explain it," he admitted with a dry chuckle. "The bottom line is, you're training and I didn't want to hinder that in any way."

I nodded, somehow understanding where he was coming from even though he hadn't elaborated.

"I know this is all… insane, but I—"

"What's insane?"

"Just…" I paused, wondering how my being in Boston must have appeared to him. To someone who didn't know the half of what I'd overcome to be here. "Trying to make a go at competing. Having a dream of essentially creating a company from scratch. My fractured family." I shrugged, suddenly feeling insecure. "It must all appear insane to you."

Trevor shook his head, then lifted his arm so that I could scoot closer to him. "Doing something for yourself is the exact opposite of insane to me."

I glanced up at him, barely able to see around the scruff on his sculpted jawline. "Really?"

Trevor placed his chin on top of my head, causing my cheek to rest on his chest. "You should always set goals for yourself. It's what keeps us all going, I think."

I longed to ask what he meant. There was so much wisdom and experience behind his words, but lying next to him while his body was wrapped around mine provided too much comfort. I was out before I could reply.

Swiping my hand across my face in search of the lone hair tickling my cheek, I wrestled three times with the blankets before freeing my foot. On the third try, a gentle hand scooped my foot up and placed it on top of the blanket.

"Morning, sleepyhead. How you feeling?"

Pushing my hand through tangled strands of my hair, I sat up slowly, took in my surroundings, and frantically sifted through my memories. I remembered Trevor picked me up from the club. I remembered him telling me he liked me, and that he wanted to make a go of it. I also recalled changing into his T-shirt. Feeling the soft cotton, I looked down and pulled it slightly away from my body with my thumb and index finger.

"Okay. Did we—?"

He chuckled and placed his hand on my hair. "No."

"Good." I hadn't realized how that sounded until he lifted my face to his. His index finger trailed my hairline until it made it all the way down to my chin. I shivered and blinked.

His lips drifted slowly toward mine, causing my nerves to come alive.

My teeth.

Are dirty.

I never imagined him picking me up three sheets to the wind and bringing me home. And I certainly hadn't entertained the idea that I'd be waking up in his bed. My thought process prior to my drunken pub crawl had never wavered from Tommy dropping me off, and I knew there was zero chance of me hooking up with *him*.

I tensed, resisting his pull, and he felt it.

His voice was barely above a whisper, and so deep. "Come here."

I shook my head and covered my mouth. "I haven't brushed my teeth. I can't have our first kiss be ruined before we even have it."

He stopped and smirked. "Hop to it, then."

I stood in the middle of his bed, ready to jump off the side, but he grabbed my bare legs and brought them to his face. I stilled as his five-o'clock shadow slowly rubbed up and down my thighs, causing goosebumps to break out across my flesh. Mere inches from the hem of his T-shirt I wore, his momentum paused, lingering dead center. Tingles shot from my stomach down to my core as the heat from his breaths tickled my most private part.

My legs wobbled, while my heart fluttered. I closed my eyes at the intimate touch, overwhelmed by the anticipation of what he'd do next. Slight kisses peppered my inner thighs, turning the slight flutters shocking my heart to violent kicks against my ribs as my body betrayed me, showing me once and for all, who was in charge.

Trevor pulled me closer to him, applying the lightest pressure to the back of my legs. Shifting his weight, he turned with me in his arms until I was off the bed, then he slowly let me slide down his body until my feet touched the floor. Knots formed in my stomach over the sweetness of the moment.

He didn't say anything, just acted as if him picking me up was something he normally did. Stumbling to the bathroom, I glanced over my shoulder at him one last time before I shut the door to his bathroom, creating some much-needed distance between the two of us.

Lord. Have. Mercy.

The last glimpse of him burned itself into my long-term memory. His bare chest rising and falling so dramatically, it was as if he was breathing for the both of us. And considering my shortness of breath, too elated from the intimacy of it all, he very well could have been.

Leaning against the door, I slid to the floor, flinching as my bare butt cheeks hit the cold tile. My thong did nothing to protect me from the chill. I crossed my arms and brought my knees to my chest.

We're doing this.

The thud from my head hitting the door caused him to stir. I heard his footsteps coming toward the bathroom, but I remained still.

"You all right in there?"

"Yeah, uh, my head—" Lord.

My head what? Hit the door because I'm stupid and had to collapse the first moment I'm alone because you're giving me too many butterflies to physically hold myself up?

I felt the door push just a fraction from the other side. He grunted once, then placed his palm flat on the floor, his fingers protruding slightly to my side of the door. They were mere inches from my butt cheek.

I hated to even doubt the possibility of us before it even got started, but I couldn't help it. With the fog from my brain semi-gone, the fact that we lived together seemed… messy. Not to mention the ludicrous personal changes I'd made only a short time ago. I didn't feel grounded, and I managed best when I had something secure in my life to hold on to.

The added stress of the unknown hit me like a ton of bricks.

"I know that wasn't fair of me, what I did last night," he said through the door.

"What exactly?"

His head thumped lightly, the same as mine had not a full minute ago. "All of it. I shouldn't have barged in on your time out with Tommy and Gage. I know you've gotten to be pretty good friends with them. I also know that I've been giving you mixed signals for a while, and you hooking up with one of them would have been perfectly normal." He sighed. "You're beautiful. They're cocksuckers who would love to have someone like you on their arm."

I remained silent, playing out his outrageous scenario in my mind.

I'd never considered Tommy or Gage in a romantic way. He had it so wrong. I would never.

"I—I just couldn't let that happen," he continued.

I shook my head, even though he couldn't see me. "That was never a possibility, Trevor."

"Well, I didn't know that. All I knew was I didn't want it to be."

I rubbed my eyes, realizing how peculiar it was that we were having such an important conversation though a closed door. "Everything is just so crazy," I began. Before I could truly voice my concerns, my anxiety reached a whole new level, which had me confessing the strangest thing. "I've only ever been in one relationship before."

Of everything I could have said, my inexperience was what I chose to convey.

His silence spoke volumes. My chest heaved by his stillness. I bit my upper lip, wondering if I'd made a mistake with my honesty. It wasn't as if he wouldn't be able to tell eventually, but maybe that was the kind of conversation normal people in relationships didn't have. Maybe discussing past relationships was kept in the past—probably where they should have stayed.

He made a small noise low in his throat, but I couldn't tell without seeing his expression what it meant.

"I wasn't trying to make you uncomfortable, I just wanted to you know ahead of time in case I'm not as good at this kind of stuff as you thought I'd be," I rambled, trying to cover my previous blunder.

More silence. Enough to swallow me whole. I closed my eyes, wishing I could take back my admission, then the insane attempt at explaining that admission.

"Open the door."

I stood, ready to meet his judgment head on.

Unlocking the door, I turned the knob and came face to face with Trevor as he leaned against the door frame with both hands tightly gripping the trim on the walls. His chest pushed through the door, leaving the muscles in his arms to bulge from holding his weight on them. I looked up at him, feeling small. His raw sexuality and confidence made me feel the size of an ant.

"I sorry if I made things weird," I started.

"Not weird, Blue." A wide grin spread across his face. His irises changed colors, swirling in his playfulness. How could I want to hug him and punch him in the stomach at the same time?

I rolled my eyes. "Like I've never heard that one before."

"You haven't heard it from me," he whispered, his gaze holding mine. "Nothing with you is ever weird."

Could have fooled me.

"It's not?"

His brows furrowed as he pushed off the frame and walked me backward until my ass cheeks hit cool marble. "No," he assured me. "It's the opposite. I've never fought my flesh so much in my life as when I'm near you. You're smart and funny." He leaned into me, pushing the thickness of his arousal into my stomach. "You're perfect."

His arms wrapped around my waist, and he lifted me in the air as if I weighed nothing, our gazes never faltering as he gingerly sat me down on top of the vanity. My breath felt heavy as his lips caressed the underside of my jawline. Closing my eyes, I willingly let his sweet, scattered kisses lull me, relaxing me so much I had to lean on him for support.

Trevor pulled away from me, breaking the spell. I opened my eyes, my gaze holding his. "So, we're doing this?" I asked. Not because I was dense—because I wanted him to be sure. We were roommates. I was training at his gym. I was bound to bug him with questions pertaining to fights, and I didn't want the crossover to be too much.

"We're doing it. So long as we're honest with each other. Something comes up? You come to me. You have a bad day? You come to me." His large palms framed my face, and he tilted my head up in question, almost as if he were waiting for me to agree to his terms.

I loved that he was a man who took control, yet he did it in a way that didn't include making me feel bossed around. There was something so alpha about Trevor and his need to protect those he cared about. It was fierce and endearing.

"Same goes for you then," I shot back.

Trevor grinned, dimples and all, then leaned in, placing his lips against mine. I quickly dodged him, remembering I still hadn't brushed my teeth.

He placed his hand on the back of my head to hold me in place. "Stop."

I covered my mouth and spoke through my palm. "I will not kiss you until I've brushed."

"Come. Here." He tried to pull me closer, but I fought back by pushing my head into his palm.

He laughed loudly. I'd never seen him so entertained. He could laugh at me all he wanted, but I was not about to have the moment of our first kiss tainted because of my bad breath.

When he didn't release me, I psyched him out by acting like I was going to kick him in the balls. When Trevor bent over to protect himself—and the boys—I spun around on the vanity, grabbed his toothpaste, and squeezed a liberal amount on my finger. Bringing it up to my mouth, I pushed it inside and rubbed it around, giggling the whole time.

Trevor, of course, wasn't hurt, but grunted as he straightened. I watched him in the mirror as he crowded my space again. He placed one hand on either side of my butt and leaned over my shoulder. "Hmm…you being a fighter may be a problem for me." He nuzzled my neck as I continued to make do.

"Or it could be invigorating?" I rinsed and turned to face him. "Or maybe even arousing?" I raised an eyebrow and grinned.

Trevor stared at me through the mirror, grabbed his own toothbrush, and smeared a healthy amount of toothpaste on it. Reaching around me, he turned the water on, then proceeded to brush his own teeth—while basically holding me in his arms. I turned my head to the side and stilled, intoxicated, completely lost in the sight of him up close and personal.

My butt cheeks were numb from the marble I had been sitting on, but I didn't care. My breath was fresh, and I was more than ready to kiss him. My gaze caught his in the mirror. Crystal blue eyes swirled, captivating me as he wiped his mouth with the hand towel. The storm in them picked up speed as I tried to decipher what he was thinking. It awakened something in me, something that seemed to have been resting dormant for so many years. I knew everything was moving quickly, but I was hypnotized, lost in him. In the lust. In the passion. In all of it.

Trevor spun me around to face him. My gaze fell to his lips, enamored with them as my tongue darted out to moisten my own. Light pink and plump, peeked out at me under the light scruff of his beard. An odd sense of confidence took over, making me feel sexier than ever before. My palms reached the sides of his neck, then wrapped tightly into two handfuls of his dark hair. Leaning forward, our lips collided once, twice, three times before our tongues twirled in perfect rotation.

Goosebumps caused my bare skin to pebble, as my flesh awakened, a renowned vigor spreading throughout me, causing my body to take on a life of its own. There was no guiding, no talking inside my own head, no overthinking.

Bringing my feet to the backs of his legs, I tugged him closer. His large hands fought the extra material from his oversized T-shirt I wore to touch the skin at my back. I sighed through our kiss, completely numb to anything other than pure satisfaction.

Trevor broke the kiss and stepped away abruptly. Licking my plump bottom lip, I watched, surprised as he pushed his hands through his hair, his chest robustly rising and falling in rapid succession. He squeezed his eyes shut, cursed harshly under his breath, then turned his back to me. I silenced my labored breaths the best I could and absently rubbed the pad of my index finger along my bottom lip. I'd never been so worked up. He could have laid me out on the bathroom floor and had me any which way he wanted.

I didn't know what to say.

"I'm sorry. I got carried away."

"Fuck me. *You* got carried away? Navie, I literally almost jizzed in my pants." He shook his head, appearing disappointed in himself.

At his words, I glanced down at his mid-section. A perfect outline of his arousal was on full display, vast and protruding; curiosity filled my brain.

"You've got to stop examining my dick. You've got to quit being so fucking cute, sitting on my sink in nothing but my T-shirt. And you damn sure have got to not kiss me like that right after I find out we need to take things slow. Got it?"

I blinked up at him and crossed my legs, knowing it was a lame attempt at covering them. Trevor walked back over to me and placed his thumb over my ear and his hand at the base of my skull, cupping my neck. Large fingers tugged at my hair softly as he held me in place, staring at me unlike any other time before. "All I'm saying is, I don't want you to regret anything, okay?"

I nodded, even though I didn't entirely agree. "Okay."

He pushed his forehead against mine, settling there. Breathing in each other's exhales, the moment that passed between us was magical and exhilarating. I wrapped my arms around his neck, only knowing I needed something to anchor me. He hugged me and kissed my neck before taking a step back.

He grimaced, as he cupped the obvious bulge in his gray sweats. "The karma I'm receiving for calling you Blue is astounding."

I chuckled, covering my mouth. "Sorry?"

"You're *sorry*?" he adjusted himself again and turned to walk out of the bathroom, noticeably not impressed with my innocent act. "The nickname sticks for sure, now," he called over his shoulder.

"You're the one who wants to go slow!" I yelled, feeling more confident by the second since he'd lightened the mood.

"Let's go, Turquoise!" He teased. "I'm cooking you breakfast, as promised."

I burst into laughter, then turned to face myself in the mirror. I was grinning like a child on Christmas. My *boyfriend* was so sexy. And a damn good kisser. He was a good man—my dad even thought so, not that it mattered—but it was just more confirmation. I had no idea what had changed Trevor's mind about us, or if we were crazy for even trying to be together while living in the same home, but I knew we didn't have a choice now. Not after what had just transpired between us. Not after he'd given me a glimpse of what we could be.

I pulled the first drawer open to my left, looking for a washcloth, and happened upon a stash of unopened toothbrushes. That dirty little...

I eyed them, shaking my head, and picked the blue one, smirking at the irony. After settling on a pair of his gym shorts I found hanging on the towel rack, I rolled them three times at the waist, knowing they looked ridiculous on me, but somehow felt okay with it because they were his.

When I rounded the corner to the kitchen, I stopped abruptly in in my tracks at the sight. I would never tire of seeing Trevor's bare back. The span of his broad shoulders caused the butterflies in my tummy to tumble again. His shorts, like the ones I was wearing, were slung low on his hips. My gaze roamed his body, and I wondered for a split second what he saw when he looked in the mirror because the sight of him caused my blood pressure to rise, my heartrate to pick up, and a feverish hot flash to rise from the tips of my toes to the top of my head.

He had a dish towel tucked into the side of his shorts. I cleared my throat.

He flipped the bacon, then turned in my direction. "God, I'll never get tired of seeing you like this."

"Like what?" I ran my hand across the top of my head. "A mess?"

"You're gorgeous, and you don't even know it. It's mind-blowing."

He plated the food he'd prepared, and brought my food over to the bar, where I'd taken a seat.

Grinning, I got comfortable. "Steele, are you hitting on me?"

"I already got you, babe." He winked. "Exclusively, because I don't share, so no…my compliments are not contingent on what I can get out of them. I told you that because we're at a place now where it's not sexual harassment to say it out loud. You've always been the most beautiful girl in the room, Navie."

"Trevor." I looked down and shook my head. He was being so romantic, so tender with me, and I found myself falling in real time. "Thank you. And I don't share either, so we're good on that front."

"Spectacular. It's settled." He took a large bite of eggs. "I am taking you to a movie tonight. Feels like we should mark the occasion, doesn't it?"

"It does," I agreed, matching his bite because my stomach growled.

Or fluttered, whichever way I decided to look at it.

CHAPTER 9
TREVOR

"SO, you finally locked that down, huh?" Gage asked the next morning, nodding toward Navie while she practiced take-downs with Tommy.

I raised an eyebrow and glared at him.

He put his hands up in mock self-defense. "Just saying it's about fucking time."

I shook my head, not in the mood to explain myself or talk about what me and Navie were or weren't doing. It was no one's business. "Don't you have something better to do besides stand here and analyze my relationships?"

He raised an eyebrow of his own, being a smartass. "Plural?"

"Get the fuck out of here." I hit his arm, making sure the contact would leave a bruise.

"Ow!" He chuckled, rubbing the spot my fist had just vacated.

I eyed Navie again, checking out her form. I made two mental notes to give her when she took a break. Going back to business, I finished up a couple of phone calls, and scribbled down the three fights I'd secured for the guys in the gym on the desk calendar. Gage would finally be getting an opponent he'd been vocal about wanting to fight. He'd be excited and thrived off hype, which was why I planned on announcing his match with Turner Lock in front of everyone.

"Hey." Navie bounced up to the counter, visibly happy about her workout.

I grinned at her enthusiasm. "Everything going all right with Tommy?"

"Absolutely." She beamed.

I tamped down the knee-jerk jealousy that seemed to easily spread throughout my body as she smiled at the mere mention of Tommy's name, knowing full well my reaction was barbaric. And also completely unnecessary.

"I'm going to dinner tonight with Willow and Lena."

"Okay."

"Payne is taking us and picking us up."

"You plan on getting blitzed again?" I teased.

"No." She dragged the "o" out, looking a little uncertain. "But if I want to have a drink, I don't want to worry about driving."

"Come here." I grabbed her hand and led her around the counter. I sat on the stool and pulled her closer to me. "You don't have to worry about a way home. You call me. For any and everything, you hear?" She nodded in understanding. "I mean it. I got you. No matter what's going on."

Her cheeks flushed, and I found myself smiling at how cute she looked. "Okay," she agreed.

"Okay." I kissed her, needing comfort from the chaos that surrounded me. I needed her touch to ground me; to keep me locked in on something certain as I processed the whirlwind of emotions I felt having her near me. Unfortunately, we were interrupted by immature assholes whistling and catcalling.

Navie broke our kiss and went back to work. But not before looking back at me and winking, lifting my spirits, even if just for the moment.

And the end of Gage's workout, I met him inside the cage. Whistling between my teeth, I got everyone's attention. "I have an announcement."

The clinking from the weights in the gym ceased. I smirked, knowing Gage was about to lose his shit. He'd waited months to fight Turner Lock. He knew it would garner a decent amount of attention, possibly enough notice to secure a contract.

"Gage, you have four weeks to prepare."

"For?" Gage asked, wiping his bare chest with his T-shirt.

"Turner Lock."

Tommy whistled and Navie clapped her hands, while everyone else cheered.

"Are you fucking with me?"

"Nope. I just secured it with his agent."

"Dude!" Gage fist-pumped, then advanced toward me. He wrapped his sweaty arms around my body, pulling me into a bear hug. "I love you. I. Fucking. Love. You," he said before placing a wet kiss on my cheek.

Everyone laughed. I didn't. Pushing him off me, I landed a killer leg sweep, knocking his feet out from underneath him. His back hit the mat, and he rolled over, groaning and chuckling simultaneously.

"Don't ever kiss me again," I warned.

"You liked it!" Tommy yelled from the outside of the cage.

"You want some?" I threatened.

Tommy held his hands up in surrender, causing the other fighters to chuckle.

As I climbed out of the cage, Navie made her way over to greet me. "That was awesome, Trevor."

"The leg sweep?" It was tempting to do so much more, but I would have felt guilty injuring him before the fight of his life.

"No, silly. Getting him that fight. You work so hard for these guys."

I stood back, watching the other fighters congratulate Gage. Glancing in Navie's direction, I realized I hoped to do even more to help her. I didn't voice it, though. It didn't seem like the right time.

"They deserve it. The goal is to garner some buzz for them. Turner Lock will do that for Gage."

We had our regulars on fight nights, but we needed fresh eyes. Eyes that hopefully belonged to agents or at least ground marketing strategist. People like Navie's father tended to listen to them, knowing they were capable of selling the talent. At the thought of Richard, the vibrant energy I'd felt only moments ago with my announcement vanished. I had a sneaking suspicion, Richard would play his hand when he found out Navie and I were together and one of my worst fears would come true. He had so much power in the profession, and I knew he wasn't afraid to wield it. Choosing between my relationship with Navie and the guys I'd become so invested in wasn't something I wanted to be forced to do.

Deciding to ignore the anxiousness circling in my veins, I nudged Navie's shoulder. "I brought us lunch."

"You did?"

I loved her smile; the way it started behind her eyes like a child's. It was one of the purest things I'd ever seen.

"You always feed me," she said, following me to my office.

Stopping at the door, I turned toward her and kissed her forehead. "I always will."

She grinned and walked straight for my desk. "So, Tommy thinks I'm ready for mounts."

"Does he now?" I raised an eyebrow, wondering why Tommy hadn't told me about Navie's progress. I placed her sandwich in front of her, along with her usual Salt and Vinegar chips.

Navie ignored the food and tilted her head to the side. "What's that supposed to mean?"

I sighed, knowing my response was out of line. "Nothing." Surely, my reaction to Tommy mounting Navie in an attempt to train her so she wouldn't get murdered inside the cage had more to do with my fear of screwing up our newfound relationship than it did him touching her in a strictly professional manner. I just wasn't sure how to process that.

Her gaze fell downward and stilled, as if she were inspecting the bread on her sandwich. It made me feel like a jerk.

"You know something you never told me?"

She glanced up at my attempt to change the subject. "What?"

"Your middle name."

Navie opened her chips and chuckled. "I don't have one."

I narrowed my eyes. I knew she was lying, if for nothing more than the way she looked away from me. "Why do you not want me to know?"

"Because you'll laugh, and I don't want you to have that much ammunition."

"How bad is it? Geraldine? Edith?" I grinned, already anticipating the cuteness she would display when she revealed her full name.

"Worse," she groaned.

"I can't imagine anything worse," I told her, popping a bite of my sandwich in my mouth.

"Pier."

"Pier?" I asked, holding a cough inside. "As in Navy Pier?"

"God, yes." She placed her hands over her face in embarrassment. "My parents met there. In Chicago."

"But your first name—" I started but she interrupted me.

"My mom wanted something more feminine, so she spelled it with an IE."

Grinning, I leaned across my desk and pulled her hands away from her face. "I could not love your name more."

"Yeah, right."

"I'm serious." At the sight of her vulnerability, I couldn't help myself. Pulling her around the desk, I wasn't satisfied until she reached my lap. The smell of her; the weight of her body resting atop mine felt so natural. "You're too special to have a name like Geraldine or Edith," I reassured.

Navie giggled, but pressed her hands into my chest, forcing as much space as she could between us. "What's your middle name?"

"Jackson."

"Of course, you have a badass middle name to match your first and last." She rolled her eyes.

"Jackson was my mother's maiden name."

Navie's eyes softened, all traces of teasing erased in a split second. I wasn't sure why I mentioned my mom in a moment of such lightness, but it didn't feel uncomfortable.

"I wish I could have met her."

I hadn't exactly told Navie the ins and outs of my mother's death, only that she never got to see me fight professionally.

"Was your mom sick when she passed?"

I took a drink of my water, my mind free-falling through a list of memories I wasn't sure I wanted to reminisce on. Yet, I didn't feel as gloomy as I normally would have.

"Yeah. She had cancer. Just really sad to watch, you know?"

Navie's hand covered mine as it rested on her waist. "I used to wonder if knowing my mom was going to die ahead of time would have been easier than answering the door to a cop I'd never met before telling me she was gone in the blink of an eye."

Interlocking our fingers, I rubbed the top of her hand with my thumb. "I think it just sucks, no matter how the people we love leave us."

Navie nodded but smiled the sweetest smile when she glanced at me. "I feel like I would have really loved your mom."

"You definitely would have." Tightening my grip on her, I squeezed, feeling immediate contentment.

"You would have loved mine too," she whispered.

Kissing her shoulder, I pulled her as close to me as I could. Maybe the loss of our mothers made me feel closer to her, I didn't know, but the fact that she understood every ounce of what I was feeling at the simple mention of my mom's name, without me having to explain it, gave me a sense of peace I hadn't realized I'd been missing.

After Navie left my office, I sat in silence, appreciating the amity, until my phone rang. Recognizing the caller's number, I picked up, more than curious why Jeremy Tillman, the Vice President of marketing and sales for the AFL from the Canadian office would be contacting me.

"Hello?"

"Trevor, hey. It's Jeremy Tillman. I heard Gage is fighting Lock."

"Man, word gets out fast. I *just* secured that."

"I'm in the loop, I guess. Listen, I'm going to be in Boston in a couple of hours if you're willing to meet up for a beer. I have a list of scouts we can discuss if that's something you're interested in."

Shocked, I let out a huge exhale. I'd spent the last half of my life doing business with people like Jeremy. Half the time, they never returned phone calls because they didn't have to. The fact that he'd called me and even expressed interest in a local gym was huge deal for not only Gage, but the other guys who trained as well. Especially given that I didn't do favors. Didn't accept them and never asked for them. I learned early on, owing people things got in the way of having a soul.

"That'd be great."

"Faltron is looking for a fresh face."

Nate Faltron was one of the best agents in the game. Even a meeting with him would garner favor in the fighting world.

"Gage won't disappoint. He's hungry."

"I'll holler at you later with the details. I should be in around six."

"Look forward to it."

I hung up, my mind contemplating the guys at the gym and which ones were somewhat ready. I grabbed the keys to my filing cabinet, pumped as I pulled each of their files by name. If Jeremy wanted to talk business, I would be prepared.

CHAPTER 10
NAVIE

"I'M ON MY WAY," Payne's voice trailed off as Preston grabbed the phone out of my hand and threw it across the room.

"Why would you call that asshole? We're having a conversation, Navie."

I narrowed my eyes at my brother, anger seething from my body. "I told you to leave."

My brother, in all his infinite wisdom, had shown up on Trevor's doorstep, demanding I go back home. I'd been gone for months. And stupidly, I naïvely assumed he and my father were over pretending to care.

"I'm not leaving without your ass in tow. Dad's threatening *my* future now since he doesn't have you around. This shit show you've got going on is now affecting *my* life. You've proven your fucking point." Preston held his arms out to the sides. "You can do without money and your belongings. Bravo. Now get your ass out to that car before I carry you there myself."

It was typical on all levels. Just when I thought the drama was dying down, my family showed up out of the blue, instantly crushing the semi-peaceful state I'd created for myself. To make matters worse, instead of talking to me about the situation, which was what I'd tried to do before I left, my father allowed me a few moments of reprieve before sending my brother in to knock over the first domino in an attempt to ruin all that I'd built.

"I'm not going anywhere. I'm trying to accomplish something here."

All I wanted was to be left alone. I'd given up on having their support. I'd thrown in the towel, knowing I'd never gain their respect. But the least they could have offered was a ceasefire.

Preston laughed, his tone menacing. To him, my argument was a joke. He never took me seriously. I was afraid he'd come by that opinion honestly. My whole life, my father had led the way for him daily, reminding us both in not so many words, I was a girl. Just a girl… who apparently was merely capable of living out a life he, himself, created for me. I despised the fact that neither of them condoned me thinking for myself. Little did they know, the independence I'd gained in such a short amount of time had already fanned the flames of my determination.

My brother clenched his teeth. "You're coming with me."

"The fuck she is," Payne's voice, harsh and unexpected, echoed off the high vaulted ceilings inside Trevor's living room.

Shifting my gaze, I relaxed my shoulders upon Payne's arrival. I glanced to my brother in time to see his eyes widen at Payne's appearance.

"What do you have to do with this? This is a family issue. You're not family, asshole."

Payne walked over to me, and stood directly in front of me, as if to shield me. "Asshole? That's rich, coming from you."

"One phone call to my father, and your ass is grass," my brother threatened him.

"Seriously? You're involving Daddy now that this"—he pointed between himself and my brother—"is man to man? Or do you only untuck your balls when you're battling your sister?"

My brother sneered, his perfect white teeth showing clear in the dimly lit space. I stepped around Payne and faced my brother head on, feeling secure now that Payne was present but knowing I had to handle the situation myself. "Preston, I'm not leaving. Don't show up here again. If Dad wants to speak with me, all he has to do is ask. This was uncalled for."

Preston stared me down, clearly hoping I would cave in submission. I didn't budge. I held my chin high, letting him know he wasn't leaving with what he'd come for. Silence stretched out as he considered his options, breaking our locked gazes to stare at Payne over my shoulder. Without so much as a goodbye, my brother stormed from Trevor's house, squealing his tires out of the circle drive.

I exhaled the breath I'd been holding and plopped down onto Trevor's oversized couch. "God, I have no idea what's gotten into him. My dad threatens him one time—*one* time—and he goes ape shit. I've lived with idle threats my whole life; I don't see why Preston can't handle it like a proper trust fund baby."

Payne didn't laugh at my joke. His lips turned downward, frowning at my situation. I already felt bad enough for putting him in a difficult position, given that he worked for my dad. The reality was one day, Preston would be signing Payne's paychecks and because of me, there would already be bad blood. I shouldn't have involved him, but I hadn't been able to get hold of Trevor when Preston showed up. I didn't know who else to call, and I knew turning to the cops would have been a PR nightmare for everyone, especially Trevor.

"Steele on his way home?" he asked.

"I have no idea. I tried to call him, but it went straight to voicemail. I guess his phone is dead."

"Lock up. I'm calling your dad."

I stood, frightened Payne was getting further involved. "No. Please don't. I don't want you tangled in this mess." When he didn't budge, I continued. "I promise, I'll call my father and settle things."

I may not have known everything when it came to my dad and his business, but I knew involving an employee in personal business would put both of us in for a world of hurt. My dad had more tactics than the US Army when someone messed with his money or the possibility of him losing it.

Payne eyed me as if he was trying to decipher my ability to lie. I wasn't lying. My plan was to call my dad as soon as he left. I was sick of them barging into my life, taking everything they deemed valuable, then leaving me with nothing but self-doubt. Whether or not they supported me as I tried to make something of myself was their own decision, but I was finally ready to tell my father I didn't appreciate it.

"I promise."

"All right. But this shit needs to stop. Your brother is volatile. I don't trust him. Not even with you."

"He's just—desperate. His dream has always been to take over the business when my dad retires, and he doesn't want anything or anyone in the way of that. Right now, I'm in the way because my dad is angry I've made a decision he wasn't a part of."

"I don't give a fuck what he wants. He doesn't get to just show up, walk in uninvited, and fuck with you. Your brother or not, that's not going to happen on my watch."

"I appreciate you. So much, but I'm good. I didn't really think he'd hurt me, but I knew he was serious about forcing me to go with him."

"That's hurting you, Navie."

Stunned, I blinked in silence while letting his words sink in. I'd put up with Preston's way of dealing with things for so long, I'd become immune on the surface. Just because my brother hadn't physically put his hands on me didn't mean he wasn't doing damage.

"You're right." Grabbing my phone off the floor, glad to see it wasn't broken, I pulled my dad's number up. "I'm calling my dad now."

I watched silently as Payne inspected the living room and seemed to relax when he saw nothing was out of place. "Lock up. Turn the alarm on," he said, turning for the front door.

I held my phone firm. "I will."

As soon as he left, I locked the door and set the alarm, just like he'd instructed. God, my family was in absolute disarray. It seemed the closer I got to living my own life, the harder they pushed back. It was time I stood up to my dad, and, in turn, stood up to Preston.

Exhaling, I took a seat on Trevor's sectional, tucking my feet underneath me as my thumb hoovered over the send button. My grip tightened, as I pressed the button to connect the call. I was nervous. Petrified, really.

"Navie."

"Hello, Dad."

"I assume you're calling for a specific reason, given the fact I haven't heard from you in months." His tone was ice cold.

"You assume correct."

"I'm listening."

"Dad—" My voice broke.

All the resolve I'd worked up moments ago drifted from my body all at once, leaving me indecisive. I swallowed, knowing whatever I said next would determine how he responded. There had never been more than a gentle hug from my father. We didn't get deep into feelings; we never had.

As I sat there, fumbling for my next words, I teared up, my tongue becoming thicker by the second. I'd never gone against him before. I'd never chosen myself and what I wanted over what he wanted. Grieving for the relationship we never had, I let the tears that had welled up in my eyes spill from my lids. I mourned the fact that so much time had passed and I still didn't know how to fix our relationship—or where to even start. Sniffing, I waited until I had my full voice, knowing I'd need all the determination I could muster to say the things necessary to make my point. The end of the line remained mute, making me feel even more anxious.

"I've never said this to you before, but… your way of doing things is not right. I don't like that you try to force me to do what you want. I'm a grown woman. I have dreams and thoughts of my own. Feelings that hurt every time you don't believe in me."

"Navie, you're being dramatic."

"I'm really not. I just want—I want a truce, Dad. I know you don't agree with my training. It's no secret you don't approve of females entering the cage, let alone having their own league. But I know I can do it. I've come so far in such a short amount of time. And as far as the business is concerned, I have the knowledge. Heck, there was no better mentor or job that could have prepared me for it. There are so many women out in the world who dream of an opportunity. I can give that to them, I know I can," I pleaded, my voice steady as I spoke with passion. "Preston showed up here tonight—"

"Where?"

Instead of responding to my plea, he interrupted at the first mention of my brother.

"At Trevor's, and he was being an asshole. He threw my phone, got in my space; he threatened to kidnap me, for God's sake."

"Trevor?" The line went silent again. "Trevor Steele?"

I grimaced. I hadn't even told him Trevor and I were technically an item, not that it was any of his business, yet I still felt a little like a teenage daughter who'd gone behind her father's back. Leaning my head back on the couch cushion, I squeezed my eyes shut. His response shouldn't have had anything to do with who I was dating or where the incident had gone down. I'd just told him my brother had shown up out of nowhere and threatened to kidnap me. Was that not enough to provoke action from him instead of reaction?

I knew I wouldn't get anywhere with him until I answered his question. "Yes."

"Why are you at Trevor Steele's house?"

"I'm staying with him."

"Well, *that's* great for business," he snapped. "My biggest athlete shacks up with my only daughter. Lovely, Navie. Just fucking lovely. No need to embarrass the family with your crazy ideas about entering the cage yourself, or hell creating a business doomed to fail—just entertain the media with your looseness."

Fury pulsed inside me. I sucked in a breath and angrily wiped the tears streaming down my cheeks. "Why do you say such insensitive things to me? Why do you want to hurt me, when all I've ever done is try to appease you?"

"Really? You've tried to appease me? Is that why you're living with Steele? Is that why you're not working for the company? Is that why you're not doing interviews with me and your brother as a united front? Do you have any idea the media shitstorm you've caused? Every time I turn around, someone's asking about you, and I have to make up some silly excuse for why you're not here. It's just a matter of time before someone makes their way back to his gym and figures out you two are playing house."

"Well, I wouldn't have been forced to *play house* if you hadn't sent my brother to do your dirty work. He bought the apartment I was renting and jacked the rent so high, I had no choice but to find another place to stay. Why can't you just let me be who I want to be? Are you that ashamed of me?"

"Right now? You bet your ass I am." He hung up, not giving me a chance to respond.

I clenched my cell phone in my hand so tightly I was surprised I didn't break the damn thing myself. I curled my body to the side, not taking up a third of the space on the sofa, while letting my father's words wash over me, leaving an undoubtable imprint on every cell. Lying my head on the cushion, I cried until I had nothing left; no tears, no energy. I was alone.

CHAPTER 11
TREVOR

MY MEETING with Jeremy took longer than expected. I turned my phone on silent, not wanting anything to interrupt the chance I had to sell him on Gage and the rest of the athletes working their asses off in my gym. By the time Jeremy shook my hand at the end of the night, telling me he had to get back to the airport, my phone had rung twice before I hopped into my Jeep. Catching the second call, I was surprised to see it was Payne who'd called both times. I knew something was up.

"Where the hell are you?" Payne's voice carried from the other line after the first ring. "Navie's been trying to get ahold of you for hours."

Placing him on speaker, I clicked over to my missed calls. My gut clenched when I saw her name consecutively in red. She'd called me three times, and I hadn't seen any of them. "What's going on?"

"Preston showed up at your house. I went over there and ran him off, but she was in bad shape when I left."

Bad shape? I would go to prison.

"He touched her?"

"Man, you know I'd never let that shit go down," Payne scoffed. "He just shook her up. Something about Richard changing things up since Navie is no longer around. I made sure her brother was gone before I left."

"I'm on my way."

Throwing my phone in the passenger's seat, I pushed the gas pedal to the floor, too preoccupied to worry about a speeding ticket. I was so pissed off, my hands shook. My white-knuckled grip on the steering wheel intensified as I pulled into my neighborhood. It took every ounce of willpower I had in my body not to call Richard and demand to know who he thought he was, sending his son to my house to accost my girl, before I spoke to Navie.

I rushed in, but settled down when I found her sound asleep on my sofa, her body curled to the side, as if she were hugging herself for comfort. Strands of her hair had fallen out of the messy bun on top of her head. Tendrils covered her face and lay haphazardly around her neck. She looked like a child who'd had no one around to hold her while she cried.

Fuck.

I tugged the ends of my hair in frustration, knowing I needed to be gentle when I woke her up. I considered letting her sleep, but as I sat quietly beside her, my body buzzed with the urge to hold her. For the first time in my life, I understood what codependency was. Was it healthy? Probably the fuck not. But did my sense of peace come from whether or not she was okay and would make me feel okay? Absolutely.

Gently, I rubbed her shoulder. From the feel of her alone, I felt the walls come down, releasing something so deep inside I didn't even recognize it at first.

Home. I was home.

Navie stirred, and I brought her into my arms, her cheek resting on my chest. I reveled in her smell as she snuggled into me.

"Baby?" I rubbed her back. "Navie, wake up."

She moaned as she stretched. "What happened? I couldn't get a hold of you."

I closed my eyes so I wouldn't hang my head in disgust. I'd ignored my phone for the sake of business, which turned out to be the most selfish thing I could have done.

Sitting up, I tightened my grip on her, bringing her into my lap. "I was in a meeting. I'm so sorry."

"Did everything go okay?"

I ground my molars. My chest tightened, as the shameful guilt crashed headfirst into every fiber of my being. Trying to further the guys' careers had always been my goal, but the fact that Navie's goals weren't in my previous equation didn't sit well with me. Especially since I'd seen firsthand what level of shit she had to wade through to even be able to attempt them. I'd not been there for her when she needed me and the first thing she thought to do was ask how my night had gone.

"It was fine." I kissed her lips, lingering longer than I should have. "Tell me what happened here."

"From what I could gather, my dad must have threatened Preston with something unless I come back to the company. Or at least he's making his life a living hell. Once again, it's all on me to make sure Preston gets what he wants." She shrugged, looking dejected.

"Don't let them put that pressure on you."

"It's already done. My dad…he wasn't happy with my recent decisions: living here, training. I spilled my guts to him. Told him about the league I envisioned and how helping other female fighter's reach their goals is important to me." She peered up at me, cautious. "He's extremely angry about me and you. He thinks I'm shaming him somehow."

The overwhelming need to punch someone took hold of me. How could her father—the man who was supposed to protect her most in the world—tell her he was ashamed of her? I'd never been more proud of someone. I slowed my breaths, knowing my anger would add to her uneasiness.

I cleared my mind the best I could and asked her the single question that needed to be answered. "What do you want?" I'd never paid so much attention to someone before. I was prepared to hang on every word she said. I would support her in whatever she decided.

Her mouth spread into the saddest smile I'd ever seen, like her facial features were fighting her brain for what they should do. "I want to be here. With you."

"Then it's settled."

"I wish that were true."

"Listen, you worry about your goals. I'll worry about your family."

"Trevor, I can't do that."

"You can't control their reactions, Navie. However they react—it's on them. I'll talk to your dad."

"No, I don't want that."

"Why not?" The last thing I intended was make her feel inferior, or like she couldn't handle her own business, but I'd had just about enough of her fucking brother. Showing up at my house to threaten my girlfriend wasn't something I was going to tolerate whether Navie liked it or not.

"I just want to sit with you. I don't want to think about them right now. I just want to be with you and think about positive things."

Navie leaned in close to me, pressing her lips at my neck. Relaxing, I settled deeper into the cushions as her warmth seeped into me from the outside. My breathing slowed; my lips lightly touching her temple. I squeezed my arms tight, soaking in every ounce of her goodness, and hoping more than anything, I was erasing all the negative energy that surrounded her. She wanted positive thoughts. That, I could totally help her out with.

"I've been meaning to tell you something," I spoke into her hair.

Navie leaned up so that we were eye to eye. I held my chuckle inside. Her mood flipped like a switch, enthralled with curiosity. "What?"

"Gage isn't the only one who'll be fighting in the near future."

Her eyes widened, and I waited as the reality of what I'd told her sunk in. "You got me a fight? A real one?"

Placing my forehead against hers, I nodded. "Yep."

"With who?"

"Wendy Whitlow."

"Wendy. Whitlow." Her brows pinched together, and I couldn't tell if she was impressed or worried.

"She's making a name for herself on the East Coast," I explained.

Navie's gaze turned serious. "I know who she is, I just can't believe she agreed to a fight with me."

It was as if every insecurity she'd ever had lay bare for me to see. Even more so than coming home and finding her curled up in a timid little ball. I didn't like it one bit.

"I promise you'll be ready," I assured her.

If there was one thing I knew without question, I would never put her in a position where I didn't see her coming out on top. Even if that meant not giving her an opportunity. It was selfish, I knew, but setting Navie up to nosedive wasn't something I had inside me.

"Okay." She snuggled back into my arms. "I trust you."

I held her tight, cuddling her until my body swallowed hers whole. Her faith cemented my initial thought. Having her undivided confidence that I wouldn't let her fail meant something to me. So much so, I realized with her in my arms, I would rather crash and burn a hundred times over than have her suffer through it once.

The following weeks, Navie's determination grew. I couldn't pinpoint the moment it happened, only that the intensity she put off while training had garnered the attention of everyone in the gym.

"Right, left, right—okay, back to one." I counted Navie off, pushing her further than ever before.

"I liked Tommy better," she huffed.

I chuckled, trying my best not to find her annoyance cute. "Do you want to win your first fight?"

"Yes," she snapped.

We kept the rigorous pace for a while. I worked her extra hard. She had to be in tip-top shape for the fight I'd arranged. It had proven difficult finding females willing to fight at the local level. There weren't many to begin with—not in our area, anyway. And most of the fighters—the ones I had contacts for—were far more advanced than Navie.

I tried to remain unbiased, treating her the same as any other rookie fighter. The only way to improve in the cage was to actually get inside the cage; to experience it. Although, I quickly realized, Navie wasn't just any rookie fighter. She was *my* rookie, and sending her into a cage with women who'd been training far longer than she had been made me nervous. But I couldn't be another man in her life who didn't support her. My job was to train her the best I could, then trust that she could get the job done. Not to mention, I didn't know many men with the work ethic Navie had. At the end of the day, there were probably hundreds of women in the country with more experience than her, but no one wanted it more. Her fortitude and potential kept me focused on preparing her.

"Why you mad, baby? I'm just cashing in my win from our ice cream bet." I kissed her sweaty cheek as we ended our session.

"Our bet was for grappling," she growled. "And it's a good thing I've only got two weeks of this, otherwise, our relationship would suffer. By the way, you've had plenty of time to cash in. Why now?"

"Because I wanted to touch you in the morning too." I grinned and swatted her ass. "Nighttime wasn't enough," I whispered in her ear.

"Shut up!" She glanced around, searching for any onlookers.

"You're doing great," I said, getting back to business. "We need to work on your speed, though. And I'll have to add more weight to your strength training. With quicker movements, you'll lose some of the force behind them."

"Okay," she answered automatically, but it was obvious her mind was a million miles away. It was as if everything she was working for was suddenly becoming real. Her face turned pale when she examined the ground, as her nerves became more prevalent with every step we took away from the cage. I could feel anxious energy coming off her in waves.

"Hey." I came to a stop, causing her to do the same. "You're going to do great. You have to believe that before anyone else. It's fifty percent soul, forty percent mind, and ten percent body. Got it?"

She nodded, relief flooding the bluest eyes I'd ever seen. I loved that blue. I loved the glimmer of her irises, and how they communicated every emotion she had inside her beautiful body.

"I'm cooking dinner for you tonight. Then I'm drawing you a warm bath." I leaned in closer, feeling her body stiffen. "After that," I whispered, letting the silence stretch out to make sure her mind was in the gutter, "the remote is yours." I grinned when her eyes narrowed. "We pile up in bed and just relax."

She sighed at my teasing and leaned into my side. Her reaction to my suggestion refreshed my soul. Nothing had to be dramatic with Navie. She wasn't hard to please. She was thankful for any and all consideration regarding her feelings. Tucking her head into my chest, I planted two kisses on the top of her head, not knowing whether to be thankful or pissed off that her family had set the bar so low.

I made good on my promise after a hard day's work. To say Navie was appreciative of the carb-loaded meal was an understatement.

"This tastes"—she took another bite of the shrimp alfredo I'd prepared for her—"like heaven, Trevor."

I studied her, not even bothering with my own bite. Not caring if I ever got another one, as long as I got to witness her enjoying my food. "I love how expressive your face is."

Her cheeks reddened. I loved that too—that I could make her blush with only a few words.

"If you say one word about an orgasm, or laugh because I just said orgasm, I will not take another bite." She narrowed her eyes in my direction but took another bite anyway and closed her eyes as she enjoyed the taste.

I smirked, but I hadn't found one ounce of amusement in her saying orgasm. In fact, I was damn near to the point of busting straight through the zipper of my jeans just thinking about it.

After dinner, I stayed true to my word, not allowing her into the bathroom until I had every single detail in place. I lit four candles and carefully placed them around the Jacuzzi tub, after filling it with the most expensive bubble bath I could find on such short notice. The lady at the boutique next door to the gym had seen me coming a mile away. I walked out of that place with three bags packed full of feminine spa treatments and a hundred and fifty dollars less in my wallet. It didn't matter. It would all be worth it, to be able to give Navie a relaxing night.

"Are you ready?" I called from the other side of the door, picturing her anticipation.

After a muffled giggle, she answered. "Yes."

"Okay, come in." I stood in the center of my large bathroom, hoping I'd done well. It wasn't like I lit candles, arranged flower petals, and drew bubble baths every day. Come to think of it, I'd *never* done it.

She walked through the door slowly, taking in my homemade

creation. At the sight of the oasis I'd crafted for her, she gasped and covered her mouth with her hands.

"Trevor, this is beautiful."

"I wanted it to be perfect for you."

"I love it. I've never seen anything like it." Her gorgeous eyes scoped out the whole room, experiencing the ambience in wonder.

"Come here," I said, holding out my hand for her. She obliged. "I want you to relax. I know you've got a lot on your mind right now. And I know how nerve-racking it all is, but you have what it takes. I wouldn't ever put you in harm's way. You know that, right?"

"I do."

"Okay, so you know that even if it was your life's dream to be the best female cage fighter who ever lived, and I didn't think you could do it—if I thought it was suicide putting you in there—I'd never allow it, right?"

She nodded.

"Good. Don't think about the fight. Don't think about your family. Just enjoy the moment."

She grinned and bit her bottom lip. "You're kind of perfect."

"I know," I agreed with a straight face.

She punched me lightly in the chest, while placing her lips on mine. My palms found her ass, my brain already projecting mental images of her naked body in the water. Erotic thoughts raced through my mind, creating a picture so vivid, it was as if it were a memory instead of my imagination. Continuing my daydream, I visualized taking my time, sliding each piece of fabric off her body, watching her step into my tub, while beads of water slid down her body, as my lips chased them.

Still holding on to her, I pushed my tongue inside her mouth, feasting on her, circling her tongue over and over. Every ounce of blood flowing through my body headed south. I grabbed two handfuls of her ass, massaging, pushing her core over my arousal as our kiss deepened. Her hands left my neck in a hurry and pushed my T-shirt up and over my head.

"I've waited so long for this," she said through hitched breaths.

I pulled back, her words just barely sinking in. Her eyes twinkled in the candlelight.

"You have no idea."

I kissed her again because my mind—and my body—wouldn't allow me to speak. I broke apart from her mouth, sliding my eager lips down to her collarbone. The potent scent of her skin propelled my arousal into overdrive. I slid the spaghetti strap of her tank top down her arm, bringing my head up to watch my fingers trace her bare skin.

"I love your skin."

"My skin loves you."

I grinned, noticing she'd closed her eyes. She was thinking out loud, lost in the moment. She couldn't have been more stunning if she'd tried.

I trailed barely-there kisses down her arm until I reached her hand. Bringing each finger, one at a time into my mouth, I sucked on them, until I'd tasted them all. She lifted her arms in the air, high above her head, giving me the go-ahead to undress her. My lungs expanded with a deep inhalation, and I sighed on the exhale while my fingers fondled the bare skin between the hem of her tank and the elastic of her shorts.

I watched intently as the fabric rolled up her chest, exposing her toned stomach. Dropping the tank on the floor next to us, I reached around her to unhook her bra. Her bronzed skin, peppered with goosebumps, was quickly becoming one of my favorite things. I placed my lips to her chest, holding them there to catch the rapid beat of her heart. Her bra slipped off her skin like it was made of the finest silk.

I closed my lips over her nipple as raw, passionate energy surged through me like an out-of-control freight train. Overtaken with greed, I picked her up with one arm, and pulled her beaded nipple deep inside my mouth. The moans and sighs that escaped her lips revved me up more. I switched breasts as her head tilted back, letting the moment of euphoria take over. I ached, my dick throbbing as it rubbed against the cotton of her shorts, dying for a chance to feel her.

I sat her on the side of the tub and kneeled in front of her. "Is this too fast?" As much as it killed me to break the moment, I needed to make sure Navie was comfortable with every move we made.

"No." She lifted herself off the tub as I folded the sides of her shorts, sliding them down her legs.

My gaze trailed from her core to the insides of her thighs. Naked

Navie was beyond measure, unlike anything or anyone I'd ever seen before. I leaned back on my heels, drinking in the moment, trying to memorize every detail. "Are you sure?" I didn't even know what I was saying anymore.

"Positive."

She leaned forward and kissed my chest, soft and measured, just above my heart. Her words intensified my hunger for her. I pulled my hands through her hair, tugging gently until my palms reached her scalp. Navie sighed, and rolled her neck twice, seeming completely relaxed.

Her lids opened, and her blue irises brightened. There appeared to be a newfound buoyancy behind them, something I'd never seen before. She stood, leaving me eye level with the most private part of her. Inhaling, I licked my lips. I couldn't wait to taste her, to touch her; to physically *feel* her excitement.

I couldn't remember a time I had ever been so patient, and it almost killed me. Literally, my chest tightened. My heart raced. I felt like I was having a heart attack.

Locking our fingers together, she guided me to a stance as she peered up at me from hooded eyes. "I've never had anyone treat me the way you do. Like…I'm special."

Conner McGregor could have sucker punched me, and it wouldn't have hurt me more. I never wanted her to feel anything but her worth. Special was the least of what she was.

"You *are* special. I'll always take care of you."

Navie smiled, then leaned up on her tiptoes to kiss my neck. I closed my eyes at the feel of her. Soft, sacred grazes roamed the underside of my jaw as her palms slid down both of my hips and down the inside of my jeans. I unbuttoned them so she could push them down my hips. In one swift move, she undressed me, and I kicked the denim, along with my boxers, off to the side. Standing before her naked body, there had never, *ever* been anything more sensual to me. Navie bared not only her body but her soul to me. It was as if I could read her inner most thoughts. I couldn't blink. I couldn't breathe at the initial sight of it.

She held my heart in the palm of her hand.

I swallowed, realizing what made the moment with Navie different. I could see through her; was able to see what was on the inside. Not one bit of her outward appearance held a candle to what was behind her eyes. Lust. Love. Vulnerability. Trust. I could see it all. And all of it was for me. Only me. It was the purest form of intimacy.

The silence between us wasn't uncomfortable. It was binding. Everything she was thinking and everything I was feeling bounced around the secure bubble we'd created in the small space between our bodies. I'd never been so connected to another human being. A clarity and confidence formed deep inside my chest as my hands roamed her body. I inhaled deep at the revelation, intent on savoring it.

Lifting her hand, I helped her into the tub and climbed in behind her, settling her back to my front. Her body lay perfectly atop mine, the water and suds causing a film of slickness between us. It was paradise. I ran my bare feet up the sides of her legs while my hands trailed perfection, all the way from her hips to her breasts. I leaned my head back and closed my eyes, basking in the feel of her.

Up and down.

Over and across.

My hands slipped across her breasts, gripping her puckered nipples between my knuckles. I leaned forward, wanting to watch her face as I fondled her. Navie tilted her head to the side, leaving her neck exposed for me to taste.

Should I taste or touch? I decided on both, licking her neck before sucking hard on the patch of skin just behind her ear. I straightened my fingers, putting pressure on the tips of her nipples in both my hands.

Her head pushed back deeper into my shoulder as her hips lifted off my legs. I continued peppering her skin with soft sweeps, then whole kisses, pulling her skin deeper inside my mouth a little more each time. My palm skimmed down her stomach, over her belly button, and down her pubic bone until my fingers reached her inner folds. Bare. Slick. Warm.

My God.

The feel of her juices made my mouth water. I wanted to lick my fingers dry. I wanted the tip of my dick to swim in her ecstasy. There was no way I was going to last. Not when every molecule in my body felt like it was on a timer, the seconds ticking away in an accelerated countdown for an explosive bomb.

Her arm swept up and curled around my neck, her fingers pulling the ends of my hair so hard, I thought she'd pull them out. My middle finger found its place, sliding inside her body as if she'd been molded just for me. Navie panted from my touch, driving me mad with lust.

"You all right, baby?" I whispered, continuing the same rhythm, only caring about making her feel good.

"My God…I can't…" Her toes curled into the tops of my feet, struggling for leverage.

"You feel so fucking good. So warm." There were probably a million other things I could have said to describe the euphoria I was feeling, but nothing else came to mind. My brain couldn't concentrate on anything other than the way her body reacted to my touch.

A gurgle began deep in her throat as I slid another finger inside her. The interior walls of her vagina made my mouth salivate. I could feel a single bead of semen seeping out from the tip of my dick. It ached with need; throbbed with want. I quickened my pace as her wetness coated my fingers. Navie tensed, almost fighting the exhilaration, so I slowed my movements. Languid, soft, in and out, I traced her delicate folds, not leaving one ounce of flesh untouched. Moments later, she fell apart in my arms, the top part of her body trembling, the bottom part quivering not ten seconds later.

I pulled her tight to my chest and kissed the top of her head.

She sighed twice and I grinned, elated to have given her a sweet escape.

"I have no words," she finally said.

"I have a shit-ton of words, but I can barely string two of them together right now."

She rolled over, chest to chest with me, and rested her chin on top of her hands. "That was amazing."

I slicked her hair back with my wet palm. "*You're* amazing."

Her lips circled my collar bone before she placed calculated kisses there. Once, then twice. Her tongue slipped out on the third peck, causing my abs to clench. My legs came together, pushing the bottom half of her body into alignment with my own. I cocked my head to the side and observed, enamored, as a smile spread across her face and she continued her sultry assault on my slickened skin.

I pulled her up beneath her arms to meet my lips for the next kiss. The tip of my hardness met her melted center, and tingles shot straight up my spine, causing my glutes to flex.

To push straight up into her would be pure bliss.

Focusing on restraint, I pulled back slightly as her folds threatened to swallow me whole.

Navie sighed, content with whispered kisses. She spread her legs, inviting me inside, leaving me feeling like a junkie seeking my next fix. Temptation slaughtered me, as if the needle was locked and loaded, sitting within arm's reach. I pushed ahead, too weak to break the connection. Rolling forward, just barely inside her, my body teased, just shy of actual penetration.

I grunted, wishing in that moment, the unbelievable wise tale about not being able to get pregnant underwater was true. My common sense won out as I collected my wits and climbed from the tub, snatching a towel off the rack. I wrapped it around my waist and grabbed her one from the closet.

Taking her hand, I helped her out and wrapped the towel around her. Drying herself off as she walked to my bedroom, I followed, hypnotized by her movements the whole way. She dropped the towel by the bed and crawled—*fucking crawled*—across the bed, finally settling near the headboard. Looking over her shoulder, Navie smirked, looking like a woman freakishly aware of her power. Her self-confidence astounded me, and I ate that shit up, dropping my own towel and following close on her heels, barely holding myself back from pouncing.

She giggled. "You liked that, did you?"

"You have no fucking idea how much I liked that."

My lips met hers without another word, while my hand landed between her legs, finding her more ready than ever. I loved the feel of her juices on my fingertips. The coating allowed me to reach every crevice inside her easily.

Navie's breathing picked up as I circled her insides, hoping like hell I was preparing her for what was to come. I didn't want to hurt her, and the need to be inside her made my balls ache so badly the skin underneath tightened. I lined us up the best I could with her hips wiggling underneath me from pure anticipation.

Her palm stretched across the side of my face, her thumb rubbing gently side to side, brushing the short scruff on my face. The look she gave slayed me. Erotic lust illuminated her gaze, locking me in place as I hovered above her.

I pushed forward once, placing most of my weight onto my forearms, my fists clenched on either side of her head. I was holding back; afraid I'd hurt her if I allowed my libido to overtake me. I couldn't remember a time I'd been so worked up. Not even as a teenager.

She gasped then slowly exhaled. I leaned forward again, squeezing my eyes shut at the exhilaration, her warm insides so slick they coated my dick, causing tingles to shoot down my legs all the way to the bottoms of my feet. The inner walls of her center pulled at me, practically massaging my tender skin, begging me to keep going.

Good God, I didn't want to sheath myself. Nothing would ever feel better than experiencing my woman bare. But I knew I had to. I had to be smart. But I sure as fuck didn't want to. Forcing myself to leave her heat, I reached across her to the bed-side table and grabbed the first wrapped piece of protection I felt. Ripping the package with my teeth, I sheathed myself and found my vacant spot still warm and inviting. Glancing up to her face, I looked into eyes so dark blue, they were navy. *Perfection*. I sank into her, pushing the slightest at first, then inched further, finding myself nestled even more. The farther I slipped inside her, the tighter she was. Still holding her gaze ransom with my own, her irises turned a shade darker right before my eyes. An appreciative grin lay hidden behind my clenched jaw.

"You good?"

"Yes." She rose a fraction, taking my mouth with her own.

Once I knew she was all right, I slowly pushed into her as far as our bodies would allow, my dick throbbing, synchronized with my own heartbeat. Guiding her leg forward, she followed my lead, rocking her pelvis to meet my plunges. Pure adrenaline spiked, causing me to feel light as air. With every thrust, Navie's inner walls contoured perfectly, clutching me tight.

Almost breaking our connection, I pulled out, dragging the tip of my dick over her clit, then pushed back inside of her. Over and over, I sped up the movement, then slowed to almost a punishing stillness. Navie's moans grew louder and louder with each tease.

With finality, my pelvis pushed into her as far as her body would allow on the last thrust, knowing she was seconds away from orgasm. Navie screamed out, her legs quivering in my hands. I watched as her eyes fluttered opened, then closed again lazily. Her rosy cheeks glowed from the dim light, and for some reason, the thing I couldn't pull my gaze away from was the sheen of sweat at her hairline. She looked so beautiful; completely peaceful and serene.

I picked up my pace, causing her eyes to open. When her gaze met mine, our fevered breaths covered each other's faces, neither of us seeming to be in control of our bodies or the frenzied desire rolling off us. I thrust over and over, until I rode out my release above her, as my heartrate skyrocketed, threatening to burst through my chest from exertion. She held me tight, her arms wrapped all the way around my chest, keeping me planted firmly on top of her. I was probably crushing her, but she took all my weight, content, it seemed.

Catching my breath, I rolled to the side, but kept my arm wrapped around her. "God, you felt so good. I could spend the rest of my life inside you and never come up for air."

She chuckled, turning her grinning face into the side of my forearm. "I have never, ever felt like that before. It was…pure bliss, Trevor."

"I know," I agreed. I couldn't have described it better myself.

Navie leaned up on her elbow. "I want to do it again," she said with enthusiasm.

"Already?"

"Yes, let's go." She patted my shoulder like we were teammates and she was trying to amp me up before a game.

"Oh, my sweet Cobalt." I circled her lips with my index finger, trailing down her body as I spoke. She giggled as I poked fun at her name. "Let me take care of this condom, then I'm going to take care of you again." Slipping from beneath the sheet, I pulled my bottom lip in between my teeth at her eagerness.

"Sorry, Steele." She shook her head. "You see, we've crossed this bridge now, and there's no turning back." Her fingertips traced her nipples, causing my mouth to water. Sexy didn't come close to what I was witnessing. "You took care of me." She paused, turning onto her side. My gaze followed her hand as she traced circles on her bare hip. "Now, I take care of you."

How had I gone so long without her in my life? It might turn out that I never knew the answer to that question, but the one thing I did know was I never wanted to ask it again. Heaviness occupied my chest as I walked toward my bathroom, a sense of loss filling me the farther I walked away from her. I quickly disposed of the condom and cleaned myself off. I couldn't wait to return to her side, and the weirdest fucking realization struck me. I'd been more afraid of her than she could have ever been of me, even entering my gym on day one to train for a sport she'd never competed in. With no family, no support, and zero confirmation I'd even allow her inside.

Navie had everything it took to fight. Hell, she had more than it took.

"Trevor!" Navie called from the bedroom.

Smirking at my reflection in the mirror, I answered her, one hundred percent committed to her. "Coming, dear."

CHAPTER 12
NAVIE

"THAT'S ALL FOR SHOW," Trevor explained while studying tape of Wendy's last fight. "You don't have to play the games most fighters do. I never did, but this is how some people get hype. Don't ever let your opponent in your mind like that. Remember what I told you before. So much of this sport is mental. You create that wall, like I taught you, and you don't let anything break that barrier."

"I understand. She's just…vocal."

"She is, but fighters like that are overcompensating. They don't rely on their skills. If they have to put on a show, they're making up for something."

"Makes sense," I agreed.

I appreciated his attention to detail, but my nerves were resurfacing with each minute that passed. The day of my fight had finally arrived, and aside from the few minutes of Trevor dissecting Wendy's mannerisms, he was driving me crazy, hovering over me as if I were an infant. Luckily, he'd scheduled a PR meeting for lunch, which didn't make me feel so bad for kicking him out of the house in hopes to calm myself alone. As much as I wanted his reassurance, I felt like keeping things casual would be best for my nerves.

I'd been training with the best fighters, and I was in the best shape of my life, but there was a little piece of my mind that kept recounting my dad and brother's mockery on replay, on a loop, like an old record that needed to be turned over.

"Right." He turned off the television, then glanced at his watch. "Since you're kicking me out, I guess I'll go to work."

"I'm not kicking you out. I have to meditate or something as productive."

"I get it, babe. "You'll find what works for you."

"Thank you. And I'm glad you found something to do other than bug me," I teased.

"When you cock-blocked me, I scheduled a meeting with a couple of agents."

I rolled my eyes at his joke. "Agents? That sounds promising."

"I hope so. Jeremy swears they're legit even though I've only heard of one of them."

"Jeremy?" I asked.

The only Jeremy I know is—

"Tillman." Trevor eyed me as if he was worried I'd be angry he was meeting with someone who worked for my father behind my back. It did surprise me, but I wasn't angry. Sometimes, you had to keep your enemies close to play the game. I wasn't naïve when it came to business. I'd practically seen it all.

Except I'd never considered my ex-boyfriend working with my current boyfriend.

"You remember him?" Trevor asked, closing his laptop. "He works in the Canadian office. I think he's been up there for like five or six years."

I swallowed and stood, figuring clueing him in was for the best even though Jeremy and I were way past over.

"So, this is a funny story," I began, but clammed up the second Trevor stood from his place on the sofa and crossed his arms.

"Go ahead," he urged.

"Remember when I told you my ex-boyfriend's name was Jeremy?"

Trevor's eyebrows rose in surprise. He cocked his head to the side. "You dated Tillman?"

I nodded, hoping he would leave after I quickly admitted my horrible history with my father's lackey.

"Um, yeah, for a little while."

His grin didn't reach his eyes. So, I couldn't tell if he was amused or just trying to play it cool. "Really?"

"It wasn't that big of a deal," I claimed, shrugging so he'd know I wasn't affected. "Anyway, good luck at your meeting. I have a righteous bath waiting for me."

"Right," he said as he took three long strides toward me.

Reading his expression, I lingered by hallway. "You're not getting the gruesome details. We dated. We broke up."

Trevor quickly grabbed me by the waist and pulled me closer to his chest. "So, you don't want to know about my past relationships?"

Did I?

There had to have been more than I'd heard about. I couldn't imagine a scenario where checking off a list of perfect tens so I could mentally compare myself to them at my most insecure moments would be an even trade.

"No. As long as they're in the past, I don't need to know about them."

Trevor nodded but didn't look convinced. Obviously, I was lying through my teeth. Of course, I wanted to know who he'd dated and for how long. I just didn't want to go into details about freaking Jeremy Tillman and how he used me for two years or the humiliating fact that I'd let him. And especially not the day of my first fight.

"You may not be the only person kicking a little ass today, Sapphire. A certain douche canoe named Jeremy better watch his back, or he'll be joining Wendy at the dentist tomorrow."

Giggling, I hugged Trevor's neck. I loved that he could always make me laugh, even when I felt like throwing my guts up. I loved that about him. He always knew what to do; always came through in the clutch. Trevor was valiant and made me feel like even though I was about to embark on something totally foreign to me, everything would be okay. It would all work out.

I just wished I could have connected with that feeling hours later, while walking down the small corridor from the locker room to the steel cage at Trevor's gym. My stomach turned, tightening in knots with each step I took. Mentally, I tried to shake it off, but I only calmed when Trevor placed his hand on my shoulder.

"It will take you a few minutes to feel it all out. Don't let that trip you up. It's common for all of us. Just keep your guard up and be present. Pay attention to the way she moves."

Instead of focusing on the differences inside the gym, with three rows of chairs lined up for spectators, I chose to zone in on the mat. "Okay. What if she comes straight out of the gate?"

"Just like in practice. Don't let her set the tone. Get a feel for her, but this is your fight. Be aggressive."

"Right. Aggressive. It's my fight." I nodded, trying to remain calm in spite of the chaos running through my mind.

"Hey." Trevor pushed down on my shoulders, grounding me in place. "Deep breaths. You know I'd never let you get in a cage if you weren't ready. You're fucking ready, Blue." He stuck my mouthpiece in, his thumb lingering on my bottom lip.

I shook my arms, in an attempt to expel the tension forming between my shoulder blades. I tried to quell the rapid scenarios running through my mind, by repeating Trevor's advice.

I was fucking ready.

I wasn't sure how, but as I met Wendy in the center of the cage, I was somehow able to push the negative thoughts out of my mind, instead, focusing on the task at hand.

Wendy had two inches and eight pounds on me. But like Trevor had reminded me not twenty minutes ago in the locker room, I had determination on my side. I was positive Wendy hadn't had anyone tell her she couldn't be what she wanted to be in life. I had.

Wendy hadn't had everything taken away from her, hadn't sacrificed everything she'd ever known for a chance of what could be. I had.

She'd not been forced to lose her livelihood and her family in order to live out her dream. I had.

I wanted it more than she did, and I knew it from the first look in her eyes. I knew I could take her. I was going to win. My dad and brother could kiss my ass.

She came out swinging, and I took an unexpected uppercut within the first twenty seconds. My teeth rattled, and I winced as pain shot straight from my bottom front teeth all the way up my jaw, throbbing landing at my temples. I shook it off and took a kick to the thigh before I threw my own punch. It landed. It freaking landed, and even though I didn't have much time to rejoice, I knew I'd never forget the feeling. In the distance, I could hear the crowd of twenty people cheering, but one solitary voice rang through crystal clear.

"Take her to the ground! Get low. Stay low."

I pushed with all my might, but she didn't budge. There wasn't one move I tried on her she didn't see coming. She blocked everything and ended up getting a good jab to my ribs. With the shock to my system, my breathing still hadn't evened out when the bell sounded.

Trevor met me on the mat and led me to the stool. "How do you feel?"

"A little dazed. Winded," I answered as Tommy squeezed some water in my mouth.

"That's okay. It's supposed to be like that. You need to try to get her on the ground. It looks like she's been concentrating on her jabs and punches, which means she'll be lax on her groundwork. Play to your strengths. Get that choke hold, arm bar—anything you can—even before you get her fully pinned. Use that for leverage."

My opponent came out stronger in the second round. I couldn't tell if I was getting more pissed at her for outmaneuvering me, or at myself for being so naïve. I knew fighting would be tough, but I felt like I'd already gone five rounds, and we were just beginning the second. All those practices and training sessions I thought were tough were nothing compared to the real thing.

One—two—three punches to my right side. With each strike, the air left my lungs, and each inhale was more labored than the last. With the final blow, she stumbled from putting all her weight on the right side, and I scooped her left leg, knowing I had to get her on the ground or I was done for.

I wasted no time wrapping my legs just so, squeezing my arm around her neck until I had a death grip on her. I pulled my forearm into my chest, feeling the veins on her neck protruding as I pulled tighter. I could faintly hear Trevor from the corner, but as I flexed my muscles and felt her body give, most everything went silent. My breaths and heartbeat seemed to be the only things I could feel or hear. The ref leaned in close, pulling my arm away from Wendy's neck. I'd nearly put her to sleep. Rolling out from under her, I stood, my fists pumping high into the air. The ref called my first match. I'd won.

I screamed so loud, I strained my vocal cords. It didn't matter. Nothing would ever match the feeling when Trevor ran to me, picked me up, and spun me around, my pride riding waves of victory. Payne, Gage, and Tommy surrounded us, and the crowd went wild, even though none of them knew who I was. I looked down at everyone who'd gathered on the mat. I scanned the audience, unable to make out any faces in particular, but heard every shout of elation. I felt high, like there was nothing that could bring me down.

CHAPTER 13
TREVOR

THE WEEK after Navie won her first fight, I wanted to celebrate her accomplishment because I was so fucking proud of her. It was pathetic, according to the guys. But I didn't care in the least what they thought. Of course, I took my girl out to commemorate the victory. And why wouldn't I give her a little gift to mark the occasion? She deserved it all, as far as I was concerned. Navie wasn't the typical fighter. She hadn't grown up in gyms, studying fighters her whole life, knowing that one day she'd get her shot. She'd fantasized secretly in the shadows, too afraid to speak her truth. The amount of courage she had, leaving everything she'd ever known behind and starting over, all for an opportunity to try, impressed me. All on her own, she took her shot, trained her ass off, and accomplished something for herself. Putting in that kind of effort alone was cause for celebration in my book.

The fight had been far from clean. In fact, it was quite messy, and I probably cringed more from the corner than I cheered. But she'd done it. She'd taken care of business, and that was rule number one in the cage. *Get it done.* And my girl had done it.

"I really appreciate all you've done, you know that, but I'm starting to feel like—"

"Like what?" I asked, taking a pull from my beer.

She glanced around my back yard, I assumed to make sure none of the guys were watching us. "Like you're surprised I won."

"Hey." Placing my palm under her jaw, I tilted her face to mine. "I knew you could do it, babe. I just want you to know how proud I am of you."

"I do, Trevor, but did you do all of these things when Payne won his first fight? Or even for yourself after defeating your first opponent?"

"No."

Placing her beer on the table, her gaze met mine. Strong, focused, and serious. "See?"

Confused, I took a seat in the lounge chair by my pool and pulled her onto my lap. "Say what you want to say."

She covered her face with her free hand and groaned. It was cute as hell, but I could tell she wanted a serious moment, so I suppressed my grin. She claimed I showed her my dimples to soften certain situations. It was true most of the time.

"I know you're proud of me, but showering me with all of this..." She held her hand up, noting the backyard barbeque I'd prepared for her and all of our friends, then looked back at me. "It makes me feel like you're shocked."

Tilting my head to the side, I furrowed my brow. Her reaction to my celebration for her was totally off base. "I'm not shocked. I'm proud."

"I know you are, but maybe my next fight, we settle in and have a candlelit dinner for just the two of us. Here, at home." She fondled the diamond tennis bracelet I'd given her earlier. "And no gifts."

Maybe I had gone a little overboard. "Okay."

"Okay?" She questioned, showing obvious surprise that I hadn't argued.

"Whatever you want, Royal." I grinned, flashing my dimples for effect since serious time was over.

She rolled her eyes but gave me what I wanted. Her palms placed firmly on my knees as she leaned her head back on my chest, sinking into me as if there was no place on earth she'd rather be.

I kissed the top of her head just as Gage ripped the plain white V-neck T-shirt he was wearing in half, grunting as if he were the Hulk. For some unknown reason, his dumbass had decided skinny-dipping in my pool was a good idea. I thought twice about kicking his ass for it, but each time, there was Navie, taking up for him, claiming he was harmless and hilarious. He was lucky the party was in my girl's honor. Otherwise, he would have been limping home.

While the weekend had been relaxing and fun, Monday morning was a doozy. Payne had a prior engagement at a charity event across town, Navie had to work a double shift because someone had called out of work, and I was stuck training two new fighters because half of my trainers were out with a stomach bug. To say I was in a bad mood was an understatement.

"Right." I leaned left. "Right."

"My body doesn't go there automatically."

I groaned in frustration. "Did I ask for excuses?" Cord was a good dude, but shit, if I wasn't over his explanation of why he couldn't just do what I told him.

"No."

"Then do what I told you, unless you want to be knocked out cold before your first match."

"Dayum." Gage whistled from the side of the cage.

"You want to do it?" I snapped.

"What crawled up your ass?" he shot back.

I jumped off the mat and told Cord to take five. I wasn't really sure why I was in such a bad mood. It wasn't like Navie and I were having problems. In fact, our relationship was getting better by the day.

Gage followed me to my office. "For real, what's up?"

"Nothing. Just a long day."

He glanced at his watch. "It's eleven-thirty."

"I'm heading out. Call me if things get crazy."

"Got it, man."

Grabbing my phone and keys, I left the gym, too distracted by my own attitude to get anything productive done. How could I tell him what was going on with me when I didn't even know? I felt on edge, waiting for the other shoe to drop. Somewhere between the weekend and the beginning of the week, my brain had decided to do a total one-eighty on me. Given that I had worked myself up enough to leave work for the day, the one thing I knew for sure was I had to see Navie. Seeing her would most definitely put me in a better mood, even if I only got to see her for a few minutes.

Pulling out onto the vacant street, I sped in the direction of the bar. I spotted her immediately and smiled. Her hair was a frazzled mess. The bun she'd thrown it up in had loose fly-a-ways on each side. I never found myself wondering how girls looked so beautiful without even trying until Navie.

Sneaking up behind her, I grabbed her hip and whispered in her ear. "Hey, Blue."

"Oh!" she screeched, throwing her hand over her heart. "Trevor, you scared me."

I chuckled. "Sorry."

I wasn't sorry.

"What are you doing here? I thought you were training Cord and Wes today."

I watched her clear a table like she'd done it her whole life. I hated that she worked like she did, especially when I had money. I knew better than to point that out again, though. The last time I'd mentioned she worked too hard, she clammed up for a day and a half.

"They're in good hands with Gage."

"No telling what he's training them in. I guess we'll find out when cage bunnies start hanging around outside the gym."

I followed behind her as she made her way to the kitchen to drop off the dirty dishes she'd collected.

Holding the door for Navie, I waved when the daytime cook nodded in my direction. "Hey, man. How's it going?" He asked.

"Good. Stopped by to keep my girl in line."

He chuckled. "I wasn't aware anyone had that much power over her."

Navie smiled, then grabbed my hand, leading me out back behind the building where the employees took their smoke breaks.

Even before the large metal door slammed, she was up on her tiptoes, lips pressed to mine. I breathed her in before pushing my tongue between her lips. My hands roamed up the sides of her chest, my thumbs finding the underside of her breasts. God, I'd never tire of them. Of her. For as long as I lived.

"I want nothing more than to bend you over—" I interrupted myself, kissing her lips again.

"Tonight," she agreed, squeezing me tight for a hug. "When I get home."

I pulled her bottom lip in between mine. My phone rang, interrupting our make-out session. "One second," I told her as I glanced at the number.

"Hello?"

"Mr. Steele? This is Cody with Ground Security. We have a code red going off at your house and wanted to make contact before we sent the police."

"Send them," I snapped and shoved my phone into the back pocket of my jeans. "I have to go. My alarm is going off."

"What?" Navie screeched, trailing behind me as I opened the back door.

"At the house. That was the security company."

"I'll come with you." She pulled the strings on her apron, already preparing to leave work.

"No!"

She flinched at my tone.

"Sorry. You stay here. It's probably nothing. I'll call you as soon as I get there."

"Wait," she pleaded, but I was already walking away from her. My feet were running toward my Jeep of their own accord. I planned on kicking ass, police present or not.

Flooring the gas pedal, I pulled onto the side road back to my house. Minutes later, I skidded to the front of my drive. Two police units were already there.

The first officer I laid eyes on questioned me. "Mr. Steele?"

"Yeah. Did you find anyone?"

"Yes, sir." He chuckled. "It was just your wife. She freaked out when the alarm sounded and couldn't remember the code. It happens more often than you think."

"Wife?" I glanced around, puzzled.

Britney appeared from the hallway, looking sheepishly, as another officer followed close behind her. I shook my head, confused. I hadn't seen her in years.

"Hey, Trev."

"What are you doing here?"

Her eyes bored straight into mine, silently begging me for mercy. "I, uh, forgot the code."

"We'll be on our way, Mr. and Mrs. Steele. Call us if you need anything else."

I watched as the officers exited my home, my brain teetering, unbalanced, seeming to go in every direction. *Wait!* I wanted to say. *She's not my wife. She's an intruder.*

"What the fuck, Britney?" I stepped closer to her, pissed that she'd conveniently shown up uninvited and made herself at home in my private space.

"I'm sorry. I—I didn't know what else to do. It's Brian," she said, her voice cracking.

I hadn't seen her brother since she and I ended things, but he and I had remained on good terms. He was stationed in California, but last I'd heard, he was overseas on some secret mission with the military. "What about him?"

"He's dead, Trev. He was killed last night in the Middle East. They showed up at Mom's house this morning and told us the news. I didn't know where else to go."

"So you decided to break into my house?"

"I just figured I'd hang out until you got here. I didn't mean any harm. I didn't realize you had an alarm now."

"One I need, apparently," I barked, but immediately guilt surfaced. She'd shown up out of the blue with the worst news possible. "I'm sorry." Her words were settling into my consciousness. Her brother was dead. "Why didn't you just call me?"

She frowned. "I didn't think you'd answer."

I blew out a frustrated breath. I needed a drink. The reprieve I'd felt earlier with Navie had been the universe's master plan to fuck me over.

"Trevor!" Navie's voice echoed from the front door.

Shit.

Meeting Navie in the foyer, my palms turned clammy, and my heartrate picked up. Nervous energy surged through my veins, causing my shallow breaths to bellow from my lungs.

"Why'd you leave work? I told you I'd call."

Navie wrapped her arms around me. I didn't hang on to her like normal, too afraid she'd be able to sense my nerves. "Well, you didn't call. And I was worried," she said.

"It's okay. The police just left."

"Did they find anyone?"

"Uh, well, about that." I gripped both sides of her face, knowing she was about to be pissed. "I need you to look into my eyes right now." Her spotting Britney before I had time to explain concerned me more than anything.

"Hey, I'm Britney."

I wanted to squeeze my eyes closed in frustration at the sound of Britney's voice, but I couldn't look away from Navie's face as her eyes widened the second she glanced over my shoulder and saw my ex-wife for the first time. I put more pressure on her cheeks with my thumbs, hoping to bring her beautiful baby blues back to me, but my plan failed miserably. She pulled away and stepped around me.

"What's going on?"

"Listen, I'll explain everything. Just give me one second." Taking a step forward, I spoke to Britney, hoping to be able to talk to Navie alone. "Britney, go to my room while I talk to my girlfriend—"

"The paparazzi must be slacking. I haven't heard anything about you having a girlfriend." Britney's voice dropped below a whisper.

Navie stood stock-still as she watched Britney walk toward the direction of my bedroom, while wiping her eyes, the tears from when she'd told me about her brother, still prevalent. Navie's face scrunched in distress when she clearly realized Britney knew where she was going, without needing verbal directions. Swallowing the bile in my throat, I approached Navie slowly, knowing I had to tread lightly with my explanation. Her eyes were glossy. Then, they were watery. And before I could say anything, tears welled and quickly rolled down her cheeks.

"Baby, listen to me."

She crossed her arms, in defense. "Who is she?"

"I'm going to explain everything."

"Who—is—she, Trevor?" She'd barely been able to speak, her voice wobbly and almost a murmur.

"She's my ex-wife."

"Your ex-*wife*?" Her wide, innocent eyes narrowed at the revelation. "You lied to me."

"I didn't lie to you," I defended.

Anger surged that she thought I'd been dishonest with her. She'd told me herself she didn't want to talk about exes, which was why I never brought up the asshole she used to see, and how doing business with him made me want to puke. But I was trying to be an adult, both with our relationship and the promise of a decent list of contacts the guys at the gym could take advantage of. Remorse filled my gut. I felt like shit for not clarifying the fact that my ex was an ex-wife, but my pride wouldn't allow me to take the fall for something she thought I'd done, when I knew I hadn't.

"You did. You never told me you were married."

My palms grasped the sides of her arms pulling her toward me just a fraction. "That's right. I never told you. I didn't lie about it. You're the one who told me we weren't going to talk about past relationships."

Navie walked out of my grip and took a seat at the bar—better than what I figured she'd do. I walked over and leaned across the granite, knowing I had to remain calm on the outside, even though I was ready to explode on the inside. I was livid over the fact that Britney had shown up at our home, forcing Navie to find out something so important about my past before I'd been able to tell her myself.

"I never went into this thing," I said, pointing from myself to her, "thinking I was never going to tell you about her. Honestly, I wasn't completely aware that you didn't know. It wasn't a huge secret; we just chose to keep most of our relationship out of the public eye. Your dad knew, so I wasn't positive you didn't."

I waited for her to respond, but she didn't. She placed a palm over her forehead, which gutted me. I'd almost rather her be pissed than obviously disappointed in me. She looked pained.

"We were only married for ten months. It was a mistake, which is why we got divorced."

"I can't believe I was so stupid," Navie said, as if she were thinking out loud.

"What? Don't say that." I leaned farther over the bar to take her hand, but she pulled away from me, clasping her hands together.

She stood and scooted the barstool under the granite counter. "I need some space."

"Hang on," I begged, moving when she did, intent on not letting her leave with things unresolved. "I know this is a lot. Just let me handle whatever is going on with her, and I'll tell you everything."

Navie silenced me, placing her hand in the middle of my chest. "Let you handle what's going on with her? And not handle what's going on with us?"

I hadn't cried since my mother died. I remembered it plain as day because it felt so foreign. The raw emotion forcefully bubbling up from my guts, with nowhere left to go. With no choice, I'd had to release it, the pain too great to carry inside. That same feeling I'd had all those years ago churned, rotated, and threatened to force its way out. I swallowed the lump in my throat, tamping the urge down.

I watched carefully as she nodded her head, almost to herself. As if she'd just realized something profound—or accepted it. "I'm going now. You go handle whatever is going on with *her*." She glanced up at me through watery eyes, throwing my own words back in my face. "I'll call you when I'm ready to talk."

"Navie, please." My voice broke.

"Don't, Trevor." She took a step back, then two more. "I can't right now."

I stared at her back as she made her way down the long hallway, her head bent, watching her feet as she walked away from me. I hung my head and squeezed my eyes shut, swallowing back a guttural scream. I slammed my fist into the bar at the sound of my front door shutting—the love of my life walking out on me. And I'd never even fucking told her.

I should have told Navie about Britney the first second I knew our relationship was going anywhere. I should have been transparent about my past. And I damn sure should have told Britney to leave my house and never come back, all the while not allowing Navie to leave me for space.

But I hadn't. I hadn't done any of those things, and now the past I'd tried so hard to keep where it belonged was smack dab in the middle of my present, leaving my future uncertain.

CHAPTER 14
NAVIE

"EVERYTHING OKAY?" My manager cornered me as soon as I'd made it back to work.

"Yeah, just a misunderstanding," I lied.

I hadn't planned on going back to work. I'd figured once I made it to Trevor's house and saw that everything was fine, we'd curl up on his couch and watch something on Netflix. I never imagined walking in to find his ex-wife standing there, as if it were completely normal for her to be there.

Britney.

I hated that I hated her name.

She was blonde. And beautiful, and looked like she belonged there, at Trevor's house. She'd been married to my boyfriend, and they'd probably shared so many special moments together; intimate moments—moments that married people shared together. The thought of him making such a commitment to someone else made me feel like some side piece. Like what he and I had wasn't special. I knew I was probably in my head more than I needed to be because I tended to overthink things, but I couldn't help it. Wife and girlfriend were not the same. And then there was the fact that he'd never even mentioned it. Maybe it hadn't been a secret and given that he once worked for my father and was even in the public eye, he could have assumed I'd already known that information, but I hadn't.

Like a robot, I continued to take drink orders. I didn't know how I managed, but I did. It must have been shock. Because as hurt as I was, I hadn't cried once since I'd left Trevor's. I was too pissed.

"One more, sweet cheeks?" A guy from the corner booth touched my arm as I passed his table.

"Yeah, sure." I continued walking as I jotted down his order.

Once I made my normal rounds for the last of my tables, I waited patiently at the bar while the bartender made the drinks. My mind still reeled from the news. And the fact that he was currently at our house comforting his ex-wife instead of begging for my forgiveness stung. He'd made his choice. How dense had I been? I was so wrapped up in our whirlwind romance, I hadn't even cared about his past, not when I thought it was a list of thirsty cage bunnies.

Feeling overwhelmed, I delivered the drinks to the patrons' respective tables, preoccupied by my emotions. Calling off work and going back home as if nothing had transpired seemed ridiculous.

"What time do you get off, baby?"

"Huh?"

"I can stick around, take you back to my place." The guy from the corner grabbed my arm and hit on me in front of the whole table, stunning me into silence. What vibe had I put off giving him the inclination I was remotely interested in him?

"This dude bothering you, Navie?" Payne's voice echoed off the side wall, surprising me.

"I can handle it."

He narrowed his eyes, staring straight at the jerk in the corner. "You sure?"

"Sorry, man." The drunk guy held his hands up in surrender. "I didn't know she was taken."

"You wouldn't know unless you asked her. And since you didn't, I guess you get what you get, yeah?" Payne shrugged and grinned, but it was a scary grin, as if he was picturing his fist swinging into Corner Guy's face.

I put my hand on Payne's shoulder, ready to put out the fire, but luckily Willow stepped up. "Keep your sleazy pick-up lines to yourself, dickface, or my husband will kick your ass, and I'll let him."

My eyes grew wide in astonishment at Willow's words. I'd never heard her talk to anyone like that, let alone a dude none of us even knew. Corner Guy's friends burst into laughter and slapped him on the shoulder, letting us know they planned on busting his chops after the scene played out.

Payne grinned like a damn Cheshire Cat; he evidently loved it when his wife got feisty.

I grinned, staring the douchebag straight in the eye. "So, I think we've established how many times you'll have your ass beat for fucking with me. But you should know I won't need my friend, even though he's chomping at the bit to crush your face into a million pieces. You ever talk to me like that again, I'll rip your balls off and shove them up your ass." I smirked, making sure the whole table got my drift. "Got it?" Before giving him a chance to respond, I walked away, blocking out the outburst of laughter behind me.

I didn't smoke, but a long drag of something would have felt righteous. Swinging the back door open, I welcomed the fresh air as it hit me in the face, ready for more than a ten-minute break. Willow and Payne followed close behind, and Willow spoke first.

"Are you okay?"

"Yes."

"Are you sure? Steele called and wanted us to—"

"He called you? Why would he call you?" The look that passed between them didn't go unnoticed. Shame swirled in my gut. "You knew," I guessed.

Willow nodded, but Payne held a firm facial expression behind his wife.

"I guess it's dumbass, party of one, then." I sighed.

"Navie." Willow embraced me, her small hands pressing into my back. I returned the hug, but it was a lame attempt. I just wanted to be alone. It wasn't that I didn't appreciate them checking on me, and I knew they meant well, but it was bad enough I had to work after having my heart ripped out. I didn't want their pity too.

Backing away from Willow, I stood up straight. "Look, I'm okay."

Payne's eyebrow rose as I made eye contact with him. "Fine," I conceded, "I'll *be* okay. I just need some time. This is a little…strange for me."

Willow nodded in understanding. "Take all the time you need. But please give him a chance to explain before you make any decisions about the future."

"I will," I promised. "I'll call you later, but I need to get back inside." Forget the ten-minute break. Getting back to work would keep my mind preoccupied, even if that meant dealing with some asshole I could split in two.

"Okay, we're here if you need anything."

Leaving them in the back alley, I tightened my apron, readying myself for the last half of my shift. Luckily, I stayed busy and didn't so much as receive another glance from the dickface in the corner. I still served the table, but the threat from myself and Payne had obviously lingered.

After punching my time card, I leaned against the wall, still not sure what to do with the rest of my night. My choices were talk to Trevor or get a hotel room. The hotel didn't sound so bad, but since I'd put some distance between us, I could admit I was curious to hear his explanation about the whole twisted situation.

I ended up not having to make the decision.

As I exited the bar, I noticed Trevor leaning up against the hood of my car. His large hands were tucked into his jeans, and a weary expression covered his face. He looked like a teenager, maybe the captain of the football team, who with zero effort, could be a clone of James Dean, only larger.

As I closed the distance, he pushed off the car, standing to his full height. "Hey."

"Hey." I gripped my keys tightly, not exactly knowing if I was ready for what he had to say.

"I—" he started.

"Later, baby!" Corner dickface yelled at me from the other side of the parking lot, causing his buddies to burst into laughter. They were practically carrying him, he was so drunk.

"The fuck?" Trevor was already walking toward them, his shoulders tensing more and more with each step he took. I scurried after him, worried his anger would get the better of him.

"Trevor!" I called, already picturing the gory outcome.

Trevor stepped up to the guy, nose to nose, pushing his friends back with his presence alone. "What did you just say?"

"Trevor!" I pulled on his arm. "I'm leaving." I let go of him, hoping my threat would do the trick since he was ignoring my vocal attempts to get him to back off. "I mean it."

Even though we were outside, Trevor's testosterone filled the air, ratcheting up the tension. It was so suffocating; so insanely palpable. I swallowed, hoping there would be no blood spilled. The drunk guy was oblivious to the fact that I was practically pleading for his life, but my attempt didn't go unnoticed by his friends, who were scared speechless.

Trevor leaned into him, and the mouthy dickface leaned away so far, he was almost doing a standing backbend. I chewed the inside of my cheek, barely able to watch. So many things went through my mind at once, but the main concern involved Trevor going to jail.

"Tomorrow, when you wake up and your head hurts, your body aches, and you feel like you could throw up, I want you to remember one thing, motherfucker." Trevor slapped the side of the guy's face, not hard, but enough that everyone witnessing their little conversation sucked in a breath. "It could have been a lot worse. And it will be, if you ever talk to my woman like that again." Trevor stepped back, still eyeing him.

The guy's eyes bulged as his hand covered his face. His buddies weren't laughing anymore. Neither was he.

"I—I got it. No worries," he blurted.

"You fuckin' better." Trevor pointed to the guy's friends. "Make sure your boy remembers this conversation. I won't have it again." Turning his back on the group of frat boys, Trevor took my hand in his and practically dragged me in the direction of our vehicles.

On top of being somewhat astonished, a little pissed, and a lot turned on, I was flabbergasted. I'd never seen him so angry before, not even in the cage. Inside the cage, Trevor was emotionless—a machine.

He never stooped to talking smack or bashing anyone in interviews. He was, for the most part, cool as a cucumber.

His grip tightened around my hand on the walk to my car. Staying silent, I worried about him. I could feel the adrenaline surging through his body. He was inside his own head, and I let him stay there, uninterrupted, until I noticed the fear in his eyes. It made me sad.

Stopping in front of my car, my palm cupped his jaw. "Hey."

He shook his head, telling me without words he wasn't ready to speak.

"Trevor. I'm okay," I reassured him.

He wrapped his arm around my neck and pulled me to him. In all the ways he'd shown me he cared about me before, he'd never poured his soul into a hug, holding me like his life depended on it. My chest heaved at the pressure he put on me with his body. I held it. I stood as tall as I could and pushed back, so he'd know I could handle it. We stayed like that for a moment while he gathered his thoughts. I chose not to break the silence, allowing him all the time he needed.

I'd been so angry at him, had felt so betrayed by his past, but for the life of me, I couldn't remember what any of that felt like with his arms around me.

"I love you, Navie. I know there are things I haven't shared with you." He pulled back, his palm brushing over his beard. "I know I can be distant and private. If I seem far away, it's because this is new to me. I'm not used to—sharing—myself with anyone. Even before, when I was in a relationship, I never felt like I had to."

My mouth opened, but I snapped it shut at his words. I'd never had anyone tell me they loved me like that…the amount of sincerity caused me to stop thinking. I swallowed, in an attempt to speak bluntly so he'd understand why I felt the way I did.

"I don't want to make you, Trevor. I want you to *want* to share yourself with me. Your past. Where you came from. Where you want to go. The people who helped you get where you are today. Those who made it hard for you, and yes…those you loved along the way. I don't have to know every single detail of your life, but the big stuff—the stuff you have to go to courthouses for—yeah. I need to know that stuff."

"Let's make a deal."

Interested in what he'd say next, I crossed my arms. "What kind of deal?"

"The kind where I give you whatever you want, and you come home with me."

If he was willing to open up, then I needed to be supportive. But I needed him to understand what I wanted from him. I needed a partner, not just a boyfriend. "I can work with that. But we have things to discuss."

"Whatever you want."

Trevor grinned, his eyes dancing with mischief as he opened the driver's side door and guided me into my seat. He kissed me on the cheek, but never responded verbally. Closing my door, he stepped back with a different demeanor. He seemed unsure of himself. I didn't like the look on him, especially since we'd just expressed our love for one another. I started my vehicle, watching intently as he pulled out of the parking lot ahead of me. My instincts told me he'd come to some sort of resolution. As I followed him the whole way back to his house, I just hoped the feelings he had for me were stronger than his fear.

CHAPTER 15
TREVOR

I MADE us each a cup of tea and splashed a finger of whiskey into mine before settling in for a long night on the couch with Navie. I had so much to tell her and needed everything to come out the right way.

I watched her sip the tea once, then again, before she placed the cup back on the saucer and nestled into the couch cushions. I took a deep breath, knowing I had to start from the beginning.

"I don't want to overwhelm you," I admitted.

"Why do you think you'd overwhelm me?"

Honesty. That's what she wanted.

"Because there are some things I haven't told you, and I don't want you to think I've lied to you because I haven't told you everything."

She inhaled deep and closed her eyes, as if she was mentally preparing herself to hear what I had to say. Or she was frustrated there was more for me to say. I couldn't tell, and I didn't want to ask, since neither scenario was good. We'd just had our first fight—over lies by omission—according to her, and I didn't want to have the same fight again in the future.

"Just start from the beginning. If we're doing this…then it has to be that way."

"All right." I faced her, and placed my elbows on my knees, bracing myself. "So, you already know about my upbringing. I told you I grew up in a trailer with my mom doing the best she could, which wasn't much now that I look back on it, but she loved me, and I guess that's all that matters." I swallowed, the words coming from my mouth surprising me. I never knew I felt that way. Not exactly.

"My dad left before I could walk. I don't remember him at all. I could have been standing next to him at the mall, and I never would have known it. I have no idea if he's still alive, and I don't care."

Navie placed her hand over mine in a show of support.

"I told you about that preacher, remember?" She nodded. "So, when I was a teenager, I started doing stupid shit, hanging around the wrong people—nothing too bad." I stopped.

I had never told anyone my life story before. I never thought about it or how it pertained to who I'd become. But those hardships early on clearly had an impact on who I was. Hence the lies by omission and the defensive walls I'd built.

"Anyway, long story short, he helped me. He gave me free boxing lessons and taught me about respect—about how it was earned." I rubbed her small hand, taking comfort in her support. "Some guys from the old league would come mentor at the YMCA. That's where I met them and began taking an interest in fighting. It was an outlet for me; and once I learned to channel my energy into improving my skills, that was it. I never looked back.

"Fast forward to me making the pro circuit. The first few years were hard for me to maneuver. I wasn't used to the attention, and it was overwhelming. My manager then screwed me out of a ton of money, and I shamefully had more than my fair share of one-night stands. Those first few years all kind of run together for me, honestly."

Navie remained poised, not one ounce of judgment coming from her gaze. Spilling my guts wasn't as difficult as I feared. But I hadn't really made it to the hard part yet. I took another breath and continued. "I tried to have a few relationships, but once I began getting notoriety, the media backlash ensued. Every woman I ran into, the press linked us together. As you can imagine, those relationships crashed and burned before they even got started.

"Once I worked my way through the public part of fighting, I vowed to become as private as possible. That's around the time I met

Britney." At the mention of my ex-wife, Navie's eyes averted, and I could tell it stung just hearing me say it out loud. I knew I had to push on if I wanted to get through everything, so I pulled her hand up to my mouth. Instead of kissing it, I rubbed my lips over the back of her hand, seeking comfort while hoping I was giving her reassurance. "We did a charity fight for the military, and she was there. Her brother was in the Army, and he and I got on immediately.

"He and his buddies were on leave, and they invited me and a couple of other fighters to hang out. I went, not looking to really hook up, but Britney seemed different. She didn't mind the spotlight, which was the exact opposite of the last couple of girlfriends I'd had.

"So, we began dating and when our relationship lasted longer than I expected, and I mistook that to mean it was supposed to last forever. We got married, but...I forced her to keep things private. We fought about it a lot. She liked being married to a semi-celebrity and she wanted me to show the world how much I loved her. But I knew what the media was capable of. I thought I was doing us both a favor by not playing that game. I figured if they never knew for sure we were married, they wouldn't report on us as much. But she got sick of it. She hated hiding and thought I was ashamed of our relationship. Months later, during an interview, some dipshit asked me if my girl was proud of me, and I answered something stupid to deflect the question. I told them my dog loved me. It was a joke, but... that was the straw that broke the camel's back. She packed and left before I made it back home from the fight."

Navie frowned but nodded. "She thought you were trying to hide your relationship when you were trying to protect it." Navie Fuller was no stranger to gossip rags and what a few cameras in your face could do to your privacy. She'd been raised in it, which proved to be a positive as I explained my reasons for my divorce.

"Exactly. It was never right. Never. I just thought because she didn't fear the lifestyle, that meant she was someone who could endure it." I shook my head, knowing it sounded bad. But looking back on the whole thing, I knew it to be true. "She tried to come back a few times, but after she left the first time, it was never the same. I didn't trust her, and honestly, I didn't love her. I cared for her, but that wasn't the same thing."

I scooted closer to Navie on the sofa. "Brian, Britney's brother, and I became close while she and I were together. Well, as close as brother-in-law's can be while living on different sides of the country. But our friendship was genuine. I loved him like a brother. When she left me, it was tough because I lost a friend too. Brian and I stayed cordial, but our Skype sessions became few and far between." I didn't want to hurt Navie, but I knew I needed to be honest about everything. "Brian died yesterday."

Sadness and understanding filled Navie's eyes.

"I know when you came in earlier, I made it seem like you and I could figure things out later, which made you feel like you weren't a priority. I swear that's not the case. It was all so shocking. Her showing up. The news about Brian. You finding out about my marriage, without me being able to explain it. It was just all—really shitty."

Navie rubbed soothing circles on the inside of my wrist with her thumb. "I'm sorry about Brian. And I'm sorry for how I reacted earlier. I suppose I could have been a little more understanding. I just—I felt so betrayed."

I ran my palm over my beard, hating that I'd made her feel that way. It was the last thing I had wanted to do, yet… I'd done it.

"I can't tell you how sorry I am about that."

Biting her bottom lip, Navie stared at me, her gaze more uncertain than I'd ever seen before. "What about Britney?"

"What about her?" I asked, not following her.

"Do you still have feelings for her? Do you still talk to her? She seemed—at home here."

Was she not listening to a word I said? Could she not see how torn up I was at even the notion that I could lose her? I had to do better. I had to make her see how much I loved her.

"No." I took her hand and pulled it into my lap. I was desperate for her closeness and wanted nothing more than to get those useless thoughts out of her head. "God, Navie." My thumb softly searched for any piece of skin it could find. "I can't see past my own nose where you're concerned. Don't you realize that? Baby, I am head-over-fucking-heels for you."

She smiled softly, causing hope to spring in my chest. "I'm crazy for you too, Trevor. I'll never understand why you hid your marriage, but…I do see where there was a lot going on today. I'm thankful you're telling me now, but you need to know as much as I care about you…" Her lips pursed in thought. "As much as I love you, I'm not going to deal with lying. It's not how I operate, and I deserve better."

I still didn't feel like I'd exactly lied to her. But I supposed the point was—she did. Seeing someone else's point of view had never been a strong suit of mine, but as I sat with her, as I felt her tenseness, I realized there was nothing I wouldn't do to ease that for her.

"I promise, Navie. No more secrets."

"All right, then. Are you going to go to the funeral?"

"No."

"Don't make that decision for me."

I shook my head. "Brian wouldn't like it. He wouldn't want people standing over his casket reminiscing about what kind of guy he was."

"I just don't want you to regret not going."

"It's not like that. I've made peace with it."

"That's really soon."

I shrugged. "It is what it is."

"Trevor."

"Navie."

She glanced up at me, a little annoyed, yet somehow endearing. It gave me hope.

"We're good?"

She nodded in agreement. "We're good."

I'd never felt so much relief in all my life. I didn't know how I'd gotten so lucky or why I'd been gifted with a woman like her, but I knew I never wanted to risk losing her again. I hugged her tight, pouring every ounce of love and affection I had into it.

"One more question."

"Shoot."

"I feel bad for Britney with the loss of her brother, but how do we know she won't be showing up here unannounced again?"

I chuckled. If she wanted honesty, honesty she would get. "I told her my girl was a fighter. Britney's been around the league enough to know what that means."

"You ass!" Navie shoved me but giggled. "You put her off on me?"

"I sure did."

"Well, hopefully it won't come down to that. I'm empathetic, but if her intentions ever go beyond anything platonic, she's a goner. You're not the only one who can growl out the word motherfucker and make it sound menacing." She winked.

I burst into laughter, and swooped one arm around her neck then brought her toward me, essentially putting her in a headlock. She fought me at first but gave in when she realized I was pulling us back into the cushions. As sad as the news was about Brian, I couldn't help but feel thankful for everything I had. Especially Navie. Lining her body up perfectly with mine, my palms caressed the sides of her thighs. "I love it when you talk dirty, Royal."

Navie rolled her eyes and placed her chin on top of her hands that were perfectly folded on my chest. I thought she'd reply with a witty comeback, but she didn't. She searched my gaze with her own. The small smile at the corners of her mouth made me smile too. "I love you," she said.

I placed my lips on her forehead, savoring the contact.

I'll never tire of feeling her love; feeling the sense of security it gives me.

My lips trembled through my thoughts. "I love you too. So much."

CHAPTER 16
NAVIE

"WHAT'S UP?" I closed the door to Trevor's office and walked toward his desk. When Gage had relayed the message that Trevor needed to see me in his office, I knew something was off, otherwise he would have come and gotten me himself.

Trevor looked up from the pile of paperwork on his desk. "Your dad called me."

"What did he want?" I probably already knew the answer to that question, but it was still insulting that my father had contacted my boyfriend before he'd tried to call me.

"You."

"Me?"

He licked his lips, nodding. I mimicked him, not knowing what to say. I knew exactly who we were dealing with and what lengths my dad would go to get what he wanted. I'd been privy to his tactics my whole life. My father having a man-to-man talk with my boyfriend should not have surprised me in the least. But it did, even after all these years.

"What'd he say?"

"Nothing I was interested in, that's for sure." Trevor paused, head tilted, seemingly gauging my reaction. Instead of responding, I held his gaze, demanding that he continue. What had been so important that my father chose to contact him, an ex-employee, instead of me, his own daughter?

"He saw your fight."

Crossing my arms, I suddenly felt the need to protect myself. It wasn't as if my dad was anywhere near me, but that was indicative of the hold he had over me. We weren't even in the same room, yet I felt the need to guard myself from his opinion. "And?"

"He didn't like it. He tried to blackmail me, using the league as leverage over the other fighters in my gym."

My eyes widened. He would ruin an athlete's future because he felt like I was disrespecting him by fighting? How could my father do something so cruel? Gage, Tommy—none of the athletes had anything to do with my matches or my future plans for that matter.

"He's butt hurt because a couple of reporters reached out to him over your win. And if you want my honest opinion, I think he's terrified you're going to put him out of business."

Shaking my head, I scoffed. "How could I put him out of business? That's not my intention. It never was."

"His ego is too big to believe that, Navie. He sees you getting traction. He thinks a female league will diminish the reputation of the AFL."

"Why would he think that? I just don't understand." I'd tried so many times to see where my father was coming from, but I couldn't. My brain didn't work like that. Either people were good or they weren't. I was his blood. He'd raised me. He knew I would never intentionally harm him. Never.

Trevor stood and walked around his desk. His arms were around my waist within seconds. His gaze leveled, nothing but pure sincerity behind them. "Baby, he's sexist. I know he's your father, but that's the gist of it. And it may be that he's from another generation, but that's still no excuse. He has zero respect for women in the league, and I've learned that much just from the things you've told me."

It seemed as if the dark cloud that was my family would continue following me until the weight of their actions came bearing down on me like a torrential down pour. Knowing them, they were hoping to drown me in the process. Trevor was right. But I couldn't fix my father or his outdated way of thinking. I just hated that he'd brought my boyfriend and his gym into a conversation that should have been reserved for me. The last thing I wanted was for my dad to use his power over Trevor or anyone else. Especially now, since I knew personally how hard they'd all worked to get where they were.

"I'm sorry—"

"You're sorry?" Trevor leaned back, shaking his head. "*I'm* sorry, Navie. It's a dick move, and he's your dad. That's low. I told him to fuck off. I hope you don't mind." He grinned, showing me his dimples.

I covered my mouth with my hand. A small giggle bubbled out. "You did?"

"I did."

"I don't know what to say. I can't believe he's acting this way."

"I'm starting to understand that I don't have the first fucking clue who Richard Fuller is." Trevor squeezed me tight, bringing me closer to him. "I'm sorry you had to live like that. If I'm being honest, having him come at me, no holds barred, made me think of a six-year-old Navie who didn't have a choice. The fifteen-year-old Navie who couldn't go against his word, and eighteen-year-old Navie who couldn't find a way to stand up for herself," he whispered in my ear.

Pulling back, I gulped. His eyes were soft as remorse filled them.

"Don't." So many people had been through so much worse. My upbringing seemed trivial almost, especially when he'd endured so much as a child himself.

"Okay. I'll let it go for now, but you need to know the next time I see him, things probably won't end well."

"You'll probably never see him again. He was pretty angry the last time we talked, plus the fact that he's threatening to blackball fighters who have nothing to do with me, I'm pretty sure he's disowning me." My eyes stung as I said the words out loud. Pushing them back, I straightened, as if on autopilot. Unfortunately, I'd had plenty of experience over the years keeping up appearances on the outside while internally falling on the sword.

"We'll see him again, babe. And when we do, whatever happens will happen."

I swallowed and nodded. I needed to get back out to Tommy. I had some rage to get rid of. And doubt. Disappointment. Embarrassment, too.

Trevor hugged me tight, attempting to calm the nervous energy engulfing me. I appreciated that about him—the effort he took to make me feel better. But nothing changed when I walked out of his office. Bile gathered in my belly, threatening with each step I took to spill out, as I made my way back out to the cage.

What am I doing? I'd fought a total of one fight. One. Yet, I was in my boyfriend's gym every day, training for a league that didn't even exist.

God, maybe my dad is right.

Rounding the corner, I lifted my chin toward Tommy who was standing on the outside of the cage. "I'll catch up with you later," I told him, making a split-second decision to leave, knowing I needed get away or else I'd succumb to my anxiety with witnesses.

"Okay. Is everything all right?"

"Yeah. Tell Trevor I had some errands to run, will you?"

The look of confusion that crossed Tommy's face made me feel like shit. I'd just come from Trevor's office, where I could have told him myself I was leaving for the day. But I hadn't. I decided on the twenty-second walk to the cage that I wasn't strong enough to deal with what my life had become. It pissed me off more than anything—the weakness I couldn't seem to push past. I knew deep down I was bailing on Tommy for nothing. Nothing more than my asshole dad making me feel like I didn't belong, speaking to me from memories past, and the worst part was—I was listening to him.

Trevor: I'm not freaking the fuck out or anything. All I need for you to do is text me my favorite shade of blue, and I'll give you all the space you need. Until tomorrow. You get one day.

I glanced at the text and mustered a small smile. I appreciated his effort, but I needed a minute. Except I didn't want him to worry about me, so I relented.

Navie: Navy.
Trevor: That's my girl.

I clicked my phone over to silent and leaned back into the leather sofa at the coffee shop, where luckily, I was the solo patron. I hated that I'd let my dad get into my head; that I'd let him decide how I felt about myself. He pecked and pecked at that one hollow spot until he drilled a gaping sized hole, making me feel empty.

"You hiding from someone?"

Glancing up, I smiled at Willow. She was like a damn bloodhound. Sniffing out any person in need. "Myself?" I chuckled.

Willow ordered a drink, then joined me on the sofa. "Sister, friend. What's up?"

"Did Trevor send you over here?"

"No," she said. "I haven't talked to him. Honestly, I just popped in for a few minutes of alone time."

"Really?"

She grinned. "What? You think I don't like my solace?"

"Honestly? You don't seem like the type of person who needs time alone. You just always look like you've got it all together."

"Shit, Navie. That's pretty much the opposite of my life."

We both laughed and leaned on each other. Willow backed away and straightened as the barrister brought her coffee over. She thanked her, then turned back toward me. "What's up?"

"Just processing everything."

"I hated you found out about Britney like that."

"Why didn't you tell me?"

"I honestly never thought about it. Conner and I didn't know all the details. I guess I assumed you knew about it, until I saw you at Melton's. It literally broke my heart."

"I'm sorry I've been avoiding you. I just haven't felt up to returning calls. And my dad is threatening Trevor now. It's just all a little overwhelming."

"He's threatening him?"

"Well, it's complicated. He is using the guys' future against him. I have no idea why he's so adamant about my coming back home. He's treating me like I'm a teenager. It's insulting."

"Have you talked to him? Asked him why he's doing that?"

I shook my head. "No. I'm beginning to see the importance of dealing with things instead of letting them pile up."

"Life happens, girlfriend. I'm always here for you."

"Thank you. I appreciate that."

Willow leaned over and hugged me. She gave the biggest hugs.

"I have the best idea."

"What's that?"

"Vegas. You. Me. And Lena. Only girls, all weekend."

"I'm so down with that."

"Pack your bags, sister. We're about to leave our problems here for a few days. They'll be here when we get back."

Toasting her, I sipped my drink. She wasn't wrong, and I needed a break. I wanted one, and thanks to her and Lena, I was going to get one.

Willow left before me, claiming she had other errands to run. I ended up spending a total of eighteen dollars on coffee and two muffins before I was ready to face Trevor. I knew after bailing on him without any explanation, he wouldn't just let my behavior go with a conversation. How would I explain the fact my trauma response came from a lifetime of rejection and self-doubt my father had bestowed upon me? I could assume he'd already gathered the information, but I hadn't. I'd never truly examined it. What sucked even more, was after hours of trying to work it all out in my mind, I still didn't have a solution when I pulled into Trevor's driveway.

Placing my purse on the entry table, I listened for Trevor, surprised he wasn't in the living room waiting for me. I worked up some courage as I walked toward the kitchen, but he wasn't there either. Was he actually asleep at nine-thirty? I quickened my steps, feeling a little relieved. Once I reached the spare bedroom, I changed into one of his T-shirts and threw my hair into a messy bun.

"Feel better?" Trevor's voice startled me.

I smirked at the huskiness. But I honestly didn't know the answer to his question. I wasn't sure how I felt. My legs weren't as wobbly as they'd been when I found out my father had called him. My heart wasn't racing, and my breaths weren't fighting my lungs for air. There had been no tears, nor were my thoughts sad. Answering his question inside my own mind made me realize the cloud of doubt I'd had earlier wasn't exactly there anymore. I just wasn't sure what it had been replaced with.

At the sight of him, peace circled my brain, trickling down to my limbs. Mentally, I was calm. Physically, I was relaxed. The only difference had been that I'd come home. Being in Trevor's space, with him made me feel safe. Maybe it was him. Maybe it was me. Deciphering the difference didn't seem plausible, but one thing I did know was I wasn't going to harp on the not knowing part. I was going to settle into the serene part. And that started with Trevor.

I turned toward him, noting his muscular body leaned up against the door frame, clad in nothing but a pair of boxer briefs, which reminded me he was mine.

My toes curled as the plush carpet softened under my footsteps. I made it a point to feel every inch of the tickling fabric as I made my way to him. "I do now," I whispered.

Trevor's eyes twinkled as he squinted. His arms opened automatically as I approached him. "You have the most beautiful soul, Navie."

"Soul?" I laughed and buried my head in his chest. "Sweet talker much?"

"I see it every time you look at me." His fingertips fondled my chin, tilting my head back until I looked straight into his eyes. "Right there. Pure. Strong. Loving. Everything I could ever want in my favorite shade of blue."

I tucked my head into his chest, overcome with emotion.

Most of the time, human beings tore others down instead of building them up. Building up was harder; there was more effort involved—more thinking. It took the center of a person, the true heart of someone, to actively consider something other than themselves. I knew better than anyone it required a selfless person who wanted to cultivate something they were passionate about.

Trevor Steele never took the easy way out. He hadn't in his career. Nor had he in his personal life. I should have known what I was feeling when I first walked into his house after a long day of questioning my total existence. Unconditional love. That's what he had given me and continued to give me every single day. His love was not contingent on my past, or my family members, or even how I felt about myself. It was pure. Total and complete from his heart which harbored zero outside influences.

I looked up at him, willing the strength to admit my insecurity. "I'm sorry I let my dad affect me like that."

"No worries, babe. You went through it. You felt it and sat in it for a while. I have no problem with you truly feeling how you feel. The problem I have is you giving his words meaning. We're gonna work on that—together."

"I love you, Trevor."

"I know." He winked, lightening the mood. I knew he loved me enough for both of us, even when I doubted myself. "Now, let's talk about this T-shirt." He tugged at the hem.

I stepped back, examining it myself. "What about it?"

"It's not your color, Periwinkle. It has to go," he said, lifting the bottom of the shirt until he pulled it over my head.

I smiled at his joke, but I was more than ready for what came next. He was going to *show* me how much he loved me, and I planned on letting him.

CHAPTER 17
TREVOR

"MY FLIGHT LEAVES IN AN HOUR. How could you let me oversleep? God, the girls are going to kill me." Navie scurried around the side of my bed, naked as the day she was born. Searching for her underwear, she complained that she'd been limp as noodle and hadn't remembered to set her alarm last night. "I'm never late!"

"Baby, you have plenty of time. We are literally ten minutes from the airport." I couldn't help but grin as I tried to calm her down. She was cute as hell.

"Trevor, this is not funny. Help me!"

I glanced at the end of the bed, quickly locating the black lace panties I'd taken off her hours before using only my teeth. A better man would have probably handed them to her, helping with her anxiety. I was not that man.

Picking her up from behind, I kissed her neck, aroused from my naked parts touching her naked parts. "We have time—ow." She broke free from me as I leaned to the side from taking an elbow to the ribs.

"No, we don't. I don't even have time to shower, and you know…I mean, I'm dirty." Her bottom lip puckered just a hair.

"Having my cum inside you does not make you dirty, Teal." I kept a straight face, even though some serious, not-so-subtle laughter bubbled up from my chest.

She narrowed her eyes in my direction while pulling a pair of sweatpants up, sans underwear, and ran to the closet for a suitcase. I watched her shake her head and mumble in what sounded like Spanish, even though I had no idea she spoke a second language.

"I'm so barely your girlfriend right now." She finished packing her makeup bag and shot me a scowl.

"You love me." I stepped into a pair of jeans and threw a T-shirt over my head. Tucking my wallet in the back pocket of my jeans, my insides softened even more as I watched her head for the front door, with one of my AFL hoodies thrown haphazardly over her satchel. She had covered up her bedhead with a plain black baseball cap turned backward, and her Ray Bans were tucked just inside of the plain, white, V-neck T-shirt she had on. She'd never looked more beautiful to me.

The ride to the airport was nothing short of entertaining as I watched Navie from the driver's side while she dug through her purse and carry on. I had no idea what she was looking for, but the sight amused me. Ten minutes later, I parked in the drop-off line and grabbed her bags.

"I'm assuming this is your fault." Lena gave me the side-eye as we arrived at the gate.

"Assume all you want, doll." I hugged her, not giving two shits if she blamed me for Navie's tardiness.

"I'm so excited!" Willow clapped her hands.

"Magic Mike, here we come!" Lena yelled.

"What the hell is a Magic Mike?" I asked.

Navie shot a look at Willow, who burst into laughter, while Lena thrusted her pelvis twice. "A show. I love you and I will call you as soon as we land."

"Love you. Be careful."

Payne and I waited with them until the girls boarded their flight. It was unnerving, knowing they were going away without either of us with them. Payne had his own reasons for not wanting Willow out of his sight, and I had mine where Navie was concerned. It was difficult, but neither one of us wanted to seem like Neanderthals. We'd discussed voicing our opinions about their all-girl get away, but ultimately decided against it. Well, I decided against it and convinced him it was better if they didn't go out of town pissed at us because we both knew they were going to go either way.

Besides, we trusted them. We were man enough to let our women go away for the weekend to a city where sin was considered part of the experience. I just wished we'd listened to ourselves a day later before we took Gage's fucking advice on how to spy on them without being detected.

I had no idea how tech savvy Gage and Tommy were until we were down at Melton's having a burger, and they casually mentioned Lena was keeping them updated on the girls trip via Instagram and Snapchat. I'd never had a personal page on Instagram and didn't know shit about Snapchat. I was shocked when Gage showed me a video clip of Navie dancing where some dipshit behind her had his eyes glued to her ass.

I punched Gage's arm to get his attention. "Wait! Rewind that." I planned to remember every detail of that bastard so if I ever saw him out, I could kick his ass.

He burst into laughter. "Can't, dude. It erases after a couple of seconds."

"What do you mean? I want to see that fucker's face again," I huffed.

"No can do. We could probably put a bit together from Lena's Insta-story though."

"Insta—what?"

"God, you're worse than my old man." He rolled his eyes.

"Pull it back up, I can't see shit on your little screen."

"Hey, maybe we could hook this up to your TV," Tommy's eyes grew at his drunken thought.

"Dude, I know how to do that," Gage said.

"What in the hell are you dumbasses talking about?" Payne's grumpy voice rang throughout the bar, letting me know his time alone hadn't been fun either.

"Gage says he knows how to hook up his phone to my smart TV," I explained.

"And that's news because?" Payne asked.

"Well, if you'd seen what I just saw, you'd want to see it live and in HD too."

"What'd you see?"

"I saw a slew of dudes eye-fucking our women as they danced up on them."

"Where?" The crease between Payne's eyebrows grew deeper.

"This is for real the last time I can play it. This app closes the videos after they're sent." Gage pressed play on the video again, as we crowded around him to view the clip.

"I'll drive," Payne barked, walking away from the group without so much as a backward glance before Gage could stand from his seat.

After a pit stop at the gym, we finally made it to my house, where I sat in a stupor, self-loathing flooding my veins as I watched Tommy type on two computers he'd hijacked from my office, and spliced more wires than I even realized were compatible with my smart TV. What had I become? What had Payne become? Neither of us had social media. Both of us had enough of the media without the social part of it, yet in an attempt to spy, we sat more than okay with getting a crash course from our younger buddies.

"Dude, I've done it like a million times." Tommy grunted when Payne questioned his abilities.

"I feel kind of creepy doing this, but—" Gage set up a corner table holding enough gadgets it could have matched the CIA, while Tommy quickly plugged everything in.

Payne chuckled. "*This* is what it takes for you to feel creepy?"

"I have a conscience, dumbass." Gage winked as he signed into the app on my TV.

"We're in!" Tommy yelled.

Payne and I both grinned at the realization we were about to see what our girls were up to without seeming like a couple of douchebags texting them every other minute for an update.

"It'll let me go back further on Instagram, so we'll start there."

I leaned forward, my elbows propped on my knees. I was excited. I was nervous. I was spying on my girlfriend and wasn't feeling one ounce of remorse about it.

"Wow. They look amazing." Gage's eyes widened as Lena, Willow, and Navie popped up onto my big screen TV.

"Shut the fuck up, I can't hear them." Payne was as enthralled as the rest of us.

First, they were shopping. Then, they recorded themselves trying on outfits. Next, they were in the hotel room, clinking glasses of champagne with no sound. Twelve stories later, they were at the club.

"Well, at least they're having fun." Tommy tried to be positive.

"Yeah, without us." I groaned.

"Oh, come on, guys. It's all child's play. Just a couple of dudes flirting. You've both done it a million times. Don't tell me you haven't looked at other women like that when you were single. I fucking know better," Gage argued.

"No shit, dummy. That's the point." Payne slapped the back of Gage's head, one step ahead of me.

"He's right. We're just getting in our feelings because we know what those guys are thinking. Neither of our girls even acknowledged them. It's cool." My attempt to tamp down any and all aggressive thoughts was stomped out from the next video.

"So that's what Magic Mike is," I whispered, still shocked at the video of Navie being circled by a half-naked dude who was clearly enjoying the lap dance he was giving her.

"Let's go." Payne stood up, undoubtedly ready to fly to Las Vegas and bring Willow home by throwing her over his shoulder like a cave man.

"Man. We can't. They'll get pissed if they know we've been spying on them."

"Like I give a fuck. Willow's ass is grass when I see her."

"Well, Navie and I just made it through some tough shit regarding trust, and the last thing I want to do is climb back inside *that* volcano. I like the outside better, where there's sunshine, and she's not pissed, and I can still kiss her special places."

"Pussy," he snapped.

"That too," I joked, hoping to keep him from jumping on the next flight.

"Look!" Tommy caught our attention, pointing at the screen again.

I glanced up in just enough time to see the crowd go wild when Lena jumped on top of the table and began dirty dancing to a sultry jazz number. I shook my head, miffed by the total disregard she had for her surroundings. It would be a damn miracle if they made back home in one piece.

Knowing I had to be the voice of reason, I spoke up. "We can't go. They'll think we don't trust them. Let's just drink some beers, get off that fucking app, and play some poker. They'll be home soon enough," I said, already pulling the cover off my poker table in the corner.

"Fine," Payne finally agreed. But he wasn't happy about it, that much was clear. Neither was I, but I knew it was the right thing to do. Even if it went against every instinct I had as a boyfriend.

I roused at the smell of bacon. Opening one eye, I squinted, the sun shining like a beacon of light through the wall of windows, hurting my eyes. Sitting up, I got a view of the scattered bodies on the various couches, all of them looking worse for wear. Apparently, no one had gone home after I passed out, and that appeared to have been a good thing. I couldn't remember the last time I'd been so intoxicated. Every time I considered hopping on a plane and all but manhandling Navie into coming home with me, I took another drink. Then another.

"Hey, man. You hungry?" Gage stood shirtless at my stove, cooking like he was my own personal chef.

"What time is it?" I asked, standing up to stretch.

"One forty-five."

"What?" We overslept. We were screwed. "We were supposed to pick the girls up at one-thirty."

I shoved Payne in the back, causing him to rouse as I slipped on the wrinkled T-shirt I'd worn the night before. I couldn't believe we'd overslept. The girls were going to be pissed, and if I knew Lena—and I did—she was going to let us know about it. Honestly, I wasn't too concerned with her, given that I could drop her off at her house—away from me where I wouldn't have to deal with her smartass mouth, but Navie… I'd have some groveling to do with that one. And to top it off,

I was going to do it with a major hangover. Grabbing the first ball cap I came across, I slicked my hair back and covered my head, calling for Payne to hurry as I ran toward the garage.

"They are going to be pissed," I told him as I reached overheard to open my garage.

"Yup," he agreed.

Knowing there was nothing more we could do, I put my Jeep in reverse, ready to burn rubber in order to make it to the airport in record time. Glancing in the rearview mirror, I stopped suddenly when I noticed a tan Camry pull into the circle drive with all three girls in tow. I threw my Jeep into park and hopped out, Payne close on my heels.

They'd had to Uber. Feeling even more guilty as I neared the vehicle, I began to speak as soon as Navie opened the back passenger's side door.

"I'm so sorry. We were just on our way." I hugged her tight, hoping she would forgive me.

"It's all right. We figured it out."

Her tone was light. Not offended in the least. That was a good sign.

Instead of picking up on the fact that it seemed like we were going to easily be let off the hook, Payne took the girls luggage from the trunk silently, not even so much as looking in his wife's direction. I cleared my throat, hoping he would pick up on my hint. The last thing we needed was him pissing Willow off after we'd screwed up. Besides, there was really nothing to argue about. Now that I'd slept on it and sobered up, Navie and her friends going out and having fun didn't seem so bad.

"I missed you," Willow said, snuggling up to her husband's free arm as we walked back inside my house.

Payne glanced down at his wife, one eyebrow cocked. "Did ya now?"

She stopped, pulling him to a stop as well.

Ah, shit, here we go.

"What's that supposed to mean?" she questioned.

He ignored her and continued walking inside.

"Hey! Get back here!" Her heels clicked across the hardwood floors a mile a minute. She was much shorter than her husband, causing her to almost jog to keep up with him.

"Uh, hey girls." Gage waved a spatula in the air.

"What'd you guys do last night?" Lena peered at me after glancing around the disheveled living room, plopping her body down on my couch as if she were too exhausted to hold up her own body weight. Obviously, she couldn't have cared less that her best friend was about to go ten rounds with her husband in front of us.

Willow stood front and center of my living room, her eyes narrowed at Payne; her hands placed firmly on her hips. "Conner, I asked you a question."

"Looked like you were doing just fine without me," he said.

I hung my head at his words. No one spoke until Lena added her two cents, which were totally and completely unwanted.

"And how would you know what she looked like when we were in Las Vegas and you were here, in Boston?" Lena's gaze followed the cords to the computer, then to the large TV mounted on my wall. It took her all of two seconds to connect the dots. "Unless you plugged your phone into this computer and spied on us through social media, which would be extremely sad if you did, but absolutely not a surprise." She faced us, eyeing each one of us with disgust.

"It was his idea." Tommy pointed to Gage.

"The hell it was. This is Steele's fault."

"Mine?" I threw my hands up in the air. "Payne was the one getting pissed. I just wanted to make sure—"

"Oh my God. Are you guys serious?" Willow scolded. "This is what you've been doing all night?"

"I don't even have social media. I didn't do anything," Payne argued.

"I know exactly who watched the videos. Don't even try to deny it Gagerulzthecage." Lena threw her head back, laughing at Gage's Instagram handle.

Gage scowled at Lena. "Fine. I did, but only because they wanted to see them. I swear." He held his hand up in a Boy Scout promise.

"Conner Payne, you ought to be ashamed of yourself," Willow snapped.

"Me? You were the one letting some dude get off by dancing for you!"

"I'd knock your ass out if there weren't any witnesses." Willow stalked toward the computer, her own phone in her hand. "You want to know what happened after we left Magic Mike?" She plugged her phone in, then proceeded to pull her own videos up.

Navie slid up next to me and folded her slender hand into mine. I squeezed, not sure what was happening. I looked down at her, but her eyes were glued to the TV. A series of videos began playing of the girls giggling.

The video had all our attention, even Gage and Tommy when Willow began to speak. "Okay, here goes nothing," Willow told Navie and Lena as she pulled a pregnancy test out of a brown paper bag.

My eyes grew wide, shocked. I couldn't help but glance at Payne for his reaction. Payne stood still, his arms crossed, and he hadn't batted an eye. Gage and Tommy stood behind me, giving Willow and Payne the center of the room. Willow continued to stare forward, her posture matching her husbands, seeming perfectly content for him to receive the news from the video.

I watched the screen as the girls waited for the test to be complete. They talked about what a good mother Willow would be, and how they were all sure if the test turned out to be positive, Willow and Payne would have a daughter. Glancing at my best friend, I still wasn't sure what he was thinking. His eyes hadn't wavered, and I wondered if he fully comprehended what was going on. Maybe he was in shock.

"It's positive!" Lena screamed, running out of the bathroom to embrace her best friend. "Willow! You're going to be a mom!"

I watched closely, realizing it was Navie who was recording. Small sniffles came from behind the camera. I peered down at my girlfriend, seeing her in a whole new light. The video shook as Willow hugged Navie, and all three of them cried happy tears.

"I cannot wait to tell Conner. He's going to be so excited!" Willow brought her palms to rest on her stomach as she peered down and spoke again. "Also, since this is the beginning of your journey, baby Payne, I just want to say that I love you so much already, and I'm getting on a plane in four hours to tell your daddy about you. I can't wait to meet you!"

The video cut off. No one said a word as we waited on Payne to speak. He didn't. He turned toward his wife, picked her up, and swung her around two times, squeezing so tight I could see the imprints of his hands on the bare skin showing between the hem of her shirt and the waist of her jeans.

"Well, that was dramatic," Gage commented as he slipped his bare feet into his sneakers. He spoke to Tommy, tipping his head toward the door, letting him know he was ready to leave. "I bet Payne feels like an asshole."

Tommy grinned but masked his facial expression when he spoke to the group. "Yeah, we should get going."

Payne followed suit, carrying Willow to the front door, so distracted by kissing her that he almost knocked her head into the wall. Understandably, they were taking their celebration home. I was happy for them, but the hangover, mixed with the adrenaline of oversleeping, then the surprise of Willow's good news seemed like too much at once.

Feeling drained, I sat on the sofa and leaned back as far as I could into the over-sized cushions. What a damn day already.

Navie sat beside me, her weight barely noticeable next to mine. "So, that was a lot."

"It was," I agreed. Payne was going to be a father. It wasn't that the idea was too much to grasp, it was just who would ever truly be ready for that kind of news? The responsibility for rearing a child was overwhelming. I would guess even to someone prepared. Which Payne was not.

"I was talking about you guys spying on us. I've known about the pregnancy for a day now."

"Right."

"I'll grab a bottle of water while you think about how you're going to explain yourself." Navie walked toward the kitchen, leaving me alone with my conscience.

I pushed my head deeper into the cushions. I'd rather fall into oblivion than tell her I was jealous. Guess we'd see if she was the kind of girl who thought staking my claim was cute, or if it just made her angry. Either way, I could handle her reaction as long as she didn't show me her own video holding a pregnancy test after I explained myself. She'd worked too hard to accomplish her goals, and I didn't exactly want to be a part of anything that stood in her way of doing that.

CHAPTER 18
NAVIE

I WAS a sucker for anything romantic. And Trevor being jealous of the beautiful specimen that was a Magic Mike dancer somehow fell into that category. Even though the notion was somewhat barbaric, it made me feel wanted and looked after. So, I took it easy on him.

"How come you went to all that trouble?" I took a seat on the end of the couch, nodding over to the table of electronics. Tucking my bare feet under my body, I leaned back on the arm, pulling a large pillow onto my lap.

Trevor growled in annoyance. But he seemed more frustrated with himself than my asking the question. "I literally have no idea what happened. We started out at Melton's. Then, before I knew it, we were arguing because Gage's cell phone screen wasn't big enough, which led us here, watching it on my hundred-inch television like you guys were some sort of reality show."

I shook my head in disappointment as he told his pathetic story. I laid it on thick for apology reasons. "Why didn't you just text me? I would have told you where we were. We weren't doing anything that would have upset you, Trevor."

"That's what you think?" His eyebrows pinched in disbelief. "You obviously don't know me very well if you think some former fucking frat boy dancing behind my girlfriend, his leather pants expanding by the second, doesn't upset me." His gaze narrowed, causing a deep indention between his brows. "It does. Very much so."

"Are you referring to the club? I thought you were upset about the show we went to."

"That too, while we're on it. How would you like it if I went to a strip club? Hmm? You'd be okay with naked women dancing around me while I enjoyed the show?"

I stared at him, dumfounded. I'd never thought about it like that. The dancers were stripping here and there, but they never got naked. For me, the show had been more about their dancing and the music than it had been about them losing their clothes or admiring their bodies.

"Okay." I sat up straight, ready to state my defense. "First of all, I never saw any frat boys. I truly have no idea what you're talking about where some guy in leather pants danced behind me. Secondly, you're right. In reference to the Magic Mike show, I never thought about the stripping part of it." He rolled his eyes and let a half laugh escape his lips. "It was more about the showmanship," I tried to explain.

"Right. Showmanship."

His mocking annoyed me. "You know what? I'm trying to be honest here. Just because your conscience won't allow you to see something like that without impure thoughts doesn't mean I'm the same. Did I enjoy the show? Absolutely. Did I envision myself going home with a fireman after? No."

"Look, it's not that I think you wanted to go home with someone after. And just for the record, I'd never cheat on you. Never. Not in the flesh and not in my mind. Got it?" His body scooted closer to mine. Before I knew it, he was holding my hand, and my lips were searching for his.

"I'm sorry." I broke away from him, intent on fixing our situation. "I wasn't trying to imply that. Just saying that you have nothing to fear."

"Same here, babe. I'm sorry too." Trevor's free hand slid down his face, covering his five o'clock shadow. He sighed, seeming frustrated. "I overreacted. It's not like you did anything wrong. I guess it just surprised me, seeing you so…free."

"I get it. I know I'm normally more reserved. But something I learned about myself recently is that it's in there, that freedom. I've just covered myself up for so long, being who other people want me to be." I blinked twice, remembering how amazing being somewhere where no one knew me or the struggles I faced daily had felt. "And you know what?"

"What?"

"I loved being that girl. I wasn't nervous or preoccupied. When I was there with Willow and Lena, I literally didn't think—or overthink—about anything. My mind wasn't constantly turning over, wondering what my next move should be, or how I was being perceived by trying to figure it all out."

Trevor frowned. "Come here." He wrapped his arms around me, hugging me so tight, I grunted. "I love you. I love who you are and whoever you want to be. I never want you to feel like your growth will alter us. You'll change. I'll change. We're human, Navie."

"I know that. I guess I've just never been completely sure why I was hiding the real me. Or why I felt like I needed to. And now that I've been living here, being around you and the girls, I actually have friends. Genuine friends. I don't have to conceal anything, and it feels a bit weird, to be honest."

Pulling me into a soft headlock, he placed a kiss on the top of my head. "That's because you're a weirdo, baby."

Swiping a quick jab to his ribs, I broke free and giggled. "Are we good? I feel like this got deeper than it should have. I made it heavy."

"We are better than good. And I'm going to work on my…newly developed jealous tendencies. While you continue to work on being honest with yourself, and we'll go from there. Sound good?"

"Thank you for supporting me. It means a lot."

"I'll love you at the beginning of your career. I'll love you in the middle of a family crisis with your dad. And I'll love you while you figure things out inside that pretty head of yours." His palm swept over my hair, causing me to close my eyes at his touch. "You're it for me. I got you. Until the day I die, I got you, okay?"

Nothing would ever soothe me the way he did. His presence was like my own personal elixir. And I knew he was it for me too.

"You're the sweetest man I know."

"Keep that between us. I can't have the guys thinking I'm soft now that I'm not in the cage anymore."

I rolled my eyes but grinned. "I'll keep our secret if you do something for me."

"Oh yeah?" he teased, reading my meaning.

I climbed on top of his lap and hauled his T-shirt over his head. "I may need you to make me forget that Magic Mike show. I know I told you earlier it was nothing, but for some reason, that fireman's abs keep popping back up in my mind, almost on replay, and—"

Before I could finish, Trevor stood with me in his lap. He held me tight with one hand, while tugging my shirt over my head with the other. His nimble fingers unhooked my bra before we entered our bedroom, and my jeans were unbuttoned before he dropped me on the bed. I giggled at his intensity, as if I was some love-drunk teenager, anticipating what would come next. Except I knew exactly what would come next. The passion blazing behind his irises emboldened me.

"You won't be able to drive past a firehouse without thinking about me by the time I'm done with you."

"My hero," I sighed as he jerked my jeans down with such vigor, I knew for a fact when he was done with me, I wouldn't be able to recall the word fireman. "But I have another idea," I crooned.

Fully naked, I wrapped my leg around his neck like I would in a take-down, but I slowly rolled him onto his back. His abdomen sank in as my fingers unbuttoned his jeans, leaving me almost giddy from his reaction. My gaze found his as I undressed him, my mouth watering at the sight of him. I loved that he had zero inhibitions. It was as if his confidence gave me a sense of buoyancy, where I knew without a doubt whatever way I chose to show him my love, he would not only accept it, he would love it.

Teasing him with my lips, I placed soft kisses from his chest to his most private part. Glancing up at him before I took him into my mouth, I licked the tip of him and smiled when he growled and closed his eyes in full appreciation.

Suckling, I took my time, hoping to show him how much I loved making him feel good. His hands massaged my head, relaxing me, almost too much. My thoughts quickly went from wanting to eat him up, to appreciating him; to learning every inch of him. Languid licks and soft kisses seemed to turn him on even more.

"I literally have no words." Trevor sighed in gratitude.

I rolled off him, dizzy from endorphins I never even knew existed. My body was completely limp. I couldn't have thrown a punch if someone had offered me money. "I like you speechless."

Feeling playful after sorting myself out, I pinched his side. His dimples showed themselves, leaving a deeper imprint the more he smiled. I leaned over, kissing his chin once before nuzzling into his neck.

"If silence is the price I have to pay, consider it my daily contribution."

"Since you've already paid today…" I scraped my teeth across the soft hairs on his jawline.

His large hands found two handfuls of my bare ass cheeks, pulling me back on top of him. The bottoms of my feet slipped up his calves, then back down to his own feet, massaging his legs as I stretched out. Rotating my hips, I ground into him, arching my back.

Trevor groaned, and with little to no effort, he flipped me on my back, taking complete control. Skin to skin, his large hand cupped my breast, massaging slightly as he took my nipple into his mouth. My toes dug deep, scratching and clawing at whatever skin I could dig into.

"God, you feel good."

"Please," I begged, arching my back.

"Please what, Blue?" The endearing sound his voice usually held when he teased me about my name was absent. He grunted as his arousal slid along my center, practically melting me on the spot.

My breathing hitched, and a moan escaped. I needed him inside me twenty seconds ago. I wiggled my hips until he aligned at my opening. My lips found his as he took my not-so-subtle hint and pushed forward, sinking inside me. I let out a small sigh, then a breathy whimper. My tummy tumbled at the feel of him entering me so deeply, creating a magical moment where I could have sworn I was floating.

Reaching for the headboard, I eagerly turned my body over to Trevor, basking in all that he was giving me.

"I cannot get close enough to you, baby. I can't. Get. Far. Enough. Inside. You." His grunts paired perfectly with each thrust. I submitted to each movement, allowing my body, mind, and spirit to align with his like the night stars. And when he collapsed on top of me, after pushing us both to our limit, I held his weight, closing my eyes until my breaths evened out, pairing with his, our hearts linking us together by their beats alone.

"Marry me."

My breathing faltered, causing me to inhale what little bit of saliva I had in my dried-out throat. I coughed once then twice, choking on my own spit. Trevor rolled off me at once, as if he'd just grasped that his words had caused a struggle.

Pushing myself up to a sitting position, I propped my back against the headboard for support. "What?"

Trevor was sprawled out, his head propped up the arm he was nonchalantly leaning on. "I'm serious. I love you. You love me. I'm not sure what we're waiting on."

"I wasn't aware we were waiting. It's just…" *It's just what?* I had no clue what I was trying to say.

"I can see by the look on your face that I freaked you out. I just thought…"

"I'm not freaked out. It's just—it's fast."

His face fell slightly, noticeably disagreeing with me, and by the look in his troubled eyes, he was disappointed.

The last thing I wanted to do was make him feel like I didn't love him. "I mean, I just got my second fight, and we were arguing a little while ago, and Willow's pregnant…" As per usual, my nerves took over, word vomit spewing every time I opened my mouth. I needed to stop talking.

But I was baffled—mostly confused by my own reaction. Why, after the best sex of my life, with the only person I'd ever truly loved, was I questioning his motive? Why was I making excuses for why we shouldn't get married? And why the hell was I not more upset by my not accepting his proposal?

"I don't see what Willow being pregnant has to do with me and you getting married. But I can see you're not ready, so let's just bury it, and when the time comes for us to discuss our future, we'll do it together—without me springing anything on you. Sound good?"

"Uh, yeah. Sure." I couldn't help but stare at him as he offered the simple solution. "Sounds good." It was obvious I'd hurt his feelings, but I didn't know how to fix it. It seemed evident I wasn't ready for marriage. My reaction alone had proven that.

My first instinct was to shower and find something to keep me busy for the rest of the day. Maybe some fresh air would give me clarity. But before I could even reach for the bedsheet to cover myself, Trevor slid out of bed and stole my idea of being alone in the shower.

I slumped down, lying sideways in his king-sized bed, feeling smaller than ever. If I'd done the right thing in turning down his proposal, why did it feel so wrong? If it had been the right thing to do, why was I lying in his bed trapped in the loudest silence I'd ever experienced, wishing like hell I could go back in time and say something different? A lone tear rolled down my cheek, his dark colored pillowcase absorbing it. I ran my fingertip across the damp fabric, praying I hadn't just found a way to ruin the best thing that had ever happened to me.

To say the rest of the day was awkward would have been an understatement. I couldn't shake the growing nerves threatening to spew from my mouth. I felt like I could puke. I needed to cry. My emotions were all over the place. I couldn't pinpoint why or how I'd gotten to a place where nothing felt familiar to me. Trevor had once said to me that he didn't know what he'd been fighting for. It scared me that I was already having those thoughts. It made me question if my training to cage fight was what I was supposed to be doing. It made me doubt myself, and I hated that feeling. Yet, there didn't seem to be anything I could do to steer my thoughts in a more positive direction.

And Trevor's shocking proposal. Had he thought about marrying me before? I'd only just found out that he'd been married previously. And as much as I loved him, it seemed too soon. I couldn't imagine planning a wedding on top of the other things I was attempting to accomplish. As an overwhelming sense of dread filled my gut, I picked up my phone. I wasn't sure if the phone call I planned to make would make me feel better or worse, but one thing I did know, was I could always count on honesty.

After quickly dressing, I hurried down the hallway and out to the back patio. Pulling my father's name up on the screen, I hit send before I had time to talk myself out of it.

"What, Navie?"

I pulled the phone away to make sure I'd dialed my father's number. "Preston?"

"What?"

"Where's Dad?"

"In a meeting."

"Without his phone?"

"He's in his office. I'm busy."

"Wait!" I whisper-yelled, afraid he was going to hang up on me. When he didn't hang up, I took the opportunity to try to have a normal conversation. "How are you?"

"Peachy. My sister's trying to ruin a company I plan on taking over in the near future, and my father can't find his ass from a hole in the ground around the office. Basically, you've ruined my life. How are *you*, sister?"

I held a groan inside and peered back at the sliding glass door. "I'm not trying to ruin anything."

"Keep telling yourself that. In the meantime, I'm working around the clock to blackball anything and everything Trevor Steele touches."

"Why would you do that?"

"Because you didn't want to do things the easy way, Navie. Maybe fucking with your boyfriend's shit will put things into perspective for you."

"You're a horrible person."

"That's what you keep telling me."

I ended the call, knowing nothing good was going to come of it. I couldn't believe my own brother was willing to go to such lengths to hurt me. Wiping my eyes with the back of Trevor's T-shirt, I sniffed and stood. If Preston was telling the truth, and I really thought he was, he would stop at nothing to ruin Trevor and there was no way I could let that happen. Not after everything Trevor had given for his gym and the people in it. Fight or flight? I wasn't intimidated, I was pissed. There was no way I'd ever set Trevor up for failure. Especially when I knew how much the gym and the guys he'd handpicked to train there meant to him. Putting Trevor's success at stake wasn't something I was willing to do. Not when I knew for a fact my brother was cavalier enough to attempt it. I knew what I had to do before my first tear dried. I'd brought the chaos to Trevor's front door, not the other way around, and that made me feel like shit. Less than—and more than anything—a burden.

CHAPTER 19
TREVOR

I FUCKED UP. Bad. As in, there was no going back or begging for forgiveness. The words had slipped from my mouth before my brain knew what I was saying. I'd asked Navie to marry me. I hadn't even asked her. I *told* her to do it. That wasn't just a lame proposal; it was downright wrong. She deserved more.

Exactly what I feared would happen came to light over the following weeks. At first, I figured I'd give her space. Maybe she felt weighed down by the heaviness of marriage. It was a huge step for anyone, including myself. Hell, I never expected myself to even consider the idea again, but Navie had changed my whole outlook on everything. I never wanted to be without her, and that offset my insecurities.

Instead of feeling burned by her immediate aversion to the idea, I tried to remain level-headed. I didn't want to take offense or feel rejected. I was well aware of how Navie operated. One ounce of doubt clouded her judgement, causing her to feel so overwhelmed by the situation, she folded like a cheap suit. So, in light of the hurt she'd caused me, I attempted a more mature approach, hoping to show her things didn't have to change between us just because one of us was ready to dive in headfirst, while the other needed time to process.

My good intentions backfired, as good deeds often did. Instead of small talk, late-night cuddles, and the occasional Adam Sandler comedy, we tiptoed around each other, only discussing her upcoming fight or things she needed to do to improve inside the cage. We'd managed to have sex exactly two times, but I had initiated the contact both times. Afterward, I held her, same as always, but things felt different.

Thinking we could straighten things out after her match, I decided not to bring up the elephant in the room, fearing the distraction would cause more harm. Besides, she was in the infancy stages of change—she'd admitted that after she returned from Las Vegas. Who didn't need time to sit alone with their thoughts in their twenties? I sure as hell did. And I gladly took more than my twenties to figure shit out. I knew better than anyone people reacted to life in all kinds of ways. There was no how-to book when it came to navigating it. Everyone was different. The last thing I should do was push Navie in a direction she didn't want to go in on her own. She'd end up resenting me, and I didn't want that.

On the night of Navie's second match, I found myself making rounds, determined to burn off some excess energy. The buzz inside the gym geared up, taking on a life of its own. Glancing around the crowd, I realized it had grown by about fifty people since her last match. That was solid progress. I'd never tell her, because it could have discouraged her, but female fights tended to struggle with a decent fan base. I wasn't sure why. Ask any dude if he'd like to watch a wrestling match between two hot girls in sports bras and tiny shorts, and one hundred percent of them would say hell yes.

I met Navie in the locker room, ready to calm her in any way I could. "You've got this, babe."

She nodded, but remained silent as we walked toward the cage. I swallowed the huge-ass lump that had gathered in my throat, my gut rumbling from the mere sight of her. I didn't have a good feeling.

"There's a lot of people here." Navie's eyes swept across the stands, a nervous air surrounding her.

"Don't worry about them. Just focus on your opponent." I rubbed her shoulders, surprised by the tightness in them. She'd had a massage just three days ago.

"Okay." She turned toward the center of the cage without so much as a nod to me. "I'm ready."

She wasn't ready. I could see it and feel it as well. I wanted nothing more than to grab her by the waist, pull her back into the corner, and end the whole thing before it even started. But something kept me from voicing my opinion. What if I said something and she didn't think I believed in her? Or worse, that I was the same as her family and didn't support her? It was her fight; her moment in time, so instead of protecting her like I wanted to do, I remained silent and watched from the sidelines as the referee signaled the go-ahead.

"Get low! Stay low, Navie!" I yelled from the corner.

Payne stood next to me. "She's not grounded," he said, just as Navie went down to the mat from a cross kick to the ribs.

Her body recoiled, and the pain in her eyes crushed me. When she had started the journey in cage fighting, I had been somewhat intrigued. Cage fighting took power, endurance, patience, and mental strength. I enjoyed watching her grow with each practice, proving to herself that she could do it. But now that she was my girl, the person I loved most in the whole world, watching her fail tortured me. Not that she didn't have what it took—I knew she did—but watching her take hit after hit, unable to defend herself the way I knew she could, made me question whether or not she even wanted it anymore. It was as if her determination; her shear willpower had left her body, leaving no more than a shell of the fighter she was only weeks ago.

The bell sounded, and she stumbled over to me.

"What's going on?" I asked, thinking she'd be able to explain.

"I fucking suck. That's what's going on," she snapped.

I flinched at her tone and looked to Payne, hoping he could give her the encouragement she needed to pull herself up and out of the hole she was in.

"Yeah, we can tell. Either woman up or quit. You're getting murdered out there, and we don't want to watch it." His eyes were crystal clear. He said what he meant and meant what he said.

I didn't disagree with him, but his delivery could have been softened a bit. Especially when he was talking to my woman. I clenched my teeth, knowing arguing with him wouldn't help Navie.

Silence surrounded us, growing thicker by the second as Navie took a sip of water then spit it out. The crease between her beautifully shaped eyebrows grew deep as she kept her response to herself. Without a word, she made her way back to the center of the cage for another round.

I glanced at Payne, who shook his head in disgust. I knew he blamed me, even though he didn't know what he was blaming me for. He hadn't known about the space that had been growing over the past couple of weeks between Navie and myself, and I hadn't offered any hints. But I was certain in that moment he knew I'd fucked with her mind somehow and was the reason she was taking a beating out there.

After three rounds, two jabs straight to the face without so much as a hand to block the onslaught, and ten seconds flat on the cage mat, the match was over. It took everything inside me not to run and catch Navie the instant I saw the second punch from her opponent was going to land firm. Payne held my arm tight, forcing me to wait until the ref called it.

Terrified, I made it to her on the mat in seconds. Seeing her so lifeless nearly broke me.

"Navie." I patted her cheek. "Come on, baby. Open your eyes."

"Trevor?"

I exhaled the breath I'd been holding. Her tender voice broke something inside of me. What was I doing letting her fight in cages? She was hurt, and I'd not only helped train her, given her free rein at my gym with professional fighters, but I'd also encouraged her.

"I got knocked out?" She tried to sit up but fell against me at the last second. The crowd buzzed, and I'd just noticed the noise for the first time. I nodded to Payne, giving him the go-ahead to start herding them out.

"Yeah. She got you pretty good. You feel okay? Remember what day it is?"

"I'm good. Just rung my bell." She sat up then attempted to stand.

With a little help, she succeeded, and met her opponent in the corner, congratulating her. Willow, Lena, Gage, Tommy, and Payne made a beeline for her when she exited the cage. I watched them follow Navie to the locker room, still stunned she hadn't so much as looked back at me on her way.

Impending doom filled my gut. I couldn't put my finger on it exactly, but it felt like the end. The distance between us had begun to take on a life itself, spreading like wildfire in an open field and the moment she was hurt and hadn't turned to me for comfort, I knew soul-deep whatever happened from that point forward, it wasn't going to be good for me.

I waited quietly in the background as Navie pulled her sweatpants over her shorts, then slipped into an over-sized hoodie. Willow hadn't left her side, and Navie continued to assure our friends she was fine. I could see from a mile away that she wasn't.

The ride home was silent. I didn't attempt to console her, and she never acted like she wanted it. I fought the urge to question what was happening between us. I realized something significant was occurring, but not knowing what that something was, had me on edge. Glancing at Navie in the cab of my Jeep, I could see plainly in the darkness, I wasn't going to receive any answers. The detachment, at least psychologically, couldn't have been further. Reading her mood, I knew I should have kept my questions and my concerns to myself, but my heart wouldn't allow that. I couldn't stand seeing her and not recognizing her. That made me feel worse than the thought of her being angry at me.

After grabbing her bag, I led us through the front door, hoping once she showered and we got settled in for the night, she'd open up. She didn't.

"Can we talk?"

"I don't want to talk, Trevor."

I looked on as she moisturized her face, then her neck, and eventually ended with her elbows. She didn't glance up at me once. I took a seat on the end of my bed, hoping to fix what seemed to have been a hell of a lot deeper than a proposal rejection. She stood, and pulled on a pair of yoga pants, along with an oversized T-shirt. Which was not her normal sleeping attire.

"Where are you going?"

"I need some space."

I stood from the bed, confused. "What kind of space?"

"Just—space. I have a lot on my mind."

"Navie, slow down."

She glanced at me as she tied the laces on her sneakers. "I'm feeling overwhelmed, and I want to be alone. It has nothing to do with you."

"Just come to bed, let me hold you, and we'll figure it all out."

Shocked, I watched as she filled an overnight bag with some of her belongings and toiletries. "I can't. I just—need a minute. I know it doesn't make any sense, but it's what I want. I need to be alone for a while."

"A while?"

After zipping the bag, she pulled it over her shoulder. Her eyes glistened with fresh tears. I remained silent as she stepped toward me. She tilted her head so that we were staring at each other.

"If this is about the proposal—"

She shook her head. "It's about me, Trevor. I feel—lost. I need to spend some time with myself. It's like I've changed and nothing feels familiar to me."

"Okay." I didn't know what else to say. I wished I could give her every reason in the world to stay, to swear to her that I would fix it all for her, but I didn't think I could. What she was describing to me sounded like an inside job, one that no one but her could even attempt.

She placed her hand on my cheek. "I love you, I do. But—somewhere along the line, I realized I don't love me. The respect and consideration I have for you, I don't have for myself. I never have." Her eyes pleaded with me—for what, I didn't know. Maybe it was understanding. Or a quiet cry for help. I couldn't decipher it, but the tears that welled up behind my eyes after her admission felt like they weighed a hundred pounds each.

Pulling her into my arms, I squeezed, harder than ever before. I couldn't speak. I couldn't swallow, I longed to fix her. Her problems, or whatever horrific thoughts had brought her to a place where she didn't love herself. Or better yet, I wanted to destroy the purpose for it, but I knew I had to let her go. Just as she knew she had to leave. Dejected, my heart shattered into a million pieces as I watched my girl walk toward what she claimed was finding herself, leaving me feeling more lost than ever.

CHAPTER 20
NAVIE

"I'M REALLY SORRY, SIS." Willow rubbed my back for the tenth time while standing at the small countertop of the one-bedroom apartment I'd been able to find on short notice.

"Me too. I'm still not sure what happened," I admitted. It was like it had all come to a boil, and spilled over before I was able to turn the heat down. My family; my loss. The thought of barging into Trevor's life so selfishly, while my brother planned his demise behind the scenes three thousand miles away. The weight of the world pummeled me like a sucker punch. Without even knowing, utter failure in all aspects of my life crushed me like a bug.

"Maybe you just need a little time." She sounded hopeful.

"Maybe." I took a small sip of my coffee, not the least bit interested in drinking it. I'd only made it because she was being sweet and had shown up to check on me.

Turned out I wasn't much for talking, and Willow picked up on that. So after ten minutes of skating around the issues plaguing me, she said her goodbyes and we promised to catch up over lunch soon.

For the rest of the night, I wallowed in self-pity in the comfort of my own room. Which just served to make me sadder, as it reminded me how much I'd loved sharing a room with Trevor. I missed him. But all the emotions and misplaced thoughts I'd had bottled up for so long had finally spilled out, transforming me into a person I didn't even recognize.

Why couldn't I have just accepted his proposal and gone on to live happily ever after? I didn't question my love for him. So, why couldn't I just have done it, without feeling an overpowering amount of self-doubt? Like I didn't deserve it. Probably because once again, my brother was an asshole, and if he did follow through on his threat, I'd drown in the guilt.

I cried until I had nothing else to give. My heart had never been in worse shape. It physically hurt to breathe. The bruise had shown itself, tender to the touch, and my chest ached from not only the loss of Trevor, but also from the embarrassment of my failed fight. Time passed, sunlight turned into darkness, and I never moved from my spot on the bed, too wounded by the direction in which my life was going. And all of it—every single ounce of sadness I was feeling was my own fault.

Hour after hour, I tossed and turned, trying to get comfortable in my own bed.

My phone lit up, glowing bright in the darkened room. I picked it up, hoping it was Trevor.

Trevor: I miss you.

Tucking my phone under my chin, I smiled. God, he couldn't even see me, but those three words gave me hope. Hope that no matter what mistakes I'd made in our relationship, he still wanted me. The possibility kept me hanging on to something other than the deafening feeling of defeat threatening to purge my soul.

Navie: I miss you too.

I sent the text, sure of the words I'd written back, even though I wasn't certain of anything else. It was the weirdest feeling to love someone so much and to know he loved me too, but to not really know myself or what role I'd played in the life that had become my own.

How could he be so sure he loved me when I didn't even know who I was?

I couldn't have told someone my favorite color at the moment, as wretched as that sounded. It didn't feel good, being so uncertain of everything. I closed my eyes, praying for a decent night's sleep. Maybe since I was aware of the problems I faced, I would be conscious of finding the answers.

The following weeks crept by. In fact, I'd been able to count them because the hours felt like days. Seven. Seven weeks passed, giving me more than enough time to be by myself. I spent most of them creating spreadsheets, mirroring almost everything I'd learned from the business side of things from my time at the AFL. There were lots of things my father had fucked up. But his business was not one of those things. I studied other female fighters, gaining a ton of information. I learned who their agents were. Who their trainers were and more importantly, I learned there were more women training in cage fighting than I could ever have imagined. I also learned I was in less than one percent of the female population who couldn't get into the first book in the Twilight series. On the other hand, I'd binged watched *Schitt's Creek* three times.

Trevor and I stayed light and sincere on the days we crossed paths at the gym. I knew he wouldn't admit it, but he'd been staying in his office more often than not, and I was sure it was an attempt to give me the space I'd asked for. I assumed he'd had a talk with the guys, namely Gage, because my usual smartass friend hadn't uttered one word to me about Trevor and me taking a break…which was so not Gage.

"Come on, girl. You gotta give me more than that," Tommy urged, pushing my shoulder, knocking me off balance.

"I'm trying," I argued, straightening my stance.

"You're coming to my match tomorrow night, right?" he asked, changing the subject.

"Of course. I even switched shifts at work so I could be there." I punched once, twice, then gave him a roundabout kick.

"Damn, girl. You're getting good at those," Gage said, rounding the corner just in time to hear the smack echo off Tommy's glove.

I grinned, for once agreeing with him. "You better recognize, fool."

He choked on the water he'd just drank and shook his head, laughing. Moments like those were happening more and more often. I was finding my footing where friends were concerned, and it felt good. It was odd—focusing on friendships. But the moments I had with each one of them when Trevor wasn't around made me realize my connection with them didn't have to solely be based on my attachment to him.

Somehow, sharing jokes, funny stories, and drinks with my friends made me feel like I was my own person. Every conversation we had was based on our interests or our own opinions. Nothing involving the AFL or Trevor was ever even brought up. I hadn't thought about it much before, but I'd gone from being Richard Fuller's daughter, to Trevor Steele's girlfriend in a matter of weeks. It made sense now that I'd stepped back from everything. My plans for my future, getting where I thought I wanted to go had always been tied to someone else. And I hadn't recognized it at the time, but that made me feel tethered. Co-dependent. Two things I'd learned made me feel suffocated and somewhat inferior.

At Willow's request, I hung out with them more, intentionally working time in my schedule for simply screwing off. Weekend barbeques, bowling, rollerblading. She'd even talked me into participating in a garage sale, even though I didn't have much to contribute. On the day of the sale, it was unorganized at best. Gage had been in charge of posting the signs, and while the rest of us expected him to complete that task without messing it up, Payne knew better.

"You guys didn't make the signs? You know he's going to fuck that up, right?" he asked.

"Conner, it's a sign." Willow rolled her eyes. "What could he screw up?"

Her growing belly was the epitome of cuteness, if you asked any of us. Ask her, though, and you'd get a different answer. *It's in my way. It's heavy. My skin itches from being stretched.*

We offered support, but the only one who could truly turn her annoyance into humility was Payne. I wasn't sure how he did it, and I never asked. Seemed to me that they were just soulmates, her yin to his yang. Either way, it worked out; they always worked it out. Unlike Trevor and me. I frowned at the thought. He'd tried. I hadn't.

"Oh. My. God." Willow's voice brought me out of my thoughts. I looked up just as the garage door opened, shocked from the crowd of strangers. "I'm going to kill him," she said through clenched teeth.

My eyes widened in surprise, and I bit my bottom lip. What time had Gage put on the signs? There were at least fifty people waiting in their driveway for us to open the sale. We had two tables set up. *Two.* And with just three out of the ten pieces of furniture we needed to set out, we were nowhere near ready for customers.

Overwhelmed, we greeted them, and began moving at speeds reserved for people who ran track. I grabbed a couple of lamps, a tote, and three picture frames from the tubs in her garage. "Umm, why are people here? It's not supposed to start for an hour," I whispered to Lena as I placed the lamps on a table.

Noticing an older woman walking toward me, I changed my facial expression and smiled as she approached me.

"These a set?" she asked, pointing at the lamps.

"Uh, yes ma'am."

"How much?"

I turned back to the garage, hoping someone would know the answer. I didn't even know whose lamps they were, and they weren't priced. Tommy was barely awake, and Payne wouldn't know, nor would he care. "Let me ask."

"Are those lamps yours?" I asked Willow, pointing toward the gaudy set.

She rubbed her belly. "No, must be Gage's."

"Of course, because he's not even here." I sighed. "What do I sell them for?"

"I'd give them away. Who the hell buys cheetah print lamps?" Payne grunted.

"I'll text him." Tommy began typing on his phone as one of the weirdest scenes I'd ever witnessed derailed in front of us.

I covered my mouth as the older woman I'd just spoken with yelled at a younger blonde. "Hey! I had them first!"

"Give me the other one, bitch—" the blonde began as she snatched up the second lamp, but was interrupted by the older woman screaming at her friend.

"Shana, grab the cord!"

We looked on helplessly as two women argued over the animal print lamps, both grabbing whichever piece of the property they could reach. Other people milled around, paying no mind to the verbal incident taking place mere steps from them. I'd never seen anything like it. Not that I'd ever been to a garage sale before. When Willow had first mentioned having a sale, I thought it'd be a good idea to get rid of the old and start new. Plus, she was excited about the baby and was eager to start the nesting period, so Lena and I supported her.

The last thing I was interested in was refereeing a pair of middle-aged women over a couple of hideous lamps, but no one else stepped in to intervene. I glanced around, hoping for one of the guys to take charge, but that seemed unlikely when I witnessed Payne physically turn his back on the spectacle. Not only did he ignore the screaming match, he walked inside his house without a backwards glance. Thankfully, Gage and Trevor walked up the driveway just as I approached the women.

"Hey, hey, ladies. What's going on?" Gage asked, in his I'm-the-man-of-your-dreams voice.

"I had them first!" One lady snapped.

"She only had one of them!" Another argued.

"I see. Well, these were actually mine. I must say that you both have impeccable taste." He grinned and wrapped both of his arms around each lady, sending them both into an awkward cougar-like swoon. "But what I'm wondering is, if there's anything I can do to make you girls see that splitting up the pair would actually be beneficial to both of you? You know, taking the *sharing is caring* approach." He squeezed them both into his side, making them grin like fools.

"Gag me," I said under my breath.

"Agreed." Trevor's voice wrapped around my neck, caressing it with the perfect amount of hot breath.

My mouth spread into a genuine grin at the sight of him. I scanned his appearance, noting the perfect red T-shirt, just a smidge tighter around his biceps. His black basketball shorts hung low on his hips. Black and gray running shoes were left untied and his hair was covered by a black baseball cap turned backward. I wasn't sure how long I stared at him. He looked handsome, but also peaceful. Confident. And more than that—relaxed.

"Hey," I greeted.

"Hey. How's it been going?" he asked.

"Pretty good, I guess. Just been training a lot. Not much new."

He didn't respond, which made me antsy. I assumed we were going to small talk it, the same way we had for the past couple of months. But he had other plans.

"Why don't you come over after this? I have a few things I want to talk to you about."

"Like what?" I held a hand up to block the sun.

Trevor grabbed my arm and turned me in a circle so that the sunlight blinded him instead of me. "Not here."

"Okay," I agreed. "I think this will be over at noon."

He cocked an eyebrow. "Noon? That's not what the signs say."

"What do the signs say?" I looked back at Gage, but he was signing his autograph on both the lamps, grinning like a fool. It seemed as though he'd talked both women into sharing the lamps as long as he gave each one of them his signature.

"Signs say the sale is from 6:00 a.m. to 4:00 p.m."

I placed my palm on my forehead. Willow was going to murder Gage, and there would be nothing any of us could do about it. He'd signed his own death wish by messing with a pregnant woman who'd given him specific instructions which he'd obviously ignored. Willow had purchased four signs which meant they were spread out with her address on them, inviting strangers to their house practically until dinner time. Folding my lips inside my mouth, I groaned. Even Payne's strength would be no match for her pregnant hormones.

"I'll break it to her." I sighed, wondering if volunteering was my best move. It seemed I had a soft spot for Gage, no matter how many times the dufus screwed up.

Willow sat behind a white table where she was collecting money from the customers who'd scooped up the merchandise as fast as we had been able to put it out. She seemed a little overcome by the number of customers in the line, so I began adding the items up from the next person in line to help.

"Aren't you Trevor Steele?"

At the sound of a young girl's voice, my gaze found Trevor, who was casually sitting right behind me in a lawn chair. She stood beside him, her mother in line to pay for their items.

Trevor grinned at the little girl. "That's me."

"Can I have a picture with you?"

"Uh, sure."

He looked uncertain and honestly a little uncomfortable. Since his retirement, he hadn't been bothered much by fans asking for photographs, and I knew he preferred the privacy.

Hoping to ease his discomfort, I tried to help. "Hey, why don't you guys step on the other side of the house? That way, no one will be gawking. That is so embarrassing, isn't it?" I asked the young girl. It wasn't, but she didn't know I was only doing it so no one else would see them and ask him for pictures of their own.

Trevor smirked and nodded, thanking me silently. I continued to add the items up for the elderly woman I'd been helping, since the little girl and her mother had finished paying.

Two, four, five, I love him.

I stuffed the shirts, shorts, and two plates in a bag, and shook off my thoughts. "That'll be five dollars, please."

"You sure are a pretty little thing," the sweet older woman complimented me.

"Oh." My cheeks reddened at her flattery. "Thank you so much."

"She is, isn't she?" Gage asked, chomping on a Pop-Tart as if he were in his own kitchen.

I shook my head and gave the woman a sincere smile, thanking her again.

I heard Gage yelp and then mutter, "Damn, man. I was joking."

I turned to see Trevor return from his picture, taking a seat in the lawn chair as if he hadn't just slapped the shit out of his friend. His demeanor was cool as ever, but Gage was rubbing the back of his head and glaring at Trevor. It didn't mean anything, not really. But the butterflies in my tummy didn't know that. They fluttered around in there the same as they always did when Trevor showed any kind of emotion regarding me. It had been a while since I'd been privy to anything but professionalism from him. It warmed my soul.

"I have an appointment to get to, but I'll be back before you close at four. I didn't get a chance to look around."

Breaking my moment of bliss, I glanced up to see the next person in line speak to Willow. The woman spoke casually, but my eyes grew wide, knowing she'd spilled the beans about Gage's incompetence before any of us had the opportunity to. With all the customers, and my heart swelling because of Trevor, I hadn't had a chance to tell her about the signs.

"Four?" Willow asked, handing the lady back her change.

"Your signs say four."

Willow inhaled so deep, her shoulders rose two inches. She gave the lady a tight smile, then stood quickly, almost turning her lawn chair over. Luckily, the woman walked away before Willow spoke.

"You!" Willow's shrill voice cut through the air, her eyes burning like a wildfire in Gage's direction. "Since you don't like to listen when I speak, *you*, my friend, will be out here with this sale until four o'clock this afternoon. My feet hurt. My back hurts. And these crowds of people have literally caused an ulcer in my stomach. My baby does not thank you, Gage Dawson."

"What? Everyone knows traffic picks up after lunch. You're pissed because I tried to get you more customers?"

"Watch it, man." Payne stared at Gage.

"I can handle myself, baby. Thank you, though." Willow kissed her husband and walked over to face Gage. She looked like a child next to him, minus the protruding belly, of course. "I get that you were trying to help, but when you want to do that, you need to ask the person having the sale, which you did not do. Look, I know I'm grumpy. I am perfectly aware that I am not myself right now. And I'm sorry, I really am, but Gage..." Willow burst into tears, bringing her palm up to his chest. She rested her head on her hand. Gage wrapped his arms around her, whispering in her ear.

"All right, I think it's time to lay down. You need to rest." Payne turned her around, then picked her up, bridal style, and carried her into their home.

Lena shook her head. "God, I feel so bad for her. This pregnancy is making her fucking crazy. I've never seen her get upset like that over something so small."

"Well, I feel like shit." Gage threw the remaining corner of his Pop-Tart in the trash.

I squeezed his bicep and gave him a small smile. "Don't. I know you were only trying to help. I'll stay here for the sale." He really should have checked with her, but I truly did feel sorry for him.

"Me too. We'll take care of it. I say we take all the money we make and get her a kick ass present for the baby," Lena suggested.

"Yes. Great idea," I added.

"Everything good, man?" Trevor asked Payne as he walked back out into the garage, sans Willow.

"Yeah, she's...overwhelmed. I told her this garage sale was a bad idea," Payne said as he looked around, taking in all the customers who were still checking out the merchandise.

Trevor whispered in Gage's ear, signaling to Tommy. I wondered what he was telling them, as they all began walking toward his Jeep. Before I could ask, they all jumped in and left without so much as a goodbye. Lena and I shared a dour look, knowing we were about to work our asses off while they chose to take a very unwelcomed break.

Thirty minutes later, two U-Haul trucks backed into the driveway, with two workers in each truck. All four men began loading the items from our garage sale into the trucks, each taking whatever handfuls they could carry.

Trevor pulled up to the curb a moment later. Meeting him at his Jeep, I asked, "What's going on?"

"These guys are going to take everything to a local shelter."

"A shelter?" I was still confused just as Lena walked up behind me.

"I bought Willow out, and I'm giving it to charity." He shrugged.

"Trevor." My hand covered my heart at his gesture. "That's really nice of you."

Trevor hopped out of his Jeep, then pulled his shades down over his eyes. "There's no sense in her having a heart attack over a bunch of junk she wants to get rid of. We'll split the money between her and you guys. Half for her, half for you guys to buy her a nice gift."

Lena beat me to him, wrapping her arms around his waist, pulling him tight. The gesture reminded me that they'd been friends long before I had come along. I followed her lead and leaned in for a quick hug, timid at first, given that it had been a while since he and I'd had any physical contact.

He waited me out, leaving the amount of contact we shared up to me. I wanted it all. All the connection he would give me. But I knew we had an audience too, and the hug couldn't last because our friends were studying our every movement. Not that I cared about being judged, I just wanted whatever moments I had with Trevor to be private. Especially since we'd spent some time forcing ourselves apart. Even though the separation was more me than him, I could tell in the times we were around each other, that he held back too.

"Thank you. That was really sweet."

"You're welcome." His Adam's apple bobbed once, then twice.

I pulled back and looked up into his eyes, my gaze hungry with anticipation. The moment was full of reminiscent thoughts. His hands on me. His giving nature. All of the things I admired in him; the things I loved about him coming to a head after months of not experiencing any of them in real time.

"I miss you, Indigo."

At the sounds of his words, I couldn't find a care in the world that our friends were still around us. I trembled at his nickname and swallowed my sigh of relief. Pulling his body back against mine, I pressed into him as hard as I could, releasing every ounce of scattered emotions I had inside me into the embrace. I nuzzled against him, sweeping my cheek across his wide chest. "I miss you too." My voice wavered.

My brother's threat lurked in the back of my mind, and I couldn't help but think he might have been bluffing. He hadn't made any moves, although that could have been because I'd distanced myself from Trevor. I hated not knowing for sure if he'd really hurt me by hurting Trevor. Yet, when I looked at Trevor, I was reminded I was miserable either way.

We held each other for meager seconds, but it felt like a lifetime. To feel him again after going so long without it made the loss more tangible.

"Let's go, lovebirds. I've got a date," Tommy interrupted us.

Trevor released me. "I'll see you at my place?"

"Okay," I agreed.

We all worked diligently, me appeasing the few straggling customers. Tommy and Gage went to remove the signs that were put out. Payne checked in on Willow, who'd fallen asleep, before he came back out to help load the trucks. He thanked Trevor over and over again. I'd heard him say something about Willow's harebrained schemes, but continued with my tasks, trying not to eavesdrop on the guys' conversation. I smirked with confirmation that men griped to each other the same as women did.

"Tell Willow I'll call her," I said to Payne as Lena and I headed out to my car once the driveway and garage were clear of any evidence of the garage sale from hell.

"Will do," he assured us.

After dropping Lena off, I tried relaxing in a bath before going over to Trevor's, but it turned out to be a lame attempt. The book I'd been knee-deep into the night before hadn't taken my mind off him either. There seemed like so much to say, but nothing I considered deemed meaningful. Nothing felt right for my reasons to need time away from him when he did nothing but make me feel good about myself. After unloading the dishwasher, I decided putting our face-to-face off any longer was only making me more anxious. We had things to square away and me avoiding them wasn't going to make them disappear. As I drove toward his house, I didn't think about the fear of my brother's desperate actions, nor did I consider ways to explain my moment of insanity to him. All I knew was I missed him.

I missed us.

CHAPTER 21
TREVOR

I'D DONE a load of laundry, watched two videos of Payne's and Tommy's next opponents, knocked the shit out of a bucket of golf balls, and rearranged the potted plants Navie had placed outside by my pool while waiting for her to arrive. My nervous energy was a foreign feeling, to be honest. I'd not felt so out of sorts since my first pro fight. Hell, probably not even then.

I reduced my racing heart by taking slow, steady breaths. I was ready to face her head on, to tell her the whole reason I'd mentioned needing to talk to her at the garage sale. Even if we weren't technically together, I knew we'd end up there eventually. There was no other option for me. Plus, I'd be damned if I let her sleazy brother turn the tables and give his sneaky version of the meeting we'd had before I had a chance to explain the situation to her myself. Richard had sworn we'd be alone for the face-to-face, but of course when I showed up, Preston was present. The last thing I was inclined to do was breathe the same air as that asshole, but I thought—naïvely—I could somehow help repair the situation. That had obviously been a mistake on my part, but I knew if I ever wanted another chance with Navie, being honest with her before Preston could lie about it, was the only way to go. I had to keep the lines of communication open.

I opened the door, stunned once again by her beauty. "Hey,

come in."

"Thanks." She slid her satchel over her head and placed it on the large table in my entry way, the same way she'd done a hundred times before. Perfectly comfortable. Perfectly normal.

Good.

"You want something to drink? Eat?"

"No, thank you."

"I know things are—up in the air right now, but I need to talk to you about something."

She took a seat on one end of the couch, losing her sneakers as she pulled her feet up on the cushions. Man, I missed that.

"I had a meeting with your father," I blurted. No use in beating around the bush.

A look of confusion crossed her face. "Why would he want a meeting with you?"

I could sense her perplexity, which was to be expected. "He—he wanted to talk to me about you." I held her gaze before divulging the rest. "And I admit, there were a few things to get off my chest too."

"What about me?"

"So, I'm not going to lie to you. He piqued my interest when he contacted me. I know it wasn't my place to meet with him and discuss you, but I was interested in finding out why he was willing to contact me, given how he acted the last time we spoke. I was curious about what his angle was, you know?"

She remained still, not speaking but nodding her head in understanding. Her blue irises were the color of dark, rolling thunder clouds. A fierce need rose to wrap my arms around her and calm the storm inside her.

"He saw your last fight. He wanted to know about your training, and—he asked about us. He wasn't aware that we were no longer an item."

"You told him we broke up?"

"I did," I admitted. The look of defeat on her face made me cringe. It was as if I'd cheated on her, the way her body folded forward and her lips turned downward into the slightest frown. It hurt me to see her like that.

"So now that he knows I'm completely by myself, he's going to strike? Is that what you're saying?"

"No. Well, I don't know. I'm just telling you that we did have a conversation about it, and he was told the truth. I'm not going to lie to anyone about me and you. Ever. I've been there and done that, and all it does is cause more trouble. I love you, Navie. I've never stopped. I won't ever stop."

She took in my words but still didn't respond, so I continued on.

"He was satisfied with a simple response. He didn't ask any more questions, and I didn't offer any answers, other than we were living separately."

"All right." She clasped her hands together. "So, that was all he wanted?"

"It's never that simple with your dad, you know that."

"Yeah." She sighed.

"He asked me about your career goals inside the cage." I paused, not wanting to be the reason she'd be upset but knowing I was about to hurt her with the truth of the matter. But if I'd learned anything during the course of our relationship, it was lying to her was not an option. Not even when the truth hurt.

"And you said?"

"I said…it concerned me."

"*Concerned* you?" Her harsh reaction caused me to flinch. I knew she'd be sad; I hadn't banked on anger.

"Most people train for the cage ten years before they make their debut. I didn't take anything away from you. This is a tough sport. You don't have any idea what it was like for me to stand on the sidelines and watch someone beat the shit out of you, especially when that person has thirty fights worth of experience on you."

"So, you never believed in me? You lied to me the *whole* time I trained with you and Tommy? And for what?" She rose to her feet, pacing back and forth. "To get into my pants? To bag Richard Fuller's daughter?"

I rose to my full height, matching her anger. My blood boiled from her insult. "That's not true and you know it. I can't believe you just said that."

"Well, what do you expect me to say? We break up, have limited contact, then you tell me after all this time that you had a meeting with my father, the one person I told you doesn't believe in me, and never has." Tears strolled down her perfect porcelain face and my heart broke all over again.

"Navie, I swear it wasn't like that. Please, sit down and let me explain."

She wiped her eyes with the sleeve of her long-sleeved tee but calmed long enough to take a seat. "Go on. It can't get much worse, I guess."

That's debatable.

"First of all, our limited contact was me giving you space. Space you asked for. I wanted so many times to wrap you up in a hug, to kiss you, to swing you over my shoulder and take you home with me—where you belong—but I didn't. Because I knew what you were going through, even if you didn't. I've been there. No matter how much I love you, if you don't love yourself and believe in yourself, we will never survive." I should have taken a breath, more so to give her time to comprehend what I was saying, but my emotions took over, getting the better of me.

"You have to be in tune with who you are and who you want to be. It's not anything to be ashamed of. Every human has to go through it. We change. We evolve. You can't expect to be the same person you were even a few years ago. Not when your biggest influence was your father."

"I'm not ashamed of feeling like I need to figure things out for myself, Trevor. I was more ashamed of never knowing the answer to that question in the first place."

"I'll give you all the time you need. There's nothing wrong with you telling me you need a break and me giving it to you. It doesn't mean I don't love you. It means the opposite. Do you have any idea what I've gone through every single day, not being with you the way I want? It breaks my heart to see you and know you're not really mine anymore, even though in my heart it feels like you've never left."

Navie's eyes watered, and I could tell she was trying hard not to let more tears spill over. I just wasn't sure which part of what I'd told her made her want to cry. She nodded, almost to herself. "I appreciate you telling me what happened."

I watched in horror as she leaned forward and slipped her feet into her shoes. She was leaving. I couldn't let that happen.

"You're leaving? Are you angry?"

"Yeah," she answered and walked toward the front door. Her shoulders weren't slumped though. Her gait was normal, and as weird as it was, she did seem okay even though she'd just admitted to being angry.

"Because I was honest with you?"

Navie slipped her satchel over her body, then looked me straight in the eye. "No, Trevor. I'm angry because you know what I've been through. You knew what my father and my brother thought about me trying to get into the cage." Her expression was subtle; indifferent even. "And you still went in there and confirmed their feelings on the matter all the while negating mine. You gave them what they wanted, while giving me the one thing I didn't need. I don't need anyone else not believing in me. I didn't need the man I loved appeasing me on the outside, while knowing all along that I'd fail in the end."

I stood speechless. Shocked that she thought so little of me. That wasn't anywhere near what had happened. In fact, it was damn near the exact opposite of what had happened. My chest tightened, causing fury to bubble from the pit of my stomach. Instead of voicing my aggravation, I studied her, knowing how thin the ice was that we were skating across. I wanted to throw my fucking couch across the room. I couldn't understand how she could be so dense. I loved her. I wanted to spend the rest of my life with her when I swore I would never marry anyone else again. At one time, I would have bet my life on it. But her words; the finality behind her eyes told me that releasing my frustration wouldn't make the situation any better.

"I'm going to go. I'll—let you know when I'm ready to talk."

At the sound of the echo of the large wooden door closing behind her, I sat down, resting my elbows on my knees. Heavy air filled my lungs, and I wished I could somehow take back the conversation we'd had. Maybe not take it back, but somehow explain my actions better. She had it all wrong in the worst way.

The single reason I'd even taken the meeting with her father was to support her. To tell him how wrong he was about her and how his actions toward her would be met with resistance now that she had me in her life. Whether she was my girlfriend or not, he wasn't going to fuck with her head anymore. Not while I was around.

Richard Fuller threatened to have me harassed by the press when I swore to him that his daughter would be more successful than him, and I'd be there the whole time making sure of it. Once I realized his meeting was more about demeaning Navie and her abilities, I exploded on him. Obviously, I agreed with him when he talked about her lack of experience and I'd told her as much, but that didn't mean I wanted or expected her to give up. No, I wanted her to lean the fuck in. Work harder than anyone ever expected. Learn more than anyone thought achievable. I wanted her to have everything she'd ever spoken of and eventually see her dreams come true right before her eyes. Dreams she made happen on her own, through her own hard work and determination.

Instead of our meeting ending professionally, I told her father he could go fuck himself and Richard threatened Payne's contract due to my lack of respect. It was to be expected. Aside from being a shit father, he was one hundred percent narcissistic. It had taken everything in my power not to knock his fucking lights out for threatening me and trying to blackmail me.

Tears stung my eyes, wondering how the hell things had gone from bad to worse. When I saw Navie earlier, when she hugged me, the last thing I imagined when we finally had time alone was my intentions being misconstrued. Nor had I considered the fact that she would think my conversation with her father was picking at an old scab when I was truly only trying to help. I'd gone there prepared to do whatever it took to get him to back off.

Placing my head in my palms, I squeezed my eyes shut tight. I had to make things right. I had to square things away with Navie. The pain resonating inside me wasn't going to go away. No, it was going to overflow, forcing me to realize my greatest fear.

Living without her.

CHAPTER 22
NAVIE

"WHAT'S GOING ON? You haven't been to the gym in two weeks."

"Nothing," I lied, stepping around Tommy to gather the empty glasses from the table I was cleaning off. I expected him to show up sooner or later. Although I hadn't thought of him coming to talk to me while I was working.

He crossed into my line of sight and folded his arms over his massive chest. "I'm not stupid, Navie. Steele's a fucking grizzly bear lately. You're nowhere to be found…"

"We just—"

"Broke up?"

"Sort of." I frowned.

He followed me to the kitchen, hot on my heels, letting me know he wasn't going to let it go so easily. "So what? Because he couldn't get his shit together, you're giving up on your dream?"

I laughed, sarcastic as ever. "Some dream."

Tommy grabbed my upper arm, pulling me to the other side of the freezer. I went willingly, not wanting any of my co-workers to witness our little spat. "Are you fucking kidding me right now? You've worked your ass off for this. The first sign of defeat in your personal life, and you're ready to give up?"

I shook my head, knowing he'd never understand. "Tommy—it wasn't meant to be."

"The fuck you say. It's *your* dream, Navie. *You* decide what's meant to be."

I covered my face with my hands, not wanting him to see me so vulnerable. He pulled them away immediately, forcing me to face him. "Don't let anyone take this from you. This is where you sew yourself back up. Where you dig deep; see what you're made of. You can do this. I know you can."

"Tommy," I began as I leaned into him, still hoping no one could see me. "My brother threatened me."

"With what?" He scowled. "He doesn't have shit that you need. Not with us by your side."

I shook my head, but kept my eyes trained on his. "He told me he'd ruin Trevor and the guys who trained with him. He threatened *your* future, Tommy, and everyone else's."

"He threatened you with me? He put that shit on you?"

I could tell he was growing angrier with each word I spoke. I hated to admit what a sideshow my family was, but I was bursting at the seams holding it all in. I hadn't told Trevor because I knew he'd fly to California to kick Preston's ass himself. And there'd been no way I could have confided in Willow. She would have told Payne, and there was no telling what damage would have been caused to his professional relationship with my dad. I just didn't feel like I had anywhere to turn.

"Navie, you have to start living for yourself."

"I could never be so selfish."

"We're all big boys. Trust me, we can handle ourselves and Trevor—"

"No," I interrupted him. "I can't do that to him."

"But you can let them do that to you?"

Pausing, I glanced down and closed my eyes. What choice did I have?

"You can't live life in fear."

"I'm just being cautious while I figure things out."

"That's a damn lie, and you know it. You're being bullied, and you're letting them do it."

I knew he was right. Logically, I understood everything. It was being positive I had the inner strength to endure it that was the problem. "I don't know if I can do it."

"Yes, you do. There are a million reasons for you to quit, Navie, but if you can find one reason to stay; one reason to stick it out, that's all you need. Give yourself a chance to see what you can do. If you never try, you've already failed."

I hugged him, tight, never wanting to let go. He was the brother I wished Preston could have been. My mind had been a chaotic mess. Going from one extreme to the other. One minute I'd be psyched up, enriched in confidence, telling myself I could be whatever I wanted to be. The next, fear and anxiety crippled me, causing me to feel defeated and silly for thinking I could accomplish something so farfetched. I had to pick myself back up. It made sense if I wanted to be successful at anything in life. Wallowing any longer would just keep me down in the dumps.

"Okay." I stepped away from him and lifted my chin. "You're right. I wanted this. I *want* this," I corrected myself. Taking the first step was the hardest. And then after that step, I just needed to keep stepping.

"You gotta know what's at stake, doll. It's not just your reputation in the sport or what your family holds over your head. It's how you feel about yourself. That's what will carry you through. Knowing, above anyone else, you're capable of anything, that way when someone tells you no, you smile and say, 'Hold my beer.'"

Taking a deep breath, I grinned and nodded. "You're still training me, right?"

"You bet your ass I am. I've got two fights back to back, but after that, I'm all yours."

"Tommy, I don't know how to thank you. I know you're working so hard to make it into the AFL yourself, and you're taking time from your own training to help me—"

"Shh..." He wrapped his arm around my neck, pulling me into a playful headlock. "You don't ever have to thank me for helping family. And you are family, Navie."

I let him hold me, comforted by how genuine his words were. He and I connected on a level I'd never felt with anyone other than Trevor, except my relationship with Tommy was purely platonic. He really was my brother. I could decide what my relationship with him meant to me however I wanted. Sadly, it seemed blood didn't mean a damn thing. "Same, Tommy."

"Then it's settled." He pushed me back and placed his hands on my shoulders. "I'll text you the time and dates."

I grinned, wondering how no one had claimed him as their own yet. Gage; I got. Tommy, I did not. He wasn't a player. He was a sweetheart, not afraid of showing anyone his heart. "I'll be there."

I waited impatiently for two weeks. Ten times, I'd walked out the front door of my apartment heading straight for the gym but something always stopped me. It wasn't just the thought of running into Trevor. The other guys there that I'd trained with in passing were keeping me away too. Not that I didn't have just about everything to be embarrassed about in general, those guys thinking I had quit, that I had given up on something they'd basically killed themselves training for made me feel less than. Like they would see me as some whiny girl who broke up with her boyfriend and was too dramatic to continue on. It was untrue first and foremost, and it disgusted me beyond belief. That was not the woman I wanted to be. It wasn't the woman I was.

Tommy won both of his fights. I hadn't gone as they'd been out of state, but I was proud of him just the same. A week later, he texted me. I responded, excited to get back to some sort of normalcy, but at the same time worried deep in my bones whether or not I was doing the right thing. I hadn't seen Trevor. I hadn't so much as texted him goodnight, which we'd done in the past even though we were taking a break. Looking back, I think the conversation we had about my father turned things around for us. I knew it did for me. I couldn't help but feel Trevor should have taken up for me. He should have yelled over the mountain tops that I was making progress and me being inside the cage was doable. He could have told my father I was improving. But he hadn't. He'd told him he was concerned. Which meant to me, his faith in me wavered.

Willow kept me updated on the day-to-day stuff of course. I

worried about her, as she hadn't taken to pregnancy as well as she'd hoped. She felt remorseful and guilty about it and had expressed her shame to me many times. Our lunch date with Lena prior to Payne's last fight before the baby would be born was no exception.

"I can't shake these nerves. I'm worried about everything, guys."

"About the fight?"

"For one. The baby…see? I keep calling it baby. We know we're having a boy. We know we're naming him Noah. Why can't I call him by his name? Do you think maybe I'm having second thoughts about the name, like maybe it won't fit him?"

"Babe, calm down. See, this is what pisses me off about society," Lena began. "You don't have to call your baby by the name you think you're going to give him while he's still in the womb. Babies have gone days, *days* without a name. Wait until you hold him in your arms to name him. You may have a totally different vibe for him once he's here."

"You're right. Once I see him, something else might come to me."

"You'll know when he's here. Intuition will take over," I tried to reassure her even though I had no experience in motherhood.

"Yes. Intuition. God, guys. I would have never guessed how damn frazzled I'd be with these hormones. I feel like I don't know which way is up." Willow took a drink of her water.

"You've definitely been hit hard, but you got this, girl. Women do it every day and have since the beginning of mankind. You're going to kick serious ass as a mom." Lena winked at her. "Switching gears, what's going on with you and that fine ass man of yours?" She eyed me, letting me know she wanted details about me and Trevor.

I waited to respond because I wasn't sure how much I felt comfortable sharing. It wasn't that I didn't trust them. I just wasn't in the mood to badmouth Trevor, and given I wasn't completely over the sting of his honesty, I couldn't exactly gather positive words for him just yet.

"We're… taking a break."

"A break? Like a Ross and Rachel break? Or a break-break as in if he dates someone else, you wouldn't consider it cheating?"

My face fell at Lena's words. Trevor dating someone else had never entered my mind. I'd been so wrapped up in my own stuff, I hadn't considered what he'd been doing in his free time now that I wasn't around, especially since I'd left him hanging, telling him I needed even more time. "Well, I—I don't really know."

"Trevor wouldn't do that," Willow interjected. "He loves you. Trust me, I know him well."

"I guess only time will tell. I'm not ready to talk to him about it yet. Everything happened so quickly. I'm just concentrating on me right now. I've got so much to strive for, you know? It's hard to do that when I'm with Trevor because all I can see is him."

"So, it wasn't like you guys were arguing or anything?" Lena asked.

We hadn't exactly argued. After he told me about the meeting with my father, I had just felt so let down on top of my own insecurities.

"No. I just realized I went straight from my dad's house to Trevor's. Everything I've ever done, even for myself, was tied to either man. I want to be Navie. I want to see what I'm made of on my own first." It wasn't exactly a lie. The more time I spent alone, the more I believed it.

"I can respect that. People ask me all the time why I'm single, and it blows my mind. I mean, I get the intimacy and everything, but there's nothing better than kicking my heels off at the end of the day and doing whatever the hell I want, you know?" Lena chimed in, sipping her wine.

Willow and I burst into laughter. Leave it to Lena to tell it like it was. I loved how proud she was to be on her own, and how it didn't matter that both her girlfriends would cry on her shoulder about their men. Our lives didn't dictate how she lived hers. It was the epitome of freedom to me.

Our conversation lightened over the last part of lunch. Lena and I continued to offer Willow support, even changing the conversation to her baby shower in an attempt to raise her spirits about the baby's upcoming arrival. She was excited; she just seemed overwhelmed with the responsibility of it all. Although I hadn't talked to him about it, Payne seemed to be taking the arrival of his son very well. With flying colors even. He smiled more these days and seemed lighter even though he was about to be boggled down with the obligation of a family. It was nice to know that Willow had such a strong partner; someone who'd be her stability during her time of insecurity she was so clearly having before the arrival. Plus, she still had her mom around, who planned on being there for the birth as well as a couple of weeks after to help the new parents adjust.

"You're coming tomorrow, right?" Willow asked as we were going our separate ways.

"I'll be there with bells on." I grinned, hugging her.

The advertising alone for Payne's fight had to be upwards of a million dollars. That was one thing my father did well. He promoted his fighters and their fights like his business depended on it. And of course, it did.

Billboards, newscasts, and social media had been promoting Payne for months. He wasn't exactly comfortable with it, but he saw the upside to it too. He and Willow were heavily involved with a local charity, and Payne's name helped when trying to raise money and awareness against drinking and driving. I'd never personally witnessed his testimony at area schools and colleges, but from what Trevor told me, he, along with Willow, had made a huge impact for the cause.

I'd been around the AFL most of my life. Lights, cameras, and the action wasn't new to me. Celebrities and old money were the norm in my family, but I'd always managed to stay disconnected from all the hoopla. It never impressed me like it had my brother. Obviously, growing up in a well-known family had its perks, but I always felt like I was an innocent bystander—watching my life from the outside. I was only learning now as an adult how much damage that had actually done to my psyche. The unknown abyss was a scary place to wander around in, and unfortunately for me, I'd been squatting there for the last fifteen years.

I walked into The Garden alone, feeling surprisingly calm. I hadn't trained in weeks. Hadn't even been inside the gym or talked about the sport giving me grief to anyone. Oddly enough, I was excited for Payne's match. He was undefeated, and as much as he seemed unbothered by the fact, his wife worried enough for the both of them.

"Navie!" Lena caught my attention next to the restrooms. We'd texted earlier to meet.

"The crowd is crazy already. We're still an hour away from the bell," I said, walking straight into her arms for a hug.

"Right? Willow's in the locker room. Want to grab our seats while we wait for her?"

"Sure."

Lena and I made our way through the throngs of crowd, most of whom were purchasing merchandise. I smirked as we passed a young boy bartering with his mother on how much money he could spend.

We hadn't been seated half an hour when I checked out on Lena mid-conversation. Trevor entered my line of sight, looking as handsome as ever. His black pants hung low on his hips and his plain gray fitted T-shirt stretched tight across his chest. The sleeves on his T-shirt were rolled twice for emphasis. And in Trevor's normal stylish way, his red Converse popped with color. The way he carried himself made me ache; so solid. His self-confidence was one of the most attractive things about him. Just the sight of him made my heart smile.

I took a sip from my beer, my eyes following Trevor's every move. My stomach flipped; my fingers tingled as I grasped the cold drink in my hand.

"See something you like, Momma?" Lena leaned into me and giggled.

"He's so fucking hot." I sighed.

"He is. But—"

"Trevor's hot, but he ain't no Payne." Hot air hit the side of my face, a stranger a little closer to me than I would have normally liked. "I'm a sucker for that boy, let me tell ya." A husky woman sitting behind us leaned over our seats, eavesdropping on our conversation.

"Phyllis," Lena said dryly.

"Lena." The older woman returned the formality, but I could see by her demeanor she wasn't Lena's biggest fan. The crow's feet around her eyes became prominent with her squint.

"So, you're a fan of Payne's?" I asked, noting her red flannel with the sleeves cut out.

"Fan?" Her belly jiggled when she chuckled. "Guys, did you hear this one?" She turned to a couple of guys who were seated to the right of her. "Wondering if I'm a fan of Payne's?" The men stared at me, then snickered. One looked young enough to be her son; the other looked old enough to be her dad.

"She's a sucker for Payne, sweetheart. His *biggest* fan." The older man said, stroking his long gray beard.

"Oh, that's cool." I hadn't been around a die-hard in a while, but it took all I had not to laugh at Lena's expression. She'd clearly come in contact with them before and wasn't the least bit impressed.

"Hey, girls." Willow scurried through the aisle, then bent to take her seat. "Oh, hey Phyllis," she greeted, and leaned forward to give her husband's biggest fan a hug.

"How you feelin', darlin'? You look stunning. Absolutely glowin'." Phyllis softened her tone when addressing Willow.

"You know, I'm doing well. It took me a while to adjust, honestly. But I've been concentrating really hard on taking care of myself, and I think it's helping. Well, with the exception of being a ball of nerves tonight."

"Oh, honey, our boy won't let us down. He's going to kick Harris's ass," Phyllis yelled the last part, to I assumed, whoever would listen.

I watched the exchange somewhat amused. But mostly proud to see Willow in such good spirits. I downed the last of my beer, deciding I was definitely having another. I was in the mood. "Hey, I'm gonna go get a drink. You guys want anything?"

"I'll take a beer." Lena reached for her wallet.

"Water for me," Willow added.

"I got it." I rushed off before they could refuse my buying for them.

The line was longer than I expected. But not long enough that the beer wasn't worth it. I pulled up my X feed, mostly to waste time while I waited. I never really read any of the articles; I just liked to see what was trending.

"What's trending?" Trevor's voice echoed behind me. I closed my eyes at the sound of it, and exhaled a steady breath, comforted by the fact he knew me so well. Smiling, I stuck my phone in my back pocket before turning toward him.

"Butterflies flocking to Canadian park on their way to Mexico, Taylor Swift, politics, horrible hobbies… you know, the usual."

"I don't know why you even care about that crap." He chuckled. He was relaxed, unlike me. His hands tucked casually into his pockets, and his eyes bright with a bit of mischief behind them. His beard was a little longer, I noticed.

"Because you never know when someone will be standing behind you in the beer line and ask about them."

He dropped his chin to his chest and grinned at my sarcasm. I'd never tire of seeing him like that; in the moments where I could picture him being a fifteen-year-old boy. The innocence of his body movements, his boyish grin; they made me giddy inside, causing me to feel fifteen again myself.

"You look beautiful." His flirty gaze twinkled at his compliment.

"Thank you." I moved up in line. "Is Payne ready?"

"More than ever. The outcome of this fight will determine his next contract." Trevor stopped abruptly, realizing by mentioning the contract, he was bringing up my dad.

I ignored it. "He's on top of the game right now. And with the baby coming… I can't see him losing focus now."

"Yeah, but that baby is going to change things."

"I guess, but this is his job. His career; the way he provides for Willow and the baby. He'll stay focused."

He nodded in agreement. "I have no doubt. I better get back there. I just saw you and… couldn't pass up the opportunity."

I smiled at his honesty. "It was good seeing you, Trevor."

"Can I—just one thing?" he held up his index finger. I nodded once, giving him the go ahead. "Are you planning on coming back to the gym?"

I swallowed and answered truthfully. "I am. Tommy and I are getting back to work soon. He wanted to get a couple of fights out of the way, and of course, support Payne. But, yeah. I'll be in soon."

"Good. That's good. I know you thought I—" He grimaced and stopped mid-sentence. "I just—I'm glad you're not quitting."

"I appreciate that." I smiled, believing my own words.

He winked at me. We stared at each other for a moment, an odd sense of peace surrounding us. We hadn't spoke of anything important, but it felt like we'd resolved something. I bit my bottom lip and stepped up to the concession as he walked away. Whatever it was, I was glad it happened.

As I made my way back to the girls, fighting heavy traffic the whole way, I realized I was grinning. It felt good. A silly five-minute conversation with him about social media and Payne. Sometimes, I supposed it was the small things. I still had things I wanted—*needed* to say to him, but it didn't seem like we were ready for that conversation. So, until we were, I could enjoy not only seeing him in a new light but seeing myself in one as well.

CHAPTER 23
TREVOR

I NOTICED Navie the minute she walked into the arena. Long tan legs exposed in one of those short jumpsuit things girls wore to drive men in-fucking-sane. Well, if that had been her intent; the cherry red garment had worked like a charm. And the heels she paired with her outfit…fuck me. I pictured myself unbuckling them with my teeth ten different ways before I made it back to the cage with Payne.

I adjusted myself not caring who saw me and jumped in the corner. Damn, it was going to be a long night. "You ready?"

"Yep." Payne answered, staring out into the crowd intent on finding his wife. He grinned when he spotted her in the second row. Willow insisted on sitting on the crowd, not in the VIP boxes at his matches. She wanted to experience the intensity with the crowd, and she loved hearing them cheer his name. I smirked when she glanced up in mid-conversation with Phyllis, the lady who'd once punched her in the face, and made eye contact with her husband. That incident still cracked me up. Phyllis never missed a fight. She actually held a special place in Payne's heart, securing her spot as his biggest fan early on. He sent her gear and merchandise every time he got something new. As far as he was concerned, she'd could have been his only fan, and he would have been happy. She supported him no matter what and she loved his wife.

It was awesome to witness his success. He'd been through so much in his life. I, on the other hand, rarely thought about life. It was what it was. People were born with a fate-dealt hand, and they played it. Except after meeting Payne—after learning his story, I came to the realization that no matter what happened in life, anyone could change their situation. It was odd that his life clued me in, given that mine hadn't exactly been peachy, and I was what most would consider successful. But the fact that my best friend had served time in prison and still managed to find happiness and positive success made me realize anyone could do it.

Sometimes bad things happened to good people. Sometimes, good people made bad mistakes, and it sucked. But seeing how far he'd come, it made me proud. He was tough; he was resilient and I loved him like a brother. Even if I was going through my own shit, it was nice to still be able to be proud for someone's victories.

We tapped knuckles, our ritual, and I stepped back in his corner behind his trainer, as anticipation grew within me by the second.

"Let's go!" Gage gripped Payne's shoulder, as did Tommy.

Payne nodded once and took his spot in the center of the cage. Michael Harris would be his fiercest competitor to date. Payne had secured a decent following before he'd even gone pro, but once he'd made a name for himself in the circuit, his opponents had gotten tougher with each fight.

I knew for a fact Richard and Preston were in the box. Fortunately, I hadn't run into either of them. That would not be the case by the end of the night, but instead of focusing on the outcome of that run-in, I chose to concentrate on Payne.

One thing at a time.

The referee gave the go ahead and Payne advanced immediately. His offense was unparalleled. He was explosive out of the gate, forcing Harris back three steps. Harris's balance wavered, giving Payne the upper hand. Taking two quick jabs to the ribs, Harris retreated to his corner, realizing immediately that had been a mistake. His eyes widened as Payne followed him, not giving him time to recover. Harris pushed his way to the center of the mat, trying to regain his composure.

"Get him on the ground!" I yelled.

"Arm bar!" Tommy shouted.

Payne never acknowledged us, but I knew he could hear us. His leg lurched up, kicking Harris in the ribs. Harris came back, his fist making contact with Payne's face. Once. Twice. Three times, before Payne ducked.

Payne spit blood out the side of his mouth and stood to his full height. He was the kind of fighter I loved to watch. When things got tough, he got tougher. Pain had never been an issue for him. In fact, he thrived on it. It hyped him up.

Both men circled each other for a couple of seconds, trying to read the other's next move. "He's waiting too long," Tommy said.

"He's almost done waiting him out. Look at his face."

"He needs to get him on the ground."

"He will." I had no doubt.

Hook. Jab. Hook. Straight into a takedown. The crowd roared as Payne wrapped his arms around Harris and took him straight to the ground. Payne hadn't gotten a good hold of him, and Harris rolled out from the takedown just as the bell rang, signaling the first round was over.

"Water," Payne barked, choosing not to sit.

Gage pumped three quirts of water into his mouth. Instead of swallowing it, Payne spit it back out onto the mat and signaled for more. His trainer offered advice, and Payne acknowledged him, but looked to me.

"That fucker is squirrely. Make sure you get a good grasp on him with your legs," I said.

Payne nodded but otherwise didn't respond. Without looking back at us, he walked back out, ready to start the second round.

Harris took a different approach in the second round. He went for Payne as soon as the bell rang. Payne took two punches to the face right off the bat. When he stood, ready to retaliate, Harris backed up, Payne moving toward him full on. Payne held his arms out wide, telling Harris he'd had his chance and now it was his turn. Payne's fans roared at his cockiness. They loved it when he showed any emotion while fighting because it was so out of his norm.

He punched once then stretched his leg straight out in attempt to kick Harris in the face. It landed and knocked him off balance. Payne pounced on him, taking him to the ground immediately. Harris went down, but rolled twice, kicking out of Payne's hold. Payne kicked once, making contact with Harris's leg, and Harris returned the kick to Payne's ribs. He punched once to the ribs and then to the face, splitting Payne's lip. Payne licked the blood, then smiled an earie blood-stained toothy grin.

Tommy and Gage traded a smirk as I leaned toward the cage. The anticipation of Payne's retaliation took my adrenaline to a whole other level. I swallowed, my gaze fully focused on his motions. Before I could get too invested, the second round ended.

"Knee him when you get a chance. He's leaving himself open on the right side."

"I'm about to fucking destroy him," Payne answered, his gaze never leaving Harris' corner.

"Go get him, boy," Gage encouraged.

Payne turned and found his wife in the crowd, winking at her just before the third round began. Being that he was dead center of the cage when he did it, cheers erupted. Not only did his fans love when he showed emotion, they loved when he showed any sentiment toward his wife. In most cases, the public tried to ruin relationships where most of the guys were concerned, but not with Payne. I wasn't sure if it was because he'd gone public with his past and they had a soft spot for him, or it was because they knew he'd stand up for his wife and their relationship at all costs. Either way, they loved Willow as much as they loved him. I felt like a proud papa witnessing it. He had made it through the toughest part of being a fighter unscathed. At the thought, complete and total understanding shot through my mind like a lightning bolt. Protecting my personal life seemed like the right choice, given my experience in the league. After all the cage bunnies over the years, and my marriage… it was the only thing that made sense. No matter what the situation had been, I thought hiding and keeping my personal life out of the public eye would have saved the integrity of any relationship I had or would have in the future.

I'd done everything wrong from the very beginning with Navie. I shouldn't have tried to conceal our relationship, which left people guessing about us. We hadn't attended any public events together and had barely gone out to dinner. Aside from our closest friends, I'd not proclaimed any right to her. For all the guys at the gym might have known, it could have been a convenient hook up. We could have been friends with benefits, and I never expressed anything different because it wasn't any of their business.

Screams of joy brought my attention back to the fight. I looked up to see Payne complete a beautiful flying knee knockout, straight to Harris's face. Payne squatted in front of him, ready to pummel him, just as the referee jumped in and pushed him out of the way. Gage and Tommy yelled, high-fived, and pushed me so hard, I nearly tumbled over, not expecting it. I laughed and pushed them back. Our boy had just completed his first year in the pro-circuit. Undefeated.

I could picture Richard's smug face in the box. He could try to fuck with Payne's contract, and even threaten it again, but he'd be the biggest fool on earth to do so. Conner Payne was the best fighter in the AFL, and after what he'd just accomplished—going undefeated—Richard wouldn't have the balls to lose a sure thing. Unfortunately, there seemed to be nothing more important to him than money, and Payne had just secured that for him.

Payne left the cage as soon as the referee announced him the winner. He hung the heavy-weight belt over his left shoulder, and grinned, just as he made eye contact with his wife. There were so many people surrounding him, between his team, the gaggle of reporters, and the crowd. I took the initiative to climb down from the cage to meet Willow and escort her to him personally.

"Oh, my God!" she squealed as I picked her up and swung her around in a circle. "I'm so damn proud of him, Trevor!"

"Never had a doubt," I said as I placed her back on her feet.

Keeping her hand secure in mine, I pushed through the throngs of people. Tommy and Gage, along with Lena and Navie, were close behind us. Once we made it to the tunnel, Willow jumped into her husband's arms as the crowd excitedly chanted his last name. The rest of us leaned up against the wall in the tunnel while Payne turned toward the crowd one last time with his wife in his arms and held his belt up for them. He waved, giving his fans what they wanted. Acknowledgement. I grinned and started toward the locker room as they all followed. No one spoke as the roars from the crowd continued to grow louder.

"Dude. You are the King," Gage slapped Payne on the shoulder as we entered the locker room.

"You're admitting this now?" Tommy chuckled. "The six-second knockout with Camden didn't do it for you?"

Willow's smile was contagious. Navie and Lena grinned too. Hell, we were all grinning. Tommy took a seat on one of the sofas and Navie followed him. Lena grabbed a chair, so I did too.

"One of your best fights to date," I told him as Willow practically dressed him in front of us as if he were a child. Payne stepped into the sweats, then took a seat next to me.

"Except for the part where you let him hit you," Willow chimed in, sitting on her husband's lap. "I hate when you do that."

Before any of us could recall our favorite moments from the fight, the door swung open and none other than Richard Fuller entered the room, his deep baritone voice echoing from the doorway. "Conner, congratulations."

Navie's movement in the corner of my eye caught my attention. Her body tensed, unease in her beautiful blue eyes. I brought my gaze back to her father who was making his way into the room, followed by her brother and… Jeremy fucking Tillman.

I glared at Richard, then pulled my bottom lip in between my teeth when my gaze crossed her brother Preston, who wore the most devilish smirk I'd ever seen. I concentrated on relaxing my hands so I wouldn't throat punch him. Jeremy, for the most part, stood stoic until his gaze landed on Navie. His eyes brightened, and he grinned.

"Navie," he greeted, walking toward her. Once he stood in front of her, he pulled her into a hug. "You look stunning."

"What are you doing here?" she asked him, ignoring dad and brother.

"Yeah, about that," Preston began, but his attention was set on me as I quickly approached them. "Steele," he crooned, holding his hand out for me to shake. "Long time no see."

I ignored Preston's hand, and stepped up to him, hovering above him a good four inches. My nostrils flared; I wanted nothing more than to stomp his guts where he stood. "What exactly are you trying to accomplish here?" I clenched my fists, knowing the second I touched him, he'd have me arrested. My brain fought my body for logic.

"Oh, bringing Tillman as my guest?" he asked, his cocky persona sending a clear signal through his shit-eating grin.

I felt the group take their spots at my back. Tommy and Gage directly on either side of me. Payne, Willow, and Lena behind them. The line had been drawn in the sand. Them against us. The only factor still unknown was Navie. Silence, so loud I could hear my own heartbeat, swallowed me whole as Navie confronted her brother. She stepped around me, coming face-to-face with him. Her father standing next to him, kept quiet; intrigued almost.

"What's going on?" Navie asked.

In his defense, Jeremy seemed as confused as she did, which told me they'd manipulated him. Unfortunately, he was about to see a side to me only a dude named Jensen Little, who'd knocked my ball cap off in tenth grade, had ever seen. Even in the cage, my opponents had always been business. Jensen had been personal.

"It looks like your brother and possibly your father brought Jeremy here thinking you'd leave with him," I said, but never took my eyes from Preston's face.

Nodding, he agreed with me in front of everyone. "Let's not blow things out of proportion when we're all here to congratulate Payne." Preston glanced over my shoulder.

"Do you think this is some kind of joke?" Navie asked.

Preston sighed and stepped toward his sister. "You literally got your fucking lights punched out in your last so-called match." He chuckled. "I think the joke is on you, and you need to pack your bags, come back to the company, and things can go back to normal, princess."

Jeremy narrowed his eyes at Preston, seemingly shocked to hear him speak to her that way. I wasn't. But it did make me respect him a little more and feel one hundred percent better about my professional dealings with him.

"You think your opinion matters to me?" she asked, her voice trembling on the last words. I knew she was shadow boxing her soul in that moment. On the surface, she'd decided to stand up to her family, but the deeper she had to dig, the more she struggled to overcome a lifetime of cavalier treatment from them.

"I know it does, otherwise you'd still be shacking up with your so-called trainer, and you're not, so…" Preston raised an eyebrow, daring her to prove him wrong.

"Honestly, I'm so ashamed to even be kin to you. What are you trying to prove? You make fun of me for working my ass off at something I'm trying to accomplish? You invite my ex-boyfriend here under false pretenses? For what? And you…" She pointed at her father. "You just allow him to do these things without so much as a word. I can't believe this." She ran her hand through her hair and pushed out a deep breath. I knew her well enough to know she was more hurt than she was angry. I wished I could have just been excited about the fact that she'd stood her ground, even with an audience. Gage and Tommy stood motionless next to me, and I could hear Willow's labored breaths. It was probably eating her alive not to say anything, but in an odd turn of events, it was if we all knew Navie had to deal with her family on her own, in her own way, even though I was sure I wasn't going to let it go too far. Unfortunately, I wasn't that chivalrous.

"Navie, don't overreact. He just worries about you, the same as me. I've told you before the cage is no place for a woman. You getting knocked out only proves that. Not to say some women aren't capable of a decent punch, but you… my beautiful daughter, are not the one." Richard's hand rose just enough to pat his daughter's shoulder, but Navie blocked it, pushing it away.

"He doesn't worry about me. Neither do you."

"That's preposterous," her father quipped.

"Do you have any idea how pathetic you are? Nobody respects me," Preston whined in a girly voice, in what I assumed was his lame attempt at mocking Navie. "Nobody loves me. Blah, blah, blah."

Pulling my bottom lip in between my teeth, I bit down, drawing blood. It would be too easy to murder him.

Willow gasped, and before I could put my hand on Navie's shoulder, Tommy and Gage stepped closer to us, closing the gap. They were ready to shred Preston, and so was I. Disgust filled my gut as I glanced at Jeremy, who'd at least had the decency to look ashamed. I couldn't believe her brother had gone to such lengths to hurt her.

"You're a piece of shit," I called out to Preston. Without waiting for a response, I turned to Jeremy. "I really fucking hope you didn't know anything about his intentions, otherwise, you and I are going to have a conversation, and I promise only one of us with be satisfied with the outcome."

Shaking his head, Jeremy held up his hands in defeat. "I didn't know."

"First of all," Navie said, eyeing her brother, "nothing… not Jeremy, not Dad, and certainly not you, will keep me from being with Trevor."

Pride swelled in my chest.

"I'm a grown ass woman," she continued. "I'll be with whomever I choose. Second, I'm going to live my life how I want to live it. I'm fighting in the cage. I'm going to gain experience so I know for a fact when the time comes, I'll be able to run my own business, knowing full-well every aspect of it, and there's nothing either of you can do about it."

Everyone from our camp remained silent, knowing Navie needed the moment all to herself. She stood taller as she walked over to face her father. "As for us," she pointed between herself and her father. "I love you. You're my dad, but if you don't support me, then stay out of my life. I'm done spending any amount of energy thinking about how I can earn your approval or your love. I shouldn't have to work so hard for you to love me, and I won't anymore. And you"—she glanced over her shoulder to Preston—"you're dead to me. Dead. I never want to see you again. You have no idea what love is, and you're beyond learning."

Preston shrugged. "So be it. You're turning into a bitch anyways."

Before he could finish what he was going to say next, Navie decked him. Full on tight-knuckled punched him in the face. I didn't allow her any time to consider her next move. I was on top of her brother before she had a chance to advance on him. I landed four punches to his face and three knee strikes to his ribs before Tommy, Gage and Payne ripped me away from him. Blood covered Preston's face, his pretty, never-been-hit-before-face, and the pleasure I felt welled up inside of me, making me feel like I had grown ten inches. I grinned at him, lying there covering his face while aimlessly searching for anyone and anything to help him breathe. I'd knocked the air out of his lungs with my swift knee-jabs. And it felt better than any match I'd ever won inside the cage.

Chaos ensued as Richard's bodyguards grabbed Tommy and Gage.

Payne looked back at Willow, speaking to her without a word. She nodded at her husband, fully supporting whatever he was about to say. Payne took his place, standing before his boss, as he made an announcement we were all privy to hear. "If your son ever makes contact with anyone I care about again, I'll leave the league, which translates to you losing the guy who brought in more than forty-two million dollars for your company this year."

Richard opened his mouth to speak, but Payne held his hand up, silencing Richard.

"If your son presses charges, I'm gone."

Richard turned to Preston, who was balled up in the corner, holding his pristine jacket up to stop the bleeding from his nose. "That won't be necessary, Conner."

"I'm sick of watching your fucked-up family prance around like you're royalty. I've done my part. Now, you'll do yours. I'll run my own conferences. I'll do my own interviews; the ones I choose to do, and you'll stay the fuck out of it. Draw your checks from my fights, and we'll call it even. And that motherfucker"—Payne pointed to Preston—"better not enter my line of sight."

Richard looked to all of us, taking his time to make it around the room. After a few silent moments, he brought his gaze to his daughter. He spoke to Payne, but never took his eyes from Navie. "You have my word that neither myself nor Preston will interfere with your career as long as you stick to your end of the contract."

"Let's go, baby." Payne grabbed Willow's hand, leading her out of the room. The Championship belt still hung from his shoulder. Willow turned back to us, and I nodded to her, letting her know I'd take care of Navie. Gage, Tommy, and Lena followed making their exit behind Payne, after they stopped beside me first.

"You good?" Tommy asked.

"I got this."

"Man, we'll wait in the hallway." Gage eyed Richard before speaking to Jeremy. "Come on. Let's give them some privacy."

Richard stared at Navie. "You're making a mistake, and you're wrong. I do love you. But I will never support you fighting. I don't think you're capable of being successful at it."

"Admit it, your biggest worry is that I'll damage your brand." Navie stood solid. Her tone never wavered.

Richard swallowed but nodded in complete honesty. "That's part of it, yes. I own the fucking League, Navie. What will people think if you're out here cage fighting on Thursday nights at some half-assed gym for a hundred dollars a fight?"

"Consider your reputation spared, Richard." I pushed forward, garnering his attention. I'd be damned if he was going to put my woman or my gym down in front of me. I had money. I had skill, but most of all, I had my name. My name in the league alone would pull top-notch endorsements. Hell, I was currently active in four different contracts, and I hadn't fought in close to a year. I'd use every ounce of influence I had just to prove him wrong.

"Why's that?" he asked.

Navie moved forward an inch. Just enough to be by my side. "Because I'm investing in a women's league and your daughter is going to fight in it. And she'll be the fucking face of it; CEO, head-hunter, agent, trainer, whatever the hell she wants to be." He would regret not supporting her, but not as much as I did. I knew in that moment, I'd succeed in lifting Navie up so high, no one would ever be able to bring her down again. I was prepared to let her stand on my shoulders if she needed to. There was nothing in the world that would stop me from making it so she never felt the sting of someone not believing in her again. Myself included. I should have been the one training her the whole time. I should have been the one to teach her the ropes. I'd never been more disappointed in myself, but I was prepared to do everything and then some to make it right.

"Trevor? What are you saying?" Navie was as surprised as I was.

"I'm saying, we don't need them. You don't need them, Navie. You have me, and I'll be enough for you, I promise." I faced her, bringing my hands up to her face.

"This is insane. A women's league will never make it." Richard rolled his eyes.

"We'll see about that." I was still holding Navie's face, my attention on her above all. I hadn't even looked at her father when I'd answered him.

"You can't do that." Preston had finally licked his wounds enough to join us.

I nodded once to Navie but couldn't pass up the opportunity with her brother. "One: I can do anything I want. Two: you ever come near your sister again, I'll kill you."

Preston wiped his nose, but somehow managed a smirk, even after I'd beaten his ass in front of everyone. But I wasn't finished, and I didn't care who heard it.

"Three: If Navie wants to speak with you, she'll contact you. You don't show up here, you don't call. I don't even want to hear about a fucking email. You got family business, you can send a lawyer."

Navie sighed. "My brother swears he'll ruin the guys."

"Your brother's ego is far bigger than I'd imagined." I shook my head. "Is this what you've been struggling with on your own? Preston?"

She nodded but remained silent.

"He can't compete with money, babe. This is a business. Preston can't bring a third of what the guys can to the league. They're the talent."

Navie's shoulders slumped. Turing toward her father, she whispered, "I love you, I do, but don't contact me unless you want a real relationship. I'm done having your back and you not having mine."

Richard looked to me, questioning my motives, I knew. It really was as simple as I'd said. He wasn't conducive to Navie's mind, body, and especially her spirit. He didn't think she'd be successful and to him, that was all that mattered. Sometimes, success was the journey. I was willing to create ten new leagues if that was what would be best for Navie. I was prepared to go broke and live on love if that's what she wanted to do. But I knew a little bit about the fighting league. If the athletes were good, no one cared whether they were male or female.

Richard exhaled. "I don't want to lose you, Navie. I'm your father regardless. I won't support the women's league because I don't think it will succeed, but I won't bother you anymore to come home. Your decision to leave the company has made trouble for me, but tough love seems pointless now."

"Tough love?" Navie gasped. "You really don't get it, do you?" Her voice fell flat, as if she'd finally accepted every ounce of energy she'd put in with her family over the last year had been for nothing.

"Leave. We've all had enough for one night," I said. She was damn near tears, and I wasn't about to let her pissant brother see it.

But the guy just had to speak up. "Until—"

"What the fuck did I tell you?" I stepped up to Preston, getting in his space. He hunkered down like a small child, knowing without a doubt I'd hit him again.

Richard grabbed his arm. "Come on. It's over." Richard led him out of the room, with their bodyguards in tow.

Navie slumped forward, placing her hands on her knees as soon as the door closed behind them. It had taken everything in her power to stand tall in front of her father. I knew that now. I'd witnessed it. She'd been so strong, so surefooted.

"Come here, baby." Her soft skin under my palms made me more determined as she leaned into me. I was never going to be without her again. I didn't care what we were going to be. I'd take her any which way she'd have me. "I'm so proud of you."

"Trevor." Her arms swung around my neck, squeezing tight. I held her small frame as it shook, and I knew she was letting go of everything negative she'd ever carried inside of her. I kissed the top of her head, wishing I could have done it for her.

Picking her up, I carried her to the couch in the corner, keeping my arms wrapped snuggly around her. Her body curled into to me, and I held her as tight as I could while still allowing her to breathe okay as she cried harder than I'd ever had the misfortune of witnessing.

"I love you, Navie. So damn much. I swear, I'll never ever let you feel like I don't. I'll do whatever it takes."

She squeezed me, but remained silent, trying to compose herself.

"I meant everything I said to your father," I told her. "We'll succeed together. As partners. What do you say?"

"Everything's so messed up," she responded, while wiping her tears. My fingers fondled the ends of her hair, waiting for her to face me. I was set to give her as much time as she needed.

Five minutes later, I was still playing with the ends of her hair, and her head hadn't left my chest. Her breaths evened out, and I remained content on holding her while she went through whatever emotions she needed to finally be okay. Fear gripped me inside. I didn't know if I was what she needed. I wasn't prepared for her to decline my proposition. I wasn't ready for her to tell me she needed more time. Hoping to persuade her, I gently pulled her away from me, praying I could convince her.

"I know I fucked up. I should have never doubted you. It wasn't that I didn't think you could do it, Navie. Me telling your dad I was concerned was me being cautious. This career is hard; it's difficult for guys who've trained their whole lives. But the whole time I've known you, you've shown me that no matter what anyone is going through, it only pushes them harder to create the future they want for themselves if that future is what they're supposed to be doing in life. You were made to run a women's league. You have all the business expertise. You've grown up in the middle of it all. You know what it takes, and the fact that you're willing to fight—to learn every aspect of the sport so your employees will respect you? I can't name one person in the world who cares enough to do that. Not one."

Pride swelled in my chest. I would never be satisfied until she took my last name. Until we had babies and experienced the love of two people who created and raised children together. I wanted it all. All of it with her.

"I should have been the man at your back, pushing you, and doing anything I could have for you. I should have been a true partner for you. For that, I'm truly sorry. I've never loved anyone the way I love you. These last few months, this confrontation with your father, all of it has made me realize my place as a man; as *your* man. I promise on my life, you'll never feel alone again. I'll kill myself doing whatever I can to make you happy, baby. I won't sleep until you've had your rest. I won't eat until your belly is full. I won't smile until your cheeks hurt from smiling yourself. Nothing or no one will come before you.

"I was wrong; it's hard to admit, but I will fight for a way to make all my mistakes up to you." Saying those things out loud humbled me. Tears stung my eyes, knowing I'd just bled my heart dry. I just admitted to the one person I cared about that I hadn't been who I needed to be for her. The fucked up part of it all was she was the one who'd been working so hard on changing. She'd been the one taking time for herself, trying to make herself better; the best possible version of herself, and I'd been the one the whole time who should have been doing it.

She pulled her hands from mine and covered her face. I waited impatiently, knowing if I spoke again it would just delay her response. I watched her wipe her tears, sniffing as she did. Her hair was wild; fly-a-ways from lying on my chest going every which way. Her makeup was smeared around her eyes, and it gutted me to see her like that, knowing I'd contributed to it. Goosebumps spread across her arms. I stared at them, wondering if she was cold.

"I don't know what to say."

"Say whatever you want; say whatever you're feeling. Do you want to be with me?" I hated to push her, but the plan in my head didn't have me leaving the room without my arm wrapped around her.

"No one can save me like you do, Trevor. I was barely breathing when I met you."

I shook my head, hating her words. I never wanted to think about a world without her in it.

"Not like that, I just mean I didn't even know which way was up. And you," she said as she placed her palm on my jaw, fondling my whiskers with her nails like she'd done so many times before. "You are so sure-footed. Solid. Something I'd never been around. You're caring and determined for people to be treated fairly. Something else I've never experienced."

"I'm sorry for that, baby."

"I know you are, and it's one of the things I love about you most." She swallowed, taking her time with her next words. "The time I've taken to be on my own has been… inspiring for me. I've paid my own bills. I've sat with myself; been the only voice inside my head. I learned a lot about who I am and who I want to be. But the one thing my time solidified for me is I don't want to be me and not share it with you. I know I'm kind of a loner." She smiled and looked away but quickly brought her gaze back to me. "You would have given me what I needed. I just didn't know how to ask for that. I do now."

"I will give you whatever you need. I'll never hinder you from doing what you want to do. I'll never stand in the way of you accomplishing your goals. That's what I'm saying. I'm going to support you from now on. And if I have a concern, I'll voice it. To you. And if you have a concern, with your family or anyone else, you tell me. We have to have each other's backs. No matter what's going on, trust me, and I'll do the same."

Her head tilted to the side, while her lips spread wide, her smile lines more prominent than ever. I'd never been so proud of myself. Not in winning my first fight in the cage. Not even when I made it pro and won my first title. No, nothing had ever made me feel so good as when I made her smile.

"What do you say we go back to my place and I make us a midnight snack and we can discuss our terms on this whole business proposition?"

It wasn't what I wanted to hear. My idea of the night ending had me throwing her over my shoulder, sending movers to her apartment, moving her back into my home—to my bedroom, and never letting her go again. But like I'd told her earlier. I'd do whatever it took; whatever she wanted, and I planned on never going back on that. So, I grinned and took her hands into mine. "I'm gonna kiss you now."

"Okay."

I leaned in, everything about her familiar yet different. I knew where her lips would be; I knew that she'd tilt her head to the right as I opened her mouth wider so I could snatch her tongue, but somehow it felt like our very first kiss. My insides wobbled around, and my palms itched to touch every inch of her.

Grabbing both sides of her face, I pushed deeper inside her mouth. Her tongue so smooth it was as if it were velvet. My fingers slid up and into her hair, my thumbs behind her petite ears. I fondled them, loving the feel of her.

"I love you. I'll never stop as long as I'm alive."

"I love you too. Thank you for tonight."

"You don't ever have to thank me, Navie. In fact, don't. Just expect it. I've got your back in every way. I seriously don't give a fuck about anyone or anything else."

"How do you do it?"

"What?"

"Make everything okay."

I grinned and brought her palm to my lips. Nibbling for a moment, I sighed. "We got this, babe. It's me and you." I squeezed her shoulder, bringing her in close. Kissing the top of her head, I sighed and breathed her in deep. My words were simple, yet profound. Exactly the way things should have been in the first place. Just me and her.

CHAPTER 24
NAVIE

FOUR WEEKS HAD PASSED since I'd began training again. And by training, I meant physically killing myself. Working six hours a day waitressing hadn't allowed me much down time in between. Trevor mentioned me quitting my job. Then, he dropped several hints about maybe going part-time. He pushed the limits on the hint dropping until I nipped it in the bud. I loved him. I knew soul-deep I would marry him one day. But until that day happened, I was hell-bent on earning my own way. And that meant paying my own bills and training four hours a day on top of working.

Trevor had taken over as my full-time trainer. Tommy gave him shit for it, as did the rest of the guys at the gym, but he didn't seem to mind. He took it all in stride. In fact, their ribbing him seemed to make him more intense about it.

"I'm going to push you."

"Okay," I answered during our warm-up.

"No." He walked into my line of sight. "I'm going to treat you like you're a fighter. It's going to be tough. *I'm* going to be tough, but if you want to be the best, then we have to train you to be the best."

"I understand, Trevor." I rolled my eyes. He'd already explained to me the way things would be with him being my trainer.

"I just don't want you to think I'm pushing too hard. This is what it takes."

"I get it, okay? This is what I want. I'm ready."

He kissed my nose. "One more," he said leaning forward for another kiss while grabbing a hand full of my backside. "Now, we work."

I ignored the whistles behind us. Ever since the run-in with my father, Trevor had made no secret about the status of our relationship. He announced it to damn near anyone who'd listen. It was sweet so I didn't make a habit of calling him out on it. The press tried to make a story out of it the first couple of weeks, and with Trevor shouting it from the rooftops, holding my hand in public, and sending me wild-flowers daily, more syndications were picking up on it. Because of course, the employees at the flower shop leaked a super racy snapshot of the card he'd sent with them. His walls were down, all of them. While Gage and Tommy kept us up to date with the latest headlines, and of course Lena's smartass photos of the rag mags from the grocery stores, we both agreed to stay away from the Internet. If I was being honest, I expected to hear from Preston, and I hadn't, which had me a little on edge. I didn't mention it though because I knew I was being in my head about it. Trevor had made it perfectly clear that Preston, nor anyone else had leverage when it came to our relationship.

"Grab the board. Let's work on balance first."

I tossed the medicine ball to him, and he tossed it back to me all while I balanced on a skateboard with no wheels. Trevor walked from side to side, forcing me to turn my body so that I could still see him. My thighs had never hurt so bad. I squatted with the last toss, as my legs shook, a burning sensation traveling all the way up to my hips. It was one of the exercises I hated most. Personally, I preferred to be inside the cage, practicing takedowns. But Trevor trained more on basics, telling me a strong foundation was key to persevering.

"Post up. I'll do twenty kicks, twenty knee jabs, then a take down. Flex your abs."

I took my spot at the mirror, placing my hands on the rails. One. Two. I flinched with every kick. I knew he was making me better, but that didn't mean he wasn't slowly killing me in the process.

"A hundred burpees. Speed is key. Give me twenty-five, then five back rolls, twenty-five more and so on."

As I finished, he gave out another round of instructions. "Bag work, then practice with the dummy on the mat. Work your rolls and mounts into each set of punches."

By the end of the day with Trevor, I knew I was entering a different level. The intensity and workload had increased. He wasn't joking when he said he was going to push me, but that was okay. I planned to succeed, and I didn't mind one bit to work for it, nor did I mind the view of him shirtless while I did it.

The next week, I found myself amused at Trevor's lack of interest while shopping in a local boutique for Payne and Willow's baby. He was so damn cute doing it though. Not to mention, I could plainly tell the three paparazzi's that had followed us from the diner we'd eaten lunch at annoyed the hell out of him. I could only assume tomorrow's headline would be that I was expecting a baby. Then, they'd talk about how much weight I had gained. In his defense, it bothered me too. I just wasn't as protective as he was. Plus, I'd grown up with people following my father around. I knew there was nothing we could do about it, so ignoring it seemed like the better option for my sanity.

"Why can't we just get some diapers and wipes? That's what they need the most," Trevor grumbled like a toddler who'd been told he couldn't ride his bike.

"We can get them that stuff too. I just want to add something pretty as well."

"Pretty? They're having a boy, babe."

"Fine. Cute then."

It wasn't as if I'd ever even understood the saying "baby fever." Honestly, I'd never been positive that becoming a mother was in the cards for me. It wasn't that I hadn't want to become a mom. It was more that I wasn't married and hadn't met someone I'd want to be attached to forever if things didn't work out. Except now… I was in love with the man I longed to marry eventually, so seeing all the tiny clothes made me think of what it'd be like if I had been shopping for my own baby. My palm rested on my stomach at the thought.

"Hey," Trevor whispered, taking my elbow in his hand.

I looked up at him, still lost in thought.

"What's going on in that beautiful mind of yours?"

I smiled, unsure if I should admit the ever so girly thoughts circling my brain. "Just thinking."

His gaze lingered on mine. After a few moments, his facial expression softened. "Thinking about what?"

"I don't know. Just stuff." I shrugged. We'd just gotten back together. Just found our footing both professional and personal. There was no way I was going to admit I wanted him to be my baby's daddy.

Slipping his hand down to my waist, he grinned showing me his dimples. His index finger circled my belly button over my shirt. "You wanting me to knock you up, Baby Blue?"

My cheeks heated at his bluntness. "No!"

"Navie…" He leaned into me, kissing my neck.

"Maybe one day, but not anytime soon, punk."

"One day. Is that a promise?

I nodded toward the large windows at the front of the store. "They're probably getting a front page picture right now."

He smirked and flipped the cameras off with the same hand that had just playfully caressed my navel. I laughed at his mischievousness. I loved that even though I'd felt like I was the one who'd needed to grow most during our time apart, it appeared he had as well. I was happy to see him so confident about our relationship. God, I felt safe with him. Free to admit my closet dream of becoming a mother even though we were nowhere near that stopping point in life. Even with the amount of love and understanding we'd both shown each other, the fact remained that we'd been through some heavy stuff. Some difficult situations, and anytime couples stumbled, they needed time to recover. We were no different.

After Trevor and I found the perfect gifts for the baby, Lena and I spent two hours decorating the foyer, living room, and dining room of Willow and Payne's home. She wanted it to be perfect, and I agreed with her.

"Do you think we need more daisies in the vases?" She asked for the fifth time.

"I think they look amazing. What about the sandwiches, though? We probably need to go ahead and put them out."

Gage walked into the kitchen rubbing his stomach. "Did I hear someone say there were sandwiches?"

"Don't you dare touch anything with your grimy hands." Lena swatted his shoulder as she whirled past him.

"They weren't grimy when they had two handfuls of your ass," he mumbled. "What's her problem?"

"She just wants it to be perfect. Here," I handed him half of a turkey club. "Don't tell anyone."

"I knew I loved you, girl."

I looked up just in time to see Gage's grin turn downward. Looking back over my shoulder, Trevor made a beeline for me. "Stop flirting with my woman, dumbass." He kissed my lips, settling his hand on my hip.

"I wasn't flirting. I was—whatever." Gage gave up. "I'm out of here. Everybody in this joint is on edge because of some eight-pound little human who isn't even here yet."

I smirked at Trevor as Gage left us alone. "Lord help the woman who procreates with him."

Trevor shook his head. "Lord help our planet if he procreates."

Just as I was finishing the final touches, Willow and Payne arrived. Willow's face lit up when she entered the front door. She covered her mouth with her hand, tearing up in the process. Payne's eyes grew wide and he placed his arm around his wife, bringing her toward him for a hug. We'd done it. Their house looked beautiful, a newborn's safe haven.

"Guys! This is the most beautiful thing. I couldn't have even imagined it." Willow's voice cracked as she rubbed her over-grown belly.

"For real. This is cool." Payne grabbed his wife from behind, his large hand engulfing hers.

My attention was brought back to Willow as she winced in pain. Before I could ask if she was all right, she winced again, and leaned against the entry table. "Conner!" she cried out, her cheeks reddened, and her eyes grew wide.

I stepped around Trevor, sensing that something was wrong. She bent her legs, almost to a squatting position, as she looked down to the puddle on the hardwood floor.

"Oh my—oh, Con—" She gasped, clearly in pain.

Realizing her water had broken, I began barking orders as I ran to grab my keys off their kitchen counter. "Payne, get her bag." I made it back to Willow's side and took her hand for support. "Trevor, help me get her to the car."

Payne returned from their bedroom, both his hands full of Willow's belongings. "Here," he said to Trevor as he handed him the luggage. Payne scooped Willow up in his arms and began walking toward the garage. "Tommy, lock up," he barked.

Trevor and I followed Payne to the hospital. Thankfully, we all made it safely despite having sped the whole way. Payne carried Willow in through the doors at the emergency room even though she argued with him the whole time that she could walk.

"Babe, I'm good," she said as we made entry into the hospital.

"Willow, don't start with this shit. I'm carrying you."

I glanced up at Trevor, who was smiling at their exchange even though Payne was in obvious distress.

"I left a note on the front door and posted on socials, advising the party was canceled," Lena told me as we rushed toward the nurse's station. God, I'd been so preoccupied when Willow's water broke, I hadn't even thought about the baby shower, or the fact that guests would be arriving at their house by now. I squeezed Lena's hand, thankful for her cool head.

Thirty-seven minutes. It had only taken a little over half an hour after Willow was admitted to the hospital before Payne walked out of the delivery room, a grin I'd never seen on him before shining bright. His posture was calm, cool even. But when I took in his watery eyes and red nose, I knew that he'd been crying. He got choked up telling us the baby had been born. "He's here." His voice broke at the end. "He's finally here."

Trevor, Gage, and Tommy rushed him, throwing their arms around Payne for a group hug. Lena and I held back, hoping he was going to give us the go ahead to visit Willow.

"When can we see him?" Lena asked.

"You guys can go ahead and go in. Willow's mom will be here in a few minutes." He wiped a lone tear away, beaming; pure joy radiating from him.

Lena and I didn't have to be told twice. We scurried around the guys, almost racing to our best friend's side.

"Will?" Lena whispered as we made our way inside the large hospital room.

"Guys," Willow's voice was quiet, barely a murmur as she held Noah close to her, breastfeeding him. She looked completely worn out but in the best way. Her hair was a mess. Her gown lay haphazardly while the newborn suckled greedily. It was the most beautiful thing I'd ever seen.

"Oh, my God. He's perfect." Lena leaned in to hug Willow, taking care not to disturb the baby.

"He's beautiful, Willow." I'd never been so mesmerized.

Noah clung to his mother, making satisfied noises every so often.

Trevor and Payne walked in, and I noticed Payne was still grinning from ear to ear. He sat on the side of the bed, curling his arm around Willow, staring adoringly at his little boy. I'd never seen so much love. It broke my heart and healed it all at once.

"You have a son," Trevor announced, gripping Payne's shoulder.

"I know." Payne didn't look at Trevor, clearly unable to remove his gaze from his wife and child.

As we sat in silence, watching Willow feed Noah, I had never been so content. There was something so peaceful about a new life coming into the world. I'd never witnessed such a miracle like that before. I'd never seen the love new parents had at first sight. It was striking. I knew, we all knew, in that moment their lives had been changed forever. They were the first of our little group to experience unconditional love, and even though none of us had ever felt it before, we were able to witness it firsthand. I could see the change in them the instant their baby was born. In Willow's smile, her loving spirit exuded from her, and I was guessing that was a mother's instinct. The love and protection in Payne's eyes would have brought anyone to their knees. He never took his hands off Willow or his eyes off Noah, even when he spoke to us.

"Now that he's here… I literally almost shit my pants, Will." Lena broke the serene silence.

Willow laughed. Payne did not. "Me too. Dr. Chapman told me the chances of him coming early were slim to none since he's my first baby. I was preparing myself to be overdue."

"Payne, you did good. You handled it perfectly," I said, hoping to relieve some of the stress on his face.

"Uh, yeah, at home, he handled it fine." Willow laughed.

"I thought we were keeping that private," Payne scoffed.

"No, baby. There's no way I'm not telling them." Willow looked up from the baby. "He almost fainted, you guys. They had to give him an icepack." She laughed again.

At my side, Trevor chuckled. "Dude. That's hilarious."

"Oh, you just wait, man. It's the coolest thing in the world but watching your wife in that much pain… then before you know it, the baby comes out. And it ain't pretty. Sorry, babe." He shuddered.

Trevor glanced at me, and I leaned into him completely content. I felt like nothing bad could touch me in that moment. Not my family. Not the fear of not succeeding. Not the unknown of what could have been considered a shaky future. No matter what happened with any of it, it was *my* journey. I was finally at peace with what would be. And from a tiny newborn baby who hadn't uttered a single word, no less… I knew everything would be okay.

CHAPTER 25
TREVOR

"WHAT'S up with this schedule, dude?" Tommy asked.

I signaled for him to enter my office, frustrated with the female fighter's agent on the end of the phone line; we'd been arguing for over ten minutes. "Man, I get it, but if you want her to make money, which makes you money, then she's gonna have to fight. Rookies or not."

Tommy took a seat in the chair directly in front of my desk. I rolled my eyes at the douchebag on the phone. Finally, he agreed. "Cool. She's down for the tenth. See you then. Holler at me if anything changes."

"You building an empire here?" He held up the next month's schedule that I'd put in their lockers.

"Something like that." I ran my hand through my hair. I had to give it to Richard Fuller. Starting a fighting league from the ground up was a hell of a lot harder than it looked.

"Hell, yeah!" Gage entered my office, without knocking. "I've got two fights this month!"

"If you guys want to advance, you've got to get more matches in. Richard's being an asshole right now and only looking at people on the West Coast. Since he won't reach out to me anymore, we've got to build an online presence for you."

"Damn, Steele. I'm impressed. And these female fights? Navie will be getting all kinds of experience," Tommy said, looking over the schedule in his hand.

"That's the idea."

"Aww, look, Tommy. Steele's pussy whipped and doesn't care who knows about it." Gage sat on the edge of my desk, grinning like a fool at Tommy.

"I'm this close"—I held up my thumb and index finger—"to coming out of retirement for you, dickface," I said, halfway ignoring him while checking for mistakes on my upcoming calendar.

"That won't be necessary, babe." Navie rounded the corner, locking eyes with Gage. "I got this one. We're working out today, right?"

"Damn, boy. You better run." Tommy laughed, rising to make his exit.

"Come on, Navie. It was all in fun. When something's funny, you laugh." Gage walked past Navie holding his balls as if she planned on kneeing him.

"Right. Lena said something about laughing the other night. What was it, Trevor?" She glanced at me, then back toward Gage at the door. "Oh, my bad. I don't think I was supposed to say anything about that." Navie placed her hand over her mouth and shrugged.

"What was she laughing at? Not me, I know for a damn fact." Gage was no longer laughing. Tommy was though.

"I don't think it was you per se… just *parts* of you."

"She's lying. I'll settle this right now," he swore and stormed out, clearly on a mission to clear his already damaged reputation.

I greeted Navie with a kiss. "That's just wrong, Violet."

"But so fucking funny." Tommy winked, leaving me and Navie alone.

"Sometimes, it's just nice to get him like he gets everyone else."

"I feel you," I said, grabbing the calendar off my desk. "Remember all the calls you put in last week?"

"The calls no one returned?" I rolled my eyes. "It's likely I won't forget them anytime soon."

"I heard back from Jessica Booker's agent."

"Jessica Booker? I thought she was selective with her fights."

"She usually is, but after listening to your voice mail, her agent called. He was intrigued. I talked him into a conference call, and the rest is history."

"This is huge."

"It is. We've got a little over a month to prepare."

"I'm ready."

"I'm really proud of you. You're working your ass off. It's going to pay off, Navie. It will."

"I know." Her hands reached for mine seemingly of their own accord. "Thank you for training me. And for helping me get the experience."

"You're welcome, baby. Always. I'm always going to help you do anything you want to do in life. I'll even learn to crochet if you want."

I placed a soft kiss on her forehead. I knew with every fiber of my being I was telling her the truth. I only hoped she believed me. I'd lost her once. Mostly because I thought I could love her from a distance. I had been under the impression having a relationship and being in one where one and the same. They weren't.

After Navie's break, I worked her for three hours. She was improving daily. Her moves were bolder. Her body was more agile. Even the guys took notice. Payne believed her kicks were stronger. Tommy bragged about her speed, and Gage swore her punches packed more weight behind them.

"Let's spar," Tommy suggested, spitting out his mouth guard.

I crossed my arms, annoyed. "If she's sparring, she's sparring with me," I dared him to push me. I had vowed to never let her feel alone again, and I meant every word of it.

"Oh, stop it. You've got work to do and I need to practice with someone other than you. Since there are no other females here…"

"Fine. I'll give, but I'm collecting tonight." I winked at her, not caring in the least that Tommy could hear me. In fact, I said it so he would hear me.

"Deal."

She was right. I had plenty of work to do, but that still didn't stop me from taking a few moments to fantasize about what was to come.

"Bye, Trevor," she said, and Tommy chuckled.

Flipping him the middle finger, I grabbed a water bottle out of the cooler. Now that all my calls had been made to every agent and promoter I'd ever met, and a few I hadn't, I had to take a look at my finances. I had a meeting with my accountant scheduled later in the afternoon, so I still had time to swing by Payne's to visit little Noah.

Before I even reached Payne's front door, I heard the baby crying. No, crying was an understatement. Had I not known they had a newborn, for instance if I had been the UPS guy, I would have thought some CIA torture shit was going on inside. The screams coming from that little man were blood curdling. I winced as I rang the doorbell.

"Hey, man." Payne answered the door. His hair was spiked in every direction. A burp cloth hung from his left shoulder and one leg of his gray sweatpants was raised to his knee. He looked like shit in the best possible way.

"Little man acting up?" I laughed because I could. There was something so satisfying about busting his balls for something that couldn't come back to haunt me.

"For fuck's sake, we can't keep him content today. Willow is about five minutes from blowing her gasket. I'm five hours past that point but holding my shit together for her."

I swung my arm over his shoulder. "You good?" I was long past worrying about his past addiction, but I also learned a lot about triggers when Payne and I first became friends. And it killed me to question him, but when I saw him struggling with something, my instinct to keep him safe wasn't something that went away. The worry and endless stress of hoping he never called me and told me he had fallen off the wagon. Even though he seemed beyond that past life, and appeared to have a handle on things, it still entered my mind from time to time. I'd always heard addicts were one bad day away. And I had such pride when he told his story, when he opened up and took ownership of it, but as someone who loved him, my guard was never fully down.

"I'm good. Just tired. And cranky as hell."

"Let's see if Uncle Trevor can alleviate some of this crankiness for you." I walked over to the little dude and his worn-out momma.

Willow was barely holding her eyes open. The baby was cradled in her arms as she calmly rocked him back and forth. Her eyes, those weren't calm. I frowned as I made my way over to her. She looked pitiful, and beautiful all at the same time.

"Hey, Momma. Let me see what I can do." I took the crying baby from her arms.

It wasn't as if I'd had any experience with babies, but it was worth a try. I cradled the baby's head, like Willow showed me and stood with the little guy. His eyes grew in size, as if he was trying to figure out who I was. I couldn't believe how much he'd grown and changed since the last time I'd seen him.

His gaze was filled with wonder, as if he was seeing things for the very first time. I smiled as he stopped crying and began yawning. He was just tired, or maybe he'd worn his little self out. Either way, I walked to and from the length of their living room, bouncing just a hair as I walked.

"Fuck, you're a baby whisperer."

"Conner! Language," Willow scolded as she yawned.

"Baby, he doesn't—"

"I don't care if he doesn't know words yet. I don't want that to be the first one he says," she interrupted him.

I smirked as my buddy apologized to his wife, plopping down on the couch beside her. Willow leaned her head on Payne's shoulder, and they both closed their eyes.

"Guys, go take a nap. I got this little dude."

Payne opened his eyes, asking his wife's permission. "Babe?"

"Absolutely not. You just got here," Willow said, her eyes still closed.

"I'll wake you if he starts up again. Look, he's content just walking around." I touched Noah's cheek and he grinned.

"Come on, Wil." Payne pulled Willow up by the hand and practically led her down the hallway. "We may not get another opportunity."

Willow stopped midway. "Thanks, Trevor. He has toys over there, a bottle in the fridge, and his pacifier is on the table."

"We're good. Go get some sleep."

Twenty minutes later, Noah had found sleep himself. I hadn't dared to sit down while he was awake, too scared he'd start screaming again.

With a little maneuvering, I carefully sat in the recliner, leaning back slowly, as to not wake him. Willow had him wrapped tight in a blanket when I took him from her arms. It didn't look the same now, and I wasn't sure how to fix it, so I just covered him the best I could.

It was an odd feeling holding a baby in my arms, but me and the little dude had some time, so I took the opportunity to study him. His features were miniature. I hadn't ever been around a baby. Hell, he was the first one I'd ever held, but oddly it didn't feel awkward.

I rocked once, then again, keeping up a steady rhythm, in awe of him. His nose was small, but wide, like Payne's. His eyebrows already forming, had a small crease as if he were subconsciously thinking while he rested. His eyelashes were jet black, the same as his hair, which laid perfectly atop his tiny head. It was so silky, it looked wet. My fingers found their way to his face; his head; his little fingers that peeped out at the top of the blanket. I couldn't help but touch him.

"You are one special little man," I whispered, still in awe of him.

"So are you." Navie stepped into the living room, her arms crossed, appreciation spread wide across her face.

I looked up, surprised she'd snuck up on me. "I didn't hear you."

"Willow gave me a key the other day when I picked up their groceries. She texted me when you got here and offered them a nap."

"Oh." I would have said more, but Noah stirred, bringing my attention back to him.

Navie took a seat on the ottoman beside me, silently focusing her gaze on Noah. A smile spread across her beautiful cheeks, so I smiled too. Neither of us said a word. There was nothing to say. We were in a world where a new human—one who would be loved beyond measure existed, and that made everything okay.

The peace baby Noah had created for us while our friends napped didn't last long. Within the hour, he cried out, waking his parents, letting his mother know he was hungry. Willow and I left their family to their own devices when the three of them snuggled on the couch, one eating, and the other two sighing contently.

Two days later, Navie shocked me by casually mentioning her father had contacted her. "My dad called me today," she told me, while taking two dinner plates from the cabinet.

"What'd he say?"

"He claimed he was just checking on me."

"Okay. So maybe he was," I offered.

I hated to give Richard the benefit of the doubt, especially since the last time I was around him, I could have flattened him and his son both for hurting my girl, but he was a dad after all, and I somehow understood that on a different level after seeing the parental bond Payne had experienced with Noah. It made me hopeful that maybe somewhere behind all of Richard's fucked up priorities, it was possible he actually did love Navie and care about her in his own way.

She plated the chicken and vegetables and brought them to the bar. "He also mentioned he saw where you and I were in a baby store and proceeded to tell me how the press would have a field day if the rumors were true."

"Hey," I slipped an arm around her and guided her onto my lap. Placing a soft kiss behind her ear, I squeezed her tight and closed my eyes. "It was on the front page. I could see where he would be curious."

"I feel like he overstepped, given our last conversation. He didn't even apologize before asking me something so private."

"I get that, just don't let this overwhelm you. Do what you're comfortable with. If you feel like talking to him, do it. If you're not ready, that's okay too."

"I don't think I'm ready. We just kind of sat there in silence once the formalities were out of the way. I mean, I'm not sure what I want to say to him, you know? Ever since Noah was born, I've gotten to see how parents are supposed to be with their child, and it made me realize, I never had that. Everything he's ever given me has been seeded with hidden, and sometimes not-so-hidden, stipulations."

I rested my chin on her shoulder, shuddering on the inside. It nearly gutted me that anyone made her feel unwanted, especially the person who raised her. I wrapped my arms around her tight, wishing like hell she could feel every ounce of love I had for her in that one simple hug.

Navie leaned her head back, exposing her neck to my lips. I kissed her there, barely skimming her skin at first. Slipping my hand up her shirt, I began caressing just under her breast, taking my time in truly feeling her. She arched her back, giving me more access. Slipping the T-shirt over her head, I kissed the other side of her neck, as her palms gripped both my knees.

"You're all I'll ever need, Blue," I whispered between kisses.

Navie sighed, and I felt every ounce of stress leave her body. As if my words were massaging her body, she went limp, leaning on me for complete support. I stood, picking her up in one swift move, leaving our food untouched. Carrying her to the bedroom, I gently placed her on the bed, our bodies never breaking contact. My lips traced her neck. I kissed every part of her flesh there before I went for her lips. Pushing my tongue inside, I sighed once I found hers. I never had to chase her. Never felt like I was the only one kissing. She matched each stroke of my tongue; almost greedier than I was.

As I concentrated on my movements, I unclasped her bra, sliding it off in one movement. She waited patiently, still as a statue. I bowed my head, skimming her satin skin from the center of her chest to her belly button. My tongue circled the small slit, admiring her shape. My lips trailed down, my mouth watering as I came to her heated center. I buried my face between her legs, taking in her scent; reveling in it. God, I could feel her, taste her, make love to her all damn day, never accomplishing anything else in my whole life and be completely satisfied.

I kissed her inner thigh, running my nose to her panty line. What I would give for more patience so I could drive her crazy, but my plan backfired. My dick throbbed; my chest aching with need. Heat rushed from the soles of my feet to the top of my head, causing a thin layer of sweat to bead across my forehead. My thoughts were no longer coherent. Focusing on Navie's body, and what her body did to mine, left little room for anything else.

Placing my fingers on both sides of her hips, I grasped the strings holding the black lace that covered the place I aimed to get at and pulled them down her body, savoring every goose bump that arose from my touch. I grinned and looked up at her. Her blue eyes glimmered, as she anticipated what came next. She bit her bottom lip, causing it to redden and plump. Long strands of her hair sprawled out on my crisp white pillowcase, looking more beautiful than I'd ever seen it.

"Trevor," her voice trembled, and I loved the sound of it. Heat rose in my chest, climbing all the way to my ears at the sound of her need.

Taking her feet in my hands, I palmed the bottoms, and pushed her legs straight up in the air. After placing each one on my shoulders, I turned my head to kiss the inside of her ankle. First the left one, then the right. I sprinkled small, open-mouthed kisses up her leg, pausing, and licking just behind her knee. She squirmed and attempted to pull her leg up near her body, trying to wiggle out of my grasp.

"I'm going to kiss you inside out, baby." I held tight to her thigh until she gave up the fight, letting it fall gracefully back onto my shoulder. I glanced up at her, noticing a small smile that crossed her face. She liked the idea of me kissing her inside out. She liked that I'd told her what I was about to do.

My tongue swiped across her center, front to back. My mouth watered as her juices found my taste buds. Eagerness surged through my veins. With more pressure, my tongue lapped her again, but this time, I found her center, and entered, pushing my tongue in as far as it would go inside of her.

In and out.

All around.

In and out.

I sighed with content, pulling the small nub into my mouth and suckling at first. Navie bucked twice, letting me know she was close. Pushing my face further into her, I gripped her clit between my teeth, then sucked it hard, pushing her over the edge. I licked her, wanting every ounce of her inside of me.

Sated, Navie sighed, her words barely audible. "I can't move."

I crawled out from under her legs, lying them gently on the bed. I kissed each one, taking my time, giving her time to recover as I made my way up to her stomach.

"You taste so good."

"You're so embarrassing." She laughed and covered her face with one hand.

I slid up her body and pulled it away. "Why am I embarrassing? Because I like the way you taste?"

"I don't know." She giggled and put her other hand up to shield her reddened cheeks.

"Baby." I pulled her other hand into mine.

Losing myself in her beautiful blue eyes, I lost train of thought. It was if her iris' pooled around, circling until I was hypnotized.

"I love you," she said.

"I love you too."

"I know you say I don't need to thank you, but I always feel like I need to. Trevor, I've—never felt like this. I've never been this focused or content. The support you show me—it just means a lot to me."

"I'm glad you feel good about it, but supporting you is my job as your boyfriend. It should never be something you *don't* expect. You know, I learned a lot in our time apart. Even though it wasn't something I wanted to experience, it was for the best. The same way you learned a little bit about yourself, so did I. I don't ever want to be without you, Navie. Ever. And that means I have to spend every single day giving you what you deserve. You mean the world to me, babe." I kissed her cheek.

Her arms wrapped around my neck, bringing me closer to her, as she kissed my lips. She didn't respond with words. But I felt every ounce of love and respect she had for me in her kiss. I fumbled with my jeans one handed, not taking my lips from hers.

Pushing them down to my thighs, we worked together to get them off. Navie picked up where my hands left off so we wouldn't have to separate. Operating like one smooth machine, her feet took control near my hips, as she pushed my jeans down my legs until I was able to kick them off the end of the bed. God, I loved when our skin touched. It took me to a whole new universe. Every time. Sight, smell, touch; all my senses were on overload when her bare skin found my own.

Making sure she was ready, I circled my hips, barely pushing inside her. As our bodies melded together, I thrust my hips again, then a third time, as I slid into her until I couldn't go any deeper. Sublime. It was fucking sublime when I was inside her. The heat emulating from her center damn near caught me on fire. Tingles from the tip of my dick all the way to my balls kept shooting up and down, like someone was attacking me with a fucking lightsaber.

Bringing my palm to her face, she kissed the inside of my wrist as I pushed in and out of her, slowly and intently. Guttural grunts echoed from deep within my chest. I felt like a grizzly bear claiming his mate. Uninhibited, Navie groaned on the last thrust, giving me just enough energy to push farther and harder than I had the last time. My release shot out, euphoria clouding my mind as I lay atop her, spent. Hot breaths covered my face, causing my lips to tingle. I sucked on her bottom lip, tired, but exhilarated all at the same time.

"That was—" she began, breathless.

"Hot," I finished.

"More than hot."

I peered up at her, bringing my chin to sit perfectly between her naked breasts. I'd never seen beauty like hers before. It was simple, yet so mesmerizing. No makeup. No expensive highlights donned her hair. She was raw and real. Minimal; but more than I could have ever hoped for. She was perfect. Perfect for me. I was going to marry her. I knew that, was more sure of that particular detail than I was anything else. Walking through the rest of my life with her by my side was a no brainer.

CHAPTER 26
NAVIE

"JESSICA BOOKER, HUH?" Tommy asked as we trained.

"Yeah. Trevor's had me watching her last few fights. She fights dirty."

"She does. You'll definitely have to watch her. It puts extra pressure on you because you're trying to concentrate to win, but you got this. You've worked your ass off, Navie. And I know some of Steele has rubbed off on you. You're gonna do what you gotta do to get where you want to go."

"Thanks, Tommy." I punched the bag, causing him to groan. Smiling, I continued. "And you're right. Trevor has rubbed off on me. I'm not letting anyone take this from me. Not even a little cheating bitch named Jessica."

"Whoa!" He chuckled, but I was serious.

She wasn't taking anything from me. No matter her experience. Anyone could do anything if they wanted it bad enough and worked hard for it. I'd learned that alone since I'd shown up in Boston begging Payne to ask Trevor if I could train with them with nothing more than the clothes on my back.

"Who you calling a bitch, babe?" Trevor appeared behind Tommy, grinning wide, exposing the cutest dimples. I never could resist when he grinned at me like that.

"No one." I punched one last time.

He winked at Tommy, as if he'd overheard our conversation.

"Change of plans," Trevor announced. "I have a girl coming in the morning. You'll spar with her."

"Who?" I was curious since there were no other female fighters who trained in his gym.

"Carly Sipes."

"Former light weight champion, Carly Sipes?"

I hadn't even realized he knew her.

Trevor nodded. "That's the one."

"How'd you pull that one off? Promise her a night with Gage?" Tommy chuckled.

"She'd rip Gage's dick off and shove it up his ass," Payne said, surprising us all by his appearance.

"Dude. You're back?" Tommy slapped Payne's shoulder.

"For now. If my wife calls, I gotta go, though."

"That might be how I like it, asshole," Gage responded to Payne's joke.

"All right, ladies. No need for name calling." Trevor walked behind me, placing his hands on my shoulders. "Carly is in town, and nice enough to help Navie out."

"Very cool, doll. I'll be around. Don't want to miss that." Tommy left with a wave to us all.

"I can't believe you got her to train with me."

Carly was the biggest name in women's cage fighting. She had been involved from the beginning. No other female had ever reached her level of success. Even without a true league, she'd gained multiple endorsements.

"She's happy to do it." Trevor ended the conversation, nodding toward the cage. "As soon as Gage is done, I have a few things I want to go over with you. Groundwork stuff."

"Okay." I kissed him and walked over to the jump box.

I was so tired after training, the last thing I wanted to do was make a pit stop before soaking in Trevor's bathtub for an hour, while drinking two glasses of wine that would undoubtedly put me straight to sleep. But it was Noah. I'd intentionally *not* visited them every day in order to give them family time, but the thought of seeing him made me happy. Plus, Willow's family had been in town the whole week to visit. Except they were gone now, so when Trevor mentioned visiting as soon as we hit the freeway, I didn't have the heart to tell him no.

Willow answered the door, looking like a new woman compared to the last time I'd seen her. "Hey, I'm so glad you guys came by."

"We ordered pizza, it's on the way." I winked.

Willow smirked, then eyed Trevor. "Trevor Steele ordered pizza?"

"No, Navie Fuller ordered pizza. Trevor Steele searched their website looking for 'good carbs.'" I hugged her and we both chuckled.

"Laugh all you want, Aquamarine. But you should appreciate someone like me who constantly thinks about your gains," Trevor teased.

The second I spotted Noah, I bent to take him from Payne. "Oh, come here little boy." He was cooing and swinging his arms, fighting to get out of his blanket. "He's grown so much."

"He has. I think he's going to be big like his daddy. I can barely keep up with his need to feed." Willow plopped down on their sofa next to Payne.

"Are you still planning on freelancing?" I asked, mesmerized by Noah's cuteness. "Or will you just keep your commitments to the charity?"

"I think for right now I'm just going to help out at Triple D. I'll never leave them," she gushed talking about the charity committed to educating the masses about drinking and driving. She'd told me multiple times she and Payne would always support them, given Payne's past. "It's hard to find time because when Noah's sleeping, I'm doing things around the house. I'll probably eventually get back at it, but for right now, I just want to stay in our little bubble." She gazed up at Payne, and he squeezed her shoulder, bringing her into his chest. He placed a kiss atop her head and nodded, agreeing with her. Their little boy had brought them a closeness I couldn't be sure either of them even realized was possible before they had him.

The doorbell rang, and Trevor answered the door to grab the pizza from the delivery guy. He took the box to the kitchen, where he made himself at home so no one had to get up. He loaded everyone up with two slices and placed them on the table.

"Go eat, babe. I'll watch over him until you're done." Trevor scooped the baby from my arms before I even had time to argue.

"Aww, look at Steele. He's already getting it." Willow patted Trevor's arm as she left the room to get her food.

I chuckled. "Right... he just wanted the baby."

He didn't argue, captivated with Noah. I wondered what Trevor was thinking. He was so focused on the little guy, seemingly in his own world. Payne joined me and Willow in the kitchen.

"You ready for tomorrow?" he asked.

"I am."

"Go hard. Benefit from someone with her experience."

"I plan on it," I confirmed. I took advantage since Payne brought it up. "Did you ever feel overwhelmed? I feel like it's all happening so fast. Like I just started training, but at the same time, it's all I want," I said taking a bite of the stuffed cheese crust.

"Yeah, it was a lot at once, but it was the best decision I ever made, career-wise. Now that I have a family, I don't worry about finances. I don't worry if something were to happen to me. I know that Willow and Noah will be taken care of.

"It's going to be different for you though. I had a million reasons to take the chance. With my past, it wasn't like I had any other options, but for you... it's a dream. And I think no one will ever believe in your dreams the same way you do. So, it's up to you to make them a reality."

I nodded, agreeing with him.

Payne was right. No matter how much my father doubted me, or even how much Trevor believed in me... it was up to me to make it my reality, which was why I spent the rest of our visit telling myself that over and over.

The next morning, I anxiously drove to the gym. I knew I had a lot to learn. I also knew Carly was a busy woman, and the last thing I wanted was for her to feel like she was wasting her time.

"I'm Carly," she greeted me, not exactly cheerful.

I shook her extended hand. "Navie. It's a pleasure to meet you."

"I know who you are, Fuller."

Her tone surprised me. I looked at Trevor, questioning her stance since I didn't know her and he did. Was it a bad thing she knew who I was? Had I insulted her intelligence and not known it?

Instead of reading the room, Trevor spoke as if our introduction had gone smoothly. "So, basically, I'm going to be taking notes and Tommy is going to record. I want to see how Navie's martial arts and speed match with yours. Obviously, she's only worked with men until now." Trevor walked to the cage, not turning back to see if we were following him.

"I'm not going to take it easy on you. Practice like you're playing, got it?" Carly barked, all business.

"Got it."

One round with Carly Sipes and I was full-blown questioning my sanity. Sweat dripped from my face as if someone had doused me in water. I was in good shape. Extremely good shape considering I'd been training hours every day. But her pace and strength had my breathing labored and my body aching from the punches and strikes she'd given me.

"When she rounds on you like that, try to get your leg above her head. If you get her in a leg lock, she'll break free," Trevor coached as I took a drink of water.

"Her ribs are concrete. Abs too."

"Don't worry so much about the punches. It's all about leverage."

I nodded and took my place in the center of the cage. I swung first, falling off balance when she kicked me in the thigh. Before I knew it, we were on the ground again. This time, I took Trevor's advice, swinging both my legs above her head. I quickly rolled to the side, taking her body with mine.

"Good, Navie!" Tommy yelled.

Before I could mentally celebrate, she countered with another roll and had me flat on my back. We continued a steady pace: punching, maneuvering, and kneeing.

At the sound of the bell, we untangled and made our way back to our corners. "Throw in an arm bar when you can. Use your core."

After a quick sip, I nodded at Trevor's instruction, and went back for more. Twenty minutes of back and forth, and I was more exhausted than I'd ever been sparring with Gage, Tommy, or Trevor. Carly hadn't taken it easy on me. She'd pushed me further than I'd ever gone before, even in a real fight.

"You did good today," she praised, but followed it up with constructive criticism. "But I'd suggest getting in a different martial arts class. You're limited in your movements. I had your weakness picked out within the first round." Carly placed her gloves in her gym bag.

"I'll do that." I made a mental note to get Trevor's opinion on it. "Thank you for today."

"I owed Trevor one." She shrugged. "I'll be in town for a week. We'll meet up again day after tomorrow."

I'd assumed our workout was a one-time thing. Excitement filled me, knowing I'd get more experience with her. "Awesome. I'll see you then."

I knocked on Trevor's office door as I entered, even though I knew I didn't have to. "Hey."

"Well, how you feeling?" His feet were propped up on the desk, crossed at the ankles.

"I'm beat, but I feel good."

"I'm proud of you. Carly is no joke. You held your own with her today." He dropped his feet to the floor and stood.

"Thank you. She mentioned owing you one…"

"Ah, it's nothing." He waved the notion away and kissed my lips.

Hmm. I was curious, but his kisses always had a way of making me lose my train of thought. His arms found their way around my sweaty body, bringing me flush with him. My feet came off the ground as he picked me up, never breaking our kiss.

I could spend all day lost in his kiss. Our lazy days at home were the best. It could have been that we hardly ever got them, but I liked to think it was because we spent most of our free time tangled up on the couch making out.

"Okay, I have to go to work now," I said around his lips.

"One more." His tongue reached for mine.

"Get a fucking room already," Gage interrupted us.

Trevor lowered me and scowled at our friend. I chuckled, kissed his cheek, and left with a wink in Gage's direction.

I needed a shower. And a magic pill for soreness. Boy, I did not want to endure six hours of filling drinks after that workout. But, alas, I wasn't the kind of woman who depended on my boyfriend to pay my way, and since I'd yet to make a dime off a fight… serving wench it was.

CHAPTER 27
TREVOR

"BABE?" I called out as I lightly knocked on the bathroom door. Navie had been in the shower for thirty minutes. I knew she was nervous. The tension radiating from her all afternoon, last night, and the night before, made me wish I could cure her insecurities with a single touch. But… I couldn't.

"I'll be out in a minute," she called over the shower spray.

We had to be at the gym in less than thirty minutes. Normally, I would have encouraged her a little more bluntly to hurry, but it wasn't the time. She'd barely said ten words in the last two hours, and I hated that her nerves were so prevalent. Mostly because I felt like she was torturing herself when she didn't need to. I had so much faith in her. Plus, I knew once people got to know her—once they saw her passion for the sport, they'd fall in love with her. Just like I had.

Navie opened the bathroom door as steam rolled out from behind her. I chuckled, but quickly found myself biting my bottom lip. She was naked. Beads of water spread across her skin where she hadn't dried off well enough and I wanted to lick them dry. My gaze traveled down until it reached a small patch of hair covering what I'd come to claim as my pride and joy. God, I could live inside her.

"Stop, pervert!" She threw her damp towel at me, then turned away from me as she stepped into a pair of black shorts.

"I will never be able to do that." I shrugged a lame apology, and snapped the towel in her direction, smacking her ass. "Sorry."

"Ow!" She giggled while pulling her sports bra over her head. "And no, you're not sorry."

"That's not a lie."

Navie shook her head. "I'm so freaking nervous."

"He's just going to ask you about your training."

"It's not just about the interview."

Navie walked around the room, swiping deodorant under arms, then placed the deodorant in her gym bag. I looked on as she parted her damp hair down the center so she could braid it. She always looked so cute when her hair was styled like that.

"Dang it." She grimaced, reaching behind her. "I need Willow or Lena here."

I could honestly say I'd never braided a girl's hair before, but there was a first time for everything. I had to calm her down. Her anxiety was getting the best of her, and personally, I couldn't stand to watch it.

I walked up behind her and pulled the strands from her hands. "Here," I offered.

Navie peered at me in the reflection of the mirror that hung from the wall in my bedroom. Her eyebrows rose and a smile played on her lips. "You're going to braid my hair?"

"I've watched you do it a million times. I've got this."

"Really?"

"Watch and learn, Cobalt."

Running my hands through her hair to comb out the tangles, I separated the strands into three sections. I'd witnessed her braid her own hair so many times. Surely, I could figure it out.

Navie continued to grin as I crossed each strand over and over, then straightened it out, then pulled the three sections over and under again. It looked like shit. And it was going to fall out before we even reached the gym. Instead of giving up, I moved to the other side and managed to make an even bigger mess of her hair there. She always made it look so easy. It wasn't. My fingers were too big, and my hands fumbled with the sections, causing me to lose my place regarding which pieces went where.

Instead of pulling my absolute failed attempt apart, she left it, then turned toward me and wrapped her arms around my neck. "I love you. So much."

My lips found hers, our mouths fitting perfectly together. I pulled away but held her firmly by her hips. "And I love you. You're going to kill it tonight. I can feel it."

"Thank you. For everything. For supporting me. For loving me. For fixing my hair when my hands were trembling."

"Just go out there and kick a little ass, and we'll call it even, okay?"

She grinned and leaned up on her tiptoes. Instead of kissing me, she circled her nose around mine, creating the sweetest Eskimo kisses I'd ever had the pleasure of making. "I'm going to win."

"Yes, you are," I agreed.

When Navie and I arrived at the gym, it was packed to capacity. Of course, Gage and Tommy had already texted me ten times with the news, but I hadn't texted them back anything other than a thumbs up. I didn't want to concentrate on the crowd. I didn't want to be side-tracked by who might be in the audience, although secretly, I was praying some of the agents I'd sent invites to would show up. None of them had confirmed, though.

Luckily, Lena was able to fix Navie's hair while Tommy, Gage, Willow, and Payne wished her luck, going almost overboard with words of encouragement. We all left the locker room together to give Navie a few minutes by herself. She'd taken Carly's advice on ways to get out of her own head. She'd been practicing meditation and it seemed to work for her, which gave me a sense of relief.

Thirty minutes later, I knocked on the door twice, letting her know it was time. She opened the door seconds later, her eyes intense, but her breathing was steady, which was a great sign.

We walked hand in hand toward the cage. I squeezed her hand when the crowd grew louder. I could just imagine what Gage was saying to them. He'd talked me into letting him MC for the night.

"Go get her." My lips brushed hers, giving her one last word of encouragement.

She nodded but didn't say anything. Her gait quickened, and she rolled her neck in an attempt to relax her muscles. Following her out, I couldn't help but look around in awe. Every seat was filled. Most of the spectators were already on their feet as Gage announced Navie's name. I grinned, overwhelmed. We were going to be able to pull it off. I could feel it deep inside my bones. This was only the beginning.

I took my place in her corner but remained stoic. I didn't want her to feed off me either way. I wanted her to set the tone, to accomplish whatever she was going to accomplish on her own. She needed that confirmation.

Navie met Jessica in the center of the cage, both women intensely staring at one another. As soon as the bell sounded, Navie went after Jessica, aggressively on the offense. I was proud of her for setting the tone of the fight, and she was clearly in control of the pace. Jessica tried to recover, landing two swift kicks to Navie's thighs. As if she hadn't felt them at all, Navie caught Jessica's chin with an uppercut.

"She's improved." Payne crossed his arms, interested in the fight once he saw some action.

"I know. Her time with Carly really helped."

Payne was about to respond but winced. I looked back at the mat in time to see Navie pinned up against the cage. I watched closely to make sure Jessica didn't grab it for leverage. She didn't, and eventually squatted, putting her shoulder in Navie's stomach. I knew Navie was in trouble because she'd lost almost all of her momentum. Jessica pushed into her, picking Navie up full on and slamming her down on the mat.

Watching matches had been part of my life for over twenty years. I thoroughly enjoyed being a spectator, where I didn't have a dog in the fight. I understood the fanfare because I was a fan too. But seeing the woman I loved be taken down so fiercely when there was nothing I could do about it didn't give me the same feeling it did when I was cheering my buddies on. My gut twisted with fear, and I realized then, more than any other time, what it was like for family members of those fighting.

It was terrifying to say the least. I knew the risk involved. I'd been injured more times than I could remember and knew the chance of Navie making it out of her career without something happening to her was slim to none. I grimaced at the thought.

I'd always been on the other side of things. I would have to find a balance, though. I never wanted my concern to come off as not believing in her. Forcing myself to clear my mind, I focused on the fight, not my girlfriend, who was in the middle of taking a pounding. I chanted her next move silently. She didn't do what I would have done, but she rolled out, kicking Jessica's leg to break her hold. Both back at standing positions, the bell rang, signaling the first round was over.

"Way to work," I greeted her.

"I have to get some knee jabs in. She's not expecting them. Hardly any cover on her sides," she said through labored breaths.

I grinned and looked back at Payne. He grinned too, visibly impressed with Navie's take on her opponent.

"Go get her!" Gage yelled from behind me.

Navie's attack in the second round was stronger than the first. She seemed to be finding her rhythm, and even got a few knee kicks in. She landed her punches, precise and strong. I could tell from Jessica's demeanor, Navie was wearing her down. Her mouth was open, letting me know she wasn't breathing through her nose. Her long, strong legs were bent, ready for Navie's next move, but I could see them trembling from where I stood.

The crowd roared, energized by Navie's next kick. She landed it, her foot making contact with Jessica's face. All at once, they chanted *Navie, Navie, Navie.* I couldn't believe the reception she was getting. I beamed, taking it all in.

Jessica fell to the ground, and Navie pounced on her, falling to her knees, punching and kneeing in a smooth pattern. The referee slammed onto the mat, calling it at once. It hadn't looked like a knock-out, and I couldn't see Jessica's face from the angle I was at.

Navie popped to her feet, her mouthpiece showing bright in the dim light. The veins in her neck protruded, straining at the scream of victory even though I couldn't hear her over the crowd.

I ran to her and picked her up, my adrenaline spiking to new levels. I was so fucking proud of her, prouder than I'd ever been for myself. I held my girl high, letting her take in the moment, the crowd, and the feeling… of victory.

"I can't believe people were asking for my autograph!" Navie squealed as we walked out to my jeep more than an hour later. I'd been ready to take her home for thirty minutes, but she spoke to every single person who waited outside for her. Too impressed by her humbleness and natural connection to the fans, I stood in the background like a delighted boyfriend. "I can't believe that feeling—when they were chanting my name. Trevor, I've never felt anything like it. How have you and Payne been feeling this for years and never mentioned it? You guys never acted like it was a big deal. God, it's exhilarating!"

"Alright, champ." I swung my arm over her shoulder. "A hundred bucks says you won't be so excited when people are following you around Target while you purchase tampons."

"Ah, good point." She frowned, but then she grinned again. "Man, the crowd was phenomenal. I don't think I'll ever get used to that. I'm in love, Trevor. Head over heels in love."

I stopped and pulled her into me just as we made it to the passenger side door. "Me too, Blue. Me too." My large palm cupped her jaw; my fingers finding their way into her hair. An idea popped into my head. I knew exactly what I needed to do and when. It was so weird how life just fell into place without so much as a warning.

CHAPTER 28
NAVIE

"YOU DIDN'T HAVE TO COME," Willow whispered as she hugged me.

"I wanted to."

I straightened my wrap-around dress even though it clung to my body like a second skin, which meant it hadn't moved since I'd put it on and hadn't needed any straightening. But I needed something to do with my hands. Payne was signing his contact with the AFL, and as per usual, my father was paying him well to do so. He had always had a flare for the dramatic, but millions above what Payne and Willow were hoping for was completely insane. Although, I was truly happy for my friends. Trevor and I discussed the pros and cons of skipping the whole shindig, but at the end of the day, I wanted to support Payne. I could tell Trevor was concerned about running into my brother and dad. I understood where he was coming from, but I just wasn't worried about it anymore. I still wasn't sure if that made me happy or sad.

Flash photography blinded me as we walked inside the venue. It seemed like there was even more press than normal. Payne's celebrity was quickly escalading. Willow was handling it well, and he seemed unbothered by the whole thing. Trevor's hand sat low on my back as we walked by the hoard of people gathered outside, yelling our names as we passed. Trevor didn't stop; neither did I. I'd grown up in the spotlight, somewhat, but no one had ever truly been that interested in me because my dad was the face of his company and my brother was, more often than not, causing a stir of some kind. He cared more about being relevant than I had, which was ironic since my boyfriend was more celebrity than Preston could have ever hoped to be.

"Umm… did anyone else see Gage and Lena?" Tommy asked once we were seated at our table.

"No. Why?" I asked. I hadn't talked to Lena in over a week, but I knew she'd show up to support Payne.

"They walked the fuckin' red carpet together."

I coughed, almost sending the wine I'd just taken a sip of down the wrong pipe. "What?"

"I shit you not. Both of them dressed to the T's and grinning like fools."

"I didn't realize Lena even liked Gage." I knew they had hooked up, but from their frequent roast exchanges, that appeared to have been a mistake.

"I think that's the appeal, babe." Trevor winked, sipping his own drink.

"Oh."

"Navie." My dad's voice, no more than a murmur, carried from behind me.

Trevor squeezed my hip, on the defense before I turned to face my father.

"Hi." I forced a smile. A public event was no time for family drama, and honestly, I wished for once, there would be none. "How are you?" So formal, it was awkward. *I* was awkward.

My dad leaned down to kiss my cheek since I hadn't stood to greet him. I afforded him the gesture, showing one of my own with a partial hug.

"It's good to see you. I hear you're making headway inside the cage."

I should have known he'd bring it up. It wasn't like we had anything else to talk about. "Yeah. Thanks."

Preston joined our circle, causing more tension. My father's gaze trailed over to Trevor, who had a vise grip on my waist. "Trevor."

Trevor didn't move, only nodded once in my father's direction. I could feel Tommy's eyes examining the situation, and I hated for him to witness our exchange.

"It seems we have business to discuss," my brother told Trevor.

"No, we don't."

"If you're going to play with the big boys—"

Trevor's hand slipped from around me as he stood to address my brother face to face. I held my breath, hoping his anger didn't get the better of him. At least not where there was an audience.

"You need to get a fucking grip," Trevor growled. Instead of focusing on Preston, he turned his attention to my dad. "You're losing your daughter in a battle no one but you and your son is even playing in. Stop fucking with her feelings. Stop being so fucking dramatic. And stop creating a beef with me that doesn't exist."

"You're playing with fire, Steele," Preston threatened.

I assumed he was referring to the financial backing Trevor had been able to secure for the female league, including Pro Con, an investor in the AFL.

I almost entered their conversation but thought better of it. It wouldn't have mattered what I said to my brother, he couldn't see past the threat of someone else being successful. I noticed for the first time my father was silent. It was Preston who was forcing the wedge between us, not my father. Although he was allowing it to happen.

Trevor had told me multiple times that he'd never had issues with my dad before. He said my father had treated him well during his time in the league. Granted, Trevor had made my father more money than he could ever spend, but just the same, there always seemed to be a mutual respect there. That didn't seem like the case as I watched him stand beside my brother, who was being so disrespectful. I was positive my relationship with Trevor had something to do with it but didn't feel like trying to hash it out now. We were there for our friend, not my personal life.

Instead of punching my brother's lights out like I knew he wanted to do, Trevor took the high road. "If you'll excuse us..." Trevor's voice trailed off, leaving his dismissal toward my father plain as day. I glanced up at my dad, hoping he would back off. He nodded at me once, and afforded me a tight smile, then left without another word.

Trevor kissed my forehead after taking his seat. "You okay?"

"Yeah. I just don't get it. I don't understand why he makes everything so difficult."

"It's his problem, okay? Not ours. If that's how he wants to live his life, we can't stop him."

He was right. I nodded in agreement and kissed his lips. It was so refreshing being around someone positive. Trevor always looked on the bright side of things. Or maybe he saw life's struggles as challenges and was determined to defeat them, but I'd grown to know whatever the reason, I wanted him on my team, no matter what we had to face in the future.

After the signing ceremony, Payne remained on stage, visibly annoyed that he had to do interviews. "Do you feel more pressure as you enter your second year of the professional circuit undefeated?" One reporter called out to him.

I'd always loved the press conference that followed my father's contract signings. Watching the fighters interact with some of the most unprofessional reporters in sports was a hoot. Mostly because the athletes didn't play the media's games. When one of them stepped over the line, most of them let the reporters know it. But I loved Payne the most because he would straight up ignore them. Just look away and not even answer them. It was entertaining for sure.

"No pressure here." Payne shrugged a shoulder. "I'll fight who I fight. I don't worry about records. I keep my mind on who I'm fighting in that moment."

I glanced at Willow after he answered. Her gaze never left him. The smile that spread across her face made me smile too. The love she had for him; the adoration was inspiring. She had his back. She supported her man no matter what was going on in the world around them. I glanced up at Trevor, his sights set on Payne as well. After a few moments, he peered down at me and kissed my cheek.

I had that too. The support.

Leaning my head on his shoulder, we waited out the questions, until eight minutes later when one of the female reporters asked Payne when he would be introducing his son to the world. He picked the water bottle up from the table he was sitting at, took a huge gulp, then got up and walked out. Willow was moving toward the side door before he'd even set the empty bottle down.

It never got old; seeing a man protect his family. Or a woman knowing her man so well, she could guess his next move without so much as a nod from him. Witnessing the love between two people so strong was beautiful.

My fingers moved barely; a soft scratch on Trevor's thigh, when he took my palm against his, pulling all my emotions with it. I sat up straight, knowing we had everything I thing I'd just admired in my friends. Protection; and love. I smiled as he brought my hand to his mouth, just as I knew he would. Soft lips caressed my skin, prompting a slight sigh to escape my lips. Two small kisses; one huge statement.

CHAPTER 29
TREVOR

"WHERE DO you want the wine glasses?" Lena asked, a couple of them dangling from her fingers.

"The table?" The wine glasses were the least of my worries.

"You asking or telling?" She laughed.

"The table is fine. Were you able to find blue roses?" Willow asked, Noah firm on her hip.

"They're in the back. Ten dozen, unwrapped and ready to go."

I wiped the sweat from my upper lip. "Fuck, this is nerve wracking."

Willow and Lena chuckled in sync with one another. "Of course it is, dummy. Not only are you asking Navie to marry you, you're making her dreams come true. I for one, can't wait to see her reaction." Willow continued with her task, chill as ever as she made it seem like it was just another day at the office.

"How many lights do you want around the cage?" Tommy asked.

"I don't know—"

"As many as you can get," Lena interrupted. "What?" She asked when I turned toward her. "Girls like things that sparkle." She rolled her eyes.

"As many as you can get around it," I agreed.

I'd been planning my proposal for months. Telling Navie about the league was the icing on top. I'd finally worked out the investors, the base headquarters, and had six contracts my attorneys had hammered out, ready to sign. Navie's was one of them. I was certain she thought she'd just sign once the kinks were worked out since she was part-owner in the league, but I wanted more for her. I wanted her to experience the adrenaline from signing her first contract. Therefore, I made sure hers was written first.

The contracts were generous, considering we were just getting off the ground. I'd been in talks with three agents and two trainers. Most of the women who trained around the country didn't have agents yet, being that there wasn't a professional cage for them to fight in, which meant the finances weren't large enough to need someone to negotiate. Some athletes kept them on for endorsements though. Hopefully, after I signed them, all of them would need one.

"What are you doing for food?" Willow asked as she bounced Noah on her hip, causing him to chuckle.

"Her favorite. Cheeseburger, garbage fries, and Twinkies."

"I can't imagine this not turning out in your favor."

"Hope you're right, Will." I ruffled Noah's hair. Damn, did I ever wish she was right.

Thirty minutes later, I pushed everyone out of the gym. Navie would arrive soon, and to be honest, I needed some time to myself. The last time I'd proposed, it hadn't gone so well.

My phone vibrated in my pocket as I prepared to light the candles on the table. It was Navie, thankfully. "Hey, baby. Are you on your way here?"

"Well, I was, but Casey called in at work. Ethan asked if I could cover, so I called Tommy to re-schedule our workout. He sounded weird, like he was sick or something, anyway. If you want, swing by for…"

I didn't hear anything else she said. Of course, her work would call her in on the night I was trying to make perfect for her. For fuck's sake. Leaning my head back on my shoulders, I squeezed my eyes shut out of frustration.

"Dude!" Tommy stormed into the gym, skidding to a halt when I held my index finger over my mouth, signaling I was talking to Navie on the phone.

"Let me call you back, I just had someone walk in." I hung up before she could reply. This was the worst case scenario.

"She just called and tried to cancel."

"I know." I scowled.

There was nothing left to do but call Ethan.

I dialed the phone number to the bar while Tommy waited. The appreciation in his face as he looked around the gym made me feel better about the situation, though.

Ethan answered on the second ring. "Hey, it's Steele."

"How's it going, man?"

"Well, not too good. I need you to call Navie and cancel her shift."

"Man, I wish I could, but I'm short-handed tonight."

Pulling a large breath through my nostrils, I exhaled, trying to keep my calm. "Ethan, not to be a dick, but I have huge plans for her tonight, and I'm not letting anything or anyone fuck that up. So, I'm asking for your cooperation as nicely as I can."

Ethan sighed. "All right, man. I'll take care of it."

"Thank you. I promise, I'll make it up to you at some point."

I pushed my cell phone back into my pocket and turned to Tommy. "Bullet dodged. Now, we wait to hear back from Navie."

"Damn, this is making me nervous, and I ain't even the one tryin' to get married." Tommy slapped my shoulder. "Keep me posted."

Once he left, I was alone. I spent most of that time pacing back and forth, double and triple checking to make sure everything was in place while I waited for Navie to call to tell me she didn't have to work. Placing blue rose petals at the door, I made a walkway to the cage, where I had a candlelit table prepared in the center. Just as I dimmed the lights, I heard the front door open.

Taking in my woman as she gasped was all I'd ever need in life. Navie's hand covered her mouth, as her eyes widened, then teared up from what I hoped was happiness. My feet moved toward her, not worried in the least that twenty minutes ago, our night could have turned out much different.

"Trevor, I don't have to—what is this?"

I took her hands in mine, grinning so big, I could hardly speak. I licked my lips, taking a moment for myself before I took the final steps to make her my mine forever.

"Do you like it?"

"It's beautiful."

Leading her to the dinner table, I pulled her chair out for her. "Have a seat, and I'll get dinner."

Navie's smile lit up the dim space as soon as she saw what we were having. I placed her meal in front of her, as her gaze zeroed in on the garbage fries.

"This is so sweet. I can't believe you did all of this." She looked around, fascinated by the twinkling lights on the cage, her favorite foods, and the wine I'd already poured in our glasses.

"I, uh—have an ulterior motive."

"Okay." She picked up the glass of wine then set it back down without taking a sip. "Should I be nervous?"

I took a knee directly in front of her, paying special attention to the anticipation behind her eyes. I'd originally planned on asking her to be my wife after I told her the news about the league, but seeing her, looking into her eyes, knowing I didn't want to wait another second without my ring on her finger, I couldn't hold out.

I reached for the ring in my pocket, then stared at her. Nothing but love and admiration. That's all I saw when I looked at her, and it was so fucking crazy, but it seemed to be shooting out of her like laser beams. For me. How could I not marry a woman who looked at me like I was the only man she'd ever loved?

"So, before I met you, I had decided marriage wasn't for me. As you know, the first time didn't go so well for me. I had no idea what it meant to be a partner. To be a husband. To be a man who was loved by his woman so much. I've always been independent—" I paused, taking a moment to collect my thoughts. I'd purposely not written anything down, or even really thought about what I intended to say to her. I wanted the moment I asked Navie to marry me to be straight from the heart. "Being alone was okay with me. Until you, Navie. I think about you every minute of every day. I don't want to exist in a world where you're not beside me. You're everything to me. My whole world, baby." I brushed my thumb across her cheek, wiping each tear as it fell.

"All I think about is how you're not my wife. Even on my happiest days with you, it's just not enough, Blue. Every morning when I wake up; every night when I go to bed, nothing else matters but you. Not anything or anyone. I know you like your space. I do. But I'd really like it if from now on, me giving you space means you're going to the next room, not your own apartment."

She chuckled, grinning wide enough for me to know she agreed with me.

"Navie Fuller." Bringing her hand up to my lips, I kissed it two times, softly and intentional. "Will you marry me?"

"Yes!"

I couldn't contain my smile as I slid the engagement ring onto her left ring finger. She threw her arms around me, squeezing me tight. I held her, knowing I never had to let her go.

Navie pulled away and stared at the ring. "Trevor, it's beautiful."

"I made sure there was blue in it," I said.

"I love it." She held her hand out farther, admiring the blue sapphire surrounded by diamonds.

"I have another surprise," I told her as we took our seats around the table.

"What could possibly top this?" She took a bite of her burger, joy embodying her as she chewed.

I placed the newly inked contract on the table. She wiped her hands on her napkin, picked up the folder and began reading. My palms itched to take it from her and just spill the beans. Her gaze shot to mine once she figured out what she was reading.

"What is this?" Papers flipped one after the other as if the explanation was hidden in a secret code that she'd be able to find like those olden flip books. I grinned, in love with her humbleness.

"It's a contract. For you to join the American Women's Fighting League."

"What?" She glanced over the papers. "When did the league become official?"

"Two days ago. I held out because I wanted to tell you here. After you agreed to marry me." I winked, pulling her onto my lap.

Navie obliged, as I scooted my seat farther from the table. I held her loosely in my arms as she gave me her full attention. Her soft palms landed on each side of my face, fondling the whiskers that had gone unshaven. Blue eyes so mesmerizing; so dense. It was as if a painter had squirted a tube of indigo blue paint on a crisp white canvas and just left it there, unattended. The sight of it damn near consumed me whole.

"It's ours, babe. With the investors, we have enough for a hard launch. I've already secured the contracts for us to start. Five females plus you. You're the first to sign."

"I can't believe this. It all feels like a dream. What about the contracts? Is everyone signing for this amount? It's too much. I don't want you to lose your money. And we—"

"Shh." I held my finger over her lips. "Hey." I tipped her chin back to me, wanting her to see all the way to my soul of how sure I was about my new business venture. "It's going to work out. It's not just your dream anymore, Navie. I go where you go." I held her ring finger up. "Forever."

Wrapping my arm around her waist, I pulled her close. "We're going to be the best team, baby. There is nothing I have now or will ever have that isn't yours too and vice versa."

Navie wrapped her arms around me while lying her head on my shoulder, submitting her full body weight onto me. I counted three times she sniffed, making it hard for her to speak. "So, we're really doing this?" She raised her head and beamed at me.

"We are."

My mouth closed around hers, knowing there was nothing left to say. I was the happiest I'd ever been. I couldn't remember a time in my life where I wasn't worried about anything. Nothing seemed too difficult to overcome when I knew I had my future wife by my side. Nothing.

Navie leaned back but kept her arms wrapped firmly around my neck. "One thing."

"Anything," I said, already knowing I was going to give in to her demand. I didn't really care what it was either. She'd said yes to my proposal, and that was all that mattered to me.

"We can't name the league American Women's Fighting League."

"Why not?"

"Because when they acronym that thing, and they will… it will be AWFL. I can't be a part of something that everyone will call 'awful,' Trevor."

I burst into laughter. Damn, I hadn't even noticed. I'd been too concerned with the proposal, the contracts, the agents, the paperwork, and the fucking bank loans. Slipping my hand up her leg, I squeezed the inside of her thigh, wrapping my thumb and forefinger damn near all the way around it. "And this, beautiful girl, is why we are getting married. You're smart, and I need you."

"I can't wait to become your wife."

"It's me and you, babe. We have our whole lives ahead of us, and I plan on making you the happiest professional female cage fighter who ever lived."

"Well, I'm a little reluctant about your statement. There seems to be only six of us, and just running the numbers in my head…" she teased.

"We'll start a new trend. You'll have the best husband out of all of them. I'll be the standard. You'll be looked up to." I winked at her.

"I can't with you." Her lips found mine.

Pulling her into me, I relaxed for the first time in three days.

I'd thought for years I had everything I could have ever needed. The problem with that mentality was I wasn't thinking about what I *wanted*. Peace. I supposed it was one of those things in life no one missed if they'd never experienced it before. I had now. It all made sense, and I never wanted to be in a position in life again where I missed the whole point. Love and being loved—nothing ever felt more natural.

EPILOGUE

NAVIE

"PLEASE WELCOME the sixth woman to sign to the WFL, Navie Fuller." The MC announced my name as I walked out to the official press conference for the grand launch to the league.

Trevor grabbed the microphone from the middle-aged man and announced to the packed room. "Uh, that'll be Navie *Steele* as of this weekend, and technically, she was the first to sign."

Cheers erupted, even from the media. Of course, I could hear Tommy and Gage above everyone else. I blushed, obviously not expecting our personal lives to be mentioned because of the formality with the league.

Standing with the five women on stage made me feel like Wonder Woman. Empowerment, confidence, and excitement filled my body. My limbs tingled, buzzing with anticipation. Eagerness swarmed me, ready to take on the world.

Trevor kept the news conference short and sweet. We answered the typical questions from the media, and with Trevor there, surprisingly there were no personal questions. I'd assumed he had a word with them before we were brought in. I didn't mind either way. I'd learned from Payne, if they asked me something I didn't want to answer, I didn't have to.

As we were filing out of the gym, glimmering gold caught my eye from the right side of the building. A Rolex. My father. Glancing up at Trevor, he nodded, giving me the courage to approach my dad. Trevor took my hand in his and walked beside me.

"I heard congratulations are in order."

"Yeah."

Trevor stiffened beside me. I realized he was preparing for battle, while I… relaxed. Something strange shifted inside me, a tranquility I hadn't felt before. With nothing left to prove, it didn't seem so daunting to face my father. I'd learned to let go of my need for his approval.

"I've been going to therapy," he announced, shocking me.

Stunned, and not completely sure I'd heard him correctly, I stood speechless. Trevor gripped my hand, more than likely to comfort me, but I couldn't react to it. I felt like I needed my dad to repeat the words again so I would be positive of what I thought I heard.

"I know—I didn't handle things the right way with you. And I know I can't possibly make up for all the times I chose the league over you or myself over your happiness." My father removed his sunglasses, allowing me unfiltered eye contact. "I'm making Preston go too."

"You are?"

"We need all the help we can get."

Nodding, I glanced at Trevor then back toward my dad. I wasn't sure what to say to him.

It turned out, I didn't have to say anything.

"I'm sorry, Navie. I know the damage has been done, but I sincerely hope you can forgive me someday."

I swallowed, hoping to find my voice. "I appreciate that. I hope we can get there."

He glanced at Trevor but didn't address him. After a few seconds, he cleared his throat. "I know you don't believe me, but I do want you to be happy."

"I *am* happy."

"Good, that's good."

"Thank you for coming here."

"It's the least I could do. It appears you were right the whole time. There is a future in a female league. I know we won't ever work together, but I hope to prove to you that I don't want to see you fail. Either one of you. I will help out wherever I can."

Trevor tensed and responded before I could. "We appreciate the offer, but the last conversation you and I will ever have, is where I ask you for anything."

I didn't disagree with him even though it felt a little harsh.

"Fair enough." My dad nodded. "The offer still stands."

"Thank you," I said, still unsure what his version of the olive branch meant.

"Can I call you later in the week?"

"Sure."

"I better get to the airport, then." I wondered for a split second if he would try to hug me. It looked like he wanted to, but he didn't. He placed his glasses back down over his eyes and turned toward the black Escalade waiting for him in the parking lot. I looked on as he took two steps before turning back around. "I wasn't going to ask because of the way things have been as of late, but it would mean a lot to me if—" He swallowed, as if was choking on deep regret. "If I could attend the wedding. I understand if you don't want me to walk you down the aisle, I just—I want to be there."

Glancing up at Trevor, I raised an eyebrow. I never thought of inviting my father to the wedding. I had always just assumed he wouldn't want to be there. Trevor wrapped one arm around my shoulder and pulled me close letting me know he supported my decision.

"I think that's a great idea."

"I'll be there." He grinned. "Thank you."

Trevor and I looked on as my dad got inside his awaiting car. "That was heavy," he finally said after the car drove off.

"Therapy was the last thing I expected him to say."

"Better late than never."

"Yeah," I agreed. "Four days." I grinned up at him.

"Ninety-six hours, Blue."

Four days later, Lena rearranged my hair for the hundredth time. "Are you nervous?"

"No. I'm ready to be Mrs. Navie Steele." I smiled and took the light blue handkerchief Trevor had given me the night before in my hand. Wrapping it around my bouquet, I held it to my chest. He was so thoughtful. I hadn't even been prepared for the normal traditions when it came to weddings, but he'd thought of everything.

"You're beautiful. Everything is perfect," Willow said, picking her own bouquet up.

"Thank you, guys, for everything. We wouldn't have been able to pull this off on such short notice if it hadn't been for all of you. I just—I'm overwhelmed with gratitude." I blinked my water-filled eyes, until the tears dried out so they wouldn't mess up my makeup.

"We got you, girl. Always." Lena hugged me. "Now, let's go get you married."

I watched as my friends walked down the aisle, nothing but bliss in my heart. My father in the front row, I inhaled deep, thankful he'd made an attempt.

"You sure you want *him*? I don't have a league or anything, but I make a mean chicken parmesan." Tommy winked as he took my hand and placed it under his arm.

I giggled. "Thank you for giving me away, Tommy."

"My pleasure, Blue."

My eyes widened at his use of my nickname. He chuckled. "Chill. I had to get one more in on Steele before it would become a death wish messing with his wife."

I kissed his cheek just in time. The music began, and we walked. We walked for what felt like forever and a few seconds all at once. My intention had been to focus on every detail until I made it to Trevor at the end of the aisle, but everything blurred together with each step I took. It almost seemed like a dream. I could remember bits and pieces, but not the whole scene. Faces faded to the background and all I could see was Trevor. His smile warmed my heart; it comforted me and calmed my nerves.

Trevor winked at me as I approached the altar. He stood tall and confident, his hands folded in front of him. The closer we got, the more his hands twitched, and I knew him well enough to know it was because he wanted to touch me. Normally, we would have already wrapped our arms around each other being so close.

Tommy took my hand, gracefully handing me over to Trevor as the Justice of the Peace asked who gave me away. Unplanned, I glanced over my shoulder at my father, who nodded once. I smiled, knowing things weren't perfect, but at least he was trying. That was all I'd ever wanted.

Trevor's large, warm palm swallowed mine, bringing me back to the present. I felt protected and loved automatically. Tilting my head, I found his gaze with mine. Like a warm, cozy fire in the middle of winter, my soon-to-be-husband wrapped his aura around mine and settled me in for a future I was proud of. One I was excited about.

Trevor leaned down and whispered in my ear. "You look beautiful. I'll never forget the sight of you walking toward me as long as I live."

I shivered. His breath tickled my earlobe, setting my body on fire like a live wire. Grinning like a fool, I leaned my head on his shoulder before he led me up one step to the altar.

Trevor took my hands into his and spoke in the most endearing voice I'd ever heard from him. It was careful and intentional. He pronounced each word of our vows with fervor. His eyes circled with charged emotion. Hypnotized, I couldn't see anything else. He searched my soul; speaking only when he knew for certain he had its attention. He vowed to love and cherish me forever, and God did I believe him.

"I, Navie Pier Fuller, take thee, Trevor Jackson Steele, to be my wedded husband, to have and to hold, from this day forward, for better, for worse, for richer, for poorer, in sickness and in health, to love and to cherish, till death do us part, according to God's holy ordinance; and thereto I pledge myself to you."

I slipped the gold wedding band I'd purchased for him on his left hand. I'd never seen him wear jewelry before. I initially wasn't sure he'd even want to wear a ring, but he'd surprised me and told me he'd never take it off.

The Justice of the Peace closed his Bible. "By the power vested in me, I now pronounce you husband and wife. You may now kiss your bride."

Our friends cheered as our lips met.

I'd never forget the joy I had as we sealed our vows with our first kiss as a married couple. So much of my life had been spent hopelessly searching for the meaning of family. It hadn't occurred to me that I'd wasted so much time trying to please everyone around me while at the same time, attempting to feed my soul. With Trevor standing next to me, vowing to love me forever, to always put me first, I realized if I kept searching for something that didn't exist, I'd never rest easy. I'd never be at peace. Life wasn't perfect. It was messy and chaotic, and more often than not, disappointing. But the security of those blissful moments of happiness in between the hectic ones balanced it all out.

So, with our first steps down the aisle as husband and wife, I let all the what ifs and insecurities go. I released them into the world and out of my being. My body lightened, floated all most, next to Trevor as I made a silent vow of my own. To myself. I'd never work so hard for someone to love me and accept me again. I'd never lose myself again, chasing approval that wasn't mine to give in the first place.

The foundation and security Trevor provided me outweighed any insecurity I'd ever felt before. Pursuing happiness wouldn't make me happy. Being happy would make me happy. It was a choice, and choosing Trevor was the first step. He was my person. He was my rock that grounded me like an anchor. More importantly, he was now my husband and as I took in the faces we passed making our first walk together, my heart ached—too full, it was bursting with pride. Trevor pulled my hand to his lips, kissing the silver band he'd just placed on my finger. I glanced up at him, elated by his gesture.

"Can I call you Steele Blue now?"

"If you want to sleep on the couch," I teased.

Trevor grinned and held my hand high in the air as our guests cheered. "You're my wife," he said, as if he needed to say it out loud.

"I'm your wife," I agreed.

ACKNOWLEDGMENTS

Being a writer is the best feeling in the world. When I finish a book, I feel like I'm on top of the world. Then, I realize I'm not anywhere close to releasing the book. That's where this portion of my book comes into play. Thank you doesn't seem like enough for the people involved in my journey. My family. My biggest supporters. They're always there, pushing me to finish and start the next one. Having people in your corner makes a difference. And if there are any writers out there who don't feel like you have that, I'm rooting for you. Write one word. Then, the next. Don't give up.

Thank you to those who've helped me edit, proofread, format, and cover this book. The amount of work these professionals have put into my story made it what it is today. I couldn't do this job without you. I appreciate all the hard work and dedication you've given to Valor of Steele. It's because of you all, this book is being released.

To anyone who read my book, thank you from the bottom of my heart. It's so surreal to put something so personal into words and hope a few people connect to it. If you've read any of my books, shared my releases, or just gave me a shot as a new author to you, THANK YOU. You're making my dreams a reality.

If you liked Valor of Steele, I hope you'll give my other books a chance. You can find them on my website at CarrieThomasBooks.com.

ABOUT THE AUTHOR

Carrie Thomas is the author of young adult and new adult romances. When she's not writing or reading, you can find her traveling or going to concerts with friends. Museums, theater, and music are at the top of her list when traveling to a new place. Writing romance is her favorite genre to write because everyone can relate to it. She lives in the South with her husband, two sons, and a dog named Oscar De Loya Meyer Weiner. She's a firm believer that book lovers should stick together.

Learn more about Carrie Thomas at CarrieThomasBooks.com.

Sign up for her newsletter and stay connected at CarrieThomasBooks.-com/Newsletter.

www.ingramcontent.com/pod-product-compliance
Lightning Source LLC
LaVergne TN
LVHW091029080826
845145LV00002B/410

* 9 7 8 1 9 5 7 7 0 0 4 2 7 *